Praise for Suzanne Rock and

At His Service

"An increasingly insightful heroine and a truly troubled hero who genuinely needs her strength make this story into something that feels refreshingly unique."

—*RT Book Reviews*

"Deliciously seductive. *At His Service* will leave you breathless in the best way possible."

—Lisa Renée Jones, *New York Times* bestselling author of the Inside Out series

"A forbidden affair, a masterful hero . . . oh, babe, get ready for some real heat!"

—Opal Carew, *New York Times* bestselling author

For His Pleasure

Suzanne Rock

St. Martin's Paperbacks

FOR HIS PLEASURE

For information address St. Martin's Press, 175 Fifth Avenue, New York, NY 10010.

ISBN: 978-1-250-05926-0

Printed in the United States of America

St. Martin's Paperbacks edition / December 2015

St. Martin's Paperbacks are published by St. Martin's Press, 175 Fifth Avenue, New York, NY 10010.

10 9 8 7 6 5 4 3 2 1

To Dan, for the evenings of Nintendo 64,
the mornings of banana pancakes, and that
afternoon on the beach when we were eighteen.
You sure know how to have fun, babe.

I love you.

Chapter 1

One Year Ago

"This is so exciting!" Arianna Perconti clasped her hands together as she watched the last car—an electric blue McLaren—pull up under the large LAPS4KIDS banner on the racetrack.

"Someone is going to get killed." Camille crossed herself and shook her head. "I can't believe Stefan talked you into this."

"Oh, stop worrying. Stefan Weisberg is a good friend. We're helping him celebrate his retirement from NASCAR, and he's helping my charity. It's a win-win." Ari grinned as the cars started their engines. "Just think of it, Camille—money. Finally I'll gain a little freedom from my brother's tight budget. We'll be able to expand the charity, helping more kids than ever before. We might even shed those horrid rumors of embezzlement in the process."

"The best thing you did was fire that slimy CFO," Camille said.

"I know." Ari sighed as she watched the staff at the track take their places. "Although my brothers and the media only see the poor decision I made in hiring him."

"Don't beat yourself up over it. It wasn't your fault. The man was a Grade A con man. There were reports of him conning other people before you." She shook her head. "But that's all behind us now."

"Yes," Ari agreed. "This fund-raiser is perfectly timed. Without it, it would be that much harder to move forward." She watched the brightly colored cars rev their engines. "The only downside is that I don't get to drive, too."

Camille turned to her, her features lit up in surprise. "Your brother would kill you."

She flashed her friend a sly grin. "But it would be worth it, don't you think?"

Camille shook her head. "I know you want to get out from under Leo's thumb, but allowing untrained trust fund kids to race their personal cars around a racetrack . . ." She crossed herself again.

"They aren't kids. Most of these race car fans are older than either one of us."

"Those cars cost more than my house."

Ari snickered. "Then you need a bigger house." She nudged Camille with her elbow. "Everything's going to be fine. It's not like they're really racing. They're not allowed to go faster than seventy-five miles an hour. We photograph them as they come in to the finish line and then I take my picture with the winner as he and Stefan hand me a big cardboard check."

Camille crossed her arms. "Hmph. I don't know, Ari. Seems as if a lot could go wrong."

"Stop worrying and enjoy the moment."

Camille smirked. "Can't help it. It's in my nature. Besides, that's what you pay me for."

Ari laughed as one of the officials signaled for the cars to start. While her private box was nice, she wished she was closer. Unfortunately, Stefan had told her that the field was off-limits until the race was over and the winner was ready to take pictures.

Ari leaned against the window as the signal went up

for the beginning of the race. The cars peeled away from the starting line in a cloud of smoke. The blue McLaren broke away early, its engine roaring as it flew past her window.

"That seems faster than seventy-five," she observed.

"It is." Camille pointed to a large computerized sign flashing the car's speed—eighty-five miles an hour. "That's way too fast. What does that guy think he's doing?"

Excitement rippled through Ari. Whoever was driving that McLaren was a guy who liked to break rules and live dangerously. It was an incredibly hot combination. "That car is magnificent, isn't it?"

"It's dangerous."

The sound of squealing brakes filled the air as the McLaren rounded a turn. "It's sexy," Ari whispered as she leaned closer.

"Good Lord, woman. You need to get out more." Camille stood on her tiptoes. "One ten. No, one fifteen. Damn, Ari. He just keeps going faster." She glanced at her friend. "Do you think Stefan will disqualify him?"

"I certainly hope not." Ari smiled and grabbed Camille's hand. "Come on."

"Where are we going?"

"Down to the finish line. When that car stops, I want to be the first out on the field so I can see who it is."

"Oh no." Camille pulled her hand away. "I'm not going down there."

"Why not?"

"It's far too dangerous. Besides, I'm not really into racing. It seems . . ." She hesitated, as if searching for the right word. "Barbaric."

"Fine. Stay up here then." Ari glanced at the cars as they sped around the track. "I'll go down without you." The electric blue McLaren stood out from the others not only because of its speed and color, but also because of the skilled way the driver was navigating the track. Whoever was behind the wheel was used to driving fast and hard, and that meant that he was the polar opposite of her conservative, no-nonsense brother.

Which, in turn, meant that Ari just had to meet him.

There was nothing quite like driving a sports car at speeds of over one hundred miles an hour. Jason Stone knew that the McLaren could go faster, and he was tempted to push the pedal to the floor, but he didn't. He might crave adrenaline, but he wasn't reckless. There were too many cars on the track, all driven by nonprofessional drivers. It was far too risky to go any faster.

He crossed the finish line and did another lap, slowly bringing the car down to a more reasonable speed. He'd had the McLaren custom made, a gift to himself for closing a multimillion-dollar deal and securing the rights to some very innovative software. It was nice to see that the car had lived up to all of the hype.

Jason pulled off the track and opened the driver's side door. As he emerged, his old friend Stefan hurried over.

"That was amazing," the retired race car driver said as he clasped Jason on the shoulder. "That car can really go, can't it? Where can I get one?"

"You can't, it's custom." Jason grinned and pulled off his helmet. "Pretty little thing, isn't it?"

"I'll say." Stefan stared at the car as he took off his baseball cap and pushed his hand over his receding hairline. "If you ever get tired of it . . ."

"Don't worry. I won't."

Stefan jerked his head up and let out a nervous laugh. It's just . . ." He rubbed his dark mustache and shook his head in awe. "It's an amazing car."

Jason relaxed and ran his fingers over the hood. "Thanks."

"I should disqualify you for going too fast, though."

Jason grinned. "But you won't."

"No." Stefan straightened and clasped his hand on Jason's back. "It would be a crime to drive that car under eighty."

"My feelings exactly."

Stefan chuckled. "Well, I'm just glad I could give you the opportunity to open it up and see what it could do."

Jason didn't have the heart to tell his friend that he had already taken the car out and stretched its legs, many times. Every time he got behind the wheel, he was growing more and more fond of that car. It might even be his favorite out of his entire collection.

"Come," Stefan said. "There's someone I'd like you to meet." He led Jason away over to the side, where the bystanders were watching and waiting to meet with the drivers.

"I told you that the proceeds of today's event would go to a charity," Stefan said as they walked.

"Of course." Stefan had mentioned the name of the charity, but Jason hadn't really paid attention. The charity itself didn't matter. All that mattered was the driving. When Jason drove his race cars, he felt free. He could outrun his past and be liberated from the stress of the future, if only for a little while.

"What I didn't tell you is that the winner around the track gets ten percent of the money raised as a prize and a picture with the charity's owner."

"I don't want your money."

"Look around. No one *needs* the money here. But it was her idea, and she was rather stubborn about it. It's supposed to help with publicity for the charity." He leaned in close and lowered his voice. "Her organization has been having some PR problems as of late."

"I see." So, this woman Stefan wanted him to meet was

a socialite trying to use him to improve her reputation. Jason wasn't impressed. He had known many women like that in his life. They all had more plastic than skin, and none of them had any common sense.

"Just play along, okay?" Stefan said, sensing his discontent. "It would mean a lot to me if you didn't start a fight with this girl. Her family's done a lot for my career."

Jason rolled his eyes. "Okay, fair enough. Just don't expect me to make small talk." Jason hated interacting with rich socialites. They were never interesting, and reminded him of a past he'd much rather forget.

They searched the crowd for about ten minutes, but Stefan couldn't find whoever he had wanted Jason to meet. With his patience wearing dangerously thin, Jason put a stop to the search by saying he had an appointment to keep. Enough was enough. At one point in his life he had sat around and waited for rich socialites to make time for him. Not anymore. He'd worked far too hard to leave that life behind. He wasn't going to be a lapdog for anyone.

"I'm sorry, Jason. I don't know where she went." Stefan looked genuinely distraught as he searched the crowd.

"It doesn't matter. Thanks for the—" Jason stopped short a few feet away from his McLaren. There, a short, curvy woman was running her fingers over the hood of his car. Her back was to Jason, which was fine by him. It gave him a perfect view of her ass. Round and firm, it looked like a ripe piece of fruit underneath her printed, flowing skirt. Her wide-brimmed hat and casual sandals seemed at odds with the tailored dresses the other socialites wore. It only added to her appeal.

She looked and acted out of place. Instead of standing around with a champagne glass and talking about benign topics like the weather and the latest fashion, she peered into the driver's side window of his McLaren and brushed her fingers against his steering wheel.

"It seems as if someone has taken an interest in my car," Jason mused. He had the keys, so she wasn't going anywhere, and it seemed as if the woman appreciated a good vehicle. That was rare in his world. This woman was becoming more and more fascinating by the second.

"Oh God, I'm so sorry." Stefan rushed forward to intercept her before she opened the driver's side door. Jason hung back and twisted his lips into a half-smile as she began arguing with his friend. She still faced away from him, but it didn't matter. He could hardly wait to meet her.

"I was just appreciating the car!" Ari told Stefan as she straightened her cream-colored blouse. "I couldn't believe how fast it went. When it took that last turn I think my heart skipped a beat." She glanced wistfully at the McLaren once more. "I just had to meet the person who drove it."

"Well, today's your lucky day, I guess."

Ari stiffened and widened her eyes at the familiar voice behind her. It couldn't be possible, could it? She slowly turned to face the man who had come up to join the conversation.

"Jason Stone." The sun was directly behind him, so she placed her hand on her head to hold her hat down and squinted up at his face. Yeah, it was him all right. Just wonderful.

She had seen his picture in magazines and watched his interviews on television, but she had never met him in person before. Here, standing this close to him, she could see why he'd been named the second most eligible bachelor of the year—right behind her brother Leo. The man looked devilishly handsome with his neatly trimmed dirty-blond hair and bright, blue eyes. Tall and muscular, he filled out his leather jacket and jeans nicely.

Perhaps a little too nicely. The man had this gorgeous bad-boy thing going, but Ari knew she couldn't give in to the impulse to flirt. He was the owner of Stone Suites, a hotel chain that rivaled her own and a thorn in Leo's side, which made him even more appealing. Jason didn't have the long history of being in the hotel business, unlike her family. Stone Suites was a pet project, a hobby he dabbled in on the side. His real income came from investing in new ideas. A venture capitalist, Jason bought up patents and copyrights, investing in technologies that gave his hotel chain an edge over Perconti Enterprises. Jason had a knack for picking the best ideas and then buying out the inventor to make the patents his. He profited off of people's hard work for a living and, according to her brother, was a first-class asshole.

Jason was bad for business, and bad for the family.

"You've heard of me." Jason tossed his large black helmet into the backseat and grinned at her. It seemed natural and carefree, just like him. He still had that close, slightly longer than military-style cut he'd had in the *Whispers* article she'd seen last week, and when combined with his dimpled smile, it gave him this boyish charm that was incredibly attractive.

Stefan sighed. "I suppose I should do introductions. Jason, this is Arianna Perconti. Ari, I see you already know Jason."

"Only through the media," Ari said as she extended her hand. "We've never met in person."

Jason seemed surprised, but quickly recovered. "I see my reputation precedes me." He grasped her fingers and raised them to his lips.

"Charmed." Ari tried to ignore the tingling heat racing up her arm as his lips pressed against her knuckles. "I've heard a lot about you."

"I believe that puts me at a disadvantage because, besides being a Perconti, I know absolutely nothing about you." He lowered her hand, but didn't let go, instead squeezing her fingers in his warm palm.

"You can thank my brother Leo for that. He likes to hide me away from the media."

"Let me go get the cameraman," Stefan said as he backed away. "I'll be right back. Don't go anywhere."

"We won't." Jason tightened his grip on Ari's fingers as he waited for Stefan to leave. Jason tugged her closer. "An intelligent Perconti woman giving back to the community on her own terms," he murmured as he slid his gaze down her body. "You must drive your brother crazy."

Ari's heart melted a little at the word *intelligent*. No one had ever called her that before. She knew that the media painted her as a dopey party girl, someone who couldn't do anything without her brothers' help. For years she had tried to change people's minds, but the reputation clung to her like tanning spray.

"Leo's just overprotective, that's all. I like to do things my own way." As she placed her hand on his chest to stop him from pulling her closer, she marveled at the ripple of muscle underneath his leather jacket. The more she talked to him, the harder it was to remember why he was off-limits. "I think I frustrate him sometimes."

Jason chuckled. "Then it appears we have something in common, Ms. Perconti."

"Do we?" She dragged her gaze away from her hand and looked at his face.

He nodded as amusement twinkled in his eyes. "I frustrate your brother, too."

Her breath caught as he flashed her his dimpled smile. "I guess we're quite the pair, huh?"

"Yes, Arianna. Quite the pair indeed." Heat rippled through her as the amusement in his features faded, replaced by something more intense and hungry.

Time seemed to stand still as the crowd around them faded away. Ari's heartbeat quickened, and her legs felt weak. God, if he could affect her like this with just a look, imagine what he could do with a touch, a kiss . . .

Off-limits, she had to yell in her mind. After a long moment, she cleared her throat and glanced at the McLaren beside her. "Your car is beautiful," she said in an effort to change the subject.

"It has nothing on you."

"Flirt." Ari felt the heat rise to her cheeks as she pulled her hand from his. "My brother warned me about you."

"Oh really?" He seemed amused. "What did he say?"

"He said that you were a manipulative asshole."

He snorted. "He'd be right—but only in the boardroom." He reclined his arm on the car and inched his fingers toward her. "Outside the boardroom, I can be . . ."

"Kind?" She dragged her gaze back to his.

"Fun," he corrected.

"Forgiving?" She leaned forward, closing the distance between them.

"Laid back." He eased his fingers closer and twirled a long strand of her hair around his fingers.

"I like laid back." She focused on his right dimple and wondered what it would feel like to run her tongue over it.

"You do?" He shifted his gaze from his fingers to her face.

She nodded. "I like fun even more."

"Well, then." He shifted his hand and hooked his finger under her chin. "It seems as if we have something else in common, Ms. Perconti."

She nodded. "I think we do. And call me Ari."

"Ari." His voice was filled with awe and caused something to flutter in her lower abdomen.

"Here we are." Stefan hurried over with the cameraman and a large cardboard check. "Sorry about the wait."

"No trouble." Ari cleared her throat and stepped away from Jason. The distance allowed her to get her bearings. What was she doing, flirting with the enemy?

"Now, if you'd stand here, Ms. Perconti," the cameraman said.

Ari moved into position and made a show of taking the oversized check from Stefan and Jason. Then they repositioned themselves as Ari and Stefan handed an equally obnoxious large check to Jason.

"I told you that I didn't want the money," Jason said to Stefan.

"You have to take it," Ari said. "It's part of the deal. The winner gets ten percent."

"But I don't need it."

"It's not about needing it. It's about sportsmanship and fun."

"Interesting," he murmured as he dragged his gaze over her curvy frame. "What if there was another way to achieve your goal, one where you got to keep your money?"

"Another way?" Ari wrinkled her brow in confusion.

"Yes."

Intrigued, Ari lowered her check. "I'm listening."

"Instead of taking the money, I take you." When she frowned, he hurried to continue. "Just out to dinner. One boring dinner, that's all I ask."

She narrowed her gaze. "So let me get this straight. I get to keep the money if I go out to some fancy restaurant with you?"

"Not a fancy restaurant. Somewhere more . . . amusing." He grinned, showing off his dimple once more. "Consider it an extra donation from a benefactor." He inched closer. "Someone who admires your passion for helping kids."

Ari glanced at Stefan, unsure. "It's a lot of money you're giving up." And she knew that Leo would frown upon her taking it from Jason. This was a dangerous game they were playing, one where she could end up in a lot of trouble with her family. "Leo would kill me for being indebted to you."

"Just some beer and wings, and your brother will never know." Jason closed the distance between them and flashed her that gorgeous, conspiratorial smile. "It will be our little secret."

"Beer and wings, huh?" The prospect of going to a restaurant with Jason was exciting. She never got to just hang out informally. Everything was orchestrated to show off her family's cultured lifestyle and elegance. Beer and wings sounded . . . divine.

Ari nibbled her lower lip. Jason may be manipulative, but she was a Perconti. If Leo could hold his own with Jason, it stood to reason that she could, too. Besides, it was only dinner. How much trouble could she possibly get into in a couple of hours?

"Okay," she said. "I'll do it."

"Perfect. It's a date."

"Can we take the picture now?" Stefan asked.

"Of course." As Jason moved beside Ari and slid his arm around her waist, warm tingles raced over her skin. She did her best to listen to the instructions and smile for the camera, but it was difficult. Jason's body heat surrounded her, making her feel safe and protected. It took most of her willpower to resist curling up next to him and burying her face in that strong, protective chest, especially when his fingers were inching down from her waist, skimming against her hip and upper thigh.

When the session was done, Stefan helped the cameraman pack up his things. Ari started to move away from Jason, but he gripped her hip tighter, holding her in place. Before she could protest, he leaned close, so close that his lips were inches away from her ear.

"I'll pick you up tomorrow at eight. Be sure to wear something comfortable." He dragged his hungry gaze down her body. "If you're good, I might even give you a ride in the McLaren."

The McLaren. Ari took a step back and watched Jason get into his car, wondering just what she had gotten herself into.

Chapter 2

Present Day

Ari fidgeted with her wedding veil as the large cement pillars of Stone Suites came into view. The hotel was both familiar and strange. For weeks she had spent almost every day in the modern, art deco hotel. Then she'd had to leave for a fund-raising event in London. That event had led to work in France, Germany, and Austria. Raising funds for her charity had kept her busy for four months, which meant she hadn't been with *him* in four long months. Just the thought of seeing Jason again was enough to make her shake with need.

Sure, she and Jason had texted and e-mailed almost every day, but a few dirty texts weren't the same as the real thing. She had meant to visit him when she had arrived in Boston a few weeks ago, but with all of the hoopla going on with her wedding over at the Palazzo, she couldn't get away. But all of that was behind her now. Sort of.

Ari sighed and toyed with her diamond necklace as she took in the passing buildings in Boston's busy financial district. She and Jason had agreed long ago that their relationship was a secret "friends with benefits" arrangement. While they had fun together, they both knew that it could be only that—fun. He was her family's competition and nothing would change that. They had agreed to keep their sexual interludes on the down low and to not discuss business or their personal lives. When they were together, they lived in the moment. Past and present didn't exist. Many times Ari felt as if she was living two lives, one she showed the world, her family, and the media, the other with Jason. One was filled with obligation and restraint, the other freedom.

Jason, in turn, had kept his word. He never spoke of their sexual escapades to Leo or the press, and even dismissed her attempts to explain herself after Leo announced her engagement to Landon Blake. Jason didn't want to hear about how Leo and Landon had made a business deal that involved her hand, or her reasons for agreeing to it. According to him, what happened outside of the bedroom didn't matter. He could care less about how Landon was using her to improve his image and how she was using him for money. As long as he could keep on seeing her, the name-only union meant nothing to him.

Ari hoped that Jason still had that same laid-back attitude after she told him what had happened during the ceremony. She needed a place to lay low for a while until everything blew over.

Ari wasn't proud of her actions. Leaving her stuffy aviation tycoon fiancé at the altar was an impulsive move, but one that felt right. While Ari felt a little guilty over her actions, she didn't dwell on it. Landon knew that this marriage was a sham and had even planned on spending their wedding night at a seedy club downtown. It wasn't as if she was breaking his heart. She was doing both of them a favor by ending this farce.

No, Landon didn't care for her, and Ari no longer wanted to be tied down in a name-only marriage. She was so tired of being manipulated by Leo. He was older but not wiser, at least when it came to her life. His actions were starting to affect the rest of her brothers' attitudes toward her. Dante and Marco were already a tad too overprotective. It would only be a matter of time before her younger brother, Gio, started ordering her around as well.

It was time to start making decisions for herself. In order to do that, she needed a place to lay low while Leo cooled his temper enough for her to reason with him. Leo had done a great job of keeping her and the rest of her siblings together after their father's death. He'd been there for her when she got into a bit of trouble in high school and again when her charity fell apart, but she wasn't a child anymore. He needed to learn to let go.

She needed to figure out a way to prove to Leo and the rest of her family that she didn't need to be coddled. She was a grown woman, an independent thinker, and she could think of no better way to liberate herself from her family than by staying with their fiercest rival. Half the time Jason and Leo weren't on speaking terms and the other half they were arguing. No one would think to look for her at either Jason's apartment or Stone Suites. And Jason, well, Jason was more than just discreet. He was entertaining, amazing, and could always be counted on for some mind-blowing sex.

Sex. It had been ages since she had done anything more than masturbate. She was more than ready for whatever the gorgeous adrenaline junkie had in store.

Excitement rippled through her as she pulled her sunglasses out of her purse and put them on. Jason was sin in a suit. He fucked like an animal and she couldn't get enough of him. Even now, as she directed the cab to the back of the hotel and waited for it to pull over, her skin tingled with anticipation.

"Excuse me, ma'am."

Ari glanced up at the wiggling fingers of the cab driver and realized that he wanted to be paid. "How much?"

"Thirty-three, seventy-two."

"What? We couldn't have gone more than a mile. That's robbery." She glanced at his name tag on the dashboard. "Do you make a habit of robbing your customers, Omar?"

"Hey, lady. You were the one who wanted to make a stop at Quincy Market. Time costs money."

Ari blew a long curl from her face and dug into her small white clutch. The cab ride was going to cost half the money Leo's girlfriend, Karin, had given her. How was she supposed to survive for the next week or two on so little?

"Here." She stuffed the bills in the driver's chubby fingers and stepped out onto the sidewalk, purposefully leaving her cell phone behind so her brothers couldn't track her. She wasn't in a position to argue. She was a runaway bride with nothing but the clothes on her back and a few twenties in her purse. It wasn't like she had a lot of options. At least the cab driver was good enough to park on one of the side streets behind the building, away from most of the pedestrians. Wearing a wedding dress on a busy public sidewalk was sure to attract attention.

"Oh." Ari stumbled as her heel stuck into a crack on the sidewalk. She tumbled forward and felt a pull on her bridal train. "Damn." The door had closed with a piece of her dress stuck in it. She reached for the door handle just as the cab started pulling away from the curb.

"Wait! My dress!" Ari dropped her purse and yelled obscenities at the driver, but he didn't listen. The cab picked up speed, and Ari felt the firm tug on her rear. Her veil fell and covered most of her face as she pulled at the tulle on her gown. A loud tearing noise ripped through the air. Within seconds her ass hit the pavement and pain vibrated up her spine.

Shit. Ari rubbed her tailbone and watched the cab pull away with a big chunk of bridal train in the door. That Vera Wang gown had been gorgeous.

Ari eased back onto her feet and picked up the back part of her dress to inspect the damage. The train was ruined, tearing about midway up her thigh in a jagged rip. At least there was enough material to cover her backside. The front remained long, so perhaps if she just stuck close to a wall, no one would notice.

She dropped the torn tulle and rubbed her tailbone as she glanced around her. A couple of people were staring, but thankfully no one seemed to recognize her. Yet.

"What are you all looking at? Go on, get out of here." She made a shooing motion with her hands as a businessman looked down his nose at her.

When he didn't move, she stuck her tongue out at him. The man huffed and hurried off, clearly annoyed that she had caught him staring. *Good riddance.*

As the pain in her tailbone receded, Ari pulled out the prepaid phone she'd purchased in Quincy Market and began to text. *Had to change phones. Coming in thru the garage.* She had sent Jason a message before getting into the cab, but didn't tell him the whole story. Boy, was he going to be in for a big surprise.

His response was immediate. *The laundry room is on the left. I'll meet you there.*

She placed her phone in her clutch as she made her way through the underground valet garage and approached the metal door. She passed Jason's large collection of sports cars and remembered how he had promised her that someday they were going to have sex in each and every one. He had made good on his promise. In a few short months they had gotten naked in all of his cars save the electric blue McLaren 650S—his favorite. Something she hoped to rectify soon. There was something exhilarating about going down on him while parked at some remote location, knowing that at any moment he'd take charge and have his way with her on the hood. She missed him and she wanted him.

As she approached the large metal door of the employee entrance, she pulled out a tissue from her clutch and used it to grab the dirty, germ-infested handle. After a quick glance around to make sure no one was watching, she stepped inside.

Placing her sunglasses in her purse, she walked over the tiles, looking for a door marked LAUNDRY ROOM. Cool, air-conditioned air blew across the back of her legs, making her shiver. Really, what had she been thinking, agreeing to this wedding sham? The union was supposed to get the Perconti family out of debt. Landon's funds would give her enough money to keep her charity afloat and she'd give him enough stability to quiet the rumors that had surfaced about his kinky lifestyle. It had sounded like a win-win situation, but as the months started ticking down to her wedding, she realized that something was missing. She wanted a real relationship, one with love, respect, and fun.

Ari heard the whirring of the washing machines before seeing the sign for the laundry room. Relief washed through her as she placed her tissue on the handle, opened the door, and stepped inside.

Industrial-sized washing machines and dryers were lined up against the walls, their humming and sloshing creating a background clamor that was a sharp contrast to the quiet hall. After a quick glance around, Ari realized that she was alone.

Now what? She nibbled her lower lip and wondered if Jason had heard about the wedding fiasco yet. There had been at least two dozen reporters at the Palazzo, waiting for a wedding that would never happen. Ari wouldn't be surprised if her hasty retreat blanketed both tabloid and mainstream news channels an hour or so from now.

Ari jumped as the door opened behind her. "Who's there?"

Jason's handsome face came into view, and she felt a familiar heat rise. There was nothing sexier than a man in a business suit, and Jason's tailor-made attire was no exception. The navy brought out the blue in his eyes, making them more sapphire than topaz. His lean, muscular frame looked positively lickable, and she couldn't wait to run her fingers through his thick, latte-colored locks. He had that seductive smile ready, complete with that dimple she loved, but when he rested his gaze on her it faltered.

"Ari," he said as he closed the door behind him. "What happened?"

"It's a long story."

"Tell me." He started to close the distance between them, then hesitated and looked at her ripped dress. "Did Landon do this to you?" Fury laced his even tone.

"No, of course not. Just hold me, Jason."

"Of course, princess." He held his arms out. "Come here."

In two steps she was next to him with her arms wrapped around his neck. "I can't even begin to tell you how happy I am to see you." Days of pent-up frustration rose up in her chest and threatened to spill out as tears.

Jason tried to gather his wits as he slid his arms around her trim waist. "I'm glad you're here too, Ari." And he was, although he'd never admit it to anyone but her.

"I had to see you," she mumbled into his chest.

He understood her feelings. It had been a long time since he'd held her. He didn't realize how much he had missed it until this moment. "Whatevah's wrong, I can fix it." He grimaced at his Boston accent, an accent he had worked hard to hide along with his past. Unfortunately, the slipups had been happening more and more around her lately. Thankfully, she didn't seem to notice.

"You can't fix this."

"Try me."

"This is my problem, not yours." She leaned back from his embrace and shook her head. "Remember our promise. No talk of business. Our lives outside of each other don't exist when we're together."

"I—of course, dahlin'." They had agreed to use their time together as an escape from their everyday lives. Up until today, Jason had honored that, biding his time until he found the right moment to use their relationship to gain an advantage over her brother, but seeing her so upset and worried gave him pause.

Something was wrong, deeply wrong, judging by her disheveled look and the way she was shaking. All thoughts of exploiting her disappeared and he just wanted to hold her and fix whatever it was that was making her so upset.

"Kiss me, Jason," she whispered. "I just need to be with you." She undid the buttons of his suit coat, popping them off one by one.

He knew she was distracting him from questioning her, and for once, he didn't mind being manipulated. It had been so long since they had been together, and he had been working too many long hours trying to put her upcoming wedding from his mind.

He kissed her hard, enjoying how her sweet taste burst on his tongue. No woman had ever tasted quite as good as Ari. No one felt as good, either. He slid his fingers down her back, sides, and hips as the air heated around them.

Ari threw herself into the kiss, meeting his tongue with enthusiasm. It wasn't long before he forgot why she had come to him, or why she wanted him to kiss her. All he could think about was burying himself deep inside her body and losing himself in her softness.

He bent his head, tasting the delicate skin of her neck and shoulder. As her familiar scent enveloped him, a sense of urgency began to take hold.

"I need to feel you inside of me," she whispered as she ran her fingers over his biceps. "Please."

Jason groaned as he slid his fingers down over her ass and pulled her close, letting her feel every inch of his rock-hard erection. She responded by widening her stance, inviting him closer.

"Hang on," he whispered into her ear.

As he lifted her from the ground, Ari tightened her arms and legs around his body, enveloping him in her warmth. He placed her on the nearest washing machine and devoured her mouth, desperate to feel her flesh against his.

Ari let out a soft moan as he stroked her tongue with his own. The sweet sound caused his cock to press painfully against the zipper of his pants.

"Do you have a condom?" he asked when he broke away a few minutes later.

"My clutch," she gasped and immediately began fumbling around on the top of the washing machine for her purse. "Oh God."

"What?"

She looked up as her eyes clouded over in pleasure. "This washing machine." She opened the clutch and began rummaging around.

"You like the vibration, don't you?" Jason reached over and turned the knob from delicate to normal.

She bit her lower lip and slid the condom out of the wrapper. "Here."

"Put it on me." He eased back, allowing her access to his zipper. As she fumbled around with his pants, he ran his fingers along the outsides of her legs, toying with her Disney garter.

"Cinderella?"

"Who else?" Ari said as she tossed the clutch to the ground.

She covered his hand and moved it around to her inner thigh. Carefully, he slid his fingers underneath the garter and inched them toward her center. "Do you like it?"

"Yeah, I do." Very much so. The garter was so typically Ari. She had this childlike passion for princesses and happy endings that he found endearing. It reminded him of her innocence. Ari's upbringing had been so different from his. In a way, he didn't think it was right for Leo to shelter her so much from the real world. Then again, it was that sheltered lifestyle that had allowed him to manipulate her so easily. If Ari had had any real sense of how dangerous he was, she never would have flirted with him at that charity function, and never would have agreed to dinner.

All rational thought left him as she dipped her hand into his pants and wrapped her long fingers around his cock. He attacked her mouth once more as desire rushed through his body. When she tightened her grip, pleasure fogged his mind, causing him to gasp.

"Ari." His accent slipped out again, but he was beyond caring. Jason shuddered as she rolled the condom down his length. Her touch wasn't delicate, but rough and needy. Just the way he liked it.

"Now, Jason," she whispered. "I want you now." She spread her thighs wider apart and positioned him at her opening.

With a swift thrust, he entered her, causing them both to groan. As her wet heat surrounded his shaft, Jason felt as if he was finally home.

"Do you hear that?" A voice rose up from outside the laundry room.

"Hear what?" a second voice responded.

Ari widened her eyes as some shuffling echoed from the other side of the laundry room door. Jason placed a finger on her lips, quieting her. The possibility of being caught gave him an adrenaline boost that made his cock swell to painful levels. As he grew, Ari's inner walls hugged him tighter, and he had to bite his lip to keep from groaning with pleasure.

"It sounded like moaning," someone said.

Ari started to giggle, so Jason put his hand over her mouth and leaned in close.

"Remember our game?" he whispered. Unable to resist, he slid his tongue around the outer edge of her ear.

She widened her eyes and nodded. Reaching around his body, she dragged her long, manicured nails over his backside. Even through the cotton fabric of his suit pants, it felt incredible.

Jason ground his teeth to keep from groaning with pleasure. Slowly, he removed his hand from her mouth and leaned over to lock the laundry room door.

"Game on," he whispered as the voices grew louder.

"I don't hear anything. Do you think it was one of the machines?" one of the voices asked.

"Possibly," her companion said. "Those things are older than dirt."

Jason slid his hands around Ari's waist and pulled his hips back until only the tip of his cock remained inside her. Then he pressed forward, biting back a moan as her muscles contracted around his shaft.

"Maybe we should just check on the laundry room," one of the maids said. "Perhaps something needs to be shifted in one of the dryers."

Ari grabbed his ass and spread her legs wider. Excitement rippled through him as he quickened the pace, performing short, shallow thrusts while he cradled her back to steady her on the machine. Ari tugged his shirt from his pants and clawed her manicured fingers down his back.

The pain made him want to cry out, but he bit it back and flashed her a devilish look.

She responded with a triumphant smile that only made him want her more.

They had played this game enough before and knew the rules. They'd fuck just out of sight of the unsuspecting staff, each giving the other as much pleasure as possible. The first one to make a noise to trigger their discovery lost.

Not once had Jason lost—ever. Ari seemed to think that she could win this round, but she forgot that Jason never lost at anything. Not anymore.

Jason cradled her shoulders and leaned her back, allowing himself to perform quick, hard thrusts into her sheath. The angle allowed him to penetrate deeper, touching that extra-sensitive spot deep inside her core.

Ari wasn't one to be outdone. She tightened her inner muscles and slipped her hands underneath his pants and boxers. Pleasure mixed with the pain as she dug her fingernails into his skin, and Jason had to bite his lip to keep from groaning.

He pumped harder, faster, as the noises from the hall floated through the cracks in the door.

"I don't know. The laundry isn't our job. Perhaps we should get Carla to do it."

Ari leaned up and placed her lips close to his ear. "Come on, tiger. You can do better than that." She bit his earlobe, then slid her tongue along his jaw. Jason tightened his grip on her back as she dug her fingers deeper into his ass, spreading apart his cheeks as she pulled him hard against her hips.

Jason bent his head over her shoulder and tried to keep from moaning as pleasure spiraled through his torso. He ran his tongue along her neck, taking in her sweet taste. Urgency bubbled through his veins, making him crazy with need. He slid his hands down to her hips and anchored her in place as he pumped faster. The voices rose up again outside the door.

"Yeah, we should ask Carla. It's her job, and she takes too many breaks as it is."

"They're going away," Ari whispered. Her voice sounded disappointed.

Jason reached behind her and turned the washing machine from wash to rinse. The hunk of metal started whirling and vibrating, causing Ari to jostle back and forth along his length.

"Come for me," Jason whispered. "I want to feel you grip my cock."

She met his gaze. "Only if you come with me."

Forgetting the couple in the hall, Jason slammed into her body with wild abandon. Ari let go of his ass and placed her hands on the wall behind her, using it for leverage. The washing machine moaned under their weight and began tipping from front to back in time with his thrusts.

"That doesn't sound right," he heard through the door. "I think we should just peek in and see if everything's okay."

Adrenaline surged through his body, moving to the drumbeat of their flesh coming together. Fuck, this was what he needed. There was nothing more intoxicating than the rush of that adrenaline high, mixing with the sharp need for rough sex. Jason needed both more than he needed air, and his sweet Ari was only too happy to give it to him.

Sharp, metal clicks of someone turning the knob filtered through the room as the washing machine wobbled from front to back. Every muscle in Jason's body tightened, every nerve ending felt like it was on fire. *Yes, God, yes.*

"The room's locked."

Ari let out a low moan and then bit her lip, as if realizing what she had just done.

Jason kept moving. He was close, so close.

"Here, let me try." More clicking followed the voice. Jason glanced behind him to see the doorknob turning.

"Come on, princess," he whispered. "Come for me."

Ari bit her fist and closed her eyes. Jason ground his teeth to keep from groaning as she spread her legs wider. The familiar tightening formed at the base of his spine.

"Who would lock the door like this?"

"I thought it would only lock from the inside."

Ari's thighs quivered and her inner walls spasmed around his cock. Jason opened his eyes to see her locked in a silent cry. The image was so beautiful, so erotic, that it unleashed a tidal wave of emotion from deep within his center.

Pleasure erupted through his system, slamming into his body like a race car missing a turn and hitting a wall. Jason gasped as the world around him faded away, numbing him to everything except pure, heavenly bliss.

"I think you're right. We need to get Carla." The words sounded as if they were spoken through a tunnel. Jason's whole body went boneless, and he braced himself on the washing machine to keep from falling over.

As footsteps retreated in the hall, Jason leaned over and captured Ari's lips once more. He could never get enough of her taste, her touch. Exhaustion overwhelmed him as he reached for the button on the washing machine and turned it off.

"That was amazing," Ari said as he broke the kiss.

"Incredible." He straightened her veil and brushed the dark hairs that had fallen across her face. "You're crazy, you know that?" Wonderfully crazy. No other woman gave him such a rush. No one even came close. Ari was like some exotic drug, and he was an addict looking for that next high.

This arrangement wasn't only good for him personally, but professionally as well. Jason could have all the sex he wanted, and he secretly had leverage over his adversary. Yes, they had agreed not to talk about their families or businesses, but that didn't stop Ari from dropping hints about Leo and the family business here and there. Jason had used the scraps of information to gain an edge over her family, and that advantage had driven his rival mad with frustration.

Leo's frustration had then doubled when the media made an issue of his dating a hotel intern, which made a wonderful distraction. While Jason had nothing to do with Karin, he didn't hesitate to take advantage of the situation. Leo's problems had given Jason enough time to fix the issues he was having with his new software. In a few short months, Jason would be rolling out a new technology that would drastically cut back on costs and revolutionize how hotels could serve their guests. With a little luck, the software would cripple Perconti Enterprises and cement his name as one of the most progressive businessmen in the twenty-first century.

Jason was playing a game he knew he could win. Ari was his ace in his pocket, and with her, he'd give both Landon and Leo a run for their money.

"I'm the one who's crazy?" She stared at him with wide eyes. "You were the one who changed the washer speed from delicate to heavy duty."

Jason smirked as he slid away from her body and helped her to stand. "Touché." He bit back a moan as she settled her skirts into place. "You didn't wear underwear to your wedding," he observed.

"I often don't wear underwear. You know that." She picked up her clutch and slipped on her jeweled heels, which had fallen off during their sexcapade.

"Feeling better?"

"Much." She flashed him a gorgeous smile. "Thank you."

"My pleasure."

"I'm sorry to be so impulsive. I just really needed . . . well, I'm glad you weren't busy." She narrowed her gaze. "I didn't interrupt anything, did I?"

"Just the usual." *Beating myself up over agreeing to such a stupid arrangement.* While Jason knew that it was in his best interest financially to let Ari enter a loveless marriage, there was something about seeing her with another man, even a man he knew spent most nights without her at the Dark Desires sex club, that didn't sit well with him. It was so disturbing, in fact, that Jason had purposefully avoided all of the media stories surrounding the Percontis and Ari's upcoming marriage.

Speaking of which . . . He glanced at his watch. "Shouldn't you be at your wedding?"

"Nah." Ari edged past him and unlocked the door. "I left."

"You blew off the reception?" He frowned and rubbed his jaw. "Leo and Landon must have been pissed."

"Not the reception, silly," she called over her shoulder. "The ceremony."

"Hold on a moment." Jason grabbed her elbow and spun her around to face him. The movement was a little more forceful than he'd intended, and before he realized what he was doing, he had Ari up against the door and his body pressed against hers.

"Jason, you're hurting me."

He immediately eased his death grip on her arm. "I'm sorry. I thought you just said that you didn't attend your own wedding."

"I didn't," Ari said.

Jason couldn't believe what he was hearing. "You left him at the altar?"

"A real runaway bride. Can you believe it?"

Jason felt relief, he knew he shouldn't but couldn't help it. "I take it Landon is furious?"

"Nah." She waved her hand in dismissal. "He'll be relieved. Trust me. I bet he's already retreating to that sex club of his. My brother is a different story. He's probably yelling and pacing like a madman even as we speak."

Jason could only imagine. He had been on the receiving end of Leo's temper on more than one occasion. He didn't envy the Palazzo staff.

He ran a hand over his face and tried to process the implications of her actions. No matter which way he looked at the facts, only one result remained. By refusing to marry Landon, Ari not only jeopardized her family's business, but stung Leo's pride. She made her brother look like a fool. Leo was no doubt beside himself with anger. If Ari was discovered at Stone Suites, Leo was going to suspect he was behind her disappearance at the altar, and Jason was going to feel the brunt of the Perconti temper. Jason would have to put his renovations on hold for several months while he dealt with the ornery Italian and the resulting media frenzy he'd create.

"Holy hell, Arianna. What have you done?"

Chapter 3

Nausea rocked Jason as he wrestled with what to do next. This was bad, really bad.

"What do you mean, what have I done? I stopped myself from entering a loveless and boring marriage." She tugged on his tie and smiled. "Now I'm free to do whatever I want." She inched closer. "With whoever I want."

"Did you even think this through? Consider the consequences?" Jason stumbled back a few steps and gripped the edge of the washing machine to steady himself.

She crossed her arms and glared at him. "Aren't you the one who always tries to get me to be more impulsive?"

Impulsive with sex, yes, but this . . . shit, this was catastrophic.

"Jason, say something." Ari put her thin, delicate hand on his elbow. "You're scaring me."

Scaring her. More like *she* was scaring *him*. With one move, Jason felt as if his role had switched from the manipulator to the manipulated.

Even more worrisome was his uncontrollable relief over her leaving her fiancé at the altar. The sudden surge of male pride made him want to whoop and spin her in the air. His impulsive urge felt foreign and wrong. Jason didn't do commitment. In fact, before Ari, his relationships had never lasted more than a couple of weeks. Hell, he hoped he didn't give her the wrong impression.

"This was a stupid move," he said.

She bristled and straightened. "It was not. I don't love Landon. Why should I marry him?"

Her words sent heat rushing through his veins. Jason pushed aside the surge of possessiveness he felt toward her. "Leo's probably looking for you."

"Of course he is." She pulled her hand away and picked up her clutch. Jason curled his fingers into a fist to keep from reaching out to her. "I'm not stupid." She lifted her chin, as if daring him to tell her different.

"Ari, running out on your wedding is not only a slap in the face to your brother, but Blake as well. They won't take something like this sitting down." He dropped his gaze to his hand. The machine was still warm from Ari's body. Even now, he craved her as much as he wanted to throttle her. He had to get his emotions under control.

"I don't expect them to, but this was the only way I could get my family's attention."

"Their attention?" He met her gaze and was once again struck by her beauty. Ari was almost a foot shorter than him, and full of curves. Her big, almond eyes narrowed with determination as they peered at him from under her mass of chocolate waves.

She crossed her arms and leaned against a nearby washing machine. "I'm tired of living my life under a microscope. For years Leo has been telling me what to do and how to act. I know he means well, but I'm a grown woman. It's time I start making my own decisions. What better way to make a statement about my independence than by leaving my own wedding and staying with . . . you?"

Jason felt the world around him spin. "You want to stay *here*?" Fuck, he loved her spirit. It was what had attracted him to her in the first place. He understood Ari's craving for excitement all too well. But this . . . this was too much. By letting her stay, he was admitting that their relationship was more than physical. He was telling her and the world that he cared about what happened to her and supported her in her decision not to marry.

"It's only for a little while," she said. "Once Leo and I come to an understanding, I'll return."

"You can't—"

"You have to see why I can't go home now, Jason. Crawling back to my brother is like admitting I'm in the wrong. Only by staying here can I make Leo understand that he can't control me."

Jason swallowed as a squeezing sensation tugged in his chest. "You have to go back," he told her.

"Haven't you been listening?" She shook her head, causing her hair to fall in front of her eyes. "I can't."

"You can." He closed the distance between them and grabbed her upper arms to keep her from bolting. "You must." She was shaking, he realized. Did Leo scare her that much?

"Damn it, Jason." She jerked out of his grip and put some distance between them. "I thought we had an understanding."

"We do." An understanding that involved sex without strings. This was getting far too serious for his comfort.

"Then let me stay with you while I work things out with my family."

"You can't stay in my apartment." It was his sanctuary, the one place he could shed his high-society persona and be himself. He wasn't going to give up that sanctuary to a Perconti, no matter how attractive she may be.

"Here then. I could stay in the penthouse suite." She inched closer. "It's just for a little while. I swear I won't bother you. You won't even know I'm here."

He gave in to the temptation to brush the stray hair from her face. It felt so smooth and perfect. "You're a stubborn woman, you know that?"

She widened her eyes. "Then I can stay?"

He hesitated, then lowered his hand. Instead of answering the question, he asked one of his own. "Why didn't you talk to your brother about this before the wedding?"

"How would you feel about telling Leo that his plans were about to blow up in his face?" She shivered and looked away. "I got cold feet."

"I see your point." While Jason would have relished the idea of throwing a wrench in Leo's plans, Ari cared about her brother and didn't want to hurt his feelings. That didn't change the fact that she couldn't stay at his hotel. If Leo caught her at Stone Suites—or worse, in a compromising position with him—then he'd be livid. Jason respected the hotelier enough to keep their rivalry to the boardroom. He had no desire to make their battle personal. Heaven knew he had enough skeletons in his closet for the Percontis to rip his reputation to shreds.

"Don't you think staying here is a bit extreme, though?" he asked. "Leo's already angry. Finding out you are staying at Stone Suites would be like rubbing his nose in the situation." While he loved the idea of spending the next several days in Ari's arms, he wanted to do it on his own terms, and without the family drama. While he cared about Ari, he wasn't ready to sacrifice his reputation and his business for her independence from her family.

"Perhaps there is somewhere else you can stay," he offered. "With a friend, maybe."

"I don't have many friends. At least none I can stay with."

"What about Camille?"

"I don't want to get her involved." She reached up and slid her finger down his cheek. "And stop worrying about me. I just need a little time to sort things out with my family, that's all."

"And have them stop controlling you."

"Yes." She flashed him a brilliant smile. "I knew you'd understand."

He understood all right. Ari was using him to get out from under her brother's thumb. Jason wasn't sure if he liked the idea of her using him to take charge of her life. He kind of liked her brothers controlling her. They kept her safe. Jason always knew where she was, and what she was doing. If Leo allowed her to do whatever she wanted, she wouldn't need him to feed her craving for spontaneity and excitement. She'd be able to get those things on her own.

In short, if Ari got the freedom she craved from her oppressive brother, she wouldn't need him anymore. He wasn't sure how he felt about that.

She ran her fingers down the lapel of his suit jacket. "So we have an understanding. I'll stay at your hotel while I try to convince my overbearing brother that I am perfectly capable of making my own decisions."

"I don't know—"

"You don't think I can make my own decisions?"

"It's not that. It's just—"

"Surely you have a vacant room in this place." She flashed him a seductive smile. "We could play catch-up. You know, enjoy each other's company." She dropped her gaze to his lips. "It can be just like old times—before my engagement was announced."

It took all of his strength to put his hands on her hips and gently push her away. "Ari—"

"It's not forever. Just . . . for now. Think of it as our little secret." She tightened her hold on his neck and brushed her lips against his. "I know how much you love a secret."

A secret . . . Yes. Jason loved secrets because they often gave him the advantage in the boardroom. This was different, however. This was personal.

"Come on, Jason. I have nowhere else to go. You don't want to see me on the streets, do you?"

"I'm a busy man, Ari."

"I know. I won't get in the way. I swear." She inched closer. "I'm just asking for a place to stay. Nothing more."

Jason pushed aside his rising panic and forced himself to consider her argument. This woman was offering him unlimited sex and a chance to irritate his adversary. He had to admit that her idea had merit, and if he kept his eyes open, an opportunity to exploit this situation might present itself. The more he thought about it, the more he liked the idea.

"Well?"

Jason grinned and captured her lips with his own.

"Is that a yes?" Ari asked when he broke for breath.

"You drive a hard bargain, princess." Jason slowly backed them both up until she was flush against the laundry room wall. As he pressed his body against her, need roared through his veins. She responded by letting out a moan and tightening her arms around his neck. He slid his fingers down over her soft curves and cupped her ass. Despite having just been with her, Jason wanted to plunge himself deep inside her once more.

"It'll just be for a few days, maybe a week," Ari promised.

Jason furrowed his brow and pretended to consider her request. "You can stay at my hotel as long as you wish, with one condition."

"Just one?" she joked.

"Ari, this is serious. What you did today is sure to create a backlash in the media, and I don't want you to be caught up in those reporters' talons."

She flashed him a skeptical look. "Since when have you been interested in my well-being?"

"Since you placed yourself in my care." This relationship was going to move forward on his own terms, or not at all. He needed control.

"Wait a minute. I didn't ask you to care for me. I just wanted a place to stay. I need to make a statement—"

"And you will, but you don't want to create a scandal in the process." She didn't seem convinced, so he plowed forward. "No shopping trips, no dining out, no going outside this hotel for any reason." If he was going to spin this to his advantage, he needed her cooperation. The last thing he wanted was her blurting to the media that she and Jason had an understanding. Those vultures would purposefully misconstrue her words and place him in a difficult position.

"You mean no freedom and no fun," Ari said.

"Not necessarily. Just hide out and relax for a few days."

"And have sex with you."

"Now that you suggest it . . ." He tried to kiss her, but she pulled away.

"It sounds like you want me to become your slave," she said.

He shifted his eyebrows suggestively and pressed his thickening cock against her lower abdomen. "Would being my love slave for the next few days be such a hardship?"

"Now that I think about it . . ." Ari grinned as she lifted her leg and wrapped it around his waist. "No, no, it wouldn't."

"Didn't think so." He wedged himself between her thighs and kissed a long, hot trail down her neck and shoulder.

A loud ringing noise pierced his lust-filled brain, but he ignored it. Nothing was going to prevent him from possessing Ari once more. Nothing.

"Jason?"

The ringing echoed through his skull again, and Ari pushed his shoulders. "Your phone."

"It will go to voice mail," he murmured as he pressed his lips against the sensitive place between her neck and shoulder.

"It might be important."

With a growl, he pulled away from Ari and grabbed the phone from his pocket. "This better be good," he said as he brought his cell to his ear.

"It is, Mr. Stone." Michaela's voice sounded nervous, as it should. Jason wasn't in the mood to deal with his assistant's politeness.

"I'm busy, Micki."

"There's someone here to see you in the lobby."

"Send them away."

"I—I really think that you should talk to this person. He seems rather insistent."

Leo. Jason glanced at Ari and tried to keep the smile from his face. "Tell him that I'll be there in a minute."

"Yes, sir."

Jason pocketed his phone. "I have to go."

"Where?"

"To meet your brother in the lobby."

"He's here?" She widened her eyes and disentangled herself from Jason's embrace. "Are you going to rat me out?"

Jason flashed her a seductive smile. "I wouldn't dream of it." He lifted her hands up to his lips and kissed her knuckles.

"Where should I go?"

He lowered her hands. "Not the penthouse suite—that's the first place they'd look. Go to the ninth floor. That's where we keep the honeymoon suites."

"The honeymoon suites?"

Uh, oh. Jason cleared his throat. "I'm renovating the floor, but there's one room they haven't touched yet. It's at the far end of the hall." He slipped his all-access card from his jacket pocket. "Wait for me there."

"Of course." Ari threw herself at Jason. "Thank you."

Jason wrapped his arms around Ari, enjoying the feel of her curves against his body. He indulged himself for a long moment, then slowly unwrapped her arms from around his neck and forced himself to stand back.

"Use the service elevator to go up to room 9002." He handed her his card. "I'll be along as soon as I can."

She lifted her brows. "Are you sure you won't tell him about me?"

He made an *X* on his chest with his finger. "You can trust me." He kissed her cheek. "I promise. Now go." He tapped her ass and urged her down the hall to the elevators.

Her features brightened as she hit the button on the control panel. "This is going to be so much fun."

Indeed. Jason kissed Ari once more, then left her to find the honeymoon suite on her own. After straightening his suit jacket, he made his way through the service area and up the stairs to the first floor. With each step, the heated desire he had felt in the laundry room faded away, replaced by the cool calm that sparked his reputation as a merciless bastard. He turned over possibilities on how to handle Leo, and decided that for the moment, he'd play ignorant. It was better to let his rival think that he had nothing to do with his sister or the wedding. For now.

Jason struggled to keep the smile from his face as he entered the lobby and found Michaela. "Where is he?" he asked when the tall, leggy Asian woman was within earshot.

Micki adjusted her black-rimmed glasses and started to reply, but was cut off by a low, familiar voice.

"I'm over here."

Jason made a slow turn and stared at an older, much bulkier version of himself. His breathing hitched, and his smile faltered.

"Deacon." The name felt like both a blessing and a curse. Deacon was the one person who knew every intimate detail about Jason's troubled past. As a result, he was the only person who had enough dirt on him to tear down his empire like a house of cards.

The man ran his hand over his stubbled jaw and flashed him a knowing smile. "It's been a long time, hasn't it, brother?"

Karin Norell nestled herself deeper into the cushions of the leather sofa and watched Leo Perconti pace back and forth.

"How could she do this to us? I don't get it, Karin. I just don't get it." Leo had taken off his suit jacket and draped it over a nearby chair. Concern etched his brow as he paced the length of the room.

"I don't know," Dante said from his position behind his laptop. He had taken over one of the easy chairs in the living area and put his feet up on the coffee table. Karin still felt uneasy about the marks he was putting into the polished table despite the fact that she was no longer cleaning the hotel room. Some habits were hard to break.

"I had everything worked out." Leo stopped pacing and placed his hands on the back of the sofa. "What went wrong?"

"Perhaps things aren't as bad as they seem." Karin thought back to her conversation with Arianna before the wedding and realized that she might have unintentionally set in motion something that was going to ruin them all. It was difficult not to let the guilt show on her face.

Leo shook his head. "This is more than just going out for air. Someone kidnapped her. That has to be it. There's no other explanation for why she wouldn't show up to her own wedding."

"Perhaps she just didn't want to marry the bastard." Dante glanced up from his computer screen.

Leo straightened. "Impossible. She told me herself that she was fine with it. She understood the importance of this marriage. Perconti Enterprises needs Landon Blake in order to remain solvent. This marriage was to secure our future." He waved his hand in the air around him. "All of this was dependent on that union. Without Landon Blake we have nothing."

"There has to be some other way," Karin said from her position on the couch.

Leo turned to face her. "Don't you think if there was something else I could do, something besides arranging a marriage for my sister, that I would've done it?"

"No one here is suggesting that you didn't look into all of your options," Dante said as he returned his gaze to the computer screen.

"You just keep tracing that phone." Leo pointed at his brother. "I need to know where she is, now."

"What are you going to do once you find her?" Karin asked.

"I don't know." Leo pinched the bridge of his nose and muttered something in Italian.

"Relax, before you have another anxiety attack." Karin patted the sofa seat next to her.

He dropped into the seat beside her. "I had every detail planned."

And that was where he went wrong, although Karin couldn't tell him that. For years Leo had been taking care of Ari and the rest of his siblings. While he had let the oldest two, Marco and Dante, grow up, Ari and her younger siblings—the twins Gio and Gianna—were a different matter. Leo had to stop dictating their lives, not only for their sakes, but for his own. His controlling nature wasn't helping his anxiety, and Karin worried about his health.

She took his hand. "Perhaps she changed her mind. It's possible that she didn't want to get married."

Leo squeezed her fingers and met her gaze. "Then why did she tell me that the marriage was okay? I'm not a heartless bastard, *cara*. If she didn't want this, I could have found some other way to secure Landon's money." He pressed his lips together for a moment in thought. "By running out on the wedding, she has made both Landon and me look like a couple of old fools. Her actions have compromised Landon's trust in us." He sighed. "The damage to our reputation is extensive—never mind our new financial problems. I don't know if I'll be able to repair all of this."

"We'll repair it." Karin squeezed his fingers. "You aren't alone anymore, remember."

He shook his head. "Ari had said that she was okay with the marriage. The girl never gave me any reason to think otherwise."

"You're not the easiest man to talk to," Dante said from his position across the room.

Leo scowled. "Of course I am." He turned to Karin. "Aren't I?"

Karin averted her gaze. "Sometimes you can be a little . . . overbearing."

Dante snorted. "A little? If big brother doesn't get his way, nobody's happy."

"You shut up," Leo snapped at his brother before returning his attention to Karin. "She's not strong like you are, Karin. I have to find her before the media eats her alive."

"What are you going to do when you find her?" Karin asked.

"I'm going to see if she's okay, then I'm going to throttle her for not coming to me first." He stood and moved behind Dante's right shoulder. "Anything yet?"

"Not yet. I think I'm close, though." Dante muttered something under his breath. "Christoff's software is eating up the memory on this laptop. Things are taking longer than they should. Just give me a few more minutes." Christoff was Dante's old high school buddy who worked as a private investigator. Soon after Dante had broken up with Sabrina, he had contacted Christoff about some tracking software. Dante had wanted to track Sabrina through her cell phone and make sure that his crazy female fans didn't create any more trouble for her. From what Karin understood, Christoff didn't part with the new technology easily, and Dante had spent quite a large amount of the Perconti funds to gain the software. At the time, Leo had been furious, but now, in light of recent developments, he had changed his opinion of his brother's purchase.

Karin started to ask if there was something she could do to help, but the elevator doors opened and Marco hurried in before she could get out the words. "What did I miss? Did you find her?"

"Not yet," Dante said as he tapped some keys on his keyboard. "But I know that she's still within the city. Give me a few more minutes and I'll have an address."

"How did things go downstairs?" Leo asked Marco as he began to close the distance between them.

"As well as could be expected, I suppose." Marco let out a long breath and went to get a drink from the bar. "I talked to Gio before he took Mamma up to her room. He hadn't had a chance to speak with Ari before the wedding, and knows nothing about her disappearance."

"And Gianna?"

"The same. She has a business meeting in the morning on the West Coast and needs to return tonight. She said to keep her informed."

"Figures," Leo muttered. "That would have been too easy."

"She has to come back," Marco said as he moved behind Dante and peered over his shoulder. "After the strike, we really can't take much more bad media."

Leo started to pace, then stopped. "Her assistant," he said, pointing at Marco. "The one who keeps track of all of her charity functions. What was her name?"

"Camille?" Dante asked.

"Yes, that's the one. She should know where our sister is hiding. You call her." Leo pulled out his cell. "I'm going to call Roberto. He had been greeting wedding guests and parking cars. Perhaps he saw something."

Dante looked up from the computer screen. "I located the phone at a diner in Southie." He shook his head. "Why would she go to South Boston?"

"I've no idea, but we're going to find out." Leo lowered his phone and glanced at his brothers. "Come on."

Dante closed up the laptop and he, Marco, and Leo strode toward the elevators.

"I'm coming with you." Karin grabbed Leo's suit jacket and handed it to him.

"You can't."

"Why not?"

Leo reached out and brushed his thumb down the side of her cheek. "Because I don't know what I'm going to find in that diner. It could be dangerous."

Karin stiffened. "I can handle it. We're partners, remember?"

"Of course we are." He smiled and kissed her forehead. "But you'd be too much of a distraction for me. I don't think I could handle worrying about you and my sister's safety at the same time." He stepped away. "Besides, I need someone to stay here in case Ari comes back. I don't want her to be alone, and Gianna has already left for the West Coast."

"Gio's here."

"He's taking care of Mamma. Please, Karin, for me."

Karin saw the sincerity in his eyes. Leo was truly frightened about what he was going to find at that diner. His words weren't coming from a need to control, but concern for her welfare. The knowledge made her uneasy. "Okay, but you owe me."

"Of course." Leo brushed his lips over her cheek.

"Just be careful."

"I'll keep you posted." The elevator doors opened and Leo and his brothers stepped inside.

"I'm counting on it." Karin let her smile fall as the elevator doors closed. She had only spoken to Ari twice, but both times she had come across as a smart woman, much too smart to go to a seedy diner in Southie by herself. She walked over to Dante's computer and ran her fingers over the map where the signal was coming from. Something wasn't right, but for the life of her, she couldn't figure out what it was . . .

Chapter 4

"What are you doing here?" Jason grabbed the sleeve of Deacon's bomber jacket and pulled him to the side of the foyer.

"Good to see you too, little brotha." Deacon chuckled and tugged his arm from Jason's grasp.

Jason glanced around the foyer and relaxed his shoulders when he realized that they were completely alone. He turned back to his brother and realized that not much had changed since they'd last seen each other. Deacon looked like an older version of himself, just a little less polished. They had the same sandy hair, but while Jason's was trimmed close to his head, Deacon had let his grow out into soft layers around his face. He wore day-old stubble and still had the same blue eyes and lopsided grin that had left a trail of broken hearts in his wake. Deacon wore a bomber jacket, white T-shirt, and jeans. The ensemble had become his uniform and all Jason could think of was that he looked just like he had when they'd had that terrible fight that had ended their relationship ten years ago. The only difference between them was the way they spoke. While Jason had worked hard to lose his Boston accent, it seemed as if his brother's had grown thicker with time.

The man could charm the panties off a nun, and yet his easygoing nature was all an act. Underneath his casual exterior, Deacon had secrets, secrets only he and Jason shared.

"What are you doing here?" Jason said. "The last time we talked, you told me you never wanted to see my face again."

"Yeah, about that." He pushed back his hair from his face and averted his gaze. "You know I didn't really mean it, right?"

"Could have fooled me." Jason stepped back in disgust. "You seemed to be rather passionate about that point, just like you were passionate about calling me a selfish asshole."

"Selfish asshole." Deacon snorted and shook his head. "It wasn't you who was the asshole, but me."

He's after something. Deacon was only nice when he wanted something from him. Jason had learned that lesson the hard way. Jason inched forward and lowered his voice. "What do you want, Deacon?"

"To bury the past."

Something wasn't right. "It's been a decade. Why now?"

He held his hands out to his sides. "I miss you, bro."

"You do?"

"We used to have a blast together. Remember the time when we—"

"Shh." Jason glanced around to make sure no one could hear them. "That was a lifetime ago," he muttered.

"Yeah, it was." Deacon dragged his gaze down Jason's body, making him hyperaware of his expensive Armani suit and loafers. "You've come a long way from our fostah home roots, little brother. I'm proud of ya."

"Thanks." Jason wanted to believe that Deacon was on the up-and-up, but there was so much between them. Could they really start over after everything that had happened?

"You really want to reconcile?" he asked.

"Yes."

"And this has nothing to do with revitalizing our former business arrangement? Because I'm telling you right now it's not going to happen. I'm a different person now."

Deacon's eyes sparkled with mirth. "No more sleeping with rich widows for money, eh?"

"For *companionship,*" Jason corrected.

"Sure, companionship." Deacon chuckled. "A dinner here, a charity function there . . . It's nothing like your gigolo past."

"It isn't." Jason glanced around to make sure no one was listening. "You know I'm not that person anymore. I've moved on."

"I see." Deacon lifted his chin and studied him for a moment before continuing. "So all of your investas wouldn't care if tomorrow morning the trending article on the Internet was called 'Jason Stone Seduces Lonely Women for Money.' "

"Keep your voice down." Jason pulled Deacon deeper into the shadows.

"Or maybe it should read 'Jason Stone Financed His Acquisitions with Sex.' "

"I didn't finance anything with sex."

Deacon crossed his arms. "You sure about that?"

Okay, maybe he'd financed a little of his empire with the money he'd gotten from those women. He wasn't proud of his past, but it was the only way he and Deacon could make ends meet at the time. Jason had seduced those unsuspecting women, but he never truly enjoyed it like Deacon did. In the beginning he didn't have to give them much—a little conversation here, a dinner there—but then things got more intense, and before he knew it, he was in over his head. It was a miracle that he'd been able to get away from it at all.

"Why did you really come here, Deacon? If you think that throwing our past in my face will get me to forgive you, then you're mistaken. I've moved on." Jason had worked hard to forget that dark time in his life. He'd always altered his personality and past for those women, becoming whoever they wanted him to be. With practice, a few hundred dollars turned into a few thousand. Soon, lying became second nature, and he didn't know where the fake Jason ended and the real one began. He wouldn't go back to that place again. He couldn't.

Deacon held up his hands in mock surrender. "I'm not here to argue, little brotha. Honest."

"Really? Could have fooled me. That part of my life is dead and buried, Deacon, and there's nothing you or anyone else can do to change that." Jason had never parted on bad terms with those women. As far as he knew, they all still adored him . . . all except for one. Fortunately, that one had done a short stint in a mental institution, so anything she said wouldn't have much merit.

"Sorry. Look, it's just . . ." Deacon rubbed his neck. "It's been a long time, you know? And you're all the family I've got."

Jason sighed with resignation. "Okay, stop playing games with me. What happened? Are you in trouble? How much money do you owe?"

"There you go again, always thinking the worst of me." Deacon chuckled and shoved his hands in his pockets. "Although, now that you mention it, I got laid off a few months ago from that factory job, and it's been hell trying to scrape enough money togetha for rent."

"You got evicted."

"Yeah." He chuckled. "Can you believe it?"

And there it was, the real reason why Deacon had ended up on his doorstep. He didn't know why he was surprised. Even when they were together, Jason was always bailing him out of trouble. Deacon had never liked to work hard, and it appeared as if his laziness had caught up with him. Again.

"I thought, maybe, I could hang out here a little while until I find anotha job. We could talk and—I don't know—maybe start ova."

Start over. While Deacon was frustrating, he was also family. Perhaps this visit was nothing more than it seemed on the surface. Reconciling would be like a dream come true. He was jealous of Leo and his army of siblings willing to support him. Perhaps with a little effort, Jason could have that support system, too. It wasn't as if Deacon was a total deadbeat, far from it. With the proper motivation, his brother could become a huge asset.

Jason saw a lot of himself in his older brother. They both loved the rush of adrenaline, and would do anything in order to get it. Jason collected fast cars and enjoyed sparring with the paparazzi, and his brother searched for that rush in different ways. Gambling, bar fights, and racing motorcycles were only a few of Deacon's vices. While he hadn't made the best life choices, Jason understood his brother's need to chase that high. For both of them, routine and stability were like a death sentence. Perhaps if Jason could prove to Deacon that running a business wasn't all routine and pencil pushing, he could get his brother excited about something other than scamming people for money.

"I'd like that," he said.

Deacon let out a long breath. "Thanks, Jason. You won't regret this. I promise."

"I hope not." He motioned one of the receptionists behind the kiosks to come over. "Please give this man one of our best rooms."

"Of course, Mr. Stone." She started to walk away, but then hesitated. "Oh, I almost forgot. A courier came by earlier with a large envelope for you. He said it was really important."

"Did he say what it was about?"

She thought for a moment, then shook her head. "Just that it was important and that you should read it right away. It couldn't wait. I left it in your office."

Jason glanced down at her name tag. "Thank you, Kiera."

"Sure thing, Mr. Stone."

Jason nodded to his brother. "I'll check in on you later to make sure you're settled in."

"Sure thing, Mista Stone." Laughter twinkled in Deacon's eyes as he pressed his lips together and bowed.

"Shut up." Jason tried not to laugh, but it was difficult. Ten years ago, no one would've called him Mr. Stone. Now it was unusual not to hear it. Respect was something that had been hard to come by in his younger years, and no one understood how much that lack of common decency had hurt him better than Deacon.

Jason grinned as he clasped his brother on the arm. "Catch you later."

Perhaps this wouldn't become the disaster he'd envisioned when he first saw his brother in the lobby. Perhaps this could mark a new page in his life, one where forming relationships became more important to him.

Just as long as the past stayed in the past. As Jason headed back to his office to check his e-mails and fetch the envelope, his thoughts turned toward Ari waiting for him upstairs. Ari was so different from Deacon, so different from him. He made a mental note to remind his brother not to talk about their childhood or escort business with anyone. He couldn't afford to let his checkered past come to light. Ari wouldn't understand his crazy, messed-up childhood, or his reasons for doing what he did. Hell, he wouldn't understand it either if he hadn't lived through it. If word leaked out to the media, they'd probably assume that she was paying him to be with her. They wouldn't care about the truth, only what sold papers and magazines. If his past leaked out to the public, not only would he suffer, but she'd suffer as well.

Arianna kicked off her shoes and settled into the lounge chair situated by the large bay window of the suite and glanced at her watch. Almost an hour had passed since Jason had left her to meet with her brother. Surely his conversation with Leo couldn't last for too much longer. She smiled to herself as she thought of Jason trying to get rid of her brother downstairs so that he could come back up and be with her. She needed another sex-therapy session. The bliss she'd felt down in the laundry room had long since given over to jitters.

It had been one heck of a day. She supposed she should tell her family where she was, but she lacked the focus and mental agility she would need to deal with her brothers. The entire experience had been exhausting, and there was nothing more that she wanted to do than to take a long nap—but not until Jason returned and updated her on her family.

She scanned the Boston skyline through the large picture window in the hotel room and then focused on the street below. She searched for something to calm and center her, but found nothing. In fact, she was surprised at the lack of activity outside of Stone Suites. The Palazzo was constantly buzzing with reporters and fans, but this hotel was eerily quiet.

Too quiet. It felt weird not having the media taking her picture, or peppering her with questions about her brothers. It was because of the reporters that Leo kept her under his thumb. He had seen what bad media coverage had done to their father, and then was the center of some bad press himself. He didn't want her to experience the self-loathing or outrage at seeing a private moment in print, so her every outing was planned as part of some grand design to make her life seem uninteresting and to keep the family company alive.

Everything in her life was monitored: how she dressed, what she ate, who she hung out with. The only freedom her brothers allowed her was her charity. In recent years even that had been restricted. Once Leo had learned that the CFO she had picked out was embezzling money from Ari's Kids, his faith in her decision-making had hit an all-time low. Her name was still on the letterhead, but all of the major decisions had to go through her brother. Sometimes Ari felt she served no other purpose than to be a pawn in her family's war with the media.

But that was about to change. No longer did she want to be under her brother's thumb, or have to worry about how some random comment would end up in a tabloid the next day. Thanks to Jason, she knew what it was like to be free from worry and just enjoy herself. She wanted to meet the paparazzi head-on and control them, not hide from them like her family. She knew that she had so much to give, not only to her family, but to her charity and society at large. She just needed the freedom to live her life the way she wanted, not how her family expected.

Not only did Ari want to make decisions about what to do with her life, but she wanted to choose who to be with as well. If she wanted to have fun, no-strings-attached sex with Jason Stone, then her brothers should let her do it and trust that she wouldn't jeopardize the family business or get her heart broken in the process. She wasn't a child, but a grown woman, and it irritated her that Leo couldn't see her as anything more than the high school kid who'd shoplifted cashmere sweaters and Jimmy Choos to cover up the pain of her best friend's death.

Jason saw her as a grown woman, and that was a big part of his appeal. As Ari started to remove her stockings she rubbed her fingers along her inner thigh and remembered how Jason had smoothed his hands along her skin. Tingles of desire raced through her as she thought about him walking through the door and taking her into his arms once more. Arianna loved his spontaneity and the rush of excitement she got whenever she was around him. Could that rush between two people last? She wanted to find out, because the alternative, living a life that was not her own, was unacceptable.

Jason jerked his head up from his desk and glanced at the clock on his office wall. It was almost seven in the morning. Had he really fallen asleep in his office? After he had read the contents of the envelope, he'd lost track of time. He must have dozed off while waiting for some e-mails.

After rubbing his face with his hands, he grabbed the pictures and leafed through them once more. All of them were grainy black-and-whites of him and Ari enjoying a passionate moment in the laundry room.

"Fuck." He tossed the pictures aside and picked up the note. It was made of newspaper cutouts, the letters in odd sizes and fonts so it looked as if it had been put together as part of a kindergarten project.

> *Someone will be by to collect the money. Settle your debts with him, or the world will learn how you stay one step ahead of Perconti Enterprises.*

Included with the note was an invoice from a loan shark in Las Vegas, totaling in excess of ten million dollars.

"This is ridiculous." He didn't owe anyone any money. In fact, he had worked quite hard to stay out of debt with his business ventures.

Someone must have stolen his identity, but Jason had been up all night searching for a way to contact this loan shark and straighten things out. He'd made little progress in exchange for a lot of frustration. No one knew of this guy. It was almost as if he didn't exist.

But he *had* to exist, because the pictures were legit. The fact that someone had been watching him and Ari was unsettling. He'd had no idea that there was someone with them in the laundry room. If he had, he never would have asked to meet her there.

Jason got up and paced once more, wearing down the Oriental rug in front of his large, immaculate desk. He had taken great pains to keep his life in order and not let any secrets come to light. The fact that some jerk was trying to hold this over him made him physically ill.

No one could know about his relationship with Ari, or his reasons for it. Yes, he had pursued her because she was Leo's younger sister, but that wasn't the only reason. Ari was a lot of fun, and their time together was a great way to let off steam. He found that he not only enjoyed their interludes, but looked forward to them. If Ari ever suspected that he was using her, she'd leave him; he was sure of it.

Not to mention the mess he'd have to deal with if their relationship was made public. He knew all too well how the media could twist words to suit their own purposes. He would be painted as evil and manipulating, and Ari as ignorant and dim-witted. Neither one of them wanted that kind of publicity nightmare.

Ten million dollars. It wasn't so much money that he couldn't afford it, but it still gave him pause. If he could just track down this loan shark and talk to him, he was sure he could straighten things out.

Frowning, he dumped the pictures, note, and envelope into the trash, refusing to devote any more time to it. He had much more important things to think about, things like the gorgeous Italian woman he had waiting for him up in the honeymoon suite. He was sure that Ari was spitting mad at him for not returning last night, and could almost picture her pacing the room, ready to give him the third degree. Some apology sex was in order, and then he had a meeting with the software developer to talk about the new rollout.

After e-mailing his head of security, a former PI who might be able to track down this loan shark using his connections, Jason picked up the phone and called the kitchen to order up some room service for the honeymoon suite. It would take time for his man to get some answers, and in the meantime Jason needed to step away from his computer. He had to refresh himself if he was ever going to find a way out of this mess. Coffee, sex, and a spin in his McLaren would hopefully get his brain functioning once more.

He let the phone ring for several seconds before he returned the receiver to its cradle in disgust. Where were they? Jason had advertised to his customers that the hotel had twenty-four-hour room service, so there should be people available to take the call. He tried again, and got the same response.

Curious, he got up from his desk, closed up his office, and went down to the hotel's restaurant to see what was going on. Stone Suites offered its patrons a free breakfast buffet every morning after they stayed at the hotel. This morning was no different. As Jason walked into the restaurant area he saw the long buffet table with different trays arranged on top, each one filled with a variety of eggs, meats, and pastries for the guests. At the far end of the buffet table was a large coffee urn and several mugs. Patrons sat at the various tables enjoying their breakfast and talking quietly amongst themselves.

As a courtesy to the guests, the large-screen TV that hung on the wall on the opposite end of the room had been turned on. The local morning show was playing and the familiar anchors sat in front of a large window overlooking the Charles River. A small crowd, including several of his staff, huddled around the television set and murmured amongst themselves. Intrigued, Jason approached the crowd to find out what was going on. He stood off to one side and crossed his arms as he listened to one of the anchors speak.

"Today we have *Whispers* reporter Amanda Vaughn. She's going to give us her take on the infamous Perconti non-wedding that happened this past weekend." The anchorwoman turned in her seat to face the woman next to her. "Good morning, Amanda."

"Good morning. It's lovely to be here today. Thank you for having me."

Jason frowned. He recognized Amanda all too well. Eighteen months ago, before he met Ari, he'd had a brief fling with the *Whispers* reporter. When he'd found out who she worked for, and her real reason for wanting to spend time with him, he had broken off the dalliance. Some people were willing to do anything in order to get a story.

"There have been a lot of rumors and speculation about what really went on at the Perconti wedding, but I know that you were there and can give us a firsthand account," the anchorwoman said.

"Yes, of course." Amanda cleared her throat. "Although the Percontis claim that Mr. Blake and Ms. Perconti loved each other, I had always suspected that the hasty nuptials were to cover up Mr. Blake's most recent scandal. Blake Corporation has been struggling with an image problem ever since those infamous photos of him at Dark Desires were released to the public. The marriage to someone with such a squeaky-clean image like Arianna Perconti would go a long way to appease his conservative investors. I have a source who tells me that the head of Perconti Enterprises had spoken with Mr. Blake days before the wedding and a great deal of money exchanged hands. Furthermore, the merging of the two companies would surely give other hotel chains like Stone Suites a run for their money."

Jason snorted and crossed his arms. *Not likely.* He inched closer to the television. "Turn it up," he told a passing employee. The staff member hurried to carry out his orders.

"So you think Arianna's wedding was being used by her brothers as part of some business deal?" the anchorwoman asked.

"I do. And I think Arianna discovered this business deal and ran away from the wedding with a broken heart. The big question now is . . . where is she, and who is she hiding with?"

"Good question," the anchorwoman said. "I don't think anyone knows the answer."

"Oh, someone knows the answer," Amanda said. "A friend, a relative . . . *a lover.*"

The anchorwoman widened her eyes in surprise. "Arianna Perconti has a lover?"

Amanda Vaughn flashed her a triumphant smile. "I suspect she does, yes. Why else would she run away from a wedding that would ensure her family's financial stability if she had no other prospects?"

Was this woman for real? Where were the facts? Everything she'd said was speculation and rumor. She was a disgrace to her profession.

Jason took another step closer to the television, his gaze fixed on the reporter and anchorwoman as they continued their conversation.

"Do you know who this lover is?" the anchorwoman asked.

"Not yet, but I'm determined to find out. I've been following the Perconti family for years and they've yet to have a secret that I haven't been able to uncover. I will find out who this lover is, it's just a matter of time."

"What does Landon Blake think of all of this?" the anchorwoman asked.

"I've tried to interview him, but he has been unavailable for comment . . ."

Jason turned away from the TV in disgust. The public's fascination with the Percontis was beyond him. People should really learn to mind their own business.

"Interesting stuff, eh?" A low, familiar voice rose up from behind him.

Jason turned and found his brother sitting at a nearby table, eating an omelet. "You're up early."

"I don't need much sleep. Besides, I've got a lot of work to do." He tapped his hand on the Help Wanted section of the morning paper. "You, on the other hand, look as if you could've used a couple more snooze buttons."

Jason sighed and rubbed his forehead. "Sorry, I've had a rather long night."

"I can see that." Deacon motioned to the seat next to him as he shoveled a forkful of eggs into his mouth. "Tell me about it."

"You wouldn't understand." Jason shook his head and started to walk away, wanting to get back to Arianna. If there was such a media circus over her non-wedding, he could only imagine what would happen if they ever learned about his relationship with her.

"You never know. I'm more knowledgeable about these things than ya think."

Jason turned to face his brother. "What's that supposed to mean?"

Deacon scooped up some more eggs onto his fork. "I'm not exactly inexperienced when it comes to listening to rich people's problems. Sometimes I even help them get out of trouble."

"I'm not in trouble."

"You sure about that?" Deacon shoveled a forkful of eggs into his mouth and waved his fork in the air. "Because from where I'm sitting, it looks like you've got the weight of the world on your shoulders." He considered Jason for a moment before continuing. "Your problems wouldn't happen to be centered around a certain Italian hotel heiress, would they?"

Jason made a sound of dismissal. "Absolutely not."

Deacon nodded. "If you say so." He returned his attention to his plate, which was piled high with pastries, eggs, and breakfast meats. "You just seemed real interested in what that reportah had to say."

"This has nothing to do with Ari."

Deacon raised his brows. "Ari?"

Jason waved his hand in dismissal. "Whatever her name is. It's not about the Percontis. I'm just very busy."

Deacon averted his gaze, but not before Jason saw the concern and sadness in his features. "Of course. You don't trust me. I get it."

No, Jason didn't trust Deacon, or anyone else for that matter. He started to walk away, then hesitated. Jason thought about Leo and his brothers, and the close connection they shared. Jason had had to build his company from the ground up by himself. He'd had no one to talk to, no one to support him.

It would feel so good to have someone to confide in, and Deacon seemed to want to help. Perhaps he should give him the benefit of the doubt . . .

Jason slid into the seat next to his brother and placed his elbows on the table. "You can't tell anyone about this."

Deacon glanced up at him, then carefully put down his fork. "My lips are sealed."

Jason took a deep breath. *Here goes nothing.* "I think someone stole my identity. Now this loan shark is trying to blackmail me to settle some debts."

Deacon widened his eyes. "Are you serious? Blackmail you with what?"

Jason shook his head. "It doesn't matter. He just has

some pictures that could be misconstrued as something scandalous."

"How much does this loan shark want?"

"Ten million."

Deacon whistled. "That's a lot of money. Are you going to pay it?"

"Of course not. It isn't my debt."

"Did you talk to this guy?"

"I can't. He didn't leave any contact information. All I have is an invoice from some loan shark in Vegas, but I haven't been able to do much with it."

Deacon considered his words. "I could track him down for you."

"No, I wouldn't want you to get caught up in this. If this really is a loan shark, then chances are this guy is dangerous."

"I can handle dangerous."

"No, I don't want anything to happen to you. This is my problem, I'll deal with it."

Deacon pushed his eggs around on his plate. "I don't know," he said after a while. "If this guy is as dangerous as you say, maybe it's better not to argue with him. Just give him the money and move on."

Jason shook his head. "I'm not going to be played for a fool, Deacon."

"Even if it means that your relationship with this hotel heiress gets out in the media?" Deacon spooned another forkful of eggs into his mouth.

"I didn't say I had a relationship with an heiress."

"You didn't need to. It's written all over your face." Deacon tilted his head and studied him as he chewed his food. "I'm willing to bet those pictures from your loan shark are of her." He speared a sausage with his fork and took a bite. "And I bet that the media isn't the only thing you'll need to worry about once they are made public."

"What's that supposed to mean?"

Deacon put down his sausage and wiped his mouth with the back of his hand. "This heiress was born into money, wasn't she?"

"What does that have to do with it?"

Deacon leaned his forearms on the table. "Her family has probably had money for generations."

"Are you trying to make a point?"

"My point is that sheltered girls who are born into money get pissed once they find out they've been conned by a blue-collar gigolo."

"I'm not conning her."

"You sure?"

Jason started to say yes, and then remembered how he had used Ari to get information about Perconti Enterprises. He might not be conning her for her money, but he was manipulating her all the same. It wasn't much better.

"Doesn't matter if you're conning her or not," Deacon said. "Once those pictures come out, it won't take much digging to find out about your past. When she hears about it, she'll assume the worst. Women always assume the worst of men." Deacon picked up a pastry and examined the intricate frosting design on top before taking a bite. "You, of all people, should know that," he said with his mouth full of food.

Jason knew that his brother was only trying to help him, but Deacon's words had struck a little too close to home for comfort. "Ari's not like that. She's different."

"Wake up, Jason." Deacon placed his elbows on the table and pointed his pastry at the television set. "You and I don't fit into their world. Never did." He took another bite. "You can stick a suit on us, perhaps give us a few bucks, but it doesn't change who we are inside." He tapped his chest. "And once those socialites get to see what's inside, they want nothing to do with us."

Every muscle in Jason's body tensed at the truth in his brother's words. "Ari's not that shallow."

"Can you be sure of that?" When Jason didn't answer, Deacon put down his pastry and patted Jason's hand. "Just pay the guy and I'm sure he'll disappear. It's not like you can't afford it."

"I'm not paying a stranger for a debt that isn't mine." This was a mistake. Deacon didn't understand him, and didn't get the pressure he was under. His profit margins were razor thin until this new software could be rolled out, and he wasn't going to start throwing money away for no good reason.

"You better prepare for the consequences, then." When Jason scowled, Deacon shrugged. "Just sayin'."

"I've got to go." Jason stood and turned to his staff, who were still huddled in front of the television set, listening to that ignorant reporter prattle on like a baby bird, hungry for attention.

"Turn that damn thing off, and get back to work." He stormed out of the restaurant before he could see their responses.

Deacon's words had unnerved him, more than he cared to admit. He marched through the foyer to the elevators. Pressing the number on the keypad, he went to the floor where the honeymoon suites were located. He needed to take Ari away from this place and let loose for a little while. It was too hard to think with so much going on around him.

A beautiful woman and a fast car would go a long way toward lightening his mood. It would also help him clear his head, and Jason needed to be at the top of his game if he was ever going to get out of this mess.

Chapter 5

"Did you find her?" Karin asked as Leo walked into the room.

"No, but I found that damn *Whispers* reporter again." He shook his head as he took off his suit jacket and tie. "A two-page spread and now we are the bumper for tonight's television show." He made a disgusted noise and tossed his clothes on the chair.

"Come here." Karin sat down on the couch and patted the seat next to her. "You're getting too emotional." Ever since they'd found Ari's cell phone in Southie, Leo had been distraught. He and his brothers had spent every waking moment looking for their sister and had yet to find her.

"It's hard to stay calm," Leo said as he collapsed beside her. "Everything is falling apart." He raked his fingers through his hair. "How are the investors coming along?"

"Not great. They all want assurances that Perconti Enterprises will remain solvent despite Mr. Blake's departure." She nudged his arm. "Turn around."

He did as she asked, turning so his back was facing her. "She must be punishing me, Karin."

"I don't think she's punishing you," Karin said as she began to massage his shoulders. "I think you're punishing yourself with all of this stress. Did you take your medication?"

"I forgot in the rush to meet Dante in Faneuil Hall. I really thought we had her this time." He pulled out his cell phone to check his messages. "We're close though, I can feel it." He swiped his screen and scowled. "Damn."

"What?" Karin stilled her hands and peered over his shoulder.

"Mr. Gasaki wants me to meet with him. I'm sure it's about his shares in the company." Leo swiped the screen again.

"That's the third one," Karin said.

"Fourth." He held up his cell to show her a text. "Kline wants to hold a meeting, too. I can only imagine that it's because he's considering a pullout as well." He shook his head. "It's impossible dealing with these things until I know Ari is okay."

"I know."

"If she'd just call me . . ." He sighed and rubbed his hand over his face.

Karin lowered her hands as she felt her own cell phone vibrate in her pocket. "Go take your medicine. You need to take care of yourself first or you won't be any good to anyone."

He turned to face her and kissed her on the cheek. "I don't know what I'd do without you."

"You'd be a basket case." Karin smiled as Leo kissed her again, this time more passionately. As he moved from her lips to her jaw, Karin felt her phone vibrate once more. Reluctantly, she pulled back and patted him on the shoulder. "Go."

Leo flashed her a seductive smile and stood. "We aren't finished here."

She leaned back on the couch, causing the tops of her breasts to peek out from her low-cut shirt. "I know."

Leo growled and went to the bathroom to take his medication, tapping on his cell as he walked. Letting out a long sigh, Karin pulled out her phone and saw that the number was unknown. Karin frowned as she swiped the screen.

"Hello?"

"Karin? It's Ari."

After a quick glance toward the bathroom, Karin moved to the kitchen. "Where are you? Is everything okay?"

"I'm okay." Her voice hitched on the words.

"You don't sound okay."

"No, I am. Just . . . tired. How are my brothers doing?"

"Stressed. That *Whispers* reporter got the wedding fiasco bumped up to a two-page spread and a TV spot on their nightly program. Investors are starting to pull out of the company. You really need to come home, Ari. We need to make a united front."

"I can't."

"What do you mean you can't?"

"If I come home, then Leo will just continue to control my life. I have to make a stand."

Karin glanced at the bathroom before continuing. "Landon's been asking for you, too."

Ari sighed. "I know. I've already spoken with him this morning. We've come to an understanding."

"You did?"

"Yeah, turns out, he was having second thoughts about the marriage, too."

"Really?"

"It wasn't as if we loved each other, Karin. I guess Landon's new boyfriend didn't really like the idea of him being married, despite the union being in name only."

"I see." Karin nibbled her lip in thought. "You need to talk to Leo, Ari. He's so worried about you."

"I will, I promise. I just have to figure out what to say to him, first."

"What do you mean? You don't have to say anything. Just tell him that you're all right—"

"Remember our conversation before I left?"

"Yes."

"This is about taking a stand and becoming my own person. Leo treats me like a child."

"But he gave you shares in Perconti Enterprises. That must show that he has faith in your abilities."

"Not really. On paper I have a good portion of Perconti stock, but I know Leo won't let me sit in on corporate meetings, or listen to my ideas. He'll control me there just like he controls my charity. I'm just a figurehead."

"I'm sure if you tell him this—"

"He doesn't take me seriously, Karin. He never did. To Leo, I'm still that poor, lost teenager with no ambitions or direction for my life. I always will be."

Karin sighed. "Okay, I'll try to talk to him."

"Thanks. I appreciate it."

"Just tell me where you are now. Leo's sick with worry and I need to let him know you're okay."

"I'm at Stone Suites."

Karin stood and blinked in shock. "Stone Suites?"

"Karin?" Leo asked as he emerged from the bathroom. "Who's on the phone?"

"Karin, are you there?" Ari asked through the receiver.

Karin blinked at Leo, unsure of what to say.

Leo closed the distance between them. "What's going on? Why are you talking about Stone Suites?"

Karin worked her jaw, but no sound came out. Leo slipped the phone from her hand and put it to his ear. "Who is this?"

Ari bit back a gasp as her brother's booming baritone came over the line. Shit. This was the last thing she needed.

Swallowing her nerves, she cleared her throat and tried to appear nonchalant. "Hey, Leo."

"Ari? Is that you?"

"Yeah, it's me."

"Where the hell are you? Did you know that some filthy cab driver has your phone in Southie?"

"Yeah, about that—"

"Are you okay? Did someone hurt you?"

"I'm fine."

"Tell me where you are. I'm coming to get you." Ari heard the jingling of keys and started to panic.

"No, you can't."

"What do you mean I can't?"

Ari took a deep breath. She really didn't want to have this conversation, but he had left her no choice. "I don't want you to come get me."

"What on earth are you talking about?"

"I don't want to go home, Leo. I want to stay here."

"Don't be ridiculous. Karin mentioned Stone Suites. Are you there?"

"Yes, but—"

"What the hell were you thinking? Do you have any idea of the scandal you'd create if the media learned you ran away from your own wedding to stay with our fiercest competitor?"

"Look, there's no need to worry—"

"Did he put you up to this?"

"Who?"

"Stone." Leo ground out the name as if it left a bad taste on his tongue.

"No, of course not."

"When I get my hands on him—"

"Leo, this has nothing to do with Jason."

"Oh, we're on a first-name basis, are we? Pack your things, Ari. I'm coming to get you."

"But—"

"And don't even think of running away from me again."

"Leo, please—" The phone went dead, and she made a frustrated sound. "God damn it, Leo. Why don't you ever fucking listen to me?" She threw the cell phone at the dresser on the other side of the room. It crashed and fell to the floor. Falling back onto her pillows, Ari let out a loud noise of disgust.

Some days she really hated her brother.

Minutes passed as Arianna lay in bed with the covers pulled up around her chin. What the hell was she going to do now?

Leo was coming after her. It had probably been a mistake to call Karin, but Ari thought that they had really connected and Karin would understand her predicament. Now she knew better. They might have bonded over champagne at the Palazzo, but her loyalties were still firmly grounded with Leo.

Well, unless her brother tied her up, threw her over his shoulder, and dragged her back to the Palazzo, Ari wasn't going home with him. One way or another, Leo was going to have to learn that he couldn't push her around anymore.

Turning onto her stomach, she buried her face in her pillow. It was so hard fighting Leo alone. The man was like a bulldozer, destroying everything in his wake. He had no finesse, no understanding of what she was going through. She had no experience sparring with her older brother, or anyone else for that matter. She needed someone on her side who knew Leo's weaknesses and could use them to her advantage.

Which led to her next problem: Jason had never come back to the room last night. He had promised he would, but it was obvious something had happened when he'd left her in the basement. Judging by the phone call this morning, Ari was beginning to suspect that it wasn't her brother who'd met Jason in the lobby. She wondered what had happened, and if Jason had had a change of heart about letting her stay.

Exhaling another small sigh of disgust, Arianna turned over, threw off the covers, and got out of bed. A quick glance at the hotel alarm clock showed that it was almost 8 a.m. She wondered if Jason would come back to the room at all. If he'd had a change of heart and thought to return her to her family, it would stand to reason that he'd soon send someone upstairs to get rid of her.

Frustrated, Ari considered the possibility that Jason wanted to get rid of her. Well, she wouldn't sit around and let the men in her life lead her around by the nose. She was going to fight them, which meant that she needed to shower and get dressed before Leo burst into her room and started making demands. It would be infinitely easier to toss him out on his ass if she was dressed to impress.

Ari grabbed a Stone Suites robe from a nearby chair as she headed to the shower. As she moved, she caught sight of the hotel emblem on the lapel. Stopping, she turned the soft, white terry cloth over in her hands to get a better look. The words STONE SUITES were sewn with crimson thread in block lettering. Underneath were a few cobblestones, forming a path that could be found in most places in Boston.

She ran her fingers over the stitching, remembering the games she had played with Jason in the laundry room. Jason had always been straightforward with the rules of their play, never manipulating her to do something she didn't want to do. When he made a choice, he acted on it, just like he did when he told her she could stay at his hotel. He had immediately given her his card and told her she could stay in a honeymoon suite. There was no debate, no dragging his feet. He just made the decision and ran with it. If Jason really wanted to send her home, he would have done it last night instead of waiting until the morning. There had to be some other reason why he didn't come up to the room last night, but what?

Frowning, she slipped on the robe and padded over to the small espresso machine on the other side of the room. Perhaps some caffeine would help her sort all of this out.

The machine was much fancier than the ones at the Palazzo, but then again everything about Stone Suites was fancier than her family's hotel. Jason wasn't one to cut corners, and always demanded the very best. It was something that they had in common. Arianna had frequently argued with her brother about the quality of the items he purchased for his hotels. She wanted the top-of-the-line conveniences for the guests, but Leo was far too practical, and would never spend money on anything he felt was unnecessary or frivolous.

It seemed as if every year Leo became more miserly with family finances, and the family donations to her charity were no exception. Because of her lack of funding, Ari had to cut corners, including hiring a CFO who was willing to work for almost nothing in pay. When it had come out that her CFO was embezzling money, Leo had wanted to shut the charity down. Ari had fought hard to keep it going, and in the end they had compromised. Ari's Kids would stay open, but only if Leo had the final say in all of the major decisions.

It was the last straw in a haystack full of oppressive demands. Ari's charity had been her only outlet, the only thing in her life that she had control over. Leo had helped her set it up as a way to help her grieve over her best friend's death from cancer. It had helped her to stop shoplifting, and did a lot of good for families in need. The thought that she might lose all of that made her sick to her stomach.

That was why, when he had suggested that she marry Landon Blake, Ari had jumped at the chance. She'd do anything to keep her charity afloat. It gave her a sense of purpose beyond being a hotel heiress. That charity was her legacy, her passion. If she lost her charity, Ari would lose herself. Entering a loveless marriage had seemed like a small price to pay to keep her sense of identity.

Slowly, she picked up the rented necklace she had tossed aside last night and put it around her neck. No, at first she hadn't minded the idea of marrying Landon. They had an understanding. He would keep doing his own thing, and she hers. The union would be in name only and at the time seemed to be the answer to everyone's problems.

But that was before she had seen Leo and his new girlfriend, Karin. Watching them interact, seeing how in love they were, made Ari realize that she wanted more than a business-deal marriage. She wanted fun and laughter. She wanted love.

As she waited for the coffee to heat, she caught sight of herself in the mirror behind the espresso machine. The diamonds looked lovely against her skin, making her look much more dignified and regal than she felt. As she considered her smooth, heart-shaped face and almond eyes, she inched open her bathrobe and ran her fingers along the upper swell of her breast. Yes, she deserved more than a loveless marriage. So much more.

She watched her fingers in the mirror as they slid down the edge of the robe, pulling it open and revealing more of her chest. The tabloids had called her a sex-obsessed party girl, and suggested that she was nothing more than a vapid socialite, focused on spending her brother's money as fast as he could make it. At one time she supposed that was true, but not anymore. Ever since Alisha had died of brain cancer in high school, Ari had shed her partying ways and focused on making the world a better place, not only for herself, but for her friend, who had always had a positive attitude, even in the darkest moments of her life.

As Ari slid the robe from her shoulders and cupped her breasts, she realized that Jason had never commented on her lack of intelligence. To him, she was both beautiful and smart, capable and fun. If only the world could see her the way Jason saw her, and not the little lost party girl of her youth.

While Jason was an improvement over Leo, he wasn't perfect, either. If Jason had any decency, he would have visited her last night to see how she was doing, or at least stop by this morning. It seemed as if he had dismissed her, which in some ways was worse than Leo treating her like a child.

Ari was so tired of not being taken seriously by the men in her life. She was going to have to do something drastic if she wanted Leo and Jason to pay attention . . . but what?

Jason straightened his suit jacket and waited for the elevator doors to open. He wished he'd had a chance to freshen up before he dragged Ari out for a little joyride, but he found he needed to be with her more than anything. Those pictures had disturbed him more than he cared to admit. If someone was watching both him and Ari in this place, then he needed to get her out of here, at least for a little while. Once he had his security team sweep the building, then he'd feel safe once more.

Once the doors parted, he made his way down the hall to her suite. On the way he passed two other honeymoon suites, both under renovation. Their doors were wide open and equipment and plastic tarps covered much of the open space. A quick check of his watch showed that it was still too early for the crew to start working. He and Arianna would be the only ones on the floor for another hour at least. This was good. He didn't want anyone snooping around where they didn't belong.

He knocked on Ari's door and when no one answered

it, keyed himself inside with his spare card. He started to call out for her, but a low, throaty noise stopped him. Curious, he placed the key card back in his pocket and made his way through the living area and into the bedroom. There he found Ari sitting in front of a small table with a Stone Suites robe gathered around her waist, frowning into the mirror. She was cupping her breasts and examining her body, like a scientist might look at an interesting finding under a microscope. A simple diamond necklace hung around her neck. It looked stunning against her smooth skin.

Jason became instantly hard as he stood in the doorway and watched her.

She was criticizing herself in the mirror, he realized. Jason wondered what she was thinking. Surely it couldn't be that she was flawed in some way, could it? Her long black hair cascaded down the smooth skin of her back, and her large, amber eyes watched through half-closed lids as she squeezed her breasts.

Within a minute or two, her frown evaporated, replaced by an expression filled with hunger and need. The change captivated him. Ari was so physically beautiful it hurt, and those little noises she made were enough to drive a man insane with lust. He longed to go to her, but at the same time, he didn't dare break the erotic spell. He didn't want to ruin such a beautiful picture.

Another low, throaty groan filled the room as she lifted her leg and settled it on the small table, next to the coffeepot. The movement tugged the belt on her robe loose, and as it fell aside Jason held his breath. Blood rushed from his head to his cock, leaving him light-headed. He leaned against the doorway as he became dizzy with need.

Ari was completely naked, and her body was just as beautiful as ever. Crossing his arms, he pretended to appear nonchalant as he spoke.

"An interesting way to fill your time."

Ari froze, her eyes going wide as if she was a deer caught in a headlight. After a long moment, she cleared her throat and lifted her chin.

"You," she said as she straightened and lowered her hands.

"Me?" Jason pushed off the wall and slowly started to close the distance between them.

"Yes. You." She watched him through the mirror and waited until he stood behind her. "You've been ignoring me, Jason."

"I'm sorry. I got tied up with work."

"All night?"

"All night."

"Does it have anything to do with whoever you met in the lobby last night?" When he didn't immediately answer, she turned away from the mirror. "I already know it wasn't my brother."

"Smart girl." He put his hands on her shoulders and was surprised to find how tense they were. "No, it wasn't Leo." Her skin was so soft and smooth, like freshly brewed coffee with lots of cream. Jason's mouth watered as he imagined tasting that skin and running his tongue over those sensitive tissues.

She turned back to the mirror and stared at him through the reflection. "Who did you meet?"

"No one important."

"Must have been at least a little important if it kept you away from me all night. Lower."

Jason shifted his hands lower and smiled when she groaned her appreciation. "The person in the lobby had nothing to do with why I didn't return. It was something else. Business." He leaned in closer to her ear. "Believe me, if I could have gotten away, I would have."

"Promise?"

Jason forced himself to look up and meet her gaze in the mirror. He immediately saw vulnerability in her eyes, something he had never seen there before.

"Promise. You know I would have come up here if I could."

"Do I?" Slowly she leaned back in the chair, exposing more of her body for his viewing pleasure. "If you're playing games with me, Jason—"

"I'm not."

"I'm not going to sit up here and wait around like your little plaything."

"Of course not." He pressed his lips against her shoulder. "You are so much more than a plaything to me, Ari."

"Am I?

"Absolutely."

"I don't believe you."

He dragged his head up and met her gaze in the mirror. "Then I'll have to convince you, won't I?"

Chapter 6

Jason slid his rough fingers over her shoulder and to the front of her chest. Her skin was so warm and soft, so inviting. As he touched her, he thought about the pictures down in his office. Were they being watched now, just like they were in the laundry room? He didn't think so, but one couldn't be too careful.

He glanced up at the security camera in the corner of the room. It was possible that someone was using the security tapes to watch both him and Ari. If that was true, then it wasn't safe to be here. It was possible that, to keep her safe, he'd have to move her somewhere else—like his apartment. The idea didn't scare him as much as he thought it would. In fact, it felt oddly right, something that both pleased and terrified him. His home was considered his sanctuary. Never before had a woman set foot over the threshold—unless it was his cleaning woman, Marta. Having Ari there would be a touch too personal. Letting her into his apartment would be like admitting that she meant something to him, and that she was different from the rest. Jason wasn't ready to make that kind of statement. He wasn't sure if he'd ever be ready.

"You're distracted," she accused, pushing his hands away.

"No, I'm not."

"You aren't even looking at me, Jason."

He grabbed a pillow, took off the case, and tossed it over the camera in the corner.

"What are you doing?"

"I don't want us to be disturbed."

She wrinkled her nose. "It never seemed to bother you before."

But before it was on his own terms. "This time, I want you all to myself." His statement seemed to mollify her somewhat, which was good. He didn't want her to think that he didn't want her. Nothing could be further from the truth. Perhaps there was a way out of this mess. A way he could keep Ari and himself safe from scandal and where he didn't have to part with such a large amount of money.

"I refuse to be cast aside, Jason."

"You aren't." He returned to her shoulders. "You won't be."

She made a noncommittal sound. "If I can't have your full attention—"

"I've just been very busy with my business," he said. "The media frenzy from your non-wedding has spilled over to the other hotel chains in the area." He slid his fingers lower, until they hovered over where her breasts began to swell. "Reporters have started hanging outside Stone Suites and a few other chains, hoping to gather information. Everyone wants to know where the Perconti heiress is hiding." He bent down until his lips were level with her ear. "But don't worry. I'll never tell a soul about our little secret."

Ari closed her eyes and shivered as desire rushed through her bloodstream. "Then you aren't trying to get rid of me?"

"Of course not." He sounded appalled as he slipped his

fingers lower. "You're just being paranoid. Any man would be insane not to want to be with you."

Ari didn't want the attention of any man. She wanted the attention of Jason. She had come here for flirtation and fun, but so far all she had done was have a romp in the laundry room like some common maid and wait for him in the honeymoon suite. She had expected more of him, and was beginning to think that coming here was a mistake. This wasn't the Jason she had craved back in the cab. This Jason seemed more serious and aloof.

She pulled away from his grasp and walked over to the security camera. With a flick of the wrist, she tugged the pillowcase from its position and let it fall to the floor.

"What are you doing?"

"Security cameras never stopped us before."

He moved toward the pillowcase, but she stopped him.

"No."

"Ari, people can see—"

"We've had sex in this hotel many times before and not once have you been concerned about the security cameras." She sat back down in her chair and crossed her arms. "What is this really about, Jason? Tell me, or you can leave and don't bother coming back."

Jason stilled, and Ari sensed a growing tension in the room. She wondered if she'd pressed too hard. She knew that she walked a fine line. They had agreed never to talk about their outside lives when they were together, but he was so obviously distressed, and wasn't behaving normally. Whatever was going on needed to be dealt with before Leo arrived. She needed to have Jason's full attention and support if she was ever going to stand up to her brother.

After a long moment, Jason moved behind her once more. His features softened as his fingers returned to her shoulders. “I told you, Ari.” He slid his fingers under her robe, touching her skin once more. “It’s just work. You need to stop worrying about what goes on outside these doors. It’s not important. The only thing that’s important is what I want to do to you.”

“I’m serious, Jason.” He was trying to change the subject. She had seen him use the classic misdirection technique many times with reporters and hated to think that he put her in the same category.

“So am I.” He slid his hands down her chest and covered her breasts, causing her to groan. “Lean back.” He slid her robe lower, exposing her entire upper body.

She slid down in her seat and rested her head against the back of the chair. “You’re not going to distract me. Something’s going on and I want to—” Ari yelped as Jason pulled her chair back, toward him.

“Put your legs up on the table,” he commanded.

“Jason—”

“Just do it.”

She nibbled her lower lip and raised her feet up onto the table.

“Good,” he soothed. “Now spread them apart.” He placed his hands between her thighs and helped her move into position. “There,” he said when he was finished. “Look at that gorgeous woman in the mirror.”

Ari blinked at her reflection. At this angle, her entire body was exposed. Embarrassed, she started to close her legs, but Jason held them apart.

“No,” he commanded. “Leave them open.” When she relaxed, he moved to her side and slid his fingers up the inside of her left thigh. “What do you see?”

She shrugged. “I don’t know.” A party girl, a socialite, a hotel heiress, all of the labels felt wrong on her. She was so much more than any of those things. Why couldn’t anyone see that?

"I'll tell you what I see." He reached the top of one leg, skipped over her folds, and caressed his way down the other. "I see a gorgeous and desirable woman, one I think about every waking moment of the day."

"You do?"

"Of course. Trust me, Ari, if I could have gotten away earlier, I would have."

"You could have called, or sent a messenger."

"I didn't think about that. All I was concerned with was finishing as fast as I could so I could return to you."

Her disbelief must have shown on her face, because he smiled and resumed touching her inner thighs.

"It's true," he said as he slid closer to her mound. The muscles in her core tightened in anticipation, but once again he skipped over her folds and traced a path down the other leg.

"Then why the pillowcase? I thought you enjoyed having sex in public places because of the fear of being caught."

"I do." He hesitated, then resumed his assault on her body. "I just had been thinking about you all night. For once I wanted to have you all to myself."

"We tried that once, remember? Neither one of us liked it very much."

He thought for a moment, while his hands massaged her breasts. Ari bit back a groan as he tugged on her sensitive nipples. "The lake house?"

"You remember."

He smiled. "Of course, I could never forget our first vacation. And you're right. I've been working most of the night and am not thinking clearly. I'm sorry."

They had been at the lake house for only a weekend, but it was one of the best of her life. She and Jason had swum naked in the New Hampshire water, ate barbeque off the back deck, and had sex in every room of his twenty-room vacation home. She twisted her lips into a half-smile. “You’re forgiven.”

He massaged her for a few moments more, quietly turning her body into a steamy pool of need. “Ever think about what someone would see if they walked in on us now?” he asked as he slipped his hand up her leg. “For example, what if someone walked in at this moment and saw me doing this?” He brushed his fingers against her folds. The brief contact sent bolts of pleasure up through her center, causing her to gasp and grip the chair with both hands.

“Jason—”

“Or this?” He leaned closer and flicked his tongue over her nipple. Ari watched him through the mirror as pleasure swept through her body.

“I’ll tell you what would happen. Anyone who stumbled in on us would become as fascinated as I am with your body.” He scraped his teeth against her nipple, causing a sharp pang of pain to pierce her pleasure. Then he rolled her sensitive tip around his tongue, quickly soothing away the hurt.

Ari parted her lips as her need escalated. She glanced down in the mirror and saw that her aching mound had become damp. Moisture glistened along her folds and she resisted the urge to reach down and alleviate some of her ache.

“Never doubt how much I want you, Ari,” Jason said as he moved to the other breast and completed the same delicious torture. As her body alternated between pleasure and pain, he continued to stroke her inner thighs, always coming close, but never touching where she needed him to be.

“Jason,” she gasped as he nipped her other breast.

“That’s it, princess,” he whispered. “Talk to me. I love

the sound of your voice." He nipped harder, then laved her nipple until she started wiggling in her chair.

"Oh, God, Jason. Please."

"Please—what?"

"I need you."

"I could never deny a beautiful woman her request." He raised his head and met her gaze through the mirror as he inched his hand closer to the apex between her thighs. Ari held her breath as he hovered over her mound, not touching, but close enough so that she could feel the heat of his fingers.

"No," he said as he moved away. "Not yet." He stood and walked behind her.

"Where are you going?"

"I don't think you truly understand how desirable you are, or how other women envy you." He reached down and placed her hands over her breasts. "Touch yourself for me."

She watched his features as she did as she was asked. His eyes darkened, and his expression alternated between possessive and hungry. The more Ari touched herself, the more intense he became. After a long moment, he moved behind her. Ari watched him through the mirror as he took off his shoes, cracked open the door to the hallway, and jammed his shoe in it.

"What are you doing?"

"Adding to the excitement," he murmured as he returned to her side.

Ari widened her eyes. While they'd had sex in public before, it was always behind a locked door, or in a forgotten alcove. Never had they been so exposed. "But the staff—"

"Are loyal to me. They won't do anything."

"Are you sure? What if they talk to the tabloids, or take

a picture? I'm sure a picture of me now, when combined with information about my whereabouts, would be worth a lot of money. What if a guest comes—"

"The other rooms on this floor are being renovated, Ari. No one is around."

"The contractors—"

"Won't be on site for another hour at least."

"Is this the same person who threw a pillowcase over the camera?"

"I changed my mind." He started to close the distance between them. "You're losing focus. Pinch harder."

She did, and curled her toes as pleasure speared her core. "Oh, God." All thoughts of embarrassment and reporters faded, replaced by desire.

"You let me worry about the risk," he said as she rubbed her palms over her nipples. "Now stop thinking about the 'what ifs' and focus on the moment." A seductive smile spread over his lips. "Remember our game from the laundry room?"

Did she ever. She'd thought she was going to explode from the excitement. She nodded to Jason as he crouched down so his head was next to hers.

"I want another round." He covered her right hand, pushing it flat against her breast. "Starting now."

He scraped his teeth against her ear. Adrenaline rushed through Ari's bloodstream as she realized that anyone could walk in at any moment and see them . . .

"You're so reckless," she whispered right before he covered her lips with his. His outrageous behavior was what she loved the most about him. Jason was always pushing her to overcome her fears. So what if someone walked in? She didn't have her makeup on, and her hair covered half her face, so all they would see was Jason, giving pleasure to a mystery woman. Adrenaline blasted through her center as she realized how much of a risk they were taking.

The jolt of energy fueled her desire, causing her skin to heat.

Jason broke the kiss and cupped her knee. With a devilish smile, he put the finger of his free hand to his lips then eased her legs farther apart. Ari glanced behind her at the door, and noticed that they were still alone, but for how long?

Jason slipped his fingers up the back of her leg, drawing her attention back to him. Ari inched down on the chair and spread her knees wider apart, silently urging him to touch her everywhere.

"That's it," he whispered. "Watch yourself. See what others will see if they walk into the room. What I see." He inched his hand up and brushed his fingers over the top of her folds.

Ari groaned as a sense of urgency welled up inside of her. "This is hardly fair," she whispered.

Jason raised his brows as he got down on his knees and took off his suit jacket, tie, and shirt.

Excitement rippled through her. "You're going to torture me, but I won't be able to do the same to you."

He shifted his gaze to her breasts as a hungry look passed through his features. "You'd like to touch me?" he murmured.

"Yes."

"To have people watch you touch me?"

"Yes."

"And you will, considering you survive the first round . . ." He ducked under her leg and positioned himself until he was eye level with her mound.

"Jason—"

He brushed his fingers over her sensitive skin once more, causing another round of need to pump through her veins. "Watch me, Ari," he whispered. "See what a bystander would see."

Ari jerked her gaze up to the mirror as Jason dipped his head and slid his tongue between her folds.

Pleasure burst up through her center, making her dizzy. She groaned and kneaded her breasts, letting the sensations roll through her system.

Jason tapped the glass behind him, and then, using his fingers, spread her apart and slid his tongue around the rim of her opening.

"Yes," she whispered. Desire spiraled around her muscles, pulling them tight with need. Jason slid his tongue around and around, never letting up on his sweet torture. Ari watched his head move in the mirror and loved the erotic picture they made. She glanced at the doorway, and still found it empty.

Jason leaned back and pushed his finger into her center. "Such a dirty little princess." He leaned forward and slid his tongue around her opening, collecting the moisture as he moved his finger in and out of her body. "I love it."

"Yes." Ari curled her toes as another round of pleasure slammed into her body. She tried to inch closer, but was unable to from her position. She leaned back on the chair and kept one eye on Jason, and another on the door. She imagined someone walking in on them and watching Jason pleasure her body. On impulse, she let go of her breasts and threaded her fingers through his hair. Both seeing and feeling him move between her legs heightened the pleasure. The air became thick and heavy as tension built. Groaning, she urged him to move faster.

Jason quickened his movements, exchanging one finger for two. He moaned as he slipped his tongue over her skin, as if he was enjoying the act as much as she.

Ari tried to widen her legs and give him better access, but she couldn't from this position. Frustrated, she tightened her grip in his hair as her body started to climb toward that unseen goal.

Ari's breathing quickened as she pinched her nipples harder. Jason slid his tongue up and rolled it over her clit, sending jolts of pleasure racing through her system. Higher and higher she went, until she felt herself hover on the edge of something amazing.

Then Jason adjusted his hands and touched a sensitive spot deep inside her core. Ari bit down hard on her lip to keep from crying out his name as her orgasm slammed into her body. The world faded away into ecstasy as every muscle in her body was enveloped in bliss.

As the last ripples of her joy faded away, Jason retreated, eased her feet down off the table, and tugged her into a standing position.

"You are so beautiful when you come," he whispered in her ear.

"No one won that round," she whispered back. "Now it's my turn."

He flashed her a seductive smile. "I'm not done with you yet." He slid his hands down her waist and grabbed her ass. Ari yelped as he lifted her into the air and set her on the edge of the table.

"Be careful, you might draw the attention of someone out in the hall." He winked as he pulled something out of his pocket and handed it to her. "Hold this."

Ari struggled not to make a sound as she took the condom and watched him peel the rest of his clothes from his body.

"Thanks, princess." Taking the condom from her fingers, he opened it and shoved it over his length. "Now, for the next part of the round." He pulled her legs apart and positioned himself at her opening.

"Cheater," she whispered as he slid into her.

"I always play to win." His smile faltered as he retreated and thrust once more. "God, Ari, you're so wet."

"What? I can't hear you." She grabbed onto his shoulders to steady herself.

"Nice try." Jason leaned forward, leveraging himself against the edge of the table. "Lean back," he commanded.

Ari leaned back until her head bumped into the mirror.

"That's it." He retreated and then thrust once more. "Just like that." Again and again he pushed himself inside of her, each time thrusting a little harder. "So beautiful," he repeated. "And all mine."

Ari curled her fingers into his back and spread her legs wide apart. She loved it when he lost control like this, it felt so wild and primal. She glanced over his shoulder and saw the doorway was still empty. She imagined someone standing there, watching them. Ari arched her back as she pictured the stranger's look of surprise turning into lust. "Yes." She dug her nails into his back as need pumped through her veins.

Harder and harder their bodies came together, until the table started to shake. Ari's head bumped into the mirror with each thrust, but she didn't care. All that mattered was the amazing feeling drawing up in her core.

"Yes," she whispered. "More."

"Ari." Jason nibbled on her ear and pushed harder. The front legs of the table lifted off the ground and fell back with a loud *thump*. The noise echoed throughout the quiet room and added to the building tension.

Thump, thump. The table moved to the rhythm of their bodies, each thrust causing it to tilt more. She could fall, she realized. Their weight and the force of their lovemaking could topple the table. Knowing this gave her another adrenaline rush and fueled her excitement.

"Fuck, yes," Jason whispered as he pushed harder. "Yes."

Ari raked her nails down his back, causing him to groan. He responded by moving his hands from the edge of the table to the mirror. The change in angle caused him to penetrate deeper. The air heated around them, and the sounds of their bodies coming together became drowned out by the thudding of the table on the floor.

"I'm close." She dragged her nails down his spine and dug them into his ass, urging him faster. Pressure built, and she made soft cries with each thrust.

The table started to teeter, and Ari spread her legs higher into the air. "Jason." She curled her fingers tighter into his ass as he pistoned in and out of her body like a machine. Need wound through her, drawing her up higher and higher. Soon she was once again hovering on the edge. She wanted to go over, but held back, determined to win the game.

The table swayed precariously and banged into the wall behind it. They were getting louder, she realized. It was only a matter of time before they'd be caught. She adjusted her hands on his ass and dug in deep, spreading his cheeks apart as she felt her body stretch toward her goal.

Jason's breathing became hard and ragged. "I'm close, baby. So close."

She knew what he needed, what would drive him to the point of no return. Sliding her finger down, she slipped it in between his ass cheeks and rubbed it against the opening in his backside.

"Yes." He let one hand go from the edge of the mirror and grabbed the back of her head. "Just like that." Pulling her close, he covered her lips in a hard, bruising kiss. Never before had Ari felt so thoroughly possessed, so wanted. She inched her finger around the rim of his opening, toying with the sensitive bundle of nerves.

"Fuck, Ari." He pulled back from the kiss and arched his back, pushing harder and harder. His voice rose up with each thrust, but not quite loud enough for anyone outside the room to hear.

She inched her finger just inside his opening.

"Oh, God." He reached in between them and spread her folds apart, allowing her clit to feel the full impact of each thrust. Pleasure surged up quickly through her body, causing her to forget her mission. She slid her hands back to his hips and held on tight as he pounded into her core.

"Harder—"

He shifted his stance, hitting something sensitive deep inside her core. Within seconds she felt the push, the exquisite moment she had been waiting for.

"Jason," she cried as pulse after pulse of joy pumped through her body, each one stronger than the last. She hung there, suspended, as her whole world blanked to nothing but pleasure.

She saw him stiffen and bite his lip. He closed his eyes as his movements became more jerky and desperate. Then, in the next moment, he moaned as he followed her over the edge.

He continued to thrust, emptying himself deep inside her body, filling her with bliss. Ari clung to Jason and buried her head in his chest, never wanting the moment to end.

Letting go of the mirror, Jason slid his arms around her and cradled her to his chest. "I won."

Reality crashed down around her as she lifted her head. Once, just once, she wished he wouldn't rush through the afterglow of sex. But that was typical Jason, afraid to show any hint of vulnerability or emotion. "You did *not* win, I did."

He raised his brows. "It wasn't me who cried out my name load enough for the entire hotel to hear."

Heat rose to her cheeks. After a quick glance at the door to confirm they were still alone, she slapped him playfully on the shoulder and buried her head in his shoulder. "I don't care."

He chuckled as he wrapped his arms around her and cradled her to his chest. "Now do you believe I want you?"

She chuckled against his shoulder. "Yes."

"Good." He slipped his hands down to her ass, lifted

her from the table, and brought her over to the bed. After placing her on the comforter, he peeked out into the hall. Satisfied, he slid his shoe out from the door and let it close.

"That was really risky," she said as he returned to the bed and sat on the edge next to her.

"Not really," he said. "Like I said, they won't show up for work for a while yet. Those workers are union members and have yet to arrive on time."

Ari grabbed a pillow from behind her head and hit him with it. "Beast."

He deflected the blow and chuckled. "Not to say it was completely safe, just unlikely that anyone would walk in on us." He reached for his clothes. After fishing around in his suit pocket, he pulled out his phone.

"Shit."

"What is it?" Ari asked.

He glanced up from the phone and stared at her. "Your brother is downstairs waiting for me. He says that he's come to bring you home."

She lifted her chin. "I'm not going home. Not you, or Leo, or anyone else can make me."

He considered her for a moment, then pulled on his pants. "Get dressed."

"But I told you—"

"I know what you told me." He stood and pulled on his dress shirt. "We're not going to see your brother."

"What?" She stood and closed the distance between them. "We have to, otherwise he's going to be angry."

"Fuck his anger."

Ari blinked. "Excuse me?"

He motioned for her to get dressed. "I've dealt with your brother's anger before." He grinned as he slid on his suit jacket.

"What are you saying?"

"I'm saying that your brother needs to learn that the

world doesn't revolve around him and his needs." He began to text. "Why aren't you getting dressed?"

"All I have is my wedding dress."

He stopped texting and glanced up at her. "It will do for now. Hurry."

She pulled on her stockings and dress. "Where are we going?"

"Somewhere we can have some fun without big brother watching over us." He finished texting and pocketed his phone. "Hurry, he's on his way up here. I don't know about you, but I'd rather not explain to him why you don't have any clothes on."

"How did he know where to go?"

"One of the staff members downstairs looked you up in the computer and told him what room you were in." He frowned. "Your brother can be rather intimidating."

"Tell me about it." She slipped on her shoes. "Okay, I'm dressed."

"Good." He grabbed her hand. "Let's go."

"Are you sure?"

"I've never been more sure about anything in my life."

Before Ari could ask him another question, he pulled her from the room and down the hall. As they started down the stairs, she heard the elevator doors open and her brother's low, booming voice echo down the hall.

"Arianna? Get out here this minute. We're going home."

Stifling a giggle, Ari hurried down the stairs after Jason. Her brother was going to be furious, but she'd deal with him later. She had her fun and exciting Jason back, and she could hardly wait to see what he had in store.

Chapter 7

Jason didn't know which guilty pleasure he enjoyed more: gorging himself on chicken wings and microbrewed beer, or watching his hotel heiress do the same in a torn bridal gown. When they had first come into the mom-and-pop restaurant about twenty minutes north of Boston, they had gotten a few stares, but the people around the North Shore were discreet and used to seeing crazy things. After a few minutes of gawking, the patrons left him and Ari alone.

"I forgot how good these were," Ari said as she licked her fingers. Jason watched her delicate tongue dart out over her thumb and imagined it running over the tip of his cock. Heat slid through his center, and he shifted in his seat to alleviate the sudden pressure against the zipper of his pants.

She reached for another wing and caught his eye. He tried to remain casual, but it was difficult. The woman was beyond hot, and it was hard to think of much of anything besides tearing off her clothes and having his way with her in the middle of the restaurant.

"What?" she asked.

"Nothing." He picked up his beer and took a swig to hide his discomfort. He smiled and imagined the other patrons' reactions if he and Ari started going at it in full view of everyone at the bar. He was tempted to try, but he didn't think that they'd ever be allowed back, and he'd miss the wings.

"I just like seeing you happy," he finally said when he could trust his voice.

She grinned as she waved a chicken wing in the air. "These make me happy."

"I know."

She took a large bite and chewed for a few minutes before responding. "My brothers would never approve of something like this."

"Why not?"

She scrunched her nose. "Too common." She pulled apart the bones with her long, slender fingers. "Leo and Marco prefer dishes with fancy names, like Oysters Rockefeller." She rolled her eyes and took another bite. "And Dante thinks we should only eat Mediterranean dishes from the old country. Eating these wings feels like a small rebellion."

Jason chuckled and took another swig of his beer. "I suppose it is." His phone chirped, and he slipped it out of his pocket to check the caller ID. "It's Leo."

"I'm not talking to him."

"He's probably mad that we ran out on him."

"I don't care. I told my brother that I wasn't going to go home with him, and yet he insisted on barging into Stone Suites and carrying me back to the Palazzo like a petulant child. Until he stops being such an ogre and listens to reason, I don't want anything to do with him."

"You have to at least tell him you're all right, he's probably worried—" Jason moved to swipe the screen and answer the call, but she put her hand over his, stopping him.

"Don't."

He glanced up at her. "You can't avoid your family forever. Eventually you're going to have to explain why you ran away from the wedding."

"I know, just let me avoid them for now." When he didn't put his phone away, she tightened her grip on his hand. "Don't ruin this moment."

She had a point. Her feud with her family was really none of Jason's business. He had much more important things to worry about.

"Remember the first time we came to this place?" Ari asked, distracting him from his thoughts.

Jason smiled as the memory instantly rose to the surface. "It was after I won that charity race." He still remembered that day like it was yesterday. "What was it called again?"

"LAPS4KIDS." Ari tossed her bones onto her plate and grabbed her napkin. After wiping her fingers, she took a sip of beer. "You donated your winnings so you could take me out to dinner." She glanced around the mom-and-pop restaurant. "I have to admit, I was expecting something a little different."

Jason shrugged. "But you liked it anyway."

"Yeah, I did." Her eyes glittered with mischief as she took another wing. "I liked the McLaren, too. Still do."

Jason chuckled. They had sped up the North Shore, letting his favorite sports car do its thing. It had felt exhilarating. "I'm glad."

"Do you think that I could ever drive it?"

"The McLaren?" He widened his eyes. "You're kidding."

"No, I'm not. It's been years since I've driven such a beautiful car."

"Have you ever driven a stick shift?"

She twitched her lips. "I'm sure you can teach me everything I need to know." She wiped her face and hands with her napkin. "You just seem to love to drive the McLaren so much. I want to know why."

Jason hesitated for a moment, trying to craft his response. "Driving the McLaren gives me a sense of freedom."

"Freedom from what?" She glanced around. "You're one of the most successful venture capitalists in the world. You have more money than most people can fathom."

"That all comes with responsibility," he said.

"I know, but you always handle things so well." She studied his face for a moment before continuing. "There's another reason why you love cars, isn't there?"

"There is. Cars are like a status symbol. Most people can't afford luxury vehicles, especially since they depreciate so quickly." He took a swig of beer. "Some can't afford cars at all, even the budget variety."

"True."

"Owning luxury vehicles is like . . . it's telling people that you are financially secure enough to be a little frivolous."

And Jason deserved to be a little frivolous after surviving his horrible childhood. After being passed around from foster parent to foster parent, both he and Deacon settled with a family who didn't have enough food on the table, let alone a car. He thought back to how he and his brother had always dreaded the trip to school each morning. Not only were they all cramped on that terrible rundown school bus, but their three older siblings, children born to Jason and Deacon's foster parents, had loved to pick on them because they weren't related by blood. They had recruited many others on that bus to help them, and mere weeks after moving in with their new family, Jason and Deacon talked about running away.

When they complained, his foster parents did nothing, of course. They only took him and Deacon in to get the money from the state to fund their drug habits. Jason had promised himself that as soon as he could afford it, he was going to buy his own car and teach himself how to drive.

"Your family didn't have a car as a kid?"

"I had a more . . . humble upbringing." He could tell horror stories for hours about the neglect and carelessness of his caregivers, but knew that Ari would never understand. Such a life was completely foreign to her and her close-knit family.

"So now you buy cars to make up for it."

"Something like that." Not liking all of the questions about his past, Jason decided to turn the tables. "So we know why I like fast cars, but not why *you* like them."

"You said that it gives you freedom." Her voice sounded very matter-of-fact, as if that explained everything.

"That's true."

She shrugged. "I want to know what freedom feels like." She leaned on the table, drawing his attention to her low-cut bridal gown. "My family's so afraid of making a bad impression in the media, that I can't do anything without Leo's consent."

"Your brothers must have allowed you *some* freedoms."

"You have no idea the kind of stress we're under. The media has been horrible to my family. They drove my father to suicide, and led Leo to take medication to help with his anxiety."

"Leo takes medication?"

She continued as if she hadn't heard him. "Etiquette classes, fashion lessons . . . every part of my life is choreographed, right down to what I eat and who I can have as a friend. I can't do anything without having the family's approval first. Leo thinks that I'm emotionally fragile. I need protection from the big bad world." She made quotation marks with her hands while saying the last three words and rolled her eyes.

Jason took a long sip of beer as he processed her words. "I had no idea."

"I want to taste true freedom, Jason. Just once." She let out a long sigh. "I thought things would get better as I got older, you know? Instead they've gotten worse."

"What do you mean?"

"My best friend died of cancer while I was in high school." She pressed her lips together and stared at her hands. "It was a difficult time for me. They say that cancer is a slow killer, but it seemed as if only a few short months passed between her diagnosis and death." Ari shook her head and looked away, twisting her napkin in her fingers. "It was so unfair. I didn't know what to do with myself."

"I'm so sorry, Ari." Jason reached out to touch her hand, but she pulled it away.

"No, let me get through this." She took a deep breath before continuing. "The pain was too much sometimes, and I had no idea how to deal with it. I started stealing things to make myself feel better. A candy bar here, a fruit punch there. Before you knew it, I was stuffing cashmere sweaters and Jimmy Choos in my handbags."

"You shoplifted?" Jason raised his brows.

"It wasn't about the money, it was about getting away with it and recapturing that rebellious streak I had shared with my friend." She let out a long breath. "Eventually, it caught up to me. Leo was more understanding than I thought he'd be. He helped me set up ARI'S KIDS as a way to process my grief in a more healthy way. For a while it helped, but then the CFO was caught embezzling money, and Leo stopped trusting me to run it by myself."

"Now he makes all of the decisions for you," Jason guessed.

"Yeah. When Leo started controlling Ari's Kids, it was as if I had lost a part of myself. I want to find it again,

Jason. I want to feel my heart race in my chest and the wind in my hair. I want that rebellious freedom you take so much for granted."

He toyed with the wrapper on his beer bottle as he considered her request. She honestly didn't know how good she had it. People cared and looked out for her. He had never considered the other side—that all of that caring might come across as restrictive and suffocating.

"Okay," he said. "But only a short ride, and I'm in the passenger seat."

Ari let out a loud feminine sound of delight and jumped out of her chair. "Let's go."

"Hold on." Jason threw a few bills onto the table as the handful of patrons around them turned to stare. He grabbed her arm. "Okay, now we can go."

Ari practically floated out of the restaurant and into the parking lot. As they approached his car, Jason started having second thoughts, but then Ari wrapped her arms around his shoulders.

"Thank you." She planted her lips on his, causing his entire body to tighten with need.

Jason tried to slide his hands around her waist, but she had already grabbed his keys and was heading for the driver's side door.

"Hold on." Jason glanced around the parking lot and noticed that it was mostly empty. He had an uneasy feeling about this, but her excitement prevented him from backing down. It had been a long time since he had seen her so happy, and he didn't want to ruin the moment.

Slowly he moved to the passenger side of the car. "I must be insane."

"Everything will be fine. You'll see." Ari grinned.

Jason wiped his hand over his face. "Just . . . put the key in the ignition, Ari. Let's get this over with."

"Where's the ignition?"

Jason ground his teeth.

"I'm joking. Sheesh." She slid the key into the ignition. "Relax. My younger brother, Gio, has a sports car in Milan. I've driven it a time or two."

"He lets you drive his car?"

"I didn't say that." She turned the key. "It's been a few years, but I think I can manage it."

"I'm not sure if this is a good idea, Ari."

"Come on, you promised."

He had promised, and doing this would make her happy. He just hoped that he and his custom-made McLaren came out of this intact.

He leaned closer to Ari and pointed at her feet. "Okay. Just ease off—"

The car made an angry sound and lurched forward.

"Wait!"

"Oh, sorry." She giggled. "I think I remember how to do it now."

Before Jason could respond, she pressed down on the gas. Turning the wheel to the left, she easily navigated the McLaren from one row to the other.

Jason relaxed his shoulders. "That wasn't too bad."

"Of course not." She glanced in his direction and winked. "I've got this. Trust me."

Jason watched as she made her way around the rows of cars, driving as if she was born behind the wheel. He smiled to himself as she navigated another turn and wondered why he had ever had any reservations about this.

"You're really good," he said.

"I know." She smirked and turned around at the end of a row. After positioning them so that they faced the far end of the parking lot, she placed the car into neutral and slid her fingers over the wheel.

"It's quite the car," she said.

"You're quite the driver." Jason inched closer and eased

his hand over her thigh. Seeing her take charge behind the wheel was sexy as hell.

"I've never seen anything like it." She inched her legs wider in invitation.

"I had it custom made," he said as he inched his fingers higher. "Everything about this car is exactly the way I like it." *And the driver.* Jason had never known a woman who had liked to drive as much as he did. Just like the McLaren, it was as if Arianna had been custom made for him.

"Did you do anything to jack up the horsepower?"

"Excuse me?"

She turned and faced the road. "Let's find out."

"We're in a parking lot."

"So?" She floored the gas. Jason jerked back, letting go of her thigh. He grabbed the door handle to steady himself as the car picked up speed.

"Now, this is more like it!" Ari grinned and tightened her grip on the wheel.

"For God's sake, slow down. You're going to kill someone." And ruin his car. He reached for the wheel, but she batted his hand away.

"Stop being a wet blanket. You're starting to sound like my brother." She stepped on the clutch and changed gears.

"Oh, God." He braced himself against the car door. "Ari, stop the car. I mean it."

She giggled as they started to gain speed as they made their way across the parking lot.

"Slow down!" He reached for the wheel again, but she hit him back.

"Stop it, I'm having fun!"

A couple left the back door of the restaurant and stepped into their path.

"Ari!" Jason yelled. "Stop the God damn cah."

"I see them. Hang on." She swerved the McLaren, narrowly missing the couple.

"Stop the cah—now!"

"Okay, okay." Ari slammed on the brakes, causing them to spin. Jason threw out his hands and braced himself on the dashboard.

"Whee!" Ari turned the wheel hard, causing them to do a one-eighty. When they righted themselves once more, she changed gears again and headed back in the other direction.

"Ari!"

"Just once more, I promise."

Before Jason could blink, they were at the other end of the parking lot and spinning in circles once more. This time when they reversed direction, Ari shifted down the gears, slowing the vehicle down and placing it in neutral before finally turning off the engine.

"Oh my God, that was so fun!"

Jason slowly released his death-grip on the dashboard and leaned his head back in his seat. Never again. He would never indulge that woman again.

"Wasn't that fun?"

Jason glanced over at Ari, taking in the flushed cheeks and wide, bright eyes. Was she laughing at him? It was hard to tell. He took one breath, then two, trying to get his thoughts—and his Boston accent—under control. "You've only driven Gio's car a couple of times?"

Ari shrugged and smiled. "Maybe more. I can't remember." She took her sunglasses out of her purse and slipped them on.

"You could've killed someone," he said as he struggled to get his heartbeat under control.

"But I didn't." She dangled the keys in front of him. "It really is a great car. Much better than Gio's Lamborghini."

Jason swore under his breath and grabbed the keys. "Get out."

As they both passed in front of the car to change places,

Ari put her hand on his chest. "Thank you." She stood up on her tiptoes and kissed his cheek. "It really meant a lot to me."

He glanced down at her and his heart began to soften. She looked so much better than she had when they'd left the hotel. More fresh and alive.

"Don't mention it."

"Can I do it again sometime?"

"Hell no. Find your own."

"Does that mean you're going to buy me a sports car?"

He flashed her an irritated look, but Ari just laughed and got into the passenger seat. "I'm joking."

Jason ran his hand over his face and glanced at the sky, quietly praying for strength. As he slid his key into the ignition, his phone rang. Sighing, he pulled it out and looked at the screen.

"If it's Leo, I'm not here." Ari buckled herself into her seat.

"No, it's not Leo. It's someone from work." It was his head of security, and this was the e-mail he had been waiting for.

Jason quickly scanned the screen. His security men had swept the hotel for bugs and cameras, but couldn't find anything out of the ordinary. They'd checked the security tapes, and found no tampering. Whoever had taken those pictures that the loan shark was using to blackmail him must have been physically close by when he or she took them.

Jason swept his gaze around the parking lot. Except for a few patrons leaving the restaurant, it seemed relatively empty.

"What is it?"

Jason held up his finger. "Just a minute." He continued to scan the e-mail, which talked about how his head of security, a former private investigator, had used his contacts to locate the bastard blackmailing him. The loan shark was legit and had a base of operations in Vegas. Unfortunately, this person ran a ruthless underground operation and used unconventional methods to get back the money owed him. While most loan sharks threatened and perhaps roughed up the person owing them money, this one went after loved ones. He had been quoted as saying that a body in a hospital bed was of no use to him. He saw much better results when a gambler's loved ones' lives were on the line.

Picture attachments came with the e-mail, depicting just how far this psycho had gone to get his money. Jason grimaced at the photographs of bruised and bloodied women, and quickly passed over the ones of children on ventilators. Each picture was more gruesome than the last and Jason wondered what kind of sick fuck would do that kind of thing to another person.

"Jason, what's wrong?" Ari asked. "You don't look so good."

Ari. Jason glanced up at the gorgeous woman next to him as the images he had just seen burned through his brain. Would he hurt Ari if Jason didn't pay him? Was that what the photographs back in his office were suggesting?

"I hafta go back to work." Jason noticed that his worry was thickening his accent as he pocketed his phone. He had to get away from Ari before he completely fell to pieces.

"What's going on?"

"Business emergency."

"Jason, what happened?

He started the car and put it into drive. "It might be a good idea to smooth things over with Leo and go back to the family."

"Why?" She took off her sunglasses and stared at him.

"Because it's safer there." He steeled his jaw as his accent thickened. He had to get his emotions under control before he did something stupid.

"Safer? What are you talking about?" She shook her head. "You know I can't go back there. Leo would think that I'm groveling and he'd continue controlling me. I *have* to stay with you for a little while longer if I want my life back. Besides, you promised I could stay with you as long as I wanted."

"You're right, I did promise." He wanted to help her, but staying at the hotel was too dangerous. There had to be somewhere else she could hide out until all of this blew over. "Maybe I overreacted before. You really want to make a statement to your brother?" he asked as he eased back onto the highway.

"You know I do."

He twisted his lips into a half-smile. "Then don't stay at the hotel. Stay with me instead."

"With you?"

He glanced at her and then returned his attention to the road. "In my apartment."

"I thought you never let anyone in your apartment."

He didn't, not under normal circumstances, but this was different. His apartment had extra security, and he could keep her closer to his side. "You don't want to stay there?"

"I do. It's just . . . you're acting really weird."

"Sorry, it's just the renovations at the hotel have hit a snag. They're going to be making a lot of noise in the honeymoon suites so you can't stay there. And I want to help you. Staying at my apartment will work out for both of us." The lie fell easily off his tongue, a little too easily. Flashbacks ran through his head of some of the other women he had lied to and manipulated. Maybe Deacon was right in saying that people like them don't really change.

Jason gripped the steering wheel tighter. No, he was a

different person now. This wasn't some con to get Ari's money, but a means to keep her safe. Besides, Jason would never think of taking those other women into his personal space. This was completely different.

"Okay, I'll do it," she said.

Jason pulled into the garage underneath Stone Suites and parked the car. "Great. Go get your things and meet me back here. I'll finish up some small projects on my desk and then take you to my apartment."

"Get my things? Haven't you been listening to me? I can't go back to the Palazzo."

"Then have someone go get them for you." He got out of the car and began to text his security man to meet him in his office. "I've got to run." He started toward the hotel, and heard Ari following in his wake.

"Jason, wait up."

He stopped at the door and turned to face her. Ari stumbled and stared at him. "What's going on? And don't tell me it's the honeymoon suite renovations."

"It's nothing." He kissed her cheek and forced himself to smile. "I'll meet you in the lobby." Jason turned his back and hurried away before she could ask any more questions.

Ari watched Jason retreat and tried to process what had just happened. She knew him well enough by now to know that something had him worried, really worried. She wanted to help, but before she could do that, she needed to get her things. She couldn't stay in this wedding dress any longer.

She was going to see his apartment. It wasn't lost on her what a significant step this was. No one saw Jason's apartment besides his cleaning staff. He considered it too personal and private. The fact that he had asked her to stay there instead of the hotel was a huge step.

A huge step toward what, she had no idea, but she wasn't going to overthink it.

Ari searched around for her cell and remembered that she had thrown it at the mirror in her room. God, she hoped it still worked. Sighing, she made her way to the service elevators and up to the ninth floor. After searching the floor for a few minutes, she found the phone under the dresser. She picked it up and let out a sigh of relief when she saw it turn on. Now, who to call . . .

There was Karin, but her last phone call to her had ended in disaster. Karin was far too close to Leo for Ari to lean on.

There was her sister, Gianna, but she hated rich, powerful men and everything to do with the hotel industry. She'd be no help. Then there was Gio. Gio was selfish. He'd just twist her problem to his own advantage and probably get her in even more trouble. While she loved her younger siblings, neither could be fully trusted.

There was only one person she could count on in this situation. Hopefully she was still at the Palazzo.

"Camille," Ari said when her friend finally picked up the phone.

"Ari! Where have you been?"

"I need a favor . . ."

Chapter 8

After a quick glance in either direction on the sidewalk, Ari slipped inside Sabrina's, a small Italian restaurant on the North End of Boston's busy Italian district. Both she and Camille had agreed to meet somewhere within walking distance of the Palazzo, since cab drivers could be bribed for information. Ari was pretty sure Camille wouldn't be followed by one of the Perconti brothers, but they couldn't be too careful. Everyone knew how close Camille was to Ari, and Ari didn't need one of her brothers showing up and ordering her back home. She wouldn't go with them, of course, but the inevitable shouting match would make quite a story for the tabloids.

Keeping her sunglasses on, Ari quickly scanned the checkered tables and Italian décor until she found Camille sitting in a booth in the far corner. A man was with her whom Ari didn't recognize. Ari thought about leaving, but realized that she was being paranoid. Jason had made her jumpy back at Stone Suites with his odd behavior. The sooner she got back to him and figured out what had made him so upset, the better she'd feel.

"Ari." Camille gasped as Ari approached the booth and removed her sunglasses. "You look . . . different."

"A lot has happened." Ari nodded at the tall, thin, blond man sitting across from her friend. "Who's this?"

"A friend," he said as he swept his gaze over her, assessing. "Karin sent me."

Ari narrowed her gaze at her friend. "I told you not to talk to anyone."

"I had to get into your room, and Karin agreed to help me if I brought him along," Camille murmured. "He seemed genuinely concerned, and is quite the sweet talker." She flashed the man a seductive smile. "Handsome, too. He promised he wasn't associated with the media, or any of the Perconti brothers."

"My name's Wes and I'm in charge of housekeeping at the Palazzo. Karin sent me because she's worried about you. She wanted to come herself, but . . ."

"I understand." Ari considered him for a moment, then shook his hand. His fingers were long and firm, his grip solid. This was a man who seemed comfortable with himself and his surroundings. "I assume you are discreet?"

"Very." He flashed her a half-smile. "If you only knew . . ."

"What happened?" Camille asked. "The last I heard you left the wedding, and then you didn't call me." She flashed Ari a hurt expression. "I thought you'd at least call."

"I'm sorry, I've been busy."

"Have you talked to Landon?"

"Things are fine with Landon. He didn't really want this wedding anyway. I've been staying at Stone Suites."

"We know that," Wes said. "But why?"

"To make a statement." Ari glanced around to make sure no one was looking in their direction. "I'm tired of Leo controlling every little aspect of my life—"

"May I take your—oh my God." A tall woman with red

hair tied back in a high ponytail shrieked and fell into the seat beside Wes. "Is that really you?"

"Hi, Sabrina." Ari crouched lower in her seat and pulled her coat up around her ears. "Could you keep it down?"

"I'm sorry." She glanced at Wes and then held her hand out to Camille. "I'm Sabrina. I own this restaurant."

"Camille. How do you know each other?"

"I used to date her brother." Sabrina scrunched her nose. "It didn't work out."

"Thanks to a crazy fan and a 'let's not get serious about anyone' pact between Leo, Marco, and Dante," Wes added. "I miss you around the Palazzo. You made things more interesting."

She patted Wes's hand. "But you're always welcome here."

"It's not the same."

"I know. Some things can't be helped, though."

Ari cleared her throat, bringing everyone's attention back to her. "Could we save this for later? The longer I stay, the greater the chances someone will recognize me." She nodded to where some of the patrons had turned and started staring. "I don't want Leo to find me and create a scene."

"Sorry." Sabrina tapped her finger. "Come into the back with me. We can all talk in my office."

Ari started to protest—she didn't want to be an inconvenience—but everyone was already moving. She had to admit, it would be safer back there. Already people were giving them strange looks. It would only be a matter of time before someone recognized her and tweeted their location.

"I'm sorry, I don't have enough chairs," Sabrina said as she entered the small office area. The walls were cream colored, accented with prints of abstract art. Her desk was simple pine, and a filled bookcase stood in one corner. Aprons, menus, and various knickknacks littered the room, giving it a homey, lived-in feel.

Sabrina scooped up a jacket from one chair and tossed it in a corner. "Someone can sit here." She removed a large, orange-colored tabby from the chair. "And here." The cat gave her an angry glare, flicked its tail, and went to lie on the coats in the corner.

"Nice cat," Camille said, studying the tabby.

"Yeah. Jazz thinks he owns the place," Sabrina said. "And I guess in a way he does. He and my gecko don't get along, so I take him down here with me when I'm working." She tore her gaze away from Jazz and glanced at Camille. "I live in the apartment above the restaurant," she explained.

"Where's my suitcase?" Ari asked, trying to steer everyone back on topic.

Camille dragged her gaze away from the bookcase and took the other empty seat. "Right here." She rolled the small carry-on luggage up to one of the chairs and sat down.

"Can I have it?"

"Not until you tell me what happened. Why did you run out on your own wedding?"

Ari glanced around the room and found everyone's attention was focused on her. "I decided that I didn't want to get married anymore." She glanced at Camille, willing her not to give away too much information. "I talked to Landon and it seems as if my running away was more of a relief to him than anything else."

Camille slapped the arm of her chair. "I knew you never should have agreed to Leo's crazy idea. The cards don't lie—"

"Why did you not want to marry him?" Sabrina asked. "The papers were making it out as a fairy-tale wedding."

"That's what Leo wanted them to believe," Ari said.

"She doesn't love him. She loves Jason Stone," Camille answered before Ari could speak.

"I do not," Ari answered, narrowing her gaze at her friend. "We're just having fun." She glanced around at all of the curious expressions. "We *are*."

"Sure." Camille crossed her arms. "I've watched your expression when he texts you. If you don't have feelings for him, then I'll eat my own foot."

"It's not serious, Camille, honest."

Sabrina leaned closer. "So you're not—"

"No." Ari shook her head emphatically. "Well, yes, we're having sex, but that's it." She made a pointed look at Camille.

Wes rubbed his hand over his jaw. "Karin knows about this, I'm assuming?"

"Yes, she does. I tried talking to her earlier, but Leo found out and came rushing down to Stone Suites to bring me home." She turned to Camille. "That's why I can't go back there right now. Leo's far too mad to be reasonable, and if he sees me I'm afraid he's just going to start controlling my life even more."

"How long has your relationship with Jason been going on?" Sabrina asked.

"We started seeing each other soon after you and Dante broke up. No one knows about us, not the media, not friends, and certainly not my family. If Leo ever found out that I'm sleeping with Jason . . . he'd kill me."

"I'll say." Sabrina huffed. "When Dante's crazy fan set my restaurant on fire, Jason was right there, sticking his nose in the media and drumming up trouble." Sabrina shook her head. "That man lives for the spotlight." She crossed her arms. "I'm surprised he hasn't already used your relationship to his advantage."

"He wouldn't do that," Ari insisted. "Jason would never use me."

"I told her it was a bad idea, but would she listen?" Camille shook her head at Ari. "The cards predicted that he'd be nothing but trouble for you."

Ari frowned. "You know I don't listen to a deck of cards."

"You should."

Sabrina leaned her hip against the corner of the desk. "I'm still not quite following this story. If you were with Jason, why did you agree to marry Landon Blake?"

Ari sighed. "The marriage was a sham. It was arranged by Leo to calm the rumors surrounding Landon and his kinky lifestyle. In exchange for my hand, my family would get use of Landon's aviation empire. Together, Leo and Landon were going to create some vacation deals to draw people away from Jason's hotels and back to us. When I told Jason about it—"

"Wait, you told Jason about Leo's plan?" Wes asked.

"Of course." She shrugged. "Shouldn't I have? We were having sex. The marriage would change that."

Sabrina shook her head. "Honey, you told your family's fiercest rival Leo's plan to outwit him."

"You gave away company secrets and compromised their plan," Wes agreed.

"I did not."

"Are you sure about that?" Camille asked.

Ari thought about it, then shook her head. "Jason wouldn't use me like that." When both of her friends frowned, she slapped the arm of her chair. "He wouldn't."

"Okay, okay," Wes said. "So what happened next?"

Ari took in a long breath. "When I arrived at the Palazzo for the wedding and saw how much Leo and Karin were in love, I knew that I couldn't enter a marriage that would be in name only, not if there was a chance that I could have that kind of love for myself." She looked down at her hands in her lap. "I'm so tired of being a pawn. I want to be loved and respected as an equal."

"What about Jason?" Wes asked.

She shrugged. "He's a diversion, that's all. He isn't really marriage material."

"No, he isn't." Sabrina crossed her arms. "Stone is much too calculating and selfish to have a real relationship. Which brings me to your wedding." She studied Ari's face for a moment before continuing. "By breaking up your marriage, Stone keeps the upper hand over the Percontis."

"He's not using me." Ari stiffened her jaw, not liking the direction this conversation was going.

"Think about it, honey," Camille said. "Think about how much Jason stands to gain if Landon and your brother don't combine their assets."

"Our relationship isn't like that. If anyone is using me, it's my family."

"Your family loves you," Wes said.

"They have always used me to improve the family image." She looked at each of them in turn. "That's why Leo is so controlling. Everything I do impacts the family and the company."

"That's a lot of pressure," Wes murmured.

"Tell me about it."

"Well, what do you want to do now?" Sabrina asked.

"What do you mean?"

"Your marriage is off, your family is worried sick . . . and as far as I can tell, Leo still has control over your life. What are you going to do about it?"

Ari lifted her chin. "Well, I'm going to take back my charity, for starters."

"The charity!" Camille shifted in her seat and faced Ari. "I totally forgot about the charity."

"What do you mean?" Ari asked.

"That reporter called—Amanda Vaughn."

Ari wrinkled her nose. "That's the same reporter who did that exposé on our CFO."

Camille nodded. "She wants to do a follow-up piece."

"Why?"

Camille shrugged. "I guess to show how the charity recovered after the embezzlement."

"More like she wants to get the inside scoop about the wedding," Sabrina murmured. "I've had run-ins with this reporter before, Ari. She's the type to twist your words to make a story."

"She gave Karin and Leo a lot of trouble, too," Wes added.

Ari clapped her hands together. "That's it."

"What's it?" Sabrina asked.

Ari turned toward Camille. "If I grant this reporter an interview, I can show Leo and the rest of the world that I'm not a silly, troubled party girl. Not only can I put the embezzlement story to rest, but fend off rumors about the wedding and show that I'm my own person."

"I don't know," Sabrina said. "It's risky."

"But it can be done." Ari moved to the edge of her seat. "This is perfect. With one brief interview, I can take back control of my life."

"What about Jason?" Wes asked.

"What about him?"

"Well . . ." Wes glanced at Sabrina and Camille before continuing. "You said that you were seeing him as a form of rebellion against your family. You also said that you were staying with him to make some sort of a statement. It seems to me that once you work things out with Leo, you won't need your relationship with Jason anymore."

Ari scrunched her nose in thought. "I suppose you're

right." Although the thought of breaking up with him didn't sit very well.

"He probably won't like being dumped," Sabrina said.

"I never said I would dump him." Ari shook her head. "Besides, I don't need to worry about that right now." She stood and turned toward Camille. "Give that reporter a call and tell her that I'll meet her at the Children's Hospital tomorrow morning."

"Are you sure?" Camille asked.

Ari nodded. "If we show her firsthand how our charity is helping kids, she's sure to paint us in a good light."

Camille stood. "You're the boss." She nodded toward the door. "Come on, I'll walk out with you."

Ari started to leave, but Sabrina stopped her. "Just be careful," she said.

"I can handle myself with that reporter."

"No, not the reporter. I'm talking about Stone." She took a deep breath. "I've seen how this guy operates, and it isn't pretty. If there's a chance he can exploit your family and make a few bucks, he'll take it."

"Don't be ridiculous. I told you, Jason isn't like that. He's changed."

"You sure about that?"

"Absolutely." Ari waved her off and said her good-byes, but as the large pillars of Stone Suites came into view once more, she remembered Jason's odd behavior, and wondered if there wasn't some truth to Sabrina's warning.

Jason tried to read the e-mail on the computer screen, but the words were fuzzy and starting to blend together. He rubbed his eyes and blinked them several times, but it was no use. He had been at his large, oak desk for far too long and on little sleep, trying to figure out some way out of this mess.

The worst part of all of this was that Jason had no idea

who could have stolen his identity, or why he was being targeted. He had made a long list of people with potential bad feelings toward him, but didn't think any of them would do something so underhanded. The type of people he knew would confront him face-to-face, not blackmail him from the shadows.

Jason glanced around the high-rise corner office, suddenly sick of the plush red carpeting and leather furniture in the sitting area. Despite the floor-to-ceiling windows with a view of the harbor, he felt as if he was in a prison and time was running out. He had no idea just how much the problems in the Perconti family would affect him. That tabloid reporter, Amanda Vaughn, had been calling, wanting to schedule an interview. She had caught wind that Stone Suites' investors had been jittery and had done some digging into the company's financials. She didn't find much, thank goodness, but Jason had built a house of cards trying to hide how much money he had sunk into this new software. All it would take was for the reporter to discover that his personal savings had been keeping the company afloat for the past two years to ruin his credibility as a savvy businessman.

"You look like you could use this, little brotha."

Jason jerked back in his office chair and stared up at Deacon, who held out a cup of coffee.

"How did you get in here?" Jason asked as he snatched the cup from his brother's hands. "My office is private."

"You left the door open." Instead of leaving like Jason hoped, Deacon made himself comfortable in the chair opposite him and dropped a long, thin, envelope on the desk. "And a couri-ah brought this by for you this morning."

Jason stared at the envelope, which looked eerily similar to the last envelope he had received by courier. Was it from the loan shark?

He forced himself to remain calm as he took the envelope from Deacon's hands and tossed it on the stack of unanswered mail.

Deacon frowned. "You look like you've been running behind on ya correspondence."

"That's none of your business."

He stared at the unopened envelope for a minute and then met Jason's gaze. "Do you think it's more pictures?"

Jason pushed his hair back from his face and leaned back in his chair. "I don't know."

"Aren't ya goin' to open it?"

Jason frowned. "No."

"Why not?"

"It doesn't matter what's in there. That loan shark isn't getting a dime from me."

"Then they'll force it from you." Exasperated, Deacon ran his hand over his face. "I know how these people work."

"You do?"

Deacon nodded. "From my underground fighting days. They get real mean when things don't go their way."

"I can handle it. I'll just explain—"

"You can't reason with these people." Deacon moved to the end of his seat and pressed his finger on the desk between them. "Let's suppose they believe you—which is a long shot considering how many other people have tried a similar excuse—but let's just say that you're able to prove that you aren't the one who racked up the debt. They'd beat you up on principle."

"I don't follow."

"By admitting that you aren't the one who owes them money, they'll have ta admit that they were conned." Deacon pressed his lips together as some indescribable emotion crossed his features. "They need to save face, or everyone will try to scam them. They'll want to make an example of us."

"There's no us. This is my problem, Deacon, not yours."

"But we're brothers. We used to be so good together. We could be that way again, you know?"

"I'm not conning these people."

"Okay, no conning, but we can still work together."

Jason flexed his fingers, eager to punch something. "Deacon, you don't want to be a part of this, believe me. He's telling me that if I don't pay him, he's going to hurt not only my staff, but my . . ." *My girlfriend.* Jason pressed his lips together, biting off the words that had almost tumbled from his lips. Ari was not his girlfriend. Girlfriend implied intimacy and trust. His relationship with Ari had none of that. It was just sex and fun, nothing more.

This mess was why he could never open his life up enough to let anyone get that close to him. His past would always catch up to him, always put those he loved in danger.

Deacon considered him for a moment. "You told her about the pictures, didn't ya?"

"Told who?"

"Your little heiress."

"Ari knows nothing about this."

Deacon nodded and was silent for a long moment before responding. "What if they come after her?"

"I'm taking precautions."

"By having her stay at the hotel?"

"No—my apartment."

Deacon widened his eyes in surprise. "But you know the rules—never let—"

"Anyone into your personal space. It makes you vulnerable and weak. I know." It was a creed they had both come up with during their conning days.

Deacon nodded. "It will give them something to use against you."

"Ari won't do that. She's not a manipulator like those other women."

"Are you sure?"

"Yes." Jason made sure his voice had a note of finality about it.

"Okay, okay." Deacon held up his hands. "But why her?"

"What do you mean?"

"Why go to such great lengths to protect her, and potentially have her find out all of your dirty little secrets?" He shook his head. "I say cut her loose and let the loan shark do whatever he wants with her. She's just a girl. You need to focus on preserving the important things. Like your company and public image."

"And Ari," Jason said. "She's innocent, Deacon. I can't throw her to the wolves."

Deacon stared at his brother for a long moment and then shook his head. "I've never seen you this . . ."

"This what?" Jason asked when he didn't continue.

"This *territorial* before. I mean, who cares if she gets hurt?"

"I care," Jason muttered.

Deacon tilted his head to the side and studied Jason's face. "You don't have feelings for her, do you?"

Jason's phone rang, and he frowned as he put it on speakerphone. "Yes?"

"Leo Perconti on line one." Michaela's voice was clear and professional, without a hint of emotion. Jason didn't particularly want to speak with the Perconti patriarch, but if it meant getting rid of his brother and his bothersome line of questioning . . .

"Okay, just give me a minute." Jason placed the call on hold and glared at his brother. "I need to get back to work. This conversation is over."

"Don't be so hasty to rule out the con. I bet if we work together, we could pull one over on them and get that loan shark to leave us alone." He clapped his brother on the shoulder. "It could be our biggest con yet."

Jason wanted to tell him no, but doing so would open debate, and right now he needed his brother out of his office. "We'll talk about this later."

Deacon grinned. "Sure. Later." He shoved one hand into his pocket and reached for the door with the other. "It will be amazing, bro. You'll see."

"Good-bye, Deacon."

Deacon chuckled and left the room, closing the door behind him. Jason let out a long breath as he realized he was alone once more. He didn't like his brother's line of questioning. The man was too astute when it came to Ari. The sooner he got rid of his big brother, the better.

Jason pressed a button and picked up the phone on his desk. "Well, well, to what do I owe this pleasure?"

Chapter 9

Ari dragged her suitcase along the cement floor of the Stone Suites parking garage and toward the employee entrance. Along the way, she once again caught sight of Jason's sports cars. As she slid her gaze over the luxury vehicles and settled on the McLaren, she remembered how wonderful it had felt to ride with Jason out past the city, letting the wind flow through her hair as they sped down the highway. Jason had looked comfortable behind the wheel, and incredibly handsome. She smiled as she remembered how she had manipulated him into letting her drive the car. The calm, cool, and collected persona he showed the world had completely disappeared. It was kind of nice.

Ari slipped through the door and dragged her suitcase down the long hallway to the elevator doors.

"I've seen you somewhere before." A low baritone rose up from behind her as she waited.

Ari jerked around to see a tall, sandy-haired man next to her. At first she thought it was Jason, but the man's hair was too long, his face too narrow.

"Who are you?"

"A friend." He took a step closer. "The more interesting question is, who are you?"

"No one." Ari turned back toward the elevator and silently willed it to hurry.

"Oh, I think that you're someone, someone very important."

The elevator doors swung open, and Ari picked up her suitcase.

"Do you always sneak into Stone Suites, Arianna Perconti, or only when your brothers are searching for you?"

She stopped, letting the elevator doors slide closed, and put her suitcase down in the hallway. "What do you want?"

The man smiled in triumph as he took a step closer. "I want to know why my brother would risk so much to be with a spoiled hotel heiress."

Jason has a brother? He had never told her about a brother before. Arianna was determined not to let her confusion or fear show. She crossed her arms and dragged her gaze over his lithe frame. "You should learn to mind your own business."

"Oh, but you see, this *is* my business." He took another step forward, forcing her to take a step back. "Anything that interests my brother interests me."

Fear rippled through Ari as she took another step back and bumped into the wall. Glancing around the hall, she noticed that they were alone. "You should talk to him, then."

"Oh, I did." He closed the rest of the distance and put his forearm on the wall behind her, next to her head. "I talked to him at some length." He crouched down until he was at eye level with her. "You see, Jason is aloof and cold, even with his own family." He slid his finger down the side of her cheek. Ari recoiled and pressed her back harder against the wall. "He prides himself on having control in every aspect of his life, but with you . . . you have managed to get past his walls."

"Jason and I are just having fun."

"Fun." He tilted his head to the side. "Did you know that I came here looking for a place to stay, and he offered me his hotel, but not his apartment?"

"He didn't?"

"No, Jason keeps his past and his private life closely guarded. No one can ever enter his apartment except his cleaning staff . . . and it seems, the younger sister of his strongest competition." He hooked his finger under her chin and lifted her head to meet his gaze. "What is it about you, Ms. Perconti, that makes my brother forget the principles he grew up with? What is it that causes him to let you in but shut me out?"

"I don't know what you're talking about." She tried to jerk her head out of his grasp, but he held firm.

He tilted his head and shifted his gaze to her mouth. "Oh, I think you do." He leaned forward until only a sliver of air separated their lips. "Yes, you do." He dropped his hands and took a step back. "You might entertain him now, Ms. Perconti, but blood is thicker than water. Soon, you shall see where his true loyalties lie."

"Get away from me." Ari hit the button for the elevator once more as the man adjusted his bomber jacket.

"If you wish to entrap my brother, Ms. Perconti, you better do it quickly. Your time is running out." He took out his sunglasses and slipped them over his eyes. "Now, if you'll excuse me. I think I'll go for a ride."

Ari watched him go out the side door toward the garage. Within moments, she heard the roar of a motorcycle engine and saw his retreating form drive out of the garage and into the street.

Jason had a brother? Ari blinked as she realized that not only did she not know anything about the guy who had just assaulted her in the hallway, but she knew nothing about Jason's past. For months she had told him about her family, her charity, and her problems, but he had shared nothing in return.

Sabrina's words echoed through her head. *He's using you*. Ari didn't want it to be true, but she had to consider the possibility. If Jason thought that he could just use her and then toss her aside, then he had another think coming.

"You know why I'm calling, Stone," Leo said.

Jason tightened his grip on the receiver. "I do?"

"Where's my sister?"

"I don't know what you're talking about."

"I'm not a fool. I know you have her. Now, send her home where she belongs."

"Ever consider the possibility that she doesn't want to go home?"

"That's ridiculous. Why wouldn't she want to come home? She can't possibly want to stay there with you."

And what was that supposed to mean, that he wasn't good enough for Ari? Jason tightened his jaw to keep from yelling. Leo was just worried, he told himself. He'd feel the same way if the situation was reversed. "Have you ever listened to her?"

"Of course."

"I mean *really* listened to her?"

"What do you mean?"

"I mean, she doesn't want to go home because she's afraid that you'll control her life."

"I don't do that."

"She doesn't see it that way." Jason let out a long breath. "Look, I think she just needs a little time to sort things out."

"She talked to you, didn't she?"

"Yes."

Leo let out a frustrated noise. "What am I doing wrong that she is more comfortable confiding in you than me?"

Jason blinked at the uncharacteristic show of emotion. "Maybe if you had a little more patience."

Leo snorted. "You don't have a sister, Stone, do you?"

"No."

"Well, I'll let you in on a little secret. They'll turn you prematurely gray." After Jason chuckled, Leo continued. "It's so hard keeping this family together. Sometimes I envy you, Stone."

"*You* envy *me*?"

"You have no one to look after, no one you're responsible for but yourself. It must be so freeing."

Jason stared at the phone, not quite believing what he was hearing. For so long he had been jealous of Leo and his large family. Now he was hearing that Leo was jealous of him. It was difficult to wrap his head around the knowledge.

"She loves you, Leo, she just wants to be her own woman."

Leo sighed. "I know. I just wish I knew how to get out of this mess."

Jason's heart softened. He didn't have a sister, but he had a brother, and he knew how difficult navigating a sibling relationship could be.

"I could try talking to her," he offered.

"I'd appreciate that, Stone. I just want her home where she belongs."

"I understand."

"Anyway, Ari wasn't the only reason why I was calling."

"It wasn't?"

"Perconti Enterprises will be pulling out of Asia."

"But you have so many hotels."

"I know that you've been trying to build a presence

there, so I wanted you to have first opportunity to take them. If you want."

"I—I don't know what to say. Are you sure?"

"Very. We can no longer afford to be so spread out. We must consolidate our efforts and focus on our image."

"How much are you looking to get for them?"

"Name your price, Stone, and they're yours."

"You're kidding."

"I wish I were."

"Well, I'll have to have my people look into it."

"Of course. Just fax over an offer to my offices and I'll have my team set up the paperwork."

"No haggling?"

"No haggling."

"What's the catch?"

Leo chuckled. "Not everyone is like you," he said. "Everything doesn't have to have an angle."

They said their good-byes, and as Jason hung up the phone, he let out a long breath. Talking to Leo had always required him to be at the top of his game. One slipup, and the Perconti patriarch would eat him alive.

This conversation had been different, however. Leo seemed to have lost a lot of his fight. The long-term potential of expanding his holdings in Asia was too good to pass up. Leo knew this. It was the one place where he held a strong advantage. It must have been why he said it was for sale. He knew that Jason wouldn't be able to resist.

The deal was perfect, but it felt wrong. Jason lived for the haggling and strategic posturing that often accompanied business transactions. By offering what Jason wanted most and accepting Jason's ridiculously low price, Leo had managed to take all of the enjoyment out of doing business.

Jason stood up from his desk and walked over to the window as he sorted through all of the information he had learned over the past few days. He wondered what Ari would think of him when he told her that Leo wanted him to purchase part of her family's empire. Taking future income from her family would be a strain on their relationship, but Ari was also a better businesswoman than her brothers gave her credit for. She'd see that Leo needed the cash in the short term in order to meet his creditors and keep his investors satisfied.

She was a sensible businesswoman, but part of him wondered if she'd have hard feelings from seeing him profit over her family's loss. The past few weeks had been hard on her and her family, and purchasing these hotels wasn't going to play out well in the media. He didn't want her to suffer more than she already had.

Jason shook his head and made a low sound of disgust. Since when did he make a business decision based on the feelings of a woman? Leo wanted him to have these hotels, had practically given them to Jason for free. He'd be a fool not to capitalize on such an opportunity.

Unless . . . unless Leo had some ulterior motive. Perhaps there was more wrong with those hotels than he'd let on. Perhaps Leo wasn't giving him an advantage in Asia, but a money pit that would drain his resources and give Leo a chance to build up his holdings in Europe.

The idea was a long shot, but not impossible. Jason would have to question Ari about those hotels.

He started to leave, but noticed the unopened envelope Deacon had given him. His brother had certainly seemed interested in it and the rest of his unopened correspondence. Frowning, Jason grabbed the envelope, ripped it open, and pulled out three thin sheets of paper.

One was a photo of him and Deacon, arguing in the front foyer of his hotel. He immediately dismissed it. The photo had been taken in a public place. It only managed to prove that he had talked to Deacon, not that Deacon was his brother.

The second photo was of him and Ari, eating chicken wings and drinking beer.

Jason's chest squeezed as he stared at the photo of them together. Ari was smiling at him with those gorgeous lips, and he looked about two seconds away from sweeping the food onto the floor and having sex with her on the tabletop.

Knowing that someone was spying on them at the restaurant made him furious. Jason had specifically chosen that place because it was out of the way. If they couldn't have a casual meal, then where could they go?

His hand shook as he looked at the third sheet. It wasn't a photo, but a note. *Give us what is precious to us, and we won't take what's precious to you.* The note wasn't signed, but it didn't take a sleuth to figure out who it was from.

Ari. If Jason didn't give that Vegas loan shark the money, they'd take both Deacon and Ari away from him. He crumpled the three sheets in his hand and tossed them in the trash. He could never tell Ari that they were being watched, and he could never let her out of his sight. Helping Leo get her home would have to wait. Things were far too dangerous.

Hell, he hadn't seen Ari since leaving her in the parking garage. For all he knew, those bastards could already have her.

Something cold seized Jason's chest. Determined, he poked his head outside his office.

"Have you seen anyone asking for me?" he asked his assistant, Michaela.

Micki stared up at him over her dark-rimmed glasses. "No, should I have?"

He shook his head. "No matter." He stepped outside

his office and closed the door. "I need to go out for a little while and run an errand. Hold all calls."

"Yes, Mr. Stone."

Worried, he made his way to the downstairs foyer, sliding his cell out from his suit jacket pocket.

Where r u? he texted Deacon.

He waited for a response but nothing came. He thought back to those pictures in his office, and the warning they represented.

On my way to a job interview, Deacon finally responded.

Jason let out a sigh of relief. At least his brother was safe. *You need to come here,* Jason texted back. *We need to talk.*

Is this about your girlfriend?

Sort of.

I knew she was behind those pictures.

Jason frowned at the screen. *What are you talking about?*

I knew that she was spying on you for her brothers. Those Percontis would do anything for each other.

Jason blinked at the screen. He had never considered the possibility that Ari might be manipulating him. The idea seemed plausible, especially considering that he was planning on using her as well. Could it be possible that she was behind all of these photographs?

Got to run, bro, Deacon texted. *I'll be by after the interview.*

OK.

He tried to clamp down on his rising worry as he stopped in front of the kiosk in the foyer.

"Has anyone been looking for me?" he asked.

"Like who?" a tall, leggy blonde asked. He recognized the woman who had first told him about the envelope yesterday.

"Short woman, dark hair, olive skin . . ."

The woman thought for a moment. "No, I don't think so."

He glanced at her name tag. "Thanks Keira." He hurried over to the elevators. Where was she?

When the elevator doors opened, Jason fought down his surprise at seeing Ari standing with her suitcase in the corner. "Jason."

"Ari." Relief washed over him as he realized she was safe. He went to hug her, but her embrace felt cold and clinical. Reluctantly, he moved away.

"What is it?" He stared at her features, looking for any sign of betrayal. He hated to think that she had visited her brother and told him insider information about Jason's company, but he had to consider the possibility.

"Did you go to the Palazzo?"

"What? No. I had Camille bring my suitcase to Sabrina's. I met her there. In fact, I was just going up to the room to get the last of my things before meeting you in the lobby."

He searched her face. "You met your brothers somewhere else, then." Leo was using her to learn Stone Suites' secrets. It was what he would have done, and the only logical explanation for her behaving so oddly.

She frowned up at him. "What are you talking about?"

He was such a fool. He should have seen this day coming when he first saw Ari at that charity event. For months she had been working her way into his heart so that she could learn all about his company, his plans to outplay Leo, and report back to her brother.

Knowing that she had beaten him at his own game made him sick to his stomach. "You went to speak to your brothas and tell them about my stretched finances." God, he was fucking losing his shit. He knew better than to think with his heart. Business decisions based on emotion were never wise.

"I don't know anything about your finances. Jason,

you're not making any sense. I did exactly as you asked. I got my suitcase and came right back."

Jason gripped the railing of the elevator to keep from throttling her. "So you deny that this is some elaborate con designed to steal my customer base?"

"You're overtired and not thinking clearly," she said.

"You saw the remodeling—"

"Every hotel undergoes remodeling. It means nothing. What has gotten into you?"

She was right, of course. Ari couldn't possibly know what they were doing next door. Upgrading the honeymoon suites to install Jacuzzis and Italian marble tubs was only the beginning. Jason was planning on building a giant balcony onto each of the rooms, giving honeymooning couples a panoramic view of Boston Harbor while maintaining privacy. All of the luxuries in each room would be operated by remote control, and the entire system would be hooked up to an internal Wi-Fi so that people could not only check in and out in complete privacy, but they could order room service, extra towels, and kinky movies, all at the press of a button.

The epitome of luxury, privacy, and convenience. To say that Ari's wedding had inspired the idea would be wrong. Yes, the timing of these renovations had coincided with her wedding, and yes, he'd even fantasized about giving her a personal and private tour of one of the suites, but the decision had been purely business. The honeymoon industry is a multibillion-dollar industry. It only made sense for him to capitalize on it.

He rubbed his brow. God, he was so fucking tired. Accusing Ari of going behind his back proved just how tired he was.

For days he had been working on almost no sleep and a constant bombardment of emotional distraction. He needed a reprieve before he did something stupid that couldn't be fixed.

"Even if I did see my brothers—which I didn't—there's nothing I could possibly tell them that they didn't already know." Ari moved a stray hair from her face and curled her fingers into her palms. The woman was stunning when she was all fired up, and Jason struggled to control his rising desire.

After adjusting his suit jacket to hide his erection, Jason crossed his arms and leaned against the side of the elevator. "You're right. I'm sorry. It's just . . . your brother offered me his hotels in Asia and I was wondering why."

"He did what?" she asked.

"Leo offered me all of the Perconti Asian interests. It doesn't make sense for him to let them go—unless there is something about them you aren't telling me."

"That bastard." Her eyes widened in shock. "He told all of us before the wedding that we'd each have a stake in the company and help make decisions." She fisted her hands. "Once again, my brothers are making decisions without consulting me—"

"So there is nothing wrong with those hotels?" he asked.

She shook her head. "I don't understand. Leo has put a lot of work into expanding in Asia . . ."

"Oh, I know, which is why I think that his proposal might have an ulterior motive." He searched her face for something—anything—that would give him a clue as to her true feelings. Was everything between them a lie? Was she helping her brother in some elaborate con?

Jason steeled his jaw. No, Ari wasn't the one who had made a living conning people. He had, and he was being paranoid.

"There shouldn't be any secrets between us, Ari." He pushed off the wall and took a step closer. "If you know something about your brother's plan for his Asian holdings—"

"I don't know anything. I swear to you, Jason. If Leo is planning to give up anything in the company, he's doing it without my consent." She shook her head. "I'm not the one holding things back in this relationship. You are."

"What?" he asked as he stopped his advance. "What are you talking about?"

She lifted her chin. "I met your brother."

"Deacon?" Shock slammed through his system. "Where?"

"Right here, in the staff hallway." She pointed her finger at his chest. "You never told me you had a brother."

"He wasn't worth mentioning."

"He seems to think he is. Is he staying with you? Why have you never spoken about him before?"

"None of your business." He turned away as fear exploded through his system. He fisted his hands as he wondered how much his brother had told her, and if he had even told her the truth. Deacon was a master at spinning facts to get someone to sympathize with him.

"Why have I never heard of him?" she asked. "You hear me talk about my brothers all the time."

"Your family is different from mine."

"I can't see—"

"It's just different, okay?" He turned to face her. "Not everyone has a good relationship with their siblings like you."

"Good relationship?" Ari took a step forward. "Good relationship? My brothers try to control me, Jason. They orchestrate my every move and smother me all in the name of family. That's not exactly ideal."

"But they care about you. They order you around because it's their way of protecting you," Jason soothed. "At least you have that."

She searched his face, but Jason couldn't imagine what she was looking for.

"What happened, Jason?" she asked after a long moment. "What happened to you to make you so afraid of trusting anyone?"

Jason stepped back. "I'm not afraid."

"You are. I can see it all over your face." She took a small step toward him. "What happened?"

"Nothing happened. I'm just realistic." Recovering from the shock, he closed the last inch of space between them and tucked an unruly strand of hair behind her ear. "Trusting someone will only make you vulnerable, princess." He repeated the movement again with a second strand, this time much more slowly. As his fingers brushed over her temple, awareness tingled over his skin and desire rushed through his veins. "People make a living out of manipulating innocents to get what they want. Things are much safer when emotion isn't involved."

She placed her hand on his wrist, stopping his movements. "You sound as if you speak from personal experience."

"I am." Jason eased his hands away from her face and around to the back of her head, slipping them through the thick strands of her hair. "I know what you think you want from me, Ari." He inched closer, so close he could smell the strawberry scent of her shampoo. An innocent scent, he reminded himself. Innocent, but oh, so intoxicating. "I can't give it to you. I won't." He stroked her hair gently, enjoying the softness against his fingers.

"Why?" The word escaped from her in a breathy exhale, causing his pulse to quicken.

Good question. Never before had he been so tempted to toss his resolve out the door. It would be so easy to give in to temptation, to tell her about his dysfunctional family and how he'd been left to survive on his own. He wanted to tell her about how much his own family had hurt him, and how, as his life crashed down around his ears, he swore that he'd never allow himself to be hurt like that again. Survival meant he needed to stay one step ahead of his emotions, and loving her, trusting her, would make him vulnerable to his enemies and a danger to himself.

"I know you aren't as heartless as everyone believes," she whispered when he didn't respond. "If you just stopped pushing people away, I'm sure that they'd see what I see."

"And what's that?"

She inched closer. "A kind man. A good man."

"You're a fool if you think that about me."

"I don't think so." She ran her fingers along the lapels of his suit.

"Good men always finish last when it comes to growing a business, princess." He curled his fingers in her hair and tugged, lifting her gaze to his and causing her lips to part in surprise. "And in case you haven't noticed, I play to win." Jason leaned forward and plunged deep inside the soft recesses of her mouth, hoping that this time it would be enough to satisfy him. Knowing that he was as much a fool as she.

Chapter 10

The kiss was hard and punishing, but that wasn't what surprised her. Jason had been rough during sex before. No, there was something more there, a desperation in his kiss that tugged at her heart. He was trying to prove to her that he was a bastard, but nothing could be further from the truth. He might be an asshole in front of the camera, but that wasn't the real him. His kiss told a different story, one that made her feel needed and cherished, and that in turn made her body heat all over.

Ari gripped the lapels of his suit jacket tighter, drawing him closer. He groaned and tilted his head, deepening the kiss. Ari felt as if she was being consumed, and loved every second of it. Her mind began to fog with lust as she slid her hands down from the lapels of his suit jacket and wrapped them around his waist.

"Take me," she said as she pulled away from his lips.

"Here?"

"Right here." Ari dragged her hands down and slid them up under his jacket. "I don't think you want to wait, either." She tugged at his shirt and pulled it from his pants. As their tongues dueled, she slid her fingers under the fabric, desperate for the feel of skin on skin.

"Ari." He pressed harder against her body as he inched down from her breast and grabbed her ass.

"Yes," she whispered as he fumbled with her skirt. After gathering the material around her waist, he nibbled a long line of desire along her jaw and neck.

Ari gasped and leaned back, resting her head against the elevator wall. She slid her hands up along his spine, feeling it curve as he bent over her body.

"Jason," she whispered.

Jason responded by nipping the sensitive spot between her neck and shoulder. She rubbed up against him, enjoying the feel of his swollen erection against her lower abdomen. She dug her fingers into his back and lifted her leg, placing it against his hip. In response he inched forward, wedging himself in between her thighs.

"Yes." She arched her back and rubbed her hips against his erection. With a groan, he slid his fingers around the curve of her ass and locked her leg in place. "Hurry."

He eased his other hand from her hair and slipped his fingers around her other leg. "This will have to be quick," he whispered.

"I like quick." She dug her nails into his skin as he lifted her other leg and pressed his body against hers, positioning her against the wall.

She moved her hands between them and attempted to undo his belt. "I need you inside of me." Ari's mind blanked with pleasure. His belt buckle came apart easily in her fingers. Within moments she'd unhooked the button and zipped down his pants. She reached inside and freed his long erection. Gripping the base, she stroked him from root to tip.

Jason groaned and broke the kiss. "God, that's good."

The elevator began to move. "Someone pushed the button," she whispered, her entire body frozen with shock.

"Hurry," he said. "Before the elevator doors open

again. The condom is in my pocket." Jason moved his fingers until her panties were pushed aside. She sheathed his cock and angled it until the tip pressed against her opening. With a swift thrust he pushed himself balls-deep inside her body.

Ari gasped and clung to his shoulders as pleasure poured through every inch of her body. "Yes."

"That's it, sweetheart," he said. "Come for me." He slipped his fingers in between her ass cheeks and around her opening. "Give yourself over to it." He eased back and thrust deep once more, pushing her hips against his fingers. She whispered his name as his finger inched inside her body.

"The elevator . . ." She glanced at the control panel. First floor, second . . .

"Ignore it." He kissed her neck. "Stay with me, princess." He moved in and out of her body, from both the front and back. Each stroke was like a caress, filling her with need.

"Yes, that's it. Keep going," he urged as he quickened his movements.

Third, fourth . . . They were moving up. Ari could feel the elevator climbing. She had no idea who had pushed the button. Waiting on the other side of those doors could be a guest, a staff member, or anyone, really. The elevator could open at any moment, on any floor. The knowledge made her dizzy with desire.

"Ari, I'm close."

Jason was so intense, and she was climbing too fast. Ari moved against him as her body began to stretch toward her orgasm. The sound of their flesh coming together filled the small space, driving her higher.

"Jason—"

"Almost there."

She could feel the elevator slowing, arriving at its destination.

"God. Jason." With a burst of energy, her orgasm blasted through her body with the force of a thunderbolt. Ari bit down on her lip to keep from crying out. Euphoria swept through her system, stealing her breath. Jason buried his head in her hair as he plunged deeper and deeper inside of her core.

"Oh, God, Ari. You feel . . ." Jason shuddered, then groaned as he emptied himself deep inside her.

The elevator dinged, signaling that they had arrived at their destination. Jason quickly retreated and set her on her feet. Ari straightened her skirt as Jason got rid of the condom. The doors opened just as Jason was sliding his cock back into his pants. Ari glanced at the control panel and noticed that they were on the fifth floor. An older couple walked in holding hands. Thankfully, they were too wrapped up in each other to notice her or Jason.

Ari started to push Jason away, but he wouldn't budge. She looked up at him and raised her brows.

Jason leaned in close and whispered in her ear. "Give me a moment."

The older man pushed the button for the tenth floor, and Jason quickly pushed the one for the ninth. When the elevator started to climb once more, he placed his back against the wall by the control panel and positioned Ari in front of him.

"Look, Duncan," the older woman said. "They remind me of us when we were younger."

Ari felt Jason slide his arms around her waist and pull her close.

"Thank you," she said as she covered his roaming hands.

"Take care of her," Duncan said, nodding to Jason. "A woman worth keeping deserves to be treated well."

"I will," Jason said as the elevator doors slid open.

Tightening his grip on her hand, he dragged Ari out of the elevator and around the corner.

"That was close," Ari said.

"I know. I just hit a button so we could get off as soon as possible."

Ari put her hand in front of her mouth to hide a giggle. "I can't believe they didn't suspect anything."

Jason smirked. "I don't think they were as oblivious as you think."

"If they knew what we'd just done, then why didn't they say something?" she asked as she tugged him toward the room.

"Would you?" He took her hand. "Come on. Since we're on this floor, we can double check the honeymoon suite to make sure you didn't forget anything."

As she followed him down the hall, Ari glanced inside one of the honeymoon suites. The place still had drop cloths and ladders, still had paint cans and long two-by-fours leaned up against the wall. There wasn't anyone working, but that wasn't necessarily unusual. Despite the lack of people, the place looked the same as it always did.

Ari thought back to their conversation earlier and how Jason had said that he had hit a snag in construction.

She dug in her heels, bringing them both to a stop.

"What is it?" he asked.

"What happened with the honeymoon suites?"

"Nothing happened, why?"

She narrowed her gaze. "You said that the renovations had hit a snag."

He dropped her hand and cleared his throat. "Yes, well, it's under control now."

"Is it?" she moved away from him and peeked into the room.

"Yes." He tried to draw her away, but she pulled out of his grasp. "Show me."

"Show you what?"

"The renovations."

"Perhaps another time." He started moving back toward her room. "Come on."

Ari crossed her arms. "What's going on, Jason?"

He stopped and turned to face her. "What?"

"You left me in a rush earlier because of problems with the renovations. Now no one is working, and you are blowing off my questions about the rooms." She tilted her head to the side and studied his face before continuing. "The problems have nothing to do with the renovations. Do they?"

He hesitated for a moment, then relaxed his shoulders. "No."

"Then what happened?"

Jason began to close the distance between them. "You remember our agreement. When we're together, there's no talk of our families or work."

"This is different."

"Why?"

"Because something's happening that is upsetting you. I can tell." She brushed her fingers against his arm. "I want to help, but I can't if you don't tell me what's going on."

"I'm not hiding anything, Ari."

"Yes, you are. For starters, you have a brother staying in this hotel."

"He has nothing to do with us."

"He does." She waved her hand in the air. "He made me realize that there's this whole side of you that I don't know, and will probably never know."

"That side of me is in the past, Ari. It's buried, and needs to stay buried."

"But—"

"We have an agreement. If that agreement isn't working for you anymore, then *we* aren't working anymore."

She stared at him for a long moment before responding. "What are you saying?"

"You came to me because you needed a break from your family."

"True."

He flexed his fingers at his sides. "You agreed that this would be nothing more than—"

"Sex, yes." Sadness crossed her features as she turned toward her room. "But sometimes things change, Jason."

Things change. Jason remembered Deacon's words from the hotel restaurant. *You can't change who you are inside.* If he opened up to Ari about his brother and his past, then she'd know all about the business he used to run with his brother, and how they'd con lonely women into giving them money.

If she ever found out about that, then he'd lose her, he just knew it. Jason couldn't risk Ari finding out about the truth. Ever.

"We don't change, Ari." He grabbed her hand and pulled her into the suite next door.

"What are you doing?"

He slammed the door closed with his foot and pulled her deep into the living area, by the ladders.

"Jason—"

He stopped and turned abruptly, tugging her toward him. Ari dropped her suitcase and crashed into his body. "Things change, but we don't," he said as he wrapped his hand around her neck. "We've been together for a little over a year now, and during that time a lot has happened. One thing has always remained the same, however, and that is my need for this."

As Jason's lips crashed over hers, Ari felt his desperation.

She felt as if she was being knocked over by a tidal wave of lust, and it was hard not to get swept up in it.

"I know you need this, too," he whispered against her skin. "It's what drove you to come to me on your wedding day, and it's what's preventing you from going back to your family now."

He was right. Lord help her, he was right. She needed Jason's fun, his live-in-the-moment attitude. Her family was so oppressive sometimes with their obsession about appearances and manners. With Jason she could leave all of that behind her and just be herself.

Ari slipped her arms around Jason's neck and focused on kissing him back. With a hungry groan, Jason inched their bodies back deeper into the suite. This suite was different from hers. It was larger, and contained a lot of equipment. Jason navigated her around the paint cans and carpenter's tools, over to the ladders in the far corner. As they moved, he slid his hands around her waist and grabbed her backside, holding her to him. When she bumped into one of the ladders, he broke away from her lips and began to kiss a hot trail along her jaw and neck.

"Jason . . ." His mouth felt hot and urgent against her skin. Desire flowed through her veins, and she found it difficult to think. "Jason . . ."

"Shh . . ." he whispered as he tugged on her shirt, pulling it free from her skirt. Before she could respond, he palmed her breast, and excitement rippled through her core.

She tilted her head back and gave herself over to the moment as he nibbled along the sensitive skin of her neck. Jason leaned back and slid her blouse up over her head, then kissed her as he tossed it to the side. Ari slipped her hands around to his chest and fumbled with his buttons as he unhooked her bra and flicked it to the floor.

"When are the workers coming back?" she asked.

"You worry too much," he said. "Live in the moment."

It was so easy to just do as he asked of her. Outside the room, they each had their own problems and issues, but here . . . here they each had a reprieve from the real world. Here, there was no family feud, no reporters, and no responsibility. They could just have fun.

While she wanted to push Jason into telling her what was troubling him, she could understand his point. By telling her about his business, they'd cross that line in their relationship, and they could no longer be each other's sanctuary. Things would turn from fun to serious, and Ari wasn't sure if she was willing to lose what they shared to satisfy their curiosity.

She undid the last button and slid his shirt off his shoulders. "I want to," she whispered as she ran her fingertips over his hard muscles.

"Prove it," he said as he ran his thumbs over her nipples, sending spirals of desire through her veins. "Give yourself over to me, Ari. Enjoy the moment."

He bent his head down and Ari gasped as he took her taut nipple into his mouth. Ari threaded her fingers into his hair as Jason nipped her tip, then ran his tongue in circles over the sensitive tissue. Again and again he tortured her body, mixing pleasure and pain until her mind fogged with lust.

"I want to feel you," she whispered. "Jason—"

"You will. Be patient." He leaned back and removed her skirt, until she was wearing nothing but her purple panties and her black heels. "God, you're so beautiful."

She reached for his belt. "Your turn."

He leaned back and watched her as she removed his pants. As the belt came undone, she dropped to her knees and slid the fabric down his legs. His boxers soon followed, and Ari slipped her fingers along his shaft, stroking him from root to tip.

"Ari . . ."

She held his gaze as she wrapped her lips around his swollen head and slowly slid his cock into her mouth.

He ran his fingers through her hair, pushing it from her face. Ari moved slowly, pushing down until the tip of his erection bumped the back of her throat before retreating. Again and again she repeated the movements, until Jason's breathing quickened and his fingers tightened around her head.

"God, Ari . . ."

She slipped him from her mouth, then ran her tongue along the sensitive underside of his shaft. Jason closed his eyes and groaned, losing himself in the moment. Ari felt powerful and desired. Being with Jason was like a drug. He always made her feel special. As she eased her tongue down his shaft and slipped it around his balls, she watched him tilt his head back in bliss. Knowing that she was the one who brought him pleasure, that it was her, not anyone else, who could bring him to his knees, was a heady feeling. As Ari retreated and then repeated the movements again, Jason tightened his grip on her hair. It hurt, but only slightly. She knew that he was clinging desperately to his control, and she wondered if she could make him lose it completely.

"Stop." Jason's word was gentle but commanding as she finished her third trip down and back up his shaft.

"I don't want to," she teased as she flicked her tongue over the tip of his cock.

"Ah, but it's my turn." Jason drew her up onto her feet and eased her back onto the ladder. She stumbled, stepping up once before settling on one of the rungs.

"Jason . . ."

"Shh." He spread open her legs and knelt before her. "Like I said, it's my turn." He knelt before her and ran his fingertips over her inner thighs.

"Yes . . ." She spread open her legs, allowing him better access.

"Hang on, sweetheart," he whispered. "It's going to be a bumpy ride."

Before she could ask what he meant, he placed his lips on her thigh, creating a tingle of sensation along her skin. Using his teeth and tongue, he kissed a trail of need up her thigh, inching closer and closer to the place she needed him to be.

The scent of her desire rose up, becoming stronger with each passing second. She wanted him, needed him. When she reached forward to grab his hair and direct him toward her center, he withdrew and grabbed her wrists.

"I said hang on," he said as he placed her palms on the sides of the ladder above her head. "Now lean back."

He rubbed his palms against her nipples, then gently pushed her back until she was leaning against the ladder for support. The metal frame wobbled with the movement, and for a second she felt as if she was going to tip over.

"Relax," Jason said as he brushed his fingers down her sides. "You won't fall. Stop worrying and enjoy the moment." He dipped his head between her legs and resumed his torture.

"Jason . . ." She leaned her head against one of the rungs and watched the top of his head as he moved closer to her center. She wanted to touch him, to hold him close and force him to pleasure her, but didn't dare move. He wanted her to stop overthinking, and she was going to do just that.

Jason pulled back and rested her knee on his shoulder, then repeated his sensual exploration on the other thigh, driving her mad with desire. Ari groaned and squirmed, but didn't touch him, and never asked for more. When he finally placed her leg over his other shoulder, she almost wept with relief.

"Please . . ." She hated begging, but she felt so needy.

He straightened and leaned forward, kissing a trail up her abdomen and then laving each breast in turn. "I could do this all night," he whispered against her skin.

Ari whimpered. She didn't know if she'd last five minutes, let alone all night.

"Focus on my mouth," he said in between nips of her breast. "And how it makes you feel."

"Jason . . ."

"Tell me what you want." He cradled her breasts in his hands and squeezed.

She forced herself to meet his gaze. "I want you."

"You want me to . . . what?" He ran his fingers down her abdomen and back down to her thighs. "Don't overthink it, just tell me."

"I want you to kiss me." She spread her legs farther apart. "Here."

Ari watched him as he dipped his head between her thighs once more and ran his tongue over her folds. She gasped, then wiggled, trying to get closer to his devilish tongue.

"Oh my God." She gripped the ladder tighter as he licked and laved, always circling around her opening, but never entering. Ari raised her legs higher in the air, hoping that he'd take the hint. Instead of entering her, he slid his tongue up and rubbed her clit, causing pleasure to burst through her system.

"Louder," he whispered. "I want to hear you when you come."

"But the workers . . ."

"Aren't here. No one is here but us." He rubbed her clit again. This time Ari groaned louder.

"More," he commanded as he moved back down to her slit. "I want to hear more." He shifted his hands and rubbed her clit in a circular motion with his thumb as he slid the tip of his tongue just inside her opening.

"Yes." She leaned her head back on the ladder. "Yes."

"Louder." Jason used his free hand to spread apart her folds, pushing her underwear to the side. He dipped his tongue into her opening, teasing her sensitive tissues.

"Oh, God." She gripped the ladder tighter. "That feels so good."

He licked harder, plunging his tongue deep. Ari slid to the edge of the rung, wanting more. The ladder shifted, and her head knocked against the wooden plank above her head. She barely noticed the bump as Jason switched places with his tongue and fingers, driving her pleasure higher.

"I'm going to come," she said as he pushed two fingers into her core. God, he felt so good. Ari closed her eyes and leaned her head back as she began the familiar race toward oblivion. "Faster."

Jason quickened his movements, pushing three fingers into her center as he rubbed his tongue over her clit.

Ari curled her legs around the sides of the ladder and inched forward on the rung. The movement caused it to sway precariously to the side. Adrenaline shot up through her system as Jason steadied the ladder, then went right back to his assault on her body.

"Yes." She inched back and forth on the rung, pumping in time to his fingers. Higher and higher she soared and with each stroke, she cried out for more.

Jason moved quicker, plunged harder, until Ari was hovering on the edge of something vast and wonderful.

"Jason, please . . ."

He leaned forward and scraped his teeth against her nipple. The blast of pain vibrated through her body, triggering her orgasm. Ari cried out his name as joy poured through every crevice and pore. Again and again, he tended to her, stretching out her orgasm for what seemed like days. Bliss wrapped around her body, and tears of happiness stung her eyes. Never before had she felt anything so wonderful.

When the last threads of her orgasm faded away, Jason eased back and glanced up at the plank situated between the two ladders.

"But it's not stable," she said, glancing at the wood. "I'm not sure if it would even hold us."

"What did I say about worrying?" Jason asked.

She turned back to him. "Don't do it?"

He motioned to the wood. "I'll take care of you."

She started to take off her heels, but Jason stopped her. "No," he gently commanded. "Leave them on."

"But I can't climb a ladder in these."

"I'll help. You can do this."

She stared at him for a long moment, then turned around and climbed the ladder up to the top. She stared at the wood beyond, unsure.

"Go on." He patted her ass. "Just crawl on out there. I'll do the rest."

She glanced over her shoulder and saw the excitement in his eyes. Swallowing the lump in her throat, she climbed up onto the thick plank of wood and crawled until she was halfway between the two ladders.

"Stop." He slipped his hands over her ass. "God, you look so beautiful." He trailed his fingers over her back and shoulder, stimulating her skin. His touch felt so good, so right. As he eased his fingers back down to her ass, she started to feel more sure of herself.

"Get down on your elbows."

She did as she was told. Jason slipped his fingers in between her ass cheeks and rubbed the opening in her backside. "We're going to try something new."

"Jason—"

He slipped an object out of his pocket and before Ari

realized it, something warm and wet was sliding between her cheeks.

"What's that?"

"Oil. It makes things more . . . pleasurable. I have been carrying it around for a few days now, looking for an excuse to try it."

She was about to ask what he meant, but then his finger returned. Jason slid it around her opening once more. This time it moved much quicker. Ari groaned and arched her back as he inched his finger into her backside.

Ari gasped at the intrusion, then moaned as her body began to adjust. Jason retreated a fraction of an inch, then pressed once more, amplifying her pleasure.

Back and forth, in and out, slowly Jason worked his way into her body until his entire finger was in her backside.

"How does that feel?"

"Strange. Good." While he had toyed with the rim of her opening before, Jason had never entered her so deep from behind. She was surprised to find the intrusion so stimulating.

"It's only going to get better." He retreated and thrust a few times, allowing her body to get used to the sensation. Then he repeated the same process with two fingers. Each time he thrust, Ari's muscles stretched, causing her to moan with delight. Each time he retreated, she whimpered at the loss of sensation. By the time he had thrust two fingers all the way inside her body, Ari was ready for more.

"Jason . . ."

"Easy. Hold as still as you can. I don't want these ladders to tip over." He positioned his cock in between her ass cheeks.

"Jason . . ." She gripped the edges of the wide plank as Jason eased himself into her backside. It didn't hurt like she'd thought it would. The pleasant stretching sensation filled her core, making her mind blank with need.

"How does that feel?" he asked after his hips pushed flush with her backside.

"Incredible." She leaned back and wiggled her hips. "Do it again."

"Vixen." He lightly slapped her hip, then retreated and repeated his movements.

The sensation was . . . amazing. Better than anything she had ever felt before. As he advanced and retreated, Ari closed her eyes and enjoyed the feeling of being full, wanting him deeper.

"You're going too slow." Ari moved back as he thrust, causing their bodies to come together with a loud slap. The ladder wobbled, but remained upright.

"Ari, you're going to kill me." Jason put his hands on her hips. "Hold still."

She tried to remain motionless, really tried, but he felt so good. As he performed shallow thrusts, Ari moved her torso against him, causing him to push harder than he intended.

The plank wobbled from side to side, but she was too wrapped up in the moment to care. What started out as quick, shallow movements became longer, harder. Ari curled her fingers into the wood and made soft, feminine noises as their bodies came together.

"Harder," she commanded.

He put a hand on her shoulder to steady himself and pushed hard, inching her forward. The plank moved a fraction, but remained mostly upright.

Again and again he entered her, driving her desire higher. Her voice rose with each thrust, blending with Jason's into an erotic chorus. The plank tipped more to one side, and Jason started to slow down.

"No," she begged. "Don't stop." What they were doing

was dangerous, but it made everything more exciting. Adrenaline mixed with her desire, causing her entire body to burn with need.

He resumed his thrusts, each one harder than the last. Back and forth the ladders swayed, causing another bolt of adrenaline to shoot through her core.

"Yes," she cried as the tension rose higher. "Harder."

Jason groaned as he thrust himself inside her once more. "I'm close."

Ari climbed higher and higher. The world around her faded away as she focused on the swaying of the plank, and the burst of movement from behind. Faster and faster their bodies came together, until Jason reached around her hips and found her clit.

"Oh my God." The ladders rattled from side to side as Ari cried out Jason's name. Pleasure exploded through her body, wrapping around her muscles and filling her mind. She closed her eyes and soaked up the moment, enjoying the connectedness she felt with the man behind her.

Jason's thrusts quickened and his grip became harder. Once, twice, on the third time he shuddered and called out her name as he emptied himself deep inside of her body.

The moment was beautiful. Magical. Ari hung on to the pleasure as tightly as she could, loving how connected she felt to the man behind her.

After a long moment, Jason retreated and wrapped his arm around her waist. Ari noticed that his breathing was ragged, as if he had just finished a marathon. "Follow me. I've got you."

Carefully, he eased her off the plank and down the ladder to the floor. As soon as Ari's feet hit the bottom, he turned her around and kissed her hard. Ari's mind blanked as she wrapped her arms around his neck and pulled him close.

"That was incredible," he whispered after the kiss was over. "I didn't know it could be that good."

He chuckled as he broke contact and picked up her clothes. "Here. We should probably do that sweep of your room and head out."

Ari knew that he was right, but couldn't help feeling that once again he had avoided the vulnerability and nakedness of the afterglow. Something amazing had happened between them. She knew it had affected him, and his moving on as if nothing had happened between them left her feeling adrift.

She glanced at his outstretched hand, not quite ready to leave just yet. "It sure looks as if you put a lot of work into this room."

Jason glanced around them. "I'm renovating all of the honeymoon suites in all of my hotels to offer the latest in technology and luxury."

"Doesn't look very luxurious to me," she joked.

"That's because it isn't finished yet. It'll have a full bar here." He pointed to one corner of the room. "And a Jacuzzi here." He strode over to the other side of the room. "We're expanding here to make a large balcony where we will place a bed for stargazing and a fire pit." He waved his hand over to the window. "Everything will be remote controlled."

"Really?"

He nodded. "People can already check out and check in through a computer. I'm working on software now so people can order room service, make arrangements in the city, do virtually anything they want from their room without ever interacting with another human being."

"Wow, that's amazing."

"It's the perfect vacation."

"Perfect? I don't know. When I go on vacation, I want to meet new people, not escape them."

He chuckled. "That's because you are an extrovert. Not everyone is like you."

"Do you want to get away from people when you go on vacation?"

"I don't know." He glanced around the room. "I haven't spent a day away from my desk in so long . . . I've forgotten what having a vacation feels like."

"We'll have to fix that, then."

"Fix it?"

She nodded. "Why don't you take the day off and come down with me to the hospital tomorrow?"

He raised his brows. "You're going to the hospital?"

She nodded. "That reporter who broke the news story of my CFO embezzling money wants to do a follow-up piece. I thought I'd use the opportunity to put to rest the rumors surrounding the wedding and show Leo that I can handle things on my own."

Jason scowled. "Change it."

"Why?"

Jason pressed his lips together for a moment, as if struggling for words. "I don't know if it's the best time to step forward."

"I don't understand. I thought you wanted to help me."

"I do. It's just, I'm not sure if this is the best way to go about it."

"Why not?"

"Do you really want to use your charity to address rumors about your family?" He shook his head. "Instead of clearing up rumors surrounding Perconti Enterprises, you might be inviting scandal and rumors to your charity."

Ari narrowed her gaze. "You don't have any faith in me, either."

"Of course I do."

"Then why are you fighting me on this?" Ari pulled away from Jason, grabbed her suitcase, and moved back into the hall. "I thought you were different, Jason."

"Now you're not being fair."

"Am I?" She pulled open the door and turned to face him. "Then tell me the real reason why you don't want me to go tomorrow." She held up her finger when he started to speak. "And don't tell me that granting this tabloid reporter an interview will bring scandal to the charity. The charity is already full of scandal with the embezzlement."

"But you could bring more."

"Like what?" When he didn't answer, she threw her hands up in the air. "Let's suppose you're right. Let's suppose for the moment that I'm just as stupid as everyone thinks and that I'll completely bomb this interview."

"I never said—"

She raised her finger in the air. "Let me finish." When he stepped back, she continued. "Do you really think that I'll bungle this one interview so badly that my charity will never be able to recover from it?"

"No, of course not."

"Then let me do this by myself. If I never try things on my own, I'll never get good at them. I'll never be independent."

"Normally, I'd agree, but not in this case."

"Why?"

He worked his jaw, but no sound came out.

Ari let out an exasperated sigh as she entered her room, then closed and locked the door behind her.

"Ari." Jason's voice filtered through the polished wood as he banged on the door. "Ari, let me in. We have to gather your things and head over to my apartment."

"I'm not going."

"You have to go."

"No, I don't. You can't order me around like my brothers, and quite frankly, the thought of spending the night with you is making me a little ill. Good night, Jason."

"Jesus, Ari."

"I said, *good night.*" She picked up the remote to the

television and turned it on. Tears stung her eyes as she pressed down on the volume and turned it up until it drowned out Jason's pleas through the door.

First her brother, and now Jason. She didn't know how much longer she could take these games. For far too long she had let other people control her life. It was time to take it back.

Chapter 11

“What are you doing here?” Ari asked as she opened the door to her room the next morning.

“I’m going to take you to the hospital.” Jason looked a mess, as if he had slept in his suit outside her door all night. She wanted to ask him if he had done just that, but there were more important things to think about.

“I can go myself,” she said.

Jason picked up her suitcase and offered her his arm. “I know. Consider this an apology. Afterward, we can go to my apartment.”

She crossed her arms. “Are you going to let me do this interview by myself, or are you going to butt in?”

He held up his hand. “The interview is all yours. I just want to . . . lend moral support. When you are through we can head over to my apartment.” He grinned, but Ari wasn’t convinced his motives were so simple.

“What about your work?”

“It can wait.”

Ari considered him for a moment, then took his arm. “Very well. Just be sure to stay out of my way.”

“I’m just trying to help. There are people out there who want to hurt you and your family.”

"Like you?"

He smirked. "I'll admit that in the past I have tried to take business away from your family's company, but that was strictly business. What I'm talking about is more . . . personal. Remember what that crazy fan did to Dante . . ."

"That was his girlfriend, not him, and you're not making any sense. I can't see how anyone would be interested in a routine visit to a hospital."

"You forget that your wedding has been called off, and you are still considered missing. People will take great interest if you suddenly show up in a public place." He took her to the garage and to his McLaren 650.

"We're taking the McLaren?"

"Yes. It's my fastest car. If we need to get you out of there quickly, this car can do it." He didn't elaborate on his irrational fear that someone would want to harm her, and Ari didn't ask questions. Something was going on though, something that was making Jason overly protective of her. She wished he'd just come out and say what it was. She didn't have time to dwell on it, however. There were more important things to think about. On the drive to the hospital, she texted Camille and told her that Jason would be coming. When they got there, he parked out of the way in a parking garage and they walked through the maze of stairs and hallways until they got to the cancer ward.

"Ah, there you are," Camille said. "Everything is in place."

"Great. Is the reporter here yet?"

"She's waiting for you in a conference room. After your meeting, I figured we can go to the playroom where there will be some children who have benefitted from your charity directly." She glanced at Jason. "I'm sorry. They requested a private meeting, and—"

"I'll wait in the playroom," Jason said as he squeezed

Ari's hand and moved away. "Be sure you come directly there after your meeting."

"I will." Ari watched him go, her mind turning over the events of the past few days.

"How . . . odd," Camille said. "I never knew Jason Stone had an affinity for children."

"Neither did I," Ari said, turning to her friend. "In fact, he's been acting quite odd over the past twenty-four hours." She thought about her conversation with Deacon and wondered if the brothers had had a little chat about her, and if that chat resulted in Jason's odd protectiveness.

"Come on, the reporter is waiting," Camille said.

"Sure." After one last glance at Jason's broad, muscular shoulders, Ari pushed him from her thoughts and followed Camille into the office area, eager to see just how the hospital was faring with their donations.

Ari had been gone for over an hour. Jason glanced at his watch again as he waited for the little girl across from him to move. The poor thing had lost all of her hair and was wearing one of Ari's wigs. The seven-year-old had picked out a blunt cut in metallic green, and he could tell that it had already given her more confidence. Her bright red lipstick and purple shadow were not only striking, but seemed to suit her sarcasm and in-your-face attitude. It was the first time he had seen Ari's charity in action. Her work with these kids proved that she could be successful on her own. Jason wondered if her family ever stopped to see the difference she was making in people's lives. If they did, they might take her opinions more seriously.

"It's your move," the girl said.

Jason frowned and moved a piece on the checkerboard, not really paying attention to where it was going. He didn't have all day for this. Where was Ari?

"I win again. You're bad at this, mister."

"I guess I am." He returned his attention to the girl. "Do you play a lot?"

"Only when we come for my chemo." She piled all of his captured pieces into little towers. "Mom says that we have to start coming more frequently."

"I'm sorry."

She shrugged. "I'm not. I mean, the chemo sucks, but they give me presents. Like this wig." She touched her hair. "Do you like it?"

"I do."

"Do you want to wear one, too?"

"Not really. They're here for you."

She considered him for a moment. "You mean kids with cancer." She began putting the pieces back on the board. "It's okay," she said, glancing up at his surprised expression. "You can say it. It's just a word."

Jason marveled at the little girl's spunk. Despite her attitude, he could see how the chemo had been taking its toll. They were sitting because she was too weak to run around and play, and the IV bags on the pole beside her were a constant reminder of why she was in a place like this.

"Want to play again?" she asked.

"Maybe some other time, kid." Jason stood and walked over to the window along the far wall. The girl reminded him a lot of Ari. They were both full of optimism, both full of life. He wondered how Ari was handling the reporter, and if she needed help.

"But I set up the board and everything." She materialized at his side. "Just one more game. Please?"

Jason glanced down at the girl with metallic hair and wondered how Ari did it. Being around sick kids all of the time must be so depressing. It must take real drive and passion to commit herself to such a cause. He admired that—her passion. Jason seemed to lack passion in his life. A lot of days he felt as if he was just going through the motions.

He nodded to a group in the corner. "Why don't you play with the others for a little while?"

"They don't like me," she said, glancing over her shoulder. "They think I'm weird."

Jason didn't want to feel compassion for this girl, and the fact that he wanted to take her into his arms and give her a reassuring hug terrified him. He knew all too well what being an outsider felt like. He just wished he could give her some profound advice to make it better.

"Well, maybe you should change so that they'd like you." It had seemed to work for him. The elite who once condemned him now accepted him with open arms.

"My mom says I'm perfect as I am." She hesitated a moment before continuing. "Do you like me as I am?"

Shit. Like her? He didn't even know her. Jason really didn't want to have this conversation with this girl, or with anyone. He really didn't know how to handle women and all of their "feelings" talk.

"Sorry, kid, I have work to do," he said, pulling out his phone and pretending to text.

"Jason," Ari said as she entered the room, drawing everyone's attention. "Have some compassion." She approached the girl and put her arm around her shoulders. "Come here, honey."

Jason watched Ari lead her away and felt a tightness in his chest. He glanced just beyond Ari to her friend Camille, crossing her arms and scowling at him. Next to Camille stood the reporter Jason recognized from the television set.

Ah hell, just the person he was afraid of running into.

"Hello, Jason." Amanda Vaughn smiled one of those fake, car-dealer-type smiles. "I'm so glad to see that nothing has changed."

Right. Jason nodded in her direction. "Amanda."

"You two know each other?" Ari said as she handed the

girl off to one of the nurses with instructions to pick out a new wig from the supply boxes.

"Somewhat," Jason admitted and forced himself to smile.

"Oh, we've known each other for quite some time. Some would say that I know Jason better than he knows himself. Isn't that right?" Amanda stepped into the room and considered him. "Which makes it a little surprising as to why you're here."

The woman was delusional. They had only been together for two short weeks and unlike Ari, the sex hadn't even been that great. Jason had had no problem getting rid of Amanda as soon as he learned that she was dating him to gather dirt for her column.

Jason slid his arm around Ari. His purpose was twofold. First, he wanted to let Amanda know that under no uncertain terms would she be able to pull her seductive stunts on him and have them work again. Second, he wanted to protect Ari from the venomous woman.

"We just came from a lovely little chat," Amanda said, glancing at Ari. "It was very enlightening."

"What did you discuss?" he asked.

"Oh, just girl stuff." Amanda waved her hand in the air. "To be honest, I had no idea that you'd be here. Now that you are, I'm wondering just what your motivation might be." She made a point of looking at his arm around Ari. "Is there anything you want to tell us?"

Something bright flashed from behind Amanda, causing both Jason and Ari to shield their eyes.

"What the hell was that?"

"That's my photographer, Mason." Jason blinked away the spots and saw a young, bearded man with a knitted hat and tight-fitting shirt standing next to Camille by the door.

"No pictures," he said, trying to keep the irritation from

his voice. "And I thought you were going to focus on the charity."

"We are—unless there is something you want us to report on." Amanda's sweet smile made his stomach turn.

"No." Jason unwrapped his arm, having had just about enough of this reporter. "And I don't want you to publicize anything that you have talked about or seen here today. And that includes the charity and how it's doing."

Ari frowned and crossed her arms. "You can't do that. This is my charity and I get to choose what can and can't be publicized. The article is supposed to demonstrate how I can handle things on my own—"

"Some other time, and with a different reporter." Jason nodded to Amanda. "This is the reporter who has been giving your brother Leo so much trouble. She's known for twisting words and telling bold-faced lies in order to sell a story."

Amanda's smile appeared forced. "Come now, Jason, you used to love it when I dragged your rivals through the mud." She took a step closer and ran her fingers along the lapel of his suit jacket. "In fact, you had this unique way of thanking me—"

Jason grabbed her wrist and removed her hand. "Not anymore."

"Hey," Mason said as he stepped up next to Amanda. "Hands off, or I'll call the cops."

Jason ground his teeth as he dropped Amanda's wrist and pulled out his checkbook. "How much?"

"Excuse me?" Amanda raised her brow.

"Jason, you can't stop this story. How else am I supposed to show the world that Ari's Kids is a viable charity and that I'm competent?" Ari touched his arm, but he brushed it off.

"I'm not going to have her spreading lies about you." He turned to Amanda. "How much to bury this little visit?"

he asked, focusing on the task at hand. The sooner he got rid of the reporter, the better. Amanda had this knack for uncovering things that were better left hidden. The less she knew about his reasons for being here, and Ari's reasons for leaving that wedding, the better.

Amanda glanced from Ari and back to him again. "If there is something going on between the two of you, the public has a right to know. As one of the most eligible bachelors, there is a great interest in Jason's love life."

Ari snorted. "You can't be serious."

Jason scribbled a number and tore off the check. "Here." He couldn't really afford such an exorbitant price, but if it kept both him and Ari out of the papers, it was worth it. Not only would their being together make things difficult with Leo, but the publicity would drive even more unwanted attention to Ari and put her life in even more danger.

Amanda took the check and raised her brows. "Business is doing well, I see."

"It is imperative that your report on the charity be only about the charity, if you know what I mean. Lives are at stake."

"Oh?"

"What are you talking about?" Ari asked. "Of course she's only going to report on the charity. I've talked about nothing *but* the charity. Seriously, Jason, you've been acting weird all day. No one's life is in danger."

"Of course not." Jason cleared his throat to cover his lie and straightened his jacket. "If Ari's family found out about me hanging around, it would make business difficult. We wouldn't want any workers to be caught up in the crossfire."

"Jason, just stop it," Ari said. "I told you that I could handle this myself." She turned to Amanda. "You don't have to listen to this."

Amanda ignored Ari and continued to stare at Jason as he forced his expression to remain passive. He knew that she sensed a story, something deeper than two billionaire socialites visiting a hospital together, but she wasn't going to get any more information from him.

"Okay," Amanda said as she pocketed the check. "You win—for now." She turned to Ari and nodded. "Good day, Ms. Perconti. I trust that you will be returning to your family soon?"

"Of course."

Amanda nodded and then glanced at Jason. "Be careful of this one." She turned toward the door. "Jason Stone is an asshole who only thinks about himself." She passed by Camille and offered her a polite nod. "Come on, Mason. We have work to do."

Jason let out a breath he didn't know he was holding as both Amanda and Mason exited the room.

"I can't believe you did that," Ari said.

Jason took her hand. "Let's get out of here." There were too many vultures in this place. The sooner they got away, the better.

Ari dug in her heels. "Not until you tell me what's going on."

"Trust me, I know that reporter better than you do. She had no intention of talking about your charity. She wanted to know the real reason why you left your wedding," Jason explained.

Ari made a disgusted sound. "We didn't even talk about the wedding until you brought it up." She crossed her arms. "You can't coddle me like this forever, you know. Eventually you and my brother will have to see that I'm capable of handling the media on my own."

"I'm not saying to stay away from the media forever, just . . . for now."

"Why?"

"Think about it, Ari. If Leo knew what we have been doing for the past year, how is that going to make him feel?" When she didn't respond, he inched closer and framed her face with his hands. "We're in the middle of negotiating a business deal, remember? Something like this could cause him to renege on his offer for those Asian hotels."

"That's all this is about—business?"

"Of course."

He could tell she didn't believe his lies. Damn, this manipulation used to be so easy. He was losing his touch.

Or perhaps, Ari knew him so well that she could read him better than most.

She studied his face for a moment. "Don't you think it's time you told me what's really going on?"

Jason glanced over his shoulder at Camille, who was talking to some hospital staff. "Can we discuss this later?"

Ari glanced at her friend. "Camille, can you give us a moment?"

The older woman shrugged. "I need to get back, anyway. Seems as if the latest order of wigs we placed has been delayed." She rolled her eyes. "Call me later?"

"Sure thing." Ari waited until she left before she continued. "Okay, now we're alone. What's going on?"

He took a deep breath and then let it out. "Things have been rough with the hotel lately."

"I can see that."

He flashed her an irritated look. "Sales have been stagnant ever since your brother announced his merger with Blake Corporation."

"But that's not happening now."

"No, but that reporter has a way of uncovering information. I'd rather not have my financials broadcasted in tomorrow's tabloid headline."

She shook her head. "I don't understand. Why is the hotel business so important to you anyway? You're a venture capitalist, an opportunist."

"That's true."

"So if Stone Suites isn't turning a profit, then why not just jettison it and focus on your other investments?"

Jason let out a long breath and wandered back over to the windows. "It's complicated."

She followed him and leaned up against the wall beside him. "Tell me."

He glanced at her, then refocused on the Boston skyline. "I told you why I like sports cars . . ."

"For the freedom, yes."

"It's the same with hotels. I like them because of the freedom they represent." When she furrowed her brow in confusion, he crossed his arms, considering how much to tell her. "When I was a kid, I used to pass by a ritzy hotel on the way to school and watch the elite go in and out of the building. I used to dream about being a part of that life." A life where he wasn't picked on, and people wanted to be around him.

"The people who stayed at that hotel seemed to have lives that were trouble-free and innocent. I wanted a part of that for myself. So that was why when an opportunity came up to invest in a hotel chain, I took it."

"I'm not sure I understand."

He turned to face her. "The building I had passed on my way to school was Stone Suites."

"Your flagship hotel?" Ari asked. "I had no idea." She lowered her arms. "So you purchased the same hotel that inspired you to dream big."

He nodded. "So you see how important it is to me to keep that hotel not only functioning, but thriving. When Stone Suites does well, not only am I keeping my own dream alive, but the dreams of other boys out there who are just like me."

"Was your childhood really so bad?" she asked. "I know you didn't have as much money—"

"We didn't have any money. There's a difference." He pressed his lips together in thought. "Our parents gave up both Deacon and me shortly after I was born."

"Why?"

He shrugged. "I have no idea, and I don't care. Growing up, Deacon and I were passed around from foster family to foster family before we finally settled with a couple who already had three children of their own."

"I didn't know you had a nice, big family—"

"They only took us in for the money. They didn't really care what happened to us. And the other children resented having Deacon and me around."

"That must have been awful."

He shrugged away from her touch. "I know you feel your brothers can be rather overbearing at times, but they really have your best interests at heart. You're lucky to have people care about you."

"You have people who care about you, too." She placed her hand on his arm.

He covered her fingers with his own and smiled. "I wish that were true." He removed her hand. "Unfortunately, Deacon and I only had each other."

"You still have Deacon."

"Not really."

"But he's your brother."

"By blood yes, but our family is different than yours. Just because he's my sibling, doesn't mean we're close. Deacon and I . . . we have very different views on life."

"Such as?"

He tugged her toward the door. "Come on."

They went down the elevator and into the parking garage in silence, but Jason could see that she was thinking about what he had said. She had that determined look about her that meant she wasn't going to let the subject drop. It was only a matter of time before she started asking questions.

"If you and Deacon don't get along anymore, then why is he at Stone Suites?" she asked once they were in the car and heading back to his apartment.

"Long story." He held up his hand before she could ask any more questions. "And I don't want to talk about it."

She seemed to think about his words for a few moments before responding. "So you had no one help you with your business, no one to lean on when times got tough?"

"No."

"No one to celebrate your milestones?"

"It's okay. Really."

"No, it isn't." When he flashed her a confused look, she continued. "No one should have to go through life alone."

He shrugged and kept his gaze focused on the road. "You get used to it."

"But you don't have to live that way anymore. You have me."

He shook his head. "I'm not one of your charity cases, Ari."

"I'm not saying you are."

"Talking is overrated." He took her hand and placed it on his leg. "What we have between us is all I need."

"Are you sure?"

"Trust me."

She looked as if she was going to press the issue, and Jason silently prayed she wouldn't. He didn't like talking about his past, not when there were much more pleasant things to think about—like her hand on his leg.

She chewed her lower lip as she curled her fingers into

his flesh. "That thing between us—is that what you need now? Is that why you've been acting all weird?" Her voice was quiet, but he caught the hint of mischief in her words.

It was hard keeping the smile from his lips. This was the Ari he knew—and the one he appreciated. "What do you think?"

"In that case . . ." Ari eased her fingers up and rubbed his shaft. Desire surged through his bloodstream, making him instantly hard.

"Oh God, Ari," he whispered. "That feels good."

"Yeah?" she asked as she started to undo his zipper. "It can feel even better."

He inched back from her touch, even though every muscle in his body screamed to let her be. "Ari, I'm driving. Wait until I can pull over."

"Since when has the great Jason Stone backed down from a little challenge?" She reached in and freed his cock from his restrictive clothing. Jason shivered as she stroked him from root to tip. "Game on, Mr. Stone."

Jason pulled up to a stoplight and watched as Ari bent over and placed her lips around his cock.

"Holy hell." Jason put his hand on the top of her head as she moved up and down his shaft. Ari felt good, too good. Jason widened his legs and pushed his hips up toward her eager mouth.

"You like that?" she asked as she flicked her tongue over the tip of his erection.

"Yes." *Fuck, yes.* The woman was reckless. If someone saw them, they could be arrested. Worse, if he didn't concentrate on driving, they could get into an accident.

The light changed to green and Jason eased onto the gas. Ari slid her delicious tongue along the underside of his shaft, causing pleasure to bloom throughout his body.

"Jesus, Ari . . ." He curled his fingers into her hair, intending to pull her away from his cock. He needed to concentrate, and the longer she tongued him, the more difficult that became.

"Just focus on driving." She resumed her sweet torture by wrapping her lips around his head and pushing him deep inside her mouth.

Baseball, spreadsheets, lost puppies . . . Jason tried to think of anything that would keep him focused on the road. It wasn't working.

With shaking hands, he pulled off of the busy street and onto a side street. As he stepped on the gas, Ari doubled her efforts, moving up and down his shaft with an intoxicating rhythm.

"God, Ari. Don't stop."

She made soft, feminine sounds of pleasure against his cock, heightening his arousal. Jason bit his lips and drove with one hand, keeping the other on her head so she wouldn't hit the steering wheel. Pressure built through his bloodstream, winding his muscles tight. Fuck, the woman had an amazing mouth. He had forgotten just how good she could be.

She cupped his balls, tugging slightly as she worked over his shaft. Jason pressed a little heavily on the gas and quickly adjusted. Adrenaline shot through his bloodstream, fueling his desire to new levels.

"Ari." This was too dangerous. Dangerous, but oh so fucking good. Normally he was the one orchestrating the sex, bringing them both to the brink of adrenaline-fueled pleasure. Now, Ari was in complete and total control, and he was loving every second of it.

Ari lightly scraped her teeth over his shaft, causing pain to mix with his pleasure. Jason groaned and stepped on the gas some more, enjoying the heady mixture of adrenaline and desire. With each stroke of her smooth, pouty lips, he was losing more and more control. The woman was nothing short of magical, and as the familiar tingling rippled along his spine, he knew that in this moment, he was lost completely.

"Jason, look out," Ari said as she lifted her head. "The lamppost."

Jason straightened in his seat and realized that in his euphoria, he was drifting off the road. He straightened and quickly turned the wheel. They avoided the pole, but not the sidewalk. Ari yelped as the car leapt up onto the curb and came to a stop inches from a mailbox.

"Fuck. My car." Jason quickly tucked his cock into his pants and got out to inspect the damage. He walked carefully around, looking for any dents or scrapes. Thankfully, there were none, but the situation could have turned out so differently. If Ari hadn't said anything, the car could have been totaled, or worse, they could have gotten hurt.

Jason imagined himself trying to explain how they had gotten injured to a doctor and frowned. He strode around to the passenger seat and threw open the door. "Get out."

"What?"

"Get out."

"I'm not hurt, in case you were wondering."

Not yet. They were lucky, incredibly lucky. As the horrible possibilities of what could have happened crossed through Jason's mind, he became more and more angry. "What the hell do you think you're doing?"

She widened her eyes, then lifted her chin and crossed her arms. "You weren't exactly complaining."

He fisted his hands. "You could have gotten us both killed."

"We're not dead. We're not even hurt, and the car is fine. No harm done."

No harm . . . ? "That was reckless, Ari."

"So was having sex on a painter's plank."

He ground his teeth. "That was different."

"How? It was still dangerous."

Back in the suite, he was in complete control. There was an illusion of danger, but no real danger. This . . . "You could have gotten us killed," he said again.

"I was in complete control." She tilted her head to the side and gave him that intoxicating pout. "That's what this is, isn't it? You didn't like what I did in the McLaren for the same reason you don't want us talking about anything outside this exact moment. Both things force you out of the driver's seat in this relationship, and you can't stand not being in control."

She was right, of course, and knowing she was right just irritated him more. Ari was pushing both him and this relationship to a place he didn't want to go.

"Just stop it," he said, closing the distance between them. He felt dirty and used. She was behaving just like those rich women had behaved during his gigolo days. Each one of them had tried to dig around into his past, looking for something they could control him with. When that didn't work, they used sex to get what they wanted from him. He had left that life long ago and he wasn't going back to that place—for anyone.

He needed to get this relationship back to familiar ground. No more questions, no more manipulation. Just pure physical fun, no strings attached.

"Stop what?"

"Stop trying to use me to feed your need for independence." He hooked his finger under her chin. "I'm not some stick shift you can switch into high gear whenever you want something."

"You shared a part of your past with me at the hospital." Her eyes shone brightly with tears. "I thought we were bonding."

"No, we weren't bonding," he said. "You asked a question and I answered it, nothing more." He tightened his grip on her chin. "I now I see that talking about my past was a mistake. It led you to believe that you could control and manipulate me, just like the rest of them did."

"Rest of them?"

"What we share is special, Ari. But don't make it out to be more than it is."

"And what is it?" she asked. "What exactly do we have, Jason?"

"We have sex, Ari. Nothing more."

Chapter 12

"What are you doing?" Ari asked as she stumbled back to the car. Instead of answering, he snaked his arm around her waist, pinning her between the hood of the car and himself.

"You and I—we don't do feelings, and we sure as hell don't try to fix things in each other's lives. All we have is fun, Ari. That's all there is."

"Jason—"

"That's all that matters." He kissed her, quickly tilting his head and swooping inside of her mouth with confidence. Ari's pulse raced as he slipped his fingers down her waist and curled them into her backside.

"What are you doing?" she asked as she pulled away.

He shook his head. "You have no idea," he whispered.

Her heartbeat quickened. "No idea of what?"

He tugged her close until his erection rubbed up against her lower abdomen. "You have no idea who you're dealing with. All you see is the hotelier. The billionaire playboy. That man is a façade, princess. An act used to cover up the monster underneath."

Before she could ask what he meant, he crashed his lips against hers once more. Ari became light-headed as desire surged through her bloodstream and a dull ache formed between her thighs. Jason shifted his hands, palming her ass and holding her close. He rubbed his erection into her lower abdomen, sending tingles of pleasure racing through her core.

Ari gasped as he broke away from the kiss and ran his tongue along her jaw. "Everyone loves a billionaire adrenaline junkie," he murmured against her skin. "But if you knew who I really am, and the things I used to do, you'd run back to your brothers at the first opportunity."

"I'd never do such a thing."

He turned and nudge her against the car. Ari yelped and fell forward on the hood. The cool metal pressed up against her torso as he slid his fingers up under her skirt.

"I use people to get what I want. I manipulate women into thinking that I care, when all I want is what they can give me." He squeezed her ass and slid one hand down between her thighs. "I never gave a second thought to anyone's feelings or needs. It was take or be taken. Fuck or be fucked."

As Ari heard the tear of a condom wrapper behind her, she sensed something inside of him breaking. Once again she tried to push herself up, but Jason pressed his hips against hers and bent over her back.

"Then you came along, princess." He leaned over her back until Ari felt his warm breath rush against her ear. "And you're like a drug. A wonderful, intoxicating drug that is better than any adrenaline rush." Jason rubbed the tip of his cock against her slit. "Instead of manipulating, I feel as if I'm the one being manipulated. Each time we come together, I feel as if I'm losing a little bit more control." With one hard thrust, he pushed himself balls-deep into her body.

Ari groaned as her muscles stretched to accommodate the intrusion. Jason placed his hands on either side of her hips and pushed her up farther on the hood, angling her so that he could penetrate deeper. They both moaned as he pushed forward, filling her to the point of breaking.

"God, Ari . . ." He began to thrust. Quick, rapid movements of a man lost in his emotions. With each push, Ari slid up on the hood of the sports car, and her breasts rubbed against the metal. She tried to widen her legs, but her position didn't allow for much movement. She felt trapped beneath him, and the sensation made her skin tingle with need.

"Jason . . ."

"Yes, say my name." He slid his hand around her hips and found her clit.

Desire roared through her center, winding her muscles tight with need. "Jason."

He moved his finger in circular motions around her clit, just the way she liked it. Ari moaned and arched her back as much as she could, pressing her ass into his hips.

"You like this, don't you?" he asked.

"Yes." God, yes. Ari closed her eyes as her muscles tightened around his cock.

He pumped faster, filling her again and again until her mind fogged with lust. Ari opened her eyes and turned her head to meet his gaze. She saw hunger and desperation, possession and urgency. "This is what it's all about, Ari. Not our pasts, or our futures. Just this moment. Just you and me." He kissed her hard, and Ari whimpered as he continued to fill her with quick, hard thrusts. When he broke away from her lips, she gasped and faced forward. Jason straightened and grabbed her shoulders, leveraging himself against his thrusts. He pumped harder, faster. Every push sent Ari closer and closer to the edge. She spread her arms out over the car in silent surrender, giving herself over to him and this moment.

"You were made for my pleasure, Ari. Just like I was made for yours. Don't ever forget it."

Ari whimpered and bit down on her lip as her orgasm slammed into her body. Pleasure burst through her bloodstream, filling every crevice, every pore. She felt weightless, as if she was floating on a cloud of bliss. She hung suspended there, in the moment, as each thrust sent ribbons of joy through her body.

Jason groaned and pushed harder. Within seconds she felt him stiffen, sensed the urgency in his thrusts. Then he too tumbled over the edge into oblivion.

As the last of her orgasm began to fade, reality settled around her, making her anxious. "Jason, we're in public."

With a groan, Jason pulled out of her and set her skirt back in place. His movements were so gentle, so loving, that Ari couldn't help her heart from melting just a little bit.

"Are you okay?" she asked as she turned to face him.

"Fine." His phone buzzed and he pulled it out of his pocket. After frowning at the screen, he pocketed it once more and then opened the car door. "But you're right. We should get out of here."

Ari hesitated. She wanted to talk about what had just happened to them. She felt she had made a hole in the wall around his heart and wanted to reach out before he closed back up again.

This wasn't the time or the place, however. After a quick glance to make sure no one else was around, she got into the passenger seat.

As Jason pulled out onto the main street and took them back to his hotel, he remained quiet, as if deep in thought.

Ari started to ask him what was wrong, but then changed her mind. Instead, she turned her attention out the side window, watching the passing buildings as they made their way through the Boston streets. Back at the hospital, she had thought that Jason was starting to confide in her, but she was wrong. It didn't take long for him to retreat into himself and push her away.

Jason wanted things between them to stay the same, but did anything ever do that? She thought of her best friend Alisha, and how lost she had felt after her death. Ari had hated the change, but it had shaped her into the person she was today. Everything changes, she realized. How you grow and adapt to the changes defines who you are as a person.

This no-strings-attached relationship couldn't go on forever. If she was going to change and become her own woman, then she couldn't allow herself to be someone's plaything anymore. She wanted more from him. Needed more. As they pulled into the parking garage at Stone Suites, she wondered for the first time if Jason was capable of changing, or if she would need to find the strength to move on with her life without him.

"I thought we were going to your apartment," she said as they pulled into a parking space.

"Later—there is something I need to do first."

"What?"

"Later, Ari." He kissed her temple. "Wait for me in the restaurant. I'll only be an hour."

"What about my . . ." She watched him turn his back as she pointed to the trunk of the McLaren. He had already dismissed her.

Ari was so tired of being pushed aside. With a sigh, she decided to leave the suitcase in the trunk and head inside toward the restaurant. She could really use a drink.

She'd only taken a few steps toward the entrance before an uneasy feeling came over her. Something wasn't right. She took a quick look around, but nothing seemed out of the ordinary. Frowning, she hugged her purse to her chest and quickened her steps toward the door.

Someone was moving behind her. She could hear the footsteps. Glancing over her shoulder, she saw a large man in an overcoat and fedora following her. He seemed off somehow. His steps were too purposeful, his stance too self-assured. He continued to close the distance between them, his long strides swallowing up two of her small ones.

Something was wrong. Ari could feel it in her gut. Panic rippled through her as she dropped all pretense and sprinted toward the hotel door. The footsteps behind her quickened, and as she placed her hand on the handle, something hard hit her on the side of the head. She tried to gasp, tried to scream, but her brain had lost its command of her body.

Ari wobbled, then crumpled to the pavement as everything went black.

Jason frowned as he made his way over to the hotel restaurant. With each step, he grew more worried. Deacon had sent him a text saying that he knew who had stolen his identity. He had rushed back to the hotel, hoping he could finally put this entire blackmail mess behind him, only to discover that Deacon was not around. He had checked everywhere, even calling Deacon's cell. The man was nowhere to be found.

Jason had no idea what had happened to his brother, but he couldn't dwell on it. If he knew Deacon, his brother was probably out following up on a lead. He'd show up when he was good and ready. Meanwhile, Jason had to get Ari back to his apartment, where it was safe.

He was feeling more and more protective of Ari, and he wasn't sure what to make of it. Things were growing way too intense between them. Seeing her with the children made him want things that he had no business wanting. Jason had spent his entire life building a wall around his heart. People knew him to be cold and heartless. He wore his reputation like a shield and had pushed everyone away before they could hurt him. Ari made him want to shed his shield and start caring once more. Hell, he had even offered to donate money his company didn't have, just to protect her reputation. His behavior reminded him of his gigolo days, when women used and manipulated him for their own purposes. After he had left that life, he had promised himself that he'd never become that vulnerable again. Yet here he was, falling into the same patterns. If he wasn't careful, Jason was going to lose more than just his time and money. He was going to lose his heart.

"Mr. Stone?" a soft feminine voice rose up as the elevator doors opened.

Jason stopped short as his assistant, Micki, materialized in front of him.

"Mr. Stone?" she asked, clutching her clipboard to her chest.

"Yes, Micki?"

She pushed her glasses up onto her nose. "We've been looking all over for you. You haven't been answering your phone."

"I've been busy." He sidestepped her and headed toward the restaurant once more.

"We, uh, we have a situation," she said as she hurried to keep pace beside him.

"Really? What?" he asked as they stepped into the bar area. The familiar theme music for the nightly tabloid show echoed throughout the room. Micki started to speak, but Jason held up his hand as he saw that reporter, Amanda, on the screen.

"Who put that garbage on?" Jason demanded. The bartender shrugged his shoulders and the waitstaff all turned away from him, fascinated with their individual tasks.

"Sir," Micki said as she stepped up beside him.

"Just a minute, Micki." He strode up to the television to change the channel, but something the anchorwoman said gave him pause.

"Today we have our correspondent, Amanda Vaughn,

who has been covering the Perconti situation and has an update for us. Isn't that right, Amanda?"

Jason lowered his hand and scowled at the television screen.

"Yes." Amanda smiled and turned to the camera. There was a certain gleam in her eye, as if she was holding in some secret she was dying to tell. The woman was in her element. Jason's stomach rolled as a sense of foreboding washed over him.

"I know why Arianna Perconti left her own wedding."

"You do? Why?"

Amanda nodded. "Because she has a boyfriend."

The anchorwoman gasped. "A boyfriend? Were they dating before the wedding?"

"I believe so," Amanda said. "I have proof." Amanda waved her hand to someone off camera. "Mason?"

Jason shook with anger as he watched footage of himself and Ari talking to the child with green hair. Instead of focusing on the child, which was the entire purpose of the trip, the camera zoomed in, showing his hand as he wrapped it possessively around Ari's side.

"Arianna Perconti is dating none other than . . ." Amanda waited until the camera panned up to show his face. "Jason Stone."

"Of all the—" Jason fisted his hands and looked around him for something to throw.

"Sir, we have a situation," Micki said.

"She told me she wouldn't show it," Jason muttered.

"What?"

Jason glanced at his assistant. "I paid that reporter not to show her footage to the public."

Micki blinked. "But she did, sir."

"I can see that, yes." He ground his teeth.

"How long have they been dating?" the anchorwoman asked.

"Does it matter? Jason Stone is having sex with his rival's sister. You have to believe that her older brothers aren't going to be pleased."

"What I wouldn't give to be a fly on the wall during the next family reunion." The anchorwoman giggled.

Jason grabbed a glass from the bar and threw it at the television. "Turn it off!" The glass crashed into the set, spraying shards all over the floor.

Jason turned and stormed out of the restaurant. His assistant followed in his wake.

"Sir?"

What was he going to do? God help him, his worst nightmare was coming true, and it was all Ari's fault for wanting to talk to the press.

No, it was his own fault for wanting to go with her to the hospital so he could protect her. Jason had no one to blame for this mess but himself.

"Sir?"

Jason slowed his steps as a thought occurred to him. "Micki."

"Yes, sir?"

"You didn't happen to see Arianna Perconti in the restaurant while we were in there, did you?"

"No, sir. She isn't in the restaurant."

"Damn." He ran his hand over his jaw. "Where the hell is she?"

"That's what I've been trying to tell you, sir."

"What?" He lowered his arm. "You've seen her?"

Micki nodded. "Ms. Perconti is out in the garage."

"What the hell is she doing in the garage?"

"Someone hit her in the back of the head. She's bleeding."

Jason marched quickly through the foyer and hall, bypassing the elevator for the stairs.

"Mr. Stone." Micki followed him, her heels clicking on the marble floors.

"What happened? Who hit her?"

"We don't know."

Panic seized him as he hurried down the stairs to the ground floor. He moved past the laundry room, toward the small crowd that had gathered by the front door.

"Out of the way." He pushed aside the staff members and made it to the center of the circle. There, on the floor, he found Deacon sitting cross-legged, cradling Ari's head in his arms.

"Get away from her." Jason dropped to the floor and gently took Ari from his brother's grasp.

"I was coming back to find you," Deacon said as Jason applied the cold pack to her head. "I found her in a heap on the pavement."

"Did you see who did it?"

"No. They were long gone."

Ari moaned and turned her head to the side. "God, it hurts."

"I'm right here, princess. I'm right here." He bent down and kissed her forehead, which made her smile. "Do you hurt anywhere else?"

"No, just my head. Damn." She winced and squeezed her eyes shut.

"Did you happen to see who did it?"

"Large man. Overcoat. Hat."

"Didn't see his face?"

She shook her head and winced again.

"It's okay." He glanced around the group. "Did someone call a doctor?"

"I did, Mr. Stone," Micki said. "They'll be here in a minute."

Thank God.

"Is there anything I can do to help?" Deacon asked.

Jason rocked Ari, keeping his gaze focused on her. "Get everyone out of here."

Deacon nodded. "Sure thing." He stood and waved his hands in the air. "Come on, everybody. Move 'em out."

"Everything will be okay, Ari." He inched the cold pack away and tried not to wince at the blood.

"I know."

Jason's phone buzzed once more, signaling an incoming text. He slid his phone out of his suit and swiped the screen. The message he found sent ice through his chest.

Thought you could get out of the deal by going to the press, did you? Give us our money, or next time, we'll really *mess up the girl.*

Chapter 13

Jason paced back and forth in front of the hospital bed in a desperate attempt to keep himself busy. He felt like a caged animal, a dangerous one that was ready to strike. He was furious at so many people. Himself included.

"I never should have left you in the garage," he mumbled as he stopped at the foot of Arianna's bed. "And you should be lying down."

"I'm fine. Honest. And quit blaming yourself. You had no idea that someone was going to hit me on the back of the head."

"Doesn't matter. I never should have left you alone."

She sighed as he started pacing once more. "Even if you did, I'm not sure if there was anything you could have done to stop it. That guy was fast."

"You should've come with me." He used both hands to push his hair from his face. He hated to think how long she had been lying there, alone and bleeding, before his brother had found her.

"Stop pacing, Jason. You're making me dizzy," Ari said. "Make yourself useful and give me the remote."

He stopped and stared at the beautiful woman sitting on the edge of the bed. They were damn lucky that she hadn't been seriously injured. She had a lump on the back of her head, and a small cut that he'd insisted on stitching, even though the doctors said it was unnecessary. None of those injuries would last, thankfully. If Ari had suffered any permanent damage, he'd never forgive himself.

"Does your head still hurt?"

"Not really, thanks to the meds." She glanced at the hospital room door. "I just wish I knew who knocked me out." She gingerly touched the back of her head. "And why. At first I thought it was a mugging, but nothing was taken from me. It seems as if it was just a random act of violence. Rather strange, don't you think?"

Not really. Jason knew exactly why she'd been attacked, and by whom. As soon as he had her safe in his apartment he was going to track down that loan shark by any means necessary and make him pay. If he had to fall back on his old ways and old contacts, including using his brother, Deacon, he'd do it. Nothing was more important than Ari's safety. Nothing.

He leaned over and placed a chaste kiss on her forehead. "I'm going to go see what's keeping the hospital staff. You should've been discharged by now." He needed to move. The longer he stayed and sat with Ari, the more time he was wasting. Just sitting around and doing nothing was driving him insane.

As soon as Jason was out of the room, he searched for the nurses' station. A few quick words with the staff revealed that her doctor would see them as soon as he was finished with his current patient. Frustrated, Jason walked a short ways to a visitor rest area. Collapsing on a couch, he pulled out his phone and began to text his brother.

Did u find anything?

It wasn't long before Deacon texted back. *Not yet, but my contacts are working on it. It was definitely that loan shark. I should have the name of the muscle that hit your girl soon.*

Jason hesitated. He hated working with Deacon. He had worked so hard to become a new man, and his brother represented a past better left forgotten. Deacon had no desire to better himself, and saw nothing wrong with using people for personal gain. Jason knew he could never go back to that dark time in his life permanently, but if it meant sparing Ari more harm, then perhaps it was worth working with his brother one last time. It was worth a shot, especially since he was running out of options.

He glanced at the clock, then returned his attention to his phone. *Meet me in my office in two hours. I have a proposition for you.*

Sure thing.

Satisfied that things were moving in the right direction, Jason pocketed the phone and returned to the room. There he found Ari, sitting on the edge of the bed, staring at the television screen with her mouth slightly open.

"What is it?" Jason asked.

Ari shut her mouth and pointed her remote at the television set. "That reporter outed our relationship."

Jason steeled his jaw as he turned to the screen. He had forgotten about the talk show in all of the commotion. It was something else he was going to have to deal with once they got out of there.

"That bitch didn't mention one word about my charity," Ari said.

Jason sat down on the bed beside her. "I told you she wouldn't."

Ari shut off the television and shook her head. "I can't believe she lied to me. I feel so . . . used."

Jason covered her hands with his. "She lies to everyone, princess. That's her job."

"I'm so stupid." Tears stung her eyes as she looked up at him. "You were right. I never should have spoken with her. I'm sorry I didn't believe you."

Jason wanted to say that it was an easy mistake to make, but the doctor chose that moment to come in and discharge Ari from the hospital.

Time passed far too slowly for Jason's peace of mind as they filled out the paperwork, promised to fill her prescriptions, and got on the road. During the entire exchange with the doctor, Ari had provided one-word answers to the doctor's questions, but was otherwise silent. She silently obeyed Jason's request to let him wheel her out of the building in a wheelchair, and once in the car, she folded her hands in her lap and stared out the passenger's side window.

Something was obviously wrong. He missed the spunky vixen who liked verbal sparring. Ari seemed defeated somehow, and he wasn't quite sure what to do about it.

"You're not stupid," he said, guessing that her mood had something to do with the nosey reporter.

"Yes, I am. My brother was right. I have no business running that charity. Instead of cleaning up the family's controversy, I seem to have added more." She wiped her eyes with the back of her hand. "I'm such an idiot."

"No, you aren't. Amanda knows how to twist what people say into a story that will sell magazines. She's a manipulator. It's why she is so good at her job."

"You didn't believe her."

He sighed as he pulled up to the security gate of his apartment complex. "At one time I did. We were two weeks into a relationship before I learned that she was using me and my connections to gain tips on stories before her competition."

The security guard nodded to him and let him pass into the underground parking area. Unlike Stone Suites, this area had cameras and security personnel constantly watching. He felt good that there would be people looking out for her welfare while he was out with Deacon getting his revenge.

Ari turned away from the window and faced him. "What did you do when you found out Amanda was using you?"

"I broke up with her," he said as he stopped the car in his designated parking spot. He turned off the engine and grinned at her. "But I ended the relationship in such a way to ensure it didn't make the headlines."

She twitched her lips. "Really? How?"

"Oh no." He waved his finger at her. "I never give away Stone secrets." He flashed her an evil grin. "Let's just say I didn't show up in that *Whispers* tabloid again until they started doing that 'Most Eligible Bachelors' feature."

She chuckled. "So *that's* why my brother is number one on that list."

"What are you talking about?" Jason hurried around to the passenger's side door and helped her out of the car. Satisfied she wasn't going to faint and fall over, he went to get her suitcase from the backseat.

"Well, I always wondered why my brother was number one and you were number two. Now it makes perfect sense. Amanda would never make someone who dumped her number one on her list."

He laughed as he closed the car door and pulled out the handle of the suitcase. "I think you're giving me too much credit."

"Doesn't it make you angry? The list is biased."

"I don't care about that list, or any other." He kissed her temple and pushed the button for the elevator. "Not anymore."

"I thought you played to win," she joked as they stepped into the elevator.

"I do." He slid his key card into the control panel of the

elevator. "But you're assuming I'm playing the game." He punched a code into the elevator and it began to climb.

"I suppose you're right. It's still not fair, though."

"It doesn't matter. The magazine is just a tabloid and doesn't carry any weight with anyone important."

"Jason Stone not caring about a competition." She glanced sideways at him and smirked. "You better watch out. If I didn't know any better, I'd think you're changing."

"Perhaps." The elevator doors opened. "Ah, here we are."

"Wow." Ari widened her eyes as she broke away from his arm and stepped into the large foyer of the penthouse suite. "This is amazing." She stumbled on a dip in the floor.

"Easy." Jason grabbed her arm, steading her. "Here, let me help."

Before Ari could react, he wrapped his arms around her knees and torso and lifted her into the air.

"Jason," she said as she put her arms around his neck. "I got hit in the head, not the legs. I'm perfectly fine and able to walk, you know."

"I know, but admit it. This is more fun."

She giggled as he swept her through the brightly lit foyer and into an art deco–styled living room.

"How . . . contemporary." She glanced at the walls, which were filled with contemporary art similar to the type she had seen at the hotel, yet more skilled. "These paintings are gorgeous."

"I like to collect art. It's another of my vices." He placed her gently down on a large crimson sofa.

She stared at the paintings, taking in the bright shapes and colors. She didn't know a lot about art, but these pieces seemed to suit his personality. They were bold and exciting, just like him. "They're quite good."

"I'll let the artists know," he said.

"You know the artists?"

He smiled and picked up a remote off the coffee table that was painted to look like a domino. "Coffee?"

"Please."

He punched a few buttons. "Of course. I fund painters, sculptors, and lots of other struggling artists." He put the remote back on the coffee table. "Don't act so surprised."

"I just didn't know that your venture capitalist activities extended into the art world."

"I invest in whatever interests me." He glanced around. "Although I have to admit, sometimes the artist interests me more than the art itself."

Something beeped from the other room. Jason stood up from the couch and went to the wall as a small section opened up, creating a shelf. On the shelf were two mugs with steam coming out of them. "Cream and sugar?"

"Yes." She nodded to the mugs. "Another invention?"

"Investment. I wanted to test the software program out before I put it in my hotels." He brought the mugs over to her. "I should introduce you to the person who developed it. She's quite the thinker."

"She?"

He nodded. "Young thing. Lots of ideas, but not the capital to do them." He shrugged. "I wanted to help her out."

"It's not the art you're investing in, but the artist." She took a sip from her mug. "This is delicious."

"The people interest me more than the things they are trying to sell. I seem to have a good eye for character." He held up his mug.

"A benevolent benefactor." She raised her mug and clinked it with his. "I like the sound of that. It suits you."

He chuckled and put his mug on the coffee table. "I wouldn't go that far. I do profit from my investments, after all."

She smirked and raised the mug to her lips. "A man's got to earn a living somehow."

"Exactly." After she drank, he plucked her mug from her fingers and placed it on the table. "Now, let me check that wound on your head."

"I told you, I'm fine." Despite her words, Ari leaned forward and let him take a look at her bandage. "It doesn't even really hurt anymore."

"That's the medication talking."

She snorted as he examined her head. If only the public knew what he did to help starving artists and small business owners. He truly cared about others, which was a rare thing in this day and age. Unfortunately, the media was more interested in who Jason Stone was dating, not the lives he made better with his money.

She supposed that they were a lot alike in that regard. They both used their money to change people's lives for the better. In both cases, the press decided to overlook the good they were doing in favor of creating scandal. Jason was the opportunistic playboy. She was the vapid party girl. .

He started to pull away, but she grabbed his wrist and pulled him close. "You're a good man, Jason. Don't let the media tell you different."

He stared at her for a long moment before responding. "You're the only one who thinks so."

The sadness she saw in his face made her heart ache. She knew that kind of loneliness all too well.

Ari placed her fingers on either side of his face. "I don't think so, I know so." She tilted her head and brushed her lips against his. It was meant to be reassuring, but soon heat flooded her system. Her heartbeat quickened at the intimate contact.

"I suppose I should thank you," she said as she inched away.

"For what?"

"For taking care of me." She shivered as she withdrew

her hands. "I was so frightened. When I saw you, I instantly felt safer."

"I'm glad." He brushed a stray hair from her face as something hungry passed through his gaze.

"It's okay, you know."

"What is?"

"I just got a bump on the head. Nothing serious." When he didn't move, she leaned forward and brushed her lips against his own.

The kiss was slow and soft, as if he was afraid she might break. She slid her arms around his neck and pressed deeper, silently willing him to explore further. He brushed his tongue in long, leisurely strokes against hers, refusing to rush the moment. Ari's heartbeat quickened as desire rushed through her core.

"Take me, Jason," she whispered against his mouth.

"But you're hurt."

"Let me be the judge of that. Just shut up and take me."

He kissed her again, and this time it was harder, more possessive. As their tongues dueled, he slid one hand down her neck and shoulder, slipping it underneath the blanket. With a swift, bold stroke, he pushed the thick fabric aside, exposing her to him.

Ari lifted her leg, positioning it along the back of the couch. Instead of moving on top of her like she had hoped, he continued to kiss her slowly, intimately, as he ran his fingers over her bare skin.

"Jason," she gasped as he cupped her breast and squeezed.

"I wish I could have been there for you," he whispered. "I could have stopped it."

"Don't beat yourself up over it," she said. "It wasn't your fault."

"You're wrong."

"What do you mean?"

"I mean, it was my fault." He kissed her again.

"Don't be ridiculous," she said when she came up for air.

He inched back. "If I never left you, you never would have gotten hurt."

"I've been by myself millions of times. There was no way you could have possibly known—"

"I'll never make that mistake again, Ari," he said as he brushed his fingers over her cheek. "I promise."

He seemed a little intense about it all, but before Ari could question him, he covered her lips once more. The pressure was gentle, more exploring than taking, more playful than possessive, and soon desire rolled through Ari once more.

She tore at his shirt, trying to lift it off his body. He caught her hand and pinned it beside her head. "No."

"I want to touch you."

"Let me do this." He kissed her neck, sending tingles of warmth across her skin.

Ari groaned as he slid his hand down from her wrist and eased it under her shirt. He touched her belly, her sides, and heat trailed wherever he brushed her skin.

Ari slid her arms up over her head, letting them dangle off the end of the couch, as he lifted her shirt and began kissing where his fingers had just trailed.

"God, Jason," she whispered. "Don't stop."

He slid his hands around to her sides. She arched her back, letting him reach around and unclasp her bra. He pushed both the shirt and bra up, exposing her breasts. Ari moistened her lips as he bent his head and flicked his tongue over her nipple.

"Oh, God." She reached down and threaded her hands in his hair, but he removed them and placed them back on the couch.

"Don't move," he ordered as he returned to his work. He dragged his tongue around her nipple, coming close, but not quite reaching the center.

"Jason . . ." He kissed the side of her breast, then underneath, taking his time to cover every inch of her skin with his teeth and tongue. Ari twisted and turned as need rolled up through her center. "Please."

He glanced up at her, holding her gaze as he flicked his tongue against her tip. She nibbled her lower lip as he leaned back and blew hot air, causing her to shiver with need.

"Jason—"

He took her nipple into his mouth, sucking and sliding his tongue over her skin. Ari moaned and turned her head, falling deeper into the moment. With every touch, she became more desperate, with every lick, more needy. By the time he'd finished with the first breast and moved to the second, she was shaking with desire.

"Let me touch you," she said.

"I want to do this, Ari," he whispered as he blew another puff of hot air against her skin. "Let me have my fun."

She watched him as he worked, helpless to do anything else. The look in his eyes suggested that what he was doing meant more to him than their normal playful romp. She wanted to know what was going on in his head, but then he scraped his teeth lightly over her nipple, and her thoughts scattered into bliss.

"Tell me what you want, Ari."

"What?" She tilted her head to look down at him.

"You said that you wanted to take charge, so take charge." He kissed the canal between her breasts and smiled up at her. "Tell me what you want."

She spread her legs apart on the couch as far as they could comfortably go. "Isn't it obvious?"

"No," he said as he kissed a long, hot trail down her abdomen. "Tell me."

That tongue. It was so sinful. As it flicked over her belly button, she imagined it dipping into another part of her body.

"I want you to make me come," she whispered.

Chapter 14

He slowly raised his head from her skin and lifted his brows. "Oh really?" He made a pointed look at her injury. "Are you sure it's safe?"

She lifted her brows right back at him and tried to look regal and in control. "I think I should be the judge of what I can and cannot handle." She cleared her throat. "Now I want you to make me come. With your mouth."

He chuckled, blowing warm air against her skin. "Yes, ma'am." He kissed her again, and as his tongue flicked across her skin, he hooked his fingers into her skirt and panties. She lifted her backside as he slid them off her completely.

As soon as the clothes were removed, he was on her again, kissing a long, sensual line down her abdomen and over her mound. Ari reached for his hair, but he gently pushed her hands away.

"Jason . . ."

"Just enjoy this, Ari." He put her hands back up over her head on the pillow. "Relax."

Perhaps it was their earlier conversation, or his request that she tell him what she wanted. Whatever the reason, Ari felt a little bold and adventurous. As he was moving back between her legs, she leaned up on her elbows and fixed him with a commanding stare.

"No."

He lifted his gaze to hers. "Excuse me?"

She twisted her lips into a half-smile. "You wanted me to tell you what I wanted."

"And you said to make you come."

"Yes, I want you to make me come with your mouth, but you didn't let me finish."

"There's more?"

"Yes." She lifted her chin. "I want you to be on your back when it happens."

"Really." He pointed to the couch. "Right here?"

"Yes." She flashed him a seductive smile as she sat up. "Right here. Right now." She placed her hands on his chest and eased him back onto the pile of throw pillows. "I want to be in complete control." She stood and waited for him to put his feet up on the couch.

"You have to realize this is a little out of character."

"So?"

"So . . . perhaps you were hit in the head harder than we thought," he joked.

"Just for that . . ." She grabbed the pillow behind his head and yanked it away. "You don't get to be comfortable."

His eyes sparkled with desire as she straddled his shoulders. "You're in control, huh?"

"Yes," she said as she raised her hips.

"I could get used to this." He slid his hands up her legs and wrapped his fingers around her ass as she inched forward and lowered herself toward his mouth.

He met her halfway, sliding his tongue over her folds like a hungry man. Pleasure rocketed up her center, and Ari grabbed the arm of the sofa for support.

"Oh my."

Jason groaned as he slid his tongue between her folds.

"Yes." She lowered herself a fraction of an inch more, allowing him better access. He slid his tongue around her opening and collected the moisture he found there. Ari made a low, throaty sound as she curled her fingers into the soft fabric.

"Wow." She inched lower, and was rewarded when his tongue slid up and flicked her clit. Need rippled through her muscles, winding them tight. She leaned forward and pressed her hips closer. "Oh, that's good."

"You taste good." Jason used his fingers to spread apart her folds and feasted on her flesh, driving her crazy with desire.

"Yes." She performed shallow thrusts against his mouth, eager for him to be inside her. Pleasure spiraled through her body and brought with it the familiar pressure of need.

"Enter me," she whispered. "Please."

He refused, instead remaining just outside her opening.

"God, Jason, you're driving me crazy."

He eased his head away. "Then don't ask for what you want. Tell me."

She hesitated, a little uncomfortable with voicing her needs out loud. Then again, this was the new Ari, the confident woman who took what she wanted instead of blindly following other people's commands.

"Put your finger inside of me." Ari widened her eyes when he moved to obey. This was working. It was really working. Sweet friction heated her core and she nibbled her lower lip as she tried to think of what to say next.

"Yes," she said as pleasure spiraled through her body. Ari moved her hips in time to his thrusts, meeting him halfway. "Just like that."

"See how easy it is, Ari?" he said as he pushed his finger deep into her center and withdrew. "For far too long you've waited around for others to figure out what you want. Stop waiting, princess. Tell them. Tell me."

"Use your tongue," she commanded.

She gasped as his tongue slid around her opening and then rubbed her clit in that back-and-forth motion that drove her wild.

"Yes," she said. "Use another finger."

He exchanged one finger for two, pressing deep inside her core and spreading it apart, stretching her inner walls.

"Yes." She straightened away from the couch and slid her hands under her shirt. Cupping her breasts, she tugged her nipples as she performed shallow thrusts toward Jason's mouth. "Go faster."

Jason quickened the pace, thrusting hard into her core. Ari tugged harder on her nipples as the pressure in her body grew. She tightened her core muscles, and Jason groaned as he slid his tongue down from her clit and ran it over her damp skin.

"No, not yet."

He slid his tongue back up over her clit, nipping hard, then soothing the blast of pain with his tongue.

Ari made soft, feminine noises with each thrust and closed her eyes as the need continued to build. Once, twice, the third time he nipped her clit, pleasure burst through her center and spread out over her body. Ari leaned her head back and screamed his name as her orgasm hit her hard, bathing her body in pleasure.

Jason curled his fingers into her flesh and drank her orgasm, performing shallow thrusts with his tongue. The added stimulation made her dizzy with desire, and Ari let go of her breasts and clung to the sofa in an effort to remain upright. Never before had she felt anything so wonderful, or so complete. Jason was relentless, milking every last drop of ecstasy from her body. By the time she was done, she was shaking and spent, her entire body bathed in bliss.

Jason eased her away from his face and back down onto the couch. Adjusting his position, he curled himself around her and brought the blanket up around them.

"That was amazing," he whispered in her ear as he gently pushed the hair from her face. "You need to do that more often."

"Take control?" she asked, her eyes still closed.

"Tell me what you want," he said. "None of us are mind readers, Ari. If you want something, if you need something, then you have to let us know."

He was right, she realized. Leo controlled her life because she had let him. While she had confronted him dozens of times in her mind, she had never told him in person how his micromanaging of her life bothered her. Nothing was ever going to change if she never took charge and demanded what she wanted.

"Thank you," she said.

"For what?"

"For making me realize why I've been miserable all of these years. I've never told Leo what I wanted."

He tightened his hold around her torso. "I'm sure if you just spoke with him and told him the truth, things would change."

Ari buried her head in Jason's neck, enjoying how good his warm body felt against hers. In this brief, wonderful moment, she felt connected and loved. Nothing stood between them, and she felt that nothing could ever get in their way.

As they lay in each other's arms, Ari was struck by how right it felt to be wrapped in Jason's warmth. It was almost as if they were made to fit together. As she snuggled closer, she couldn't imagine being anywhere else in that moment. It was then that she realized something very important.

Jason hated the postcoital afterglow. Ever since she had known him, he had been finding an excuse to hurry through the after-sex snuggling or avoid it altogether. This time, however, things were different. He wasn't running away. Why?

"Did you like it?" she asked.

"It was amazing," he admitted. "I never would have thought to try something like that." He grabbed her fingers and kissed them. "I'm glad you suggested it." He turned her hand and kissed her palm. "I'm just relieved that you're all right. When I think of what could have happened . . ."

"Shh." She twisted her hand so that she covered his mouth. "Don't think about it. I'm fine."

"I could have done more. I *should* have done more." He nuzzled his face in her hair. "I'm so sorry, Ari."

"There's nothing you could have done about it. It was a random attack, made by a random person."

"I wish that were true."

"What?" She turned her head so she could see his face. "What are you talking about?"

He steeled his jaw as something dark passed through his eyes.

"Jason." She tried to push away, but he held her tightly against him. "What aren't you telling me?"

After a long moment, he relaxed his jaw and closed his eyes. "What happened to you wasn't a random attack."

"Someone targeted me?" She pushed away from him again. This time he let her go. Ari sat up and stared at him, unbelieving. "Who on earth would target me, and why?"

Slowly he opened his eyes. The guilt and pain she saw there tore at her heart. "It was a message."

"A message?"

"For me." He pushed his hair from his face and adjusted the pillow beneath his head. "A few days ago, I got a package from a courier. The package contained a note saying that I was delinquent on some gambling debts in Las Vegas."

"I didn't know you gambled."

"I don't." He let out a long breath and toyed with the end of her hair. "But this loan shark thinks I do. He says I owe him ten million dollars and if I don't pay it, that he'll hurt not only me, but those I care about."

"Can you just explain to this guy that you aren't who he thinks you are?"

"For a while I couldn't locate him. Then when I did . . ." Jason shrugged. "I sent someone to try to explain it to him, but he wouldn't listen to me." He dropped his hand from her hair and rubbed his face. "I guess I'm not the first person who has used the same excuse. He thinks I'm lying to try to get out of paying him the money."

"But you can prove that you didn't rack up those debts."

"I wish it were that simple. Someone stole my identity."

"Who?"

"I wish I knew. At one point Deacon thought he had the name of the thief, but the lead was a dead end."

"Wow. I'm so sorry, Jason."

"Me too, but that's not all. This loan shark . . . he's known for using unusual tactics to get people to pay him. He took pictures of us, Ari."

"What? When?"

"In the laundry room when you first arrived, then again at that restaurant where we got chicken wings. He said that if I didn't pay my debts, then our relationship will be made public. And if I tried to go public . . ." He waved his hand at the bump on her head. "Then he'd hurt you."

She widened her eyes. "And then that tabloid reporter talked about us . . ."

He nodded. "He thought I was trying to get out of paying him by taking our relationship to the media."

"And that's why he came after me." Ari fisted her hands. "That bastard."

"I'm so sorry."

She forced herself to relax her hands. "I'm not."

"You're not?"

She shook her head. "I didn't get hurt, not too badly anyway. And now not only have we taken away his hold over you, but you've told me what is going on." She took his hand. "All of our secrets are out in the open, Jason. He has no more control over us." She squeezed his fingers. "So you're in the clear. It's over."

He tightened his jaw and let go of her hand. "I wish that you were right." He eased away from her and sat up on the couch beside her.

"What are you talking about? Of course it's over."

"Not all of my secrets are out in the open."

"What do you mean?"

He ran his hand over his face and leaned back against the couch. "You've met my brother, Deacon."

"Yes."

"He . . . he's a lot like me."

"How do you mean?"

"We both thrive on taking chances. We like to live life on the edge. While I get my fix by taking risks in the boardroom and with my race cars, Deacon does other things."

"What kind of things?"

"Gambling, mostly, but he also races motorcycles and fights a little."

"Fights, like a boxer?"

"Underground fighting."

She sat back in her chair. "That's illegal."

"That's part of the reason why he does it. Skirting around the law gives him a thrill."

"I see." She nibbled her lip and tried to digest this

information. Jason's brother beat people up for money. It was hard to wrap her head around. "But you're not like that."

Jason averted his gaze. "At one time, yes, I *was* like that, Ari. I was very much like Deacon."

"You beat people up for money, too?"

"No." He sighed and shifted in his seat. "I told you that Deacon and I were raised in a series of foster homes."

"Yes."

"We were passed around like popcorn in a movie theater. When people thought that they'd had enough of us, they'd hand us off to someone else."

"I'm so sorry."

"That family you are trying so hard to break away from? I wish I had that." He shook his head. "You claim that Leo is suffocating you. Well, I wish I had someone who's as interested in my life as he is in yours. No one cared about what happened to us, Ari. Not one person. All that mattered were those damn checks."

Meeting his gaze, she took his hand and thought about their first meeting. Back then she had thought he was an arrogant playboy. She couldn't have been more wrong. Jason was so much more complex than people realized. More human. She couldn't imagine the loneliness he had gone through as a child.

"It's okay," he said.

Perhaps, but the loneliness she saw in his eyes hinted that it wasn't. Jason was a man who didn't typically let people get close to him. She felt honored that he was trusting her with his secrets, and knew that she'd never do anything to betray that trust. The more he opened up to her, the more she was drawn to him. Her heart ached not only for that little boy, but for the man he ultimately became.

"What happened when you got older? Did you eventually find a family?"

"Not really. As soon as Deacon turned eighteen, he

pulled me from the system. We ran away and found odd jobs to make ends meet. It was just us against the world." He looked down at his hands in his lap. "We were so young."

"What kind of work did you do?"

"Waitstaff mostly. Later Deacon learned how to tend bar, which paid more in tips. By the time I was twenty, we both worked for a catering company out of New York doing high society events."

"That doesn't sound too bad."

"It wasn't, until one night when we were working one of these events . . . an older woman approached me, thinking that I was someone else. Deacon and I were waiting tables at a fancy cocktail party, and when she approached me, I was hanging out by the bar with Deacon, waiting for my drink order. I guess the tux made her think that I was a guest, not a waiter. I think . . . I think it was just easier to lead her on than to tell her the truth. One lie covered another until I was no longer her friend, but a friend of a friend, and had recently moved to the States. Things snowballed after that."

"What do you mean?"

Jason returned his gaze to his lap. "Deacon and I realized that night that we could make more money being friends with lonely women than waiting tables."

"So you stopped working?"

"It depends on how you look at it. We provided a service. The women were lonely and needed company. We provided that company for them. We just never told them who we really were."

"What did you do with these women?"

"We attended luncheons where they could show us off to their friends. We also went to family reunions, charity functions, boating trips . . ." He shrugged. "Whatever they wanted."

"So you just provided company for them?"

"Sometimes." He shifted in his seat and averted his gaze. "Sometimes, we provided a little more."

She widened her eyes as his meaning hit home. "You had sex with them for money?"

"We never specifically set a fee. The women were just very . . . grateful for our services. We were gifted with cars and clothes and trinkets. Sometimes, if they needed our services for a specific period of time, we'd stay at their house with them."

"In their room?"

"If the situation called for it." When she didn't respond, he inched closer. "It was just a job, Ari. None of those women meant anything to me."

"But you meant something to them. They thought it was a real relationship."

"We gave them confidence and reassurance to overcome whatever difficulties they were having in their lives. Is that so bad?"

Pain sliced through Ari's chest. Jason was a professional con artist. He manipulated poor, lonely women into giving him trinkets and money. People like her.

Was he conning her, too? She thought back over their relationship and couldn't remember a time when she had given him cash or gifts. At least, nothing expensive and significant that he couldn't get himself. He had never let her pay for gas or dinner, never let her buy him mementoes when they traveled together. In fact, whenever she had tried to pay for something, he had looked damn uncomfortable.

Then again, perhaps he wasn't after her money. Ari had other things someone like Jason would find valuable. Connections, information . . . *oh shit.*

Sabrina was right. Jason was pursuing her for information on her family, and she'd been all too eager to talk about how her brother was spending his money and his business deal with Landon. Ari closed her eyes as the full impact of what she had done hit home.

When did the con begin? Was their entire relationship a lie? Ari thought back through their time together, picking out the things that were said, and more importantly, things that were not said between them.

"That charity race was planned, wasn't it?"

"What?" he asked. "What are you talking about?"

"LAPS4KIDS. The race we met at a year ago. You planned to go to that charity to seduce me."

"Of course not." He looked appalled, but she noticed that he couldn't quite look her in the eye.

"I'm such an idiot." She stood up from the couch, desperate to put some distance between them. "I trusted you, Jason."

"You can still trust me." He reached for her, but she walked a few steps away.

"You asked me out on a date because you knew I was a Perconti and had a reputation of being a stupid party girl. You thought you could say a few compliments, take me to bed a few times, and then have enough information to run my family into the ground."

"Ari—"

"Admit it. The only reason why you dated me was to get information about my family."

He hesitated then stood and tried to close the distance between them. "It might have started out that way—"

"Oh my God, you admit it!" She retreated around the couch, putting the large piece of furniture between them.

"Initially, yes, but Ari—Ari!"

She covered her ears. "Get out."

"This is my apartment."

God damn foul man. He always had to be right, didn't

he? "I said get out!" Tears stung her eyes, and she blinked them back. First Leo, then her CFO, and now Jason. When was she going to stop letting people manipulate her?

He grabbed her wrists and wrenched her hands away from her ears. "Listen to me, damn it. Okay, yes, it might have started out that way, but it isn't like that anymore."

"I don't believe you. Once a gigolo, always a gigolo."

He let go of her and stepped back, as if stung. "You don't mean that."

"Oh, yes, I do." God, her head hurt. She needed air.

He swallowed and took a step away from her. "This . . . this is why that loan shark's blackmail is so effective. It's because of people like you." He waved his hand at the windows behind her. "If my past ever got out into the media, then the public will think just like you."

"Damn right they will. I bet Deacon came here because you already got all of the information you needed from me to run my family into the ground. The two of you were probably going to have some grand champagne and toast to my family's failure."

He shook his head. "Come on, Ari. You know me. I'd never do something so cruel."

"You're probably already doing it behind my back." She grabbed a pillow.

"Ari—"

"Get out." She threw the pillow at him. "Get out!"

He dodged the pillow and pointed at her. "I don't deny what I once was, but people change, Ari." He pointed to himself. "I've changed." He grabbed the handle on the door. "I thought you, above all people, would understand that."

Ari stared at him in shock as he opened the door. Yes, she was a different person now than when she was younger, but the situation wasn't the same. She'd just stolen a few items from a few department stores. She didn't use people, and would never sleep with anyone for money under any circumstances.

"I see that you've already judged me, despite everything I've done for you," he said.

Ari made a very unladylike sound. "Don't flatter yourself. You've done nothing for me but scratch an itch." As soon as the words left her mouth she recognized them for the lie they were. Judging by the expression on Jason's face, it seemed as if he didn't believe her, either.

He jerked open the door. "I need to meet someone, but this isn't over, Ari. I'm going to make you understand me, one way or another. We're more alike than you realize. We need each other."

"I don't need anyone."

"It took me a long time to see it, but we belong together, Ari. Don't ever forget it."

Ari stared at the door in shock as the throbbing in her head returned. This was too much, way too much. She glanced around the empty penthouse and knew she had to get out of there. Every second she stayed in Jason's home, she felt as if she was suffocating.

Ari searched through her suitcase for her phone, tossing clothes aside like a madwoman. As soon as she found it, she collapsed on the couch and began to dial.

"ARI'S KIDS," Camille said after the second ring.

"Hi, Camille. It's me."

"Ari! How are you doing?"

"I've been better."

"What's wrong, child?"

"I'll explain a little later. Right now, I need a place to crash. I was wondering . . ."

"Say no more. I couldn't stay in that hotel for one minute more than necessary with all of your brothers pacing the floor like caged animals. Got a small apartment in Southie to wait things out. There's plenty of room."

Ari let out a relieved breath. "Thanks, Camille."

"That's what friends are for, darlin'. Just tell me where to pick you up, and I'll send a cab over to get you . . ."

Chapter 15

More pictures. Jason couldn't believe that those loan sharks had sent him more pictures. This time they didn't send them through a courier, but through his personal phone. He had no idea how these thugs had gotten his number, but now that they had it, Jason wasn't getting a moment's peace. This time, the pictures were of them leaving the hospital and were accompanied by a message reminding him what could happen if he didn't show up with the money at eight o'clock tomorrow night.

Things were getting way too personal. It was time to put a stop to this nonsense once and for all.

Knowing that he was in over his head, Jason had spent the better of the past hour thinking long and hard about his next move. As far as he could see he had two options. The first would be to agree to work with Deacon to clear his name, something that may or may not work, and something that could very well result in more people getting hurt. The second option would be to just pay the money and hope that he wasn't opening himself up to this loan shark turning around and blackmailing him for even more. Neither option appealed to him.

At the hospital he had been so sure of the first option,

but now, after the adrenaline rush of seeing Ari hurt had passed, after seeing these pictures with their obvious invasion of privacy, Jason was convinced that this loan shark had gotten to someone close to him. A staff member, perhaps, or someone staying at the hotel. One thing was for certain, this guy had resources and wouldn't hesitate to use them to his advantage.

In Jason's mind, there was only one way he could guarantee Ari's safety. She might not care about him anymore, but that didn't mean he didn't care about her.

"You looking for me?"

Jason glanced up from his phone and saw his brother leaning in the doorway. "Yes." He waved his hand in the air. "Close the door."

Deacon did as he was asked and sat in the office chair on the opposite side of Jason's desk. "What's up?"

Jason frowned as his brother put his feet up on the expensive wood and folded his hands in his lap. Deacon looked dirtier than normal. Large black smudges dotted his arms and face, and his clothes were torn and full of grit. As his feet hit the desk, gravel tumbled out of the soles and landed on Jason's important papers.

"Where the hell have you been? You're a mess. And put your feet down," Jason growled. "That's my stuff."

"I was in the garage, working on my bike."

"Working on your bike? You were supposed to be helping me by finding information on this loan shark."

"And I am, but these things take time, bro. You know that."

"I need answers now."

"Be patient."

"I'm done being patient." Jason slammed his fist on the desk, startling his brother. "Too many people have gotten hurt, Deacon. I need to end this. Today."

Deacon shook his head and put his feet back on the

floor. "I can't believe how uptight you are. You used to be so much more relaxed."

"That persona doesn't exist anymore," Jason muttered as he picked up his phone and flicked the screen. "He died the moment Ari got hurt and I got sent more pictures." He held up his phone to his brother, showing him a picture of him and Ari in an intimate embrace.

"It's just a picture."

"You don't understand."

Deacon stared at him for a long moment before responding. "Who are you, bro? Since when did ya care so much about a girl?"

"She's not 'just a girl.' She's more than that."

"Obviously." Deacon leaned back in his chair.

"I can't risk her getting hurt again—or you. I have to give them the money."

Deacon pressed his lips together in thought. "Paying them might not make a difference, you know."

"What do you mean?"

Deacon leaned forward in his chair. "Word on the street is that they're here."

"Here? What do you mean 'here'?"

"I mean, the plane just landed at Logan Airport."

"You're kidding." Things were much more serious than he'd thought. This only cemented Jason's decision in his mind.

"No. And it's not just one person. It's a whole entourage." He crossed his arms. "My contacts are saying that this loan shark is tired of having you string him along and wants to make an example of you."

"Jesus." Jason let out a long breath. "Deacon, I can't do this anymore. Things have gotten too dangerous."

"I thought you thrived in dangerous situations."

"I did once, but not anymore. I have too much to lose. Because of this"—he held up his phone—"and Ari's injury, I've decided to just pay this loan shark the money and be done with it."

"You're kidding." Worry lines creased Deacon's brow as he straightened in his seat. "You can't do that."

"What do you mean? In the restaurant you told me to pay this guy off."

"That was before. Now things have changed."

"Changed how?"

"Before you wanted to do things by yourself. Now you want to work together." Deacon shifted in his seat. "This loan shark is cunning, far too smart for you to handle on your own, but with me helping you . . . We'll show those goons who they're dealing with. People will think twice before they try to mess with the Stone brothers again."

"No," Jason said. "I've already put in a request with my banker for the money."

"You're kidding, right?"

"I'm afraid not. I don't want to see anyone else get hurt."

"You mean you don't want to see *her* get hurt. Please tell me you aren't giving up your pride for the sake of some woman."

"This has nothing to do with pride. If it was just the two of us, it would be different, but I have other people to consider now."

Deacon stiffened his jaw for a moment, then slumped in his chair. "Exactly how firm are you with this decision?"

"Very."

"This is going to change things. If you don't want to work with me . . ." Deacon frowned and rubbed his forehead. "I can't believe you're passing up this amazing opportunity to make a name for ourselves in the Las Vegas circles. The opportunities we'd have—"

"I'm not going to risk her life for this—or yours."

Deacon stood and paced back and forth in front of the

desk, deep in thought. Suddenly he stopped and widened his eyes. "I've got it."

"Got what?"

"The answer to our problems."

"Yeah?"

"Yeah—we leave."

"What?"

"We could just leave. Pack up and take off into the night." He straightened and grinned. "It's perfect."

"I have a business to run, Deacon, and Ari has her family. There's no way we could disappear, not like we used to." Jason shook his head.

"Forget the girl. We'll go together."

"I can't."

"But—"

"This is the way that it has to be, Deacon. I mean it."

Deacon sighed and rubbed his chin in thought. After a long moment, he stood. "Well, at least let me be the one to hand it to them."

"I couldn't—"

Deacon held up his hand. "Hear me out. You and I look a lot alike, enough so that people who don't know us well might get us confused." He nodded and put his hands in his pockets. "Like you said, this is a dangerous situation. There's no guarantee that even if you give them the money, that they won't turn around and try to hurt you, or extort you for more. You have a business to run, and a girl." He averted his gaze. "I don't have those things to worry about."

"Deacon—" Jason stood, but his brother stepped away from him.

"No, it's the truth. You have more to lose than I do. I know these people, and have played their game far longer than you have. If anyone has a chance of getting through this with their skin intact and without them asking for more money, it's me."

"I can't put you in harm's way. You have nothing to do with this."

"Take your girl and go down the coast for a few days. Stay at that run-down family place the Strands used to take us as kids. No one would think to find you there." He shrugged and looked away. "When you come back, it will all be over."

Jason flexed his fingers at his sides. His brother had a point. Deacon was far more skilled at this than he was, and would probably fare far better. Still, there were so many years of unresolved issues between them. Could he really trust Deacon to do this for him and not screw it up? "I can't run away and leave you in danger."

"I can take care of myself, Jason. Always have." Deacon looked up at him and grinned. "That's what family's for, anyway. I want to show you that I've changed too, and I can think of no better way to do that than to take the heat for this."

"They could hurt you."

"I've been roughed up before." He tapped his front teeth. "Partials. Had them knocked out during a match right before I bashed the guy's face in. Wish you could have been there to see it . . ." He cleared his throat and stared at his shoes. "Let me do this for you, Jason. I want to help." He shoved his hands in his pockets and looked up at his brother. "Perhaps it can begin to make up for letting that relationship you had with Felicia go on for so long."

"God, that woman was a nightmare. Whatever happened to her after I left?"

Deacon shrugged. "I never should have let you take one for the team like that. I owe you. Let me do this, bro."

Jason took in a deep breath and then let it out. "Tomorrow night, just before the exchange, the suitcase with the money will be just inside my office." He held up a key. "Promise me you'll be careful."

"I will." Deacon took the key and smiled.

Jason picked up his phone. "I can alert my head of security and he could—"

"No, no security. No cops." When Jason flashed him a questioning look, he hurried to continue. "If these guys think that we're double-crossing them in any way, things could go south, fast. If I'm going to do this, then I need to do it alone."

"I can't let you do this alone."

"Don't worry about me. I'll be fine."

Jason hesitated, then swiped the screen on his phone. "I'll arrange to have the exchange done in the garage. You'll wear a beeper. If anything should go wrong, just hit the button and my entire team will be there within seconds."

"But—"

"I'm not compromising on this, Deacon."

Deacon steeled his jaw for a moment as he stared at his brother. Then, gradually, he relaxed his shoulders and tapped him on the arm. "Thanks, man."

"No problem." Jason smiled and patted his brother on the shoulder. "And thank you."

As the door shut behind Deacon, Jason dialed his head of security. If they ever got out of this mess it would be a miracle.

Wes leaned against the large, marble kiosk in the foyer of Stone Suites and raised his brows. "I'm looking for a woman. Arianna Perconti."

The receptionist's cornflower blue eyes turned steely gray. "I'm sorry, we don't give out names of the patrons staying here."

Wes flashed her what he hoped was a charming smile. "Okay, then, I'd like to talk to the owner, Jason Stone."

"Everyone wants to talk to him," the woman said. "This is only my second week on the job, and already I've had more people asking for Mr. Stone personally than asking for rooms."

"It's important." Wes glanced down at her name tag. "Keira."

"You can get in line." Keira rolled her eyes. "A representative from Perconti Enterprises came in an hour ago looking for him."

"Oh?" Wes straightened. "You wouldn't happen to know who it was, would you?"

The woman shook her head. "He didn't leave a name, but his card instead."

"Can I see it?"

"I don't know." She frowned. "That's rather personal."

"Business cards aren't personal, darlin', and I promise to give it right back." He leaned on the counter and winked at her. "It can be our little secret."

She smiled and handed Wes a card that belonged to Marco. Seeing the familiar lettering made Wes's stomach tie up in knots. Marco was probably at Stone Suites for the same reason Wes was there. They both wanted to talk to Ari. Good thing they had missed each other. Seeing him would just dredge up all of the hurt and embarrassment that man had caused him over the past couple of weeks.

"Two men in suits came in an hour before that," Keira continued, oblivious to Wes's pain. "They didn't leave their names, either."

"Did they leave cards as well?" he asked, handing it back to her.

"No, they said that they'd be back to speak with him personally."

"I see. And when will Mr. Stone be returning?"

"Hard to say." She squinted at the computer screen. "His schedule says that he's going to be off site for the remainder of the day."

She placed her hands on the keyboard behind the kiosk.

"Want me to take down your name and give him a message?"

"No, that won't be necessary. I'll come back some other time."

She shrugged. "Suit yourself."

Wes pulled out his phone to text Karin an update as he strode toward the revolving doors at the front of the building.

Jason's out, and reception won't give me Ari's room number.

Okay, thanks. You tried.

I'm worried.

Me, too. She hasn't answered her phone. I wish we could confirm what that Whispers reporter said–that she was hit in the head.

I haven't given up yet. I'll hang out in the restaurant for a while and see what I can find.

Thanks, I appreciate it.

"Interested in finding Mr. Stone, are ya?"

Wes looked up from his phone and found a tall, sandy-haired man leaning against the wall by the door to the restaurant.

"How did you—"

The man tapped his temple and straightened. "Even if I didn't overheah the conversation, I can see da worry all over your face." He shoved his hands into his jeans pockets, drawing Wes's attention to how snugly his T-shirt and pants clung to his muscular body. The man was hot, and his thick Boston accent was even hotter. He also seemed a little familiar.

"Who are you?" Wes asked as he approached.

"A friend." The man flashed him a seductive smile and held out his hand. "The name's Deacon."

"Wes." Wes shook his hand. "Yeah, I'm looking for Mr. Stone. You didn't happen to see him, did you?"

"I saw him about an hour ago. He said he was going to head out of the city with his girl." Deacon shrugged and averted his gaze, but not before Wes saw something flash through his features. Hurt? Anger?

"A girl?" Wes asked, drawing closer. "Do you know what she looks like?"

Deacon considered him for a moment. "Curvy, long curly brown hair, dark eyes. A real spitfire." Deacon nudged his elbow. "I bet she's a wildcat between the sheets."

"Yeah," Wes said absently. It certainly sounded like Arianna. If they were both leaving the city, then Wes had no idea how he was going to find either Jason or Ari and tell them about the rumors.

"Or, perhaps you don't like the dark, feminine type," Deacon said, inching closer.

"Huh?" Wes widened his eyes as he focused on Deacon's hungry expression. "I, uh . . ."

"Into a little bit of everything, eh?" Deacon dragged his gaze down Wes's torso and lingered on his hips. "I bet my brother's girl isn't the only one who likes it freaky in the bedroom."

"Brother?"

Deacon smiled. "Surprised?"

"A little. I didn't know Jason had a brother."

"There's a lot about him you don't know, I'm sure." He tilted his head to the side and studied Wes's face a moment before continuing. "Perhaps I could tell you more. Say, over drinks."

"I don't really go out," Wes said, shoving his hands into his pockets. "I mean, I did, once. But not anymore."

"How come?"

Wes shook his head as he pushed the image of Marco from his mind. "It's complicated."

"It doesn't have to be."

"I'm afraid it does."

Deacon inched closer, and his leathery scent caused desire to shoot straight into Wes's cock. "Too bad. I'm new here and was looking for a place to party. I have certain . . . tastes that are sometimes hard to fulfill."

"You do?" Wes widened his eyes in surprise.

"Yeah, and Jason's no help." Deacon leaned in close and lowered his voice so only Wes could hear. "His preferences can be a little too vanilla, if you know what I mean." He leaned back and winked. "I tend to like things a little more wild."

"You're into the scene?" Wes guessed.

Deacon nodded. "Although I'm not much of a player. I prefer to watch."

Wes raised his brows. "A voyeur?"

"Something like that." He considered Wes for a moment before continuing. "I've had the privilege of watching Jason and his girlfriend a few times now. While it's been very educational, it has been, shall we say, less than satisfying."

"Did they know that you were watching them?" Wes noticed that his voice sounded a little breathless, but didn't care.

"That's the thing." Deacon pulled one hand out of his pocket and brushed his fingers along Wes's arm. "They had no idea I was there. While I was sharing the experience with them, I still felt totally alone."

Wes felt he should be scandalized over Deacon being a voyeur, but instead it turned him on. It had been a long time since he had been with anyone, and Wes wasn't very good with staying celibate. Deacon was both rugged and rebellious, a complete and total opposite to his former boyfriend. Perhaps he was just what Wes needed to jerk himself out of this funk and stop feeling sorry for himself.

Wes swallowed as his cock pressed playfully against his jeans. "What would have made it better?"

Deacon leaned forward, brushing his stubbled cheek against Wes's as he whispered in his ear. "If one of them knew I was watching."

Wes shivered as Deacon inched away. "You like to watch, knowing that one member of the couple knows you're there?"

Deacon nodded. "You see, in situations like that, the moment becomes more intimate. It's less about the couple having sex, and more about me and the one who knows I'm there." He shifted his gaze to Wes's lips. "It becomes a show for me and me alone."

"And when it's over?"

Deacon dragged his gaze back up to meet Wes's. "When it's over, the couple says their good-byes, and then I take the one who knows about me up to my room and show my appreciation for his wonderful performance."

Wes's heartbeat quickened and he struggled to get his desire under control. Clearing his throat, he forced himself to keep his voice even. "I could take you by this club, Dark Desires." He shrugged and hoped he looked nonchalant. "Who knows, you might find what you're looking for there . . ."

"Oh, I've already found what I'm looking for." Deacon flashed him a seductive smile. "Your club sounds like it would be just the thing I need." He slid his finger along Wes's jaw and smiled. "Pick me up in this lobby at ten."

Wes's entire body felt like butter as he watched the handsome bad boy stride away. He had a date. An honest-to-goodness date. Even before his breakup with Marco, it had been a long time since anyone had wanted to go out in public with him. To be seen in a popular sex club with a fine piece of man candy on his arm . . . It would be just the thing to extinguish his torch for Marco Perconti for good.

Chapter 16

Jason specifically remembered telling Arianna that she was to remain in his apartment. Staying put was for her own safety. She knew this, so why wasn't she there when he went to retrieve her?

He steeled his jaw and made another frustrated sound as he stepped on the gas pedal of his BMW. No matter how hard he pressed, he couldn't seem to outrun his demons.

Ari had pushed him to come clean about his time with Deacon and when he did, she'd behaved just as he had feared. She hated him. Hell, he hated himself for sleeping with all of those women. He deserved a chance to explain himself, however, and she had robbed him of that chance.

After calling her repeatedly on her phone, Jason was no closer to finding her. He ground his teeth and hit the steering wheel in frustration. Things never used to be so complicated. He had everything: a booming business, a beautiful girl, and Leo Perconti on the ropes. Now everything was shot to hell.

He was losing control. Deacon had said that the loan shark was in the city. If that was true, then it was only a matter of time before they found Ari. Jason had to get her away, but that seemed like an impossibility considering the circumstances. He had no idea how he was going to convince her to do anything when she wasn't speaking to him.

He was going to have to up his game. The quickest way he knew to get back on her good side was to appeal to her sense of adventure. He thought back to when he'd let her drive the McLaren, and how hot she looked behind the wheel. If he could give her that same sense of freedom and danger, then he'd have her eating out of the palm of his hand.

The only question left was how to do it. He thought about the sexual games they played, and how each felt like a thrill ride. He wanted to create the ultimate thrill for Ari, something that would turn her attention and focus back to him. By using their need for an adrenaline rush, he could show her how good it could be when she didn't overthink things and went with the moment. It was a long shot, but he was running out of time.

If he was going to create the ultimate sexual adventure, then he'd need some help. Jason changed direction and drove to an out-of-the-way shop called the Sex-It-Up and purchased just the right piece for his plan. He ignored the curious glances and smirks as he paid for his purchase and then took the back roads home, wanting the time to plan out the encounter in his head.

He'd start out by inviting her to a public place, somewhere where he could put the sex toy to good use. Then, when the moment was right, he'd drag her into his McLaren and whisk her away from the city—

The loud blast of a car horn pulled him from his thoughts. Jason jerked back and swerved out of oncoming traffic and back onto his side of the road. The street turned a hard right, and Jason overcompensated. His priceless race car swerved and rammed into a nearby streetlamp.

"Watch where you're going, asshole," the guy in the other car shouted as he passed.

Jason gave him the finger and then rested his head on the back of his seat. Things couldn't possibly get any worse.

After glancing at his Rolex, he considered calling a tow truck, but going to the station to have it fixed would take time, and showing up at a mechanic with a broken BMW would only draw media attention. He didn't want to give those damn reporters any more fodder for their magazines.

Pressing his lips together in frustration, he pulled out his cell and swiped the screen. He made it only halfway through his list of contacts before he stopped and realized that although he had a list filled with hundreds of acquaintances, there was no one close enough for him to call when he was in trouble.

Rubbing his hands against his eyelids, Jason came to the horrifying conclusion that, despite all he had done to distance himself from his brother, Deacon was the only person who would care enough to come help him. The realization made him feel like a heel. Ever since he had arrived at Stone Suites, Deacon had proven to him that all he wanted was to be a part of Jason's life, and Jason kept pushing him away. While Deacon wasn't exactly refined, he did try hard, and his heart seemed to be in the right place. He was family, and Jason was tired of being alone.

He flexed his fingers and then dialed the number of the one person he knew would not only understand him, but come to his aid.

"Hey." Deacon's carefree baritone filled the line.

"It's me."

"Little brother?" Deacon sounded genuinely surprised. "I didn't think you knew how to dial."

"Ha-ha, very funny. Look, let's quit the niceties. I have a problem."

"Oh?"

"Yeah, I need you to come pick me up. I'm about three

blocks from the Prudential Center." Jason gave him the address.

"Car problems?" Deacon asked.

"You could say that."

"Do you want me to bring my tools?"

"There's no time. Just get my keys to the Jag from my office and come get me. Don't tell anyone where you're going."

Deacon chuckled. "Okay, little brother. I have to say, it feels nice to be needed again."

"Yeah, just hurry." Jason gave him the address and hung up. Leaning his head back against the seat, he thought back to when he and Deacon were close. While he'd never con women like that again, he did enjoy the comradery he'd shared with Deacon. His brother made him laugh, and was the first in line to help Jason when he got in over his head. They'd stood up for each other more times than Jason cared to admit.

Once he settled things with Ari, perhaps he could find his brother a place in his hotel chain. Deacon had a head for numbers and was good at negotiations. Together, they'd make quite the team. He bet they could give Leo a run for his money.

"I can't believe you didn't tell me, Camille." Ari crossed her arms and scowled at her friend.

"You had your wedding to plan. I didn't want to ruin it with such trivial things."

"Trivial? Camille, we don't have the money we need to fully supply Children's Hospital like we had planned. You sat there in my meeting the other day and let me tell those people that we were going to do things we don't have the funding to do."

"I'm sorry, Ari. I thought this donor would come through, but . . ."

Camille didn't need to finish. The donor had backed out after her non-wedding became front-page news. No one wanted to donate to a charity where the person running it was surrounded in scandal.

"I wish you had said something. We really needed that money." Ari picked up her tea, then put it back down on the kitchen table of the small apartment.

"What would you have done? Gone crawling back to your brother and marry Landon?" Camille leaned forward and placed her elbows on the table. "You know how I felt about that decision. I still feel the same way. Marrying Landon would have been the biggest mistake of your life. His, too."

Ari waved her hand in dismissal. "I could have gotten money from somewhere else."

"From where? The only other person you know is Jason Stone, and after what happened, I don't think you want to go asking him for money."

Ari rubbed her forehead and leaned back in her chair. "I know. I'm sorry." She shouldn't be so mad at Camille. The poor woman was doing the best she could. Ari needed to get her act together and focus on her charity before it fell apart.

That wasn't the only reason why she needed to get back to work. She had only been at Camille's apartment for a couple of hours, but she already felt as if the walls were closing in on her. Camille was sweet, but a slob, and the place really needed a good maid. Dishes in the sink looked like they had been left there for days. Clothes and Power-Bar wrappers were strewn all over the floor, and a musty smell that Ari couldn't quite place permeated the bedroom and bath. Ari didn't know how much longer she'd be able to stay with her friend before she hired movers and a cleaning staff to bleach the entire apartment.

"What are you going to do now?" Camille asked.

"I honestly don't know," Ari said. "I feel kind of lost. I can't go back to my brother without first showing him that I can stand on my own two feet, and I can't stay with Jason knowing that he was using me to gain information about my family. It feels as if the rug has been ripped out from under me, you know?" She shook her head. "I don't have anyone I can lean on."

"You have me." Camille reached across the table and took her hand. "You always have me."

Ari smiled and squeezed Camille's fingers. "And I thank you for that. I don't know what I did to deserve you, but I'm so grateful for your friendship." She let go of her friend's hand and leaned back in her chair. "The funny thing is, I think Jason is genuinely sorry for what he did to me."

"Did he apologize?" Camille asked.

"Not exactly, but he did try to explain himself. He said that he's changed. When he was younger, he was poor and desperate. Back then he'd do whatever it took to gain the upper hand. He insists that he doesn't do that now, but I don't know. Can people really change?"

"I believe they can. People often become desperate when they need to find a way to survive, and resort to things that they normally wouldn't do. Back when I was taking Jasmine to and from the hospital, it was so difficult coming up with money for her cancer treatments. I'm not sure what I would have done if you hadn't helped me out."

"I'm sure something else would have turned up."

"Maybe." Camille nibbled her lower lip in thought. "But your donation sure made things easier."

"What are you saying, Camille?"

"I'm not justifying what he did. Believe me. It's just . . ."

"What?"

Camille sighed. "Like I said, people who are desperate

do desperate things." She looked up and met Ari's gaze. "Just look what you were about to do to save your charity."

"But I didn't sleep with Landon."

"Not yet." Camille shrugged. "But you were going to get married. For now Landon agreed to keep his hands off of you, but things change. Who knows what you would have done to stay married and keep the money flowing in to both your charity and your family?"

Ari stared at her friend as Camille's words sunk in. She was right, of course. As much as Ari wanted to believe that she was different from Jason, she really wasn't. They had both used people to get what they wanted.

"That doesn't explain his seducing me for information about my family."

Camille considered her for a moment. "Are you sure that's why he's seeing you?"

"That's what he told me."

"I know that's what he said, but honey, I've seen him look at you, especially when he thinks no one is watching him. It's as if his entire universe revolves around you. That man has feelings for you. Trust me."

"If what you say is true, then he has a horrible way of showing it." She took her teacup to the sink, so Camille couldn't see the tears stinging her eyes. She really had made a mess of things, hadn't she? All she wanted was a little independence, and look where it had gotten her. Perhaps running away from the wedding and her family had been a mistake. If she had stayed, she would have been financially secure. She never would have learned about Jason's problems with the loan shark or his sketchy past.

"Don't be so hard on yourself," Camille said. "Perhaps coming here was for the best. Heaven knows that the man needs a good kick in the pants to wake him up."

Ari looked for a place to put her cup, but there wasn't

any counter space. After balancing it precariously on the pile of dishes, she moved back to her seat.

"I don't want to focus on Jason anymore," she said. "I'd much rather think about other things, like how we can get Ari's Kids out of this mess."

"We could do another fund-raiser . . ."

Ari shook her head. "It takes too much planning and time. We'd have to front the money for the fund-raiser and we don't have that kind of cash." She averted her gaze. "The only way I can think of getting quick cash is by patching things up with my brother."

"What are you going to say to him?"

"I have no idea. I won't marry Landon, that's for sure. I'm pretty sure that ship has sailed, anyway."

"Are you sure you want to go crawling back to Leo?"

"If you can think of a better idea, I'd love to hear it." When Camille didn't immediately answer, Ari sighed. "You know things can't go on like this. The charity needs money, and I need a place to stay, which means I need my family."

"What about your independence? What about taking a stand against your brother and being your own person?"

"Those kids are more important than my pride, don't you think?" Ari pulled out her phone and placed it on the table between them. "Perhaps I can convince Leo to meet me halfway."

"It will be difficult. Your brother's holding all of the cards. I wish we had another option."

"Me, too."

Camille stood up and hugged her friend. "I'll give you some privacy."

"Thanks." Ari waited until Camille was out of the kitchen. Ignoring her full voice mail box, she took a deep breath and dialed Leo's number.

"Hello?" Karin said.

"Hey, Karin, it's Ari. Why are you on Leo's phone?"

"I sent him to rest. He's so worried about you. We all are."

"I know. I'm sorry."

"Where are you? We've been trying to reach you for hours. Someone told us that there was a mugging at Stone Suites. Are you all right? Is Wes with you?"

"Wes? No. Why would he be?"

"When you didn't return my calls I sent him over to see if you were all right. He texted me a few hours ago, but I haven't seen or heard from him since."

"He's missing?"

"Yes. And I'm worried. Why weren't you answering your phone?"

"I was busy. And . . . I'm not at Stone Suites anymore."

"Where are you?"

"With a friend—and I'm fine. Honest."

"What's going on? Leo has been worried sick—"

"Is that her?" Leo's voice boomed from the other line. "Let me see the phone."

Ari tightened the grip on her cell as her brother came on the line.

"Ari, is that you?"

"Hey, Leo."

"Oh, thank God." His voice was filled with genuine relief. "Did you get hurt? We heard that there was some sort of mugging at Stone Suites—"

"I'm fine. Sorry I didn't call you sooner, but I was busy. I'm not at Stone Suites anymore. I'm . . . somewhere else."

"Where are you?" When she didn't immediately respond, Leo's heavy sigh filled the line. "What are you doing, Ari? What's this all about?"

Ari took a deep breath. "I want to come home, but only if it's on my own terms."

"Does this have to do with the wedding? Because if

you'd just told me how you felt before we announced the engagement—"

"It's more than just the wedding, Leo. It's the fact that you never let me do anything by myself."

"That's not true."

"Unfortunately, it is."

"I'm only trying to look out for your best interests."

"I know, and I appreciate it. I just don't think I need your protection anymore. I want to make my own decisions and live my life how I see fit."

"You do that already, and once you come back and take your place in the company, the rest of the world will see how strong the Perconti family can be."

"That's the thing. I'm not sure if the family business is right for me." The thought of working day in and day out, and running every minor decision by her older brother didn't sit well with her.

"What are you talking about? Of course it's right for you. Marco and Dante—"

"That's just the thing. Marco and Dante push me around, too. Too many times the three of you have told me that I have an equal say, only to find that my voice only counts if I agree with you."

"We would never do that, *passerotta*. We agreed to split the company evenly amongst us all. Come home, so we can discuss everything in more detail. I'm sure we could work things out with Marco and Dante and come to a decision that benefits everyone."

"What about the twins?"

"Gio and Gianna don't have an interest in the company. They wish to remain as investors. They'll go along with all of our decisions, however, so that we maintain a controlling interest."

"Are they there now?"

"Gio had a photo shoot in Milan. He's on a plane now

with Mamma. As soon as it was apparent that there wouldn't be a wedding, Gianna flew back to Oregon."

"She always did hate the city."

Leo chuckled. "She couldn't get away from the commotion fast enough."

Ari closed her eyes as she realized that her younger brother and sister had traveled halfway around the world to attend her wedding, and she hadn't even spoken to them. Her entire family had shown up for the big event, and she had brushed them all off in a moment of selfishness. Tears stung her eyes as she realized how much she missed her siblings.

"I'm sorry for the mess I caused," Ari said.

"It doesn't matter. The media is always making things more dramatic than they should be." He hesitated before continuing. "Has Stone done anything to you?"

Yes, but not in the way he was implying. "He hasn't hurt me Leo, no." At least not physically. "He's been a good friend."

"Friend." She could hear the skepticism in his voice. "A friend would tell you to not let your family worry."

"And he did that, Leo. The decision not to call was mine, not his."

Leo hesitated a moment before continuing. "You need to be careful, *passerotta*. People always act with an ulterior motive."

"People like Jason, or like you?"

"I never said we weren't one and the same." Ari smiled at the humorous tone in his voice.

"My charity is suffering, Leo."

"Come home, Ari. We'll sort everything out."

"I won't give it up. And I want to make my own decisions. Not what's best for the family, but for me."

"No one is asking you to do anything you don't want to

do." Leo let out a long breath. "I've been talking to Karin, and know that I can be a bit controlling at times."

"A bit?"

Leo chuckled. "Whatever is bothering you, we'll make it right, but we can't do that unless you are here with us, where you belong."

Ari struggled to keep the tears from her eyes. God, she loved her family. Every last dysfunctional one of them.

"I'm coming home, Leo. I promise. I just need to do something first." She needed to figure out a few things, not the least of which was what to do about Jason. Camille was right about the past being in the past, but that didn't change the fact that their relationship was built on a lie. He was sleeping with her for information, and she wasn't so sure if she could just forgive that and move on, at least not without some serious changes to the relationship.

"Okay. *Mi manchi, passerotta.*"

Ari blinked back tears. "*Mi manchi, anche.*"

"Don't take too long."

"I won't. I promise."

After finishing their good-byes, Ari hung up the phone and rubbed her forehead.

"Are you okay?" Camille asked as she stepped into the kitchen.

"Yes." Ari straightened. "What time is it?"

"A little after nine."

No wonder she was so tired. Maybe if she had a glass of wine and a good night's sleep, she'd know what to do about her charity—and Jason.

"You wouldn't happen to have a bottle of Moscato hanging around, would you?" she asked. "I could really use a drink."

Camille grinned and pulled one out of her refrigerator door. "Absolutely. It's good to have you back, *mon cheri.*"

She grabbed a couple of glasses and brought everything over to the table. "We've all been lost without you."

"I told you to pick me up in the Jag, not the McLaren," Jason mumbled as he fell into the passenger seat.

Deacon chuckled. "Don't worry, I took better care of this little baby than you did your BMW." He ran his hands over the steering wheel. "Was this customized?" He reached for the climate control, but Jason swatted his hand away.

"Yes, and stop playing with the controls. You'll end up breaking something." Jason frowned and leaned his elbow along a ridge in the passenger's side door. "Just take me back to Stone Suites." He'd have his assistant, Micki, deal with the BMW later. Right now, he just wanted to get away from the whole mess.

"I always wondered why you keep your car collection at the hotel rather than your penthouse."

"There's no room in the garage. Even if there was, it's twice as expensive to park there than at my hotel."

"Since when did you start pinching pennies?"

Jason scowled at his brother. "Just drive, will ya? And on second thought, bring me to my apartment."

Deacon looked thoughtful as he turned the key in the ignition. "You look like you could use a good fuck, my friend."

Jason flashed his brother an annoyed look and lowered his arm. "No, I don't use fucking to escape my problems anymore."

"You don't? Then what do you call that nice piece of ass waiting for you at your apartment?"

Jason pointed at his brother. "You leave Ari out of this."

The streetlight changed from red to green, and Deacon stepped on the gas. The car lurched forward like a dry heave.

"Hey, this has a clutch, you know." He shifted in his seat. "Pull over. I'll drive."

"You're too edgy to drive. You'll just crash this car like you did the last one."

"Fuck you, Deacon."

"You're just proving my point. You need to loosen up, bro. If I didn't know any better, I'd think that you were the one giving over the money tomorrow night, not me."

They rode in silence for a long moment before Jason spoke again. "She wasn't at the apartment."

"Where is she?"

"I wish I knew." Jason let out a long breath and pushed his hand through his hair. "I told her about my past and she left me."

"You told her about us?"

"Yeah, pretty stupid, huh?"

"I'm sorry, bro. I tried to tell ya."

"I know."

Deacon changed lanes and settled in at a stoplight. "I heard about this club. Sounds really freaky. You want to come? It might be a good chance to blow off some steam."

"You still go to sex clubs?"

Deacon shrugged. "It's easy to find someone there to scratch an itch, you know? And they are more than willing to give you anything you need without the messy emotional stuff."

Jason ran his hand over his face. "Thanks for the offer, but I'll have to pass. I can't be seen in a place like that. I have my reputation to think about."

"Places like that have a confidentiality policy, I'm sure." He nudged Jason. "You'll probably find some of your colleagues there, looking for the same thing."

"No." Jason waved his hand in the air in dismissal. "I have more important things to think about."

"Like the girl?"

Jason scowled at his brother.

"Look, this just proves my point. Girls like her don't want anything to do with guys like us." He nudged Jason with his elbow. "Come on, go out to the club with me. You don't need to do anything. Most of the time I just sit and watch. It's great entertainment, much better than any porno—and if you play your cards right, one of the members of the scene might even go home with you."

"No." Jason's voice was a little more forceful than he'd intended, if his brother's surprised expression was any indication.

"Look at you. You're successful, rich, and respectable. Money comes easy for people like you."

"It really doesn't."

"Don't lie to me."

"I'm not." Jason shifted in his seat. "It takes just as much work to make money legitimately as it does to con someone."

"Maybe, but conning is more fun." Deacon grinned, causing Jason to roll his eyes.

"Have you ever thought of reaching out and creating your own future instead of conning people out of theirs?" Jason asked.

"The same could be said of you."

"I don't con anyone."

"No?" Deacon glanced at him and then returned his eyes to the road. "What do you think that fight with your girl was really about, bro?"

"It was about my past." Jason scowled and looked back out the window.

"No, it was about the fact that this woman wants more from you than you're willing to give."

"What are you talking about?"

"Come on, bro. Use ya head. If your relationship was truly nothing more than sex, then your past wouldn't matter to her. She's mad because she thought you two shared something special and you basically told her that she's just like all of the other women you've been with."

Jason frowned. "Ari knows our relationship is purely physical."

"Does she?"

"We discussed it."

Deacon made a noncommittal noise. "But how long ago was that discussion?" He shook his head when Jason didn't respond. "Women are fickle, my friend. They change their minds. Being your fuck-buddy might have been fine a few months ago, but any asshole can see that it's not all right now."

Jason scowled. "Don't tell me what to do."

"I'm not telling you what to do. I'm just telling you what I see." Silence descended around them for a moment as Deacon turned onto a main street.

"Look, we both know you have no intention of settling down. It's not in your blood."

On that one point, Jason could agree with his brother.

"So forget about her," Deacon said.

"What?"

"Cut her loose. If you go back and patch things up now, you're feeding her belief that your relationship means something. It's cruel to keep her thinking that you two have a future together when we both know you don't. The most humane thing you can do is let her go."

"I can't do that," Jason muttered.

"So you're admitting she means something?"

"I'm not admitting anything."

"I see," Deacon said as he pulled into the garage at Jason's apartment complex. Jason flashed the security guard a badge, and after being checked, Deacon pulled forward into one of the parking spots. "You want your cake and to eat it, too."

Deacon shut off the car engine and stared at his brother. "You want to continue to fuck your woman and do what you want with your company without anyone getting in the way. I'm telling you that you can't do that, bro. Despite what you think of her, she's just a socialite, and all socialites start to become too attached at some point. Remember our rule."

"Get out before you get tied down."

"Exactly. You've stayed too long, bro. It's time to get out while you still have your heart—and your finances—intact."

He had a point. Unfortunately, it might already be too late. The thought of leaving Ari made Jason sick to his stomach. He didn't want to leave her, just get things back to the way they were—strictly physical and fun.

Deacon clasped Jason's shoulder. "Tell you what. Why don't you sleep on it? Things always look brighter in the morning."

"Good idea." He was exhausted. Perhaps after a good night's sleep, he'd know just what to say to get Ari back into his arms once more.

"Great." Deacon got out of the car and headed toward the building.

"Hey, where are you going?" Jason asked.

Deacon stopped and pointed at the door to the building. "To your apartment."

"You can't go in there."

"Why not?"

"I need someone to drive the car back to the hotel."

Deacon slowly returned to the car. "You don't want me in your apartment."

"That's not it."

"You let *her* into your apartment."

"Deacon, be reasonable. I'm exhausted, and this car can't stay here. I already have my Lamborghini here and

I only paid for one spot. The McLaren needs to go back to Stone Suites."

"At least let me come with you and make sure you get in okay."

"Maybe some other time, Deacon. I've kind of got a lot on my mind. I'd make terrible company."

Deacon steeled his jaw and looked down at the keys in his hands, turning them over and running his finger over the bright blue tag Jason used to distinguish the McLaren keys from the others in his collection. After a long moment, he relaxed his muscles and smiled at Jason. "Sure thing, Mr. Stone."

Jason snorted and playfully punched his brother in the arm. "I'll make it up to you, I promise."

"Don't worry about it. That's what family's for, ya know?"

"Absolutely. Thanks, bro." Jason watched his brother get into the car and then made the long trek up to his penthouse suite. In the morning he'd find Ari and set things right. By this time tomorrow night, the loan shark would be paid off and he'd have Ari back in his arms. He could hardly wait.

Chapter 17

The next morning, as the elevators opened on the foyer of Stone Suites, Wes squinted at the bright incandescent light.

"Ah, hell." He slipped on his sunglasses and pulled his jacket closer around his thin frame. Last night had been . . . enlightening. He had never experienced anything quite like it. He wasn't sure if he wanted to experience anything like that ever again.

As he walked by the kiosk, he passed by a strangely familiar figure peering at one of the receptionists.

"I'm looking for Jason Stone," the man said. "Please tell him that Landon Blake is here to see him."

"He's not here right now, Mr. Blake. Would you like to leave a message?"

"Do you know when he'll be back?"

"I believe he's out for the day. I'm sorry. But if you want to leave a message . . ."

Landon. Wes detoured his path and pushed his sunglasses up on his head. "I'll take care of this," he told the receptionist as he looped his arm with Landon's and steered him away.

"What's the meaning of this?" Landon asked. "Who are you?"

"A friend of Arianna's. I work at the Palazzo. Is everything all right, Mr. Blake?"

"Of course." He glanced at Wes. "Stone phoned me yesterday and since I was in the area—"

"Yes, of course." Wes tugged on his arm, and Landon followed him outside into the crisp, morning air. "I'm so glad I found you."

"I'm sorry, I don't—I mean you look strangely familiar, but . . ."

"My name's Wes. Like I said, I work over at the Palazzo. I was one of the people who was in charge of getting the place ready for your wedding."

"Ah, that." He looked away and cleared his throat. "I should have known." He adjusted his jacket. "I suppose you're looking for compensation of some sort. Not that I blame you. Well—"

"No, no, it's nothing like that. In fact, I didn't want to talk to you about the wedding at all."

"You didn't?"

"Not exactly." Wes pulled him into the shadows of the building, where it was more private. "I wanted to talk about last night."

"Last night?"

Wes glanced around them to make sure no one was listening. "Yeah, last night."

"I'm afraid I don't know what you mean."

Wes rolled his eyes. "Don't play dumb with me. I saw you at Dark Desires."

"I don't know what you're talking about."

"Come on, Landon. I know you were there with your boyfriend."

"Who dumped me for a tiny Asian," Landon muttered.

"Yes, well, a lot of crazy things happened last night."

Landon widened his eyes. "You're the man who was part of that scene."

"Yes." Wes cleared his throat and pushed the images from last night out of his mind. He liked kink just as much as anyone, but there was something about the domme Deacon had paired him with that seemed . . . off. She had made him uncomfortable, but Deacon seemed to be really into it. So Wes suffered through the scene, hoping to please Deacon and get what he really needed later on—intimacy.

He never got it. Deacon's lovemaking was just as cold and clinical as the domme's orchestrated scene. Both her flogger and Deacon's cock were unforgiving and left Wes feeling empty. Neither of them did anything wrong exactly, but the whole night felt . . . cold. Detached. After the scene, the domme seemed to lose interest, rushing through aftercare and dumping him off on Deacon without a second glance. Deacon was far too anxious to get back to the hotel to care about Wes's sore back. He hurried Wes along, accidently touching him in sensitive areas and making him wince.

On the way out of the club Deacon and the domme exchanged nods, just enough to suggest that they were friends, but nothing more. Wes thought it odd, considering Deacon supposedly just got into town a week ago, but before he could think much about it, Deacon had his arm around Wes's shoulders and was leading him to his motorcycle.

Sex with Deacon was like the scene with the domme. Hot and erotic, but devoid of anything real. Wes caught himself comparing Deacon to Marco and found him lacking in every way. While sex with Marco had been kinky, it was also intimate. Deacon didn't want to touch or kiss, and he didn't want to snuggle in the afterglow. He just wanted a fuck and to fuck hard. Wes obliged and tried to get into the moment, but in the end he felt more used than anything else.

When Wes woke up in the morning, he wasn't surprised

to find Deacon gone. He *was* surprised to find a note, however. It was an invitation to meet him back at the club that night.

"Yes. About that," Wes said. "I used to frequent Dark Desires, but have been away from the scene for a few months. Did you happen to notice if the woman I was with had been in the club before?"

Landon thought for a moment. "I think this was the first time I've seen her, although I have to admit that I haven't been to the club as often since the engagement."

Wes nodded. "How are you doing about that, by the way?"

Landon shrugged. "I'm okay. Just wish that the media would leave it alone." He caught Wes's curious expression and looked away. "The marriage was in name only," he explained. "More like a business deal. I barely knew the woman. I don't—I don't normally go for her type."

"The billionaire socialite type?"

"The female type."

Wes snorted. "Yeah, I had heard that."

Landon frowned and averted his gaze. "Most people have. And that's why I'm struggling with my investors."

"Because you're gay?"

"Shh." Landon glanced around. "It's more complicated than that, but yes, being gay is part of it."

Wes considered him for a moment before continuing. "Did you see the guy I was with last night when the scene ended?"

Landon's eyes widened. "Yes. Are you two . . ." He waved his fingers in the air between them.

"Oh, nah." He shoved his hands into his pockets. "It was just a one-night thing. I thought perhaps it could turn into something more, but it didn't work out."

"I see. So you wouldn't mind if I . . ."

Wes smiled. "No. Knock yourself out." He pulled out Deacon's note and handed it to him. "He'll be going to Dark Desires again tonight."

"Thanks. It's been a long time since I did more than watch. I owe you one."

"No, consider it a gift. I know what it feels like to be poked fun at over who you are." Wes patted his arm. "Just do yourself a favor and stay away from that woman."

"Why?"

"There's something not right about her." He ran his hand over his lower back, remembering the flogging he had gotten the night before. "She tends to be a little rough on her subs."

"Ah, well. Like I said, I tend to shy away from the more feminine clientele."

"Then you shouldn't have a problem." Wes dropped his arm and adjusted his sunglasses down onto his nose. "You shouldn't have any problem at all."

"What's wrong?" Camille asked as she came into the kitchen.

Ari frowned and grabbed the bottled water from her hand. "This charity is in worse shape than I thought."

"I know. I had to let the accountant go."

"Another one?" Ari rubbed her forehead. "Why?"

Camille slipped into the seat opposite her. "She wasn't working out."

"Meaning . . ."

"Meaning, she had more interest in banging our public relations coordinator than balancing the books."

"So we don't have a public relations person, either?"

"I'm afraid not."

"So we lost half of ARI'S KIDS' governing board."

"Just you and me." Camille patted her friend's shoulder. "Sorry."

Ari threw down her pen. "What a nightmare." Nothing was going right. She'd been up half the night trying to figure out what to do about Jason. Balancing the books was supposed to be a nice distraction, but it was turning into a headache. "Do you have any ibuprofen?"

"Sure." Camille hesitated, nibbling on her lip. "I'm really sorry, Ari. I wanted to tell you, but you had been so busy with the wedding."

"It's okay, Camille. I understand."

"You've been so upset and distracted this morning. Why don't you take a break?"

"I wish I could." She patted her friend's hand. "I'll be fine, Camille. Honest."

"Are you sure?"

"I'm sure."

"Okay, if you say so." She didn't look convinced, but went to get Ari the medicine anyway.

Ari waited until Camille went to retrieve the medicine before she closed her eyes and rubbed her temples. This charity was an organizational nightmare. So much so that she wasn't sure if she was going to be able to repair all of the damage without some help. Picking up her pen, she flipped through the stack of receipts Camille had given her about an hour ago and tried to see if there were any more corners they could cut, at least until she could get her hands on some money.

"Here you go." Camille reentered the kitchen a few minutes later and handed her two pills and some water.

"Thanks, Camille." Ari looked up at her friend, but her gaze was drawn to a movement over her shoulder. She widened her eyes. "Jason."

"Ari." He gave her a half-smile, looking rather uncomfortable.

"I called him this morning," Camille said. "I hope you don't mind."

Ari dragged her gaze away from Jason and stared at her friend.

"You mentioned right before bed last night that you wanted to talk to him." Camille averted her gaze. "I thought I'd help things along."

Ari wasn't quite sure what to say. "I have to go over the books."

"Just a few moments, Ari," Jason said. "That's all I'll need."

"Talk to him, Ari," Camille said. "I've been watching you all morning. You're not focusing. You need to clean up one mess before you even think of tackling another."

Ari shifted her gaze between Camille and Jason, feeling a little ambushed. "Fine. Just a few moments."

"I have to go grocery shopping, anyway," Camille said.

Ari waited until Camille left before she looked at her watch. "You have five minutes."

"You weren't at the apartment," he said.

"Did you really expect me to stay? You've been lying to me, Jason. Our whole relationship is a sham. You aren't who I thought you were."

"And your reaction was the exact reason why I waited so long to tell you." He slid into the seat next to her.

Ari crossed her arms and leaned back in her chair. "I don't want to stay with someone who tries to manipulate me."

"I'll admit that in the beginning, I asked you out to dinner because I thought that I could learn more about your family, but after dinner . . ."

"Yes?" she asked when he didn't continue.

He looked down at the receipts scattered on the kitchen table. "I felt differently."

"So you never used any of the information I gave you to edge out my family in the hotel business?"

He jerked his gaze back up to meet hers. "I didn't say that."

Ari snorted. "I've heard enough. I can't be with someone I don't trust. Good-bye, Jason."

"Wait. You can't expect me to unhear things, Ari, especially when it has to do with my competition."

She turned away from him, hoping that he'd just go away.

"Having said that, I never actively went out looking for information." He brushed his fingers over her arm, then took her hand. "And when I did use information, it was only to protect myself and my assets, never to take advantage of your family. Once I realized that I cared about you I never wanted to hurt you, Ari. You mean too much to me."

Ari frowned and pulled her hand away. "How do I know you aren't trying to con me now?"

"The same way I know that you aren't some ignorant party girl who never thinks beyond a good time." He leaned in closer. "You're more than your past, Ari . . . and so am I."

She inched closer and lowered her voice. "You slept with all of those women for money and information. Do you have any idea how dirty that makes me feel?"

"I'm sorry, Ari. If I could take it all back, I would. It happened a long time ago, before we met." He sighed and pushed his hand through his hair. "And since that charity race I haven't been with anyone else."

She raised her brows. "Seriously?"

"Seriously." He shifted to the edge of his seat. "If I was really the dirty con man you're making me out to be, don't you think that my photograph would be in the papers every day with a different girl hanging on my arm? Wouldn't I have already tried to tear your family down?"

She narrowed her gaze. "How do I know you haven't tried and failed?"

He flashed her his irresistible dimple. "Since when have I ever failed at anything?"

"You have a point." She tried not to smile, but his easy, self-satisfied grin was contagious.

"The truth is, I like having your brother around. He provides healthy competition and keeps things interesting. Without your family, things would get stale and boring." He took her hand in his again. "In case you haven't noticed, I don't like being predictable."

She smirked and avoided his gaze. "No, you don't."

"This business with the loan shark is unpredictable, but not in a good way." He squeezed her fingers as his smile faded. "I've thought about it for days, and still can't figure it out."

"What do you mean? Your identity was stolen. There's nothing to figure out."

"Perhaps." Her rubbed his chin. "But I can't shake the feeling that all of this isn't some random coincidence. The amount I owe is a round number—ten million. One would think that if it was a true gambling debt, it wouldn't be so vague. The number would be something more specific, perhaps with change."

"Perhaps you can only borrow in round numbers."

"Maybe." He shook his head. "But it's also large. It would be bad business for a loan shark to let debt climb so high without some sort of collateral, don't you think?" He rubbed his chin. "I don't gamble, so I don't know. I just have this feeling that this is all some sort of elaborate set up."

"I don't understand. Why would anyone target you?"

He lowered his arm and shrugged. "Because I have money. Because my name is recognizable. Who knows?" He let go of her hand and leaned back in his chair. "I've gotten where I am today based on instinct and right now my instincts tell me that there is more to this loan shark business than we know."

Ari frowned as she considered the possibilities. "Maybe one of the women you've slept with is attempting retribution? Someone must have made the connection by now. Your face is all over the media."

"Yes, but it was such a long time ago, and most of the women have no hard feelings. They knew what they were doing and consider the money they spent on me as part of the deal."

"You said 'most.' "

Jason considered her for a moment. "There was one woman who was bitter. I guess I got too good at my craft. She believed that we'd have a future together. Her tastes were . . . eccentric. She liked to hurt people in the bedroom. Both physically, with floggers and clamps, and emotionally through humiliation."

"Oh." Ari's features took on a look of concern. "She hurt you?"

"Like I said, it was a long time ago."

"Do you . . . Did you enjoy it?"

He offered her a sad smile. "She was the tipping point. After being with her a couple of times I knew I could no longer continue being something I wasn't. While she enjoyed sadomasochistic bedroom games, I did not."

"What happened?"

"I confronted my brother and told him that I wanted out. He didn't like it, but once I made up my mind, there wasn't much he could do."

"Instead of letting others use you, you were able to take control of your life, get a job, and do things on your own."

He nodded. "I became a different person after that. Stronger."

"I envy you for that," she murmured. "All my life my

brothers have controlled what I say and do. I'd kill to be able to push away their money like my sister, Gianna, and be independent."

"And you *can* do that, Ari. That same determination I had back then is inside you now. I can see it."

Ari smiled and turned away from him to look out the window. "What happened to Deacon?"

"What do you mean?"

"You said that you were running the con together. When you decided to go legit, what happened to him?"

Jason sighed. "Unfortunately, Deacon never really saw things the way I did. I think he resents my leaving him to start my own business."

"And the woman you left? Was she angry?"

"She was at first, but Deacon smoothed things over. I haven't heard from her since."

"So you really have no idea why you're being targeted."

"No, all I know is that we both need to keep a low profile for a while."

"We?" She shook her head. "I have nothing to do with this."

"Unfortunately, they know that you're connected to me. That puts you at risk." He nodded to her head. "You've seen what they can do. These people are volatile. I plan on paying what they ask, but there's always a chance that they could turn around and want more, or want to make me suffer in other ways for taking too long to pay them."

Ari rubbed her forehead. "I can't stay here, Jason. I need to live my life."

"You can't leave this apartment. Not yet, anyway. I'm on my way to get the money for the exchange. Deacon is going to handle everything for me. Once I have it all lined up, I'll come for you."

"Then what?"

"We'll lay low for a while until all of this blows over."

"Lay low? You know me, Jason. I can't just hang out somewhere indefinitely. I need to stay busy. If I don't have my charity, then I won't know what to do with myself."

"You won't be alone. I'll be with you."

"And that changes things . . . how?"

Something hot and hungry flashed through his gaze as he inched closer. "I can help keep you from being idle."

She raised her brows. "Oh really?"

He nodded and slid his fingers over her bare arm. "If I remember correctly, we're quite good at finding ways to fill the time."

Warm tingles spread over her skin as she thought about their impulsive sex games. "We are pretty good at that, aren't we?" She smiled and pressed her forehead to his. "Okay, you've convinced me."

"Good." He inched away and pulled a small package out of his suit jacket. "Here."

"What's this?"

"Meet me in that coffee shop we used to go to in Faneuil Hall in two hours and wear what's in that package."

She started to fold the paper back. "What does this package have to do—"

"Just promise me."

She jerked her gaze up to meet his. "Okay."

He kissed her temple. "Two hours."

"Okay."

As Jason left, she opened the large envelope and dumped the contents on the table. There was a flash of black silk and lace, enough to make her heartbeat quicken. Slowly she held up the garment and inspected the tiny scrap of fabric. There was something in the lining . . .

"Vibrating underwear." She ran her fingers over the black lace in surprise. What was Jason thinking?

She looked inside the envelope once more and noticed that there was no remote. How odd. Shrugging, she cleaned up the kitchen and took the package upstairs to change. She had no idea what Jason was up to, but she was determined to find out.

Chapter 18

Ari settled herself in one of the outside tables of the small café and glanced around the crowd, looking for him. The place was packed. Good weather had brought out the tourists, and the popular spot was filled to the brim with shoppers. She sipped her latte and tried to ignore the driver Jason had sent to take her to the café, who insisted that he hang out with her until Jason arrived "just in case something happened."

She wasn't an idiot. The man was larger than an eighteen-wheeler and looked as if he could muscle a bull to the ground and not break a sweat. Jason had sent him to protect Ari from the loan shark.

Not that she minded. It showed that Jason cared.

"There you are." Deacon came over and sat in the seat across from her. "I've been looking for you everywhere."

"You have?"

"Yes." He turned the chair around and straddled it. "I came to tell you that you're going to develop a bad cold and not be able to run away with him tonight."

"Why?"

"Because things have changed. The loan shark caught wind of our plan and now wants to make the exchange in person. It seems that he's interested in more than just money." He ran a hard, calloused finger over her arm. "You're making my brother careless, my dear. If he had been paying attention, then he'd know exactly what was happening, and what he needed to do. But no, my brother has gotten soft, and it's up to me to remind him of who he really is."

"Go to hell." Ari jerked her arm away.

"I'm already there, honey."

She narrowed her gaze. "Why did you really offer to do the exchange tonight?"

"For his protection."

"Bullshit."

"Be careful, my dear. I offered my protection to him, not to you." Deacon leaned in close and sneered. "And when my brother finally sees you for the self-centered socialite you are, *he* won't protect you, either."

Ari started to stand, but he tugged on her hair, making her wince and sit down once more.

"Don't create a scene." He let go of her hair and placed his finger on her chin, turning her gaze to meet his. "Jason used to always be so willing to do whatever I asked. Now he's a wild card, and a dangerous one at that." He tilted his head to the side and studied her face. "I want to know what it is you did to him so I can change him back."

"If Jason has changed, it's because he wanted to. It had nothing to do with me."

He ignored her outburst. "Perhaps I should fuck you on a washing machine, too. Maybe then I won't care so much about the debts I owe, or what will become of me if I don't pay them."

"Stay away—wait. What are you talking about? You owe someone money?" She jerked her chin out of his grasp.

His smile looked positively predatory. "No, not money, but I must pay it back all the same."

Ari had no idea what he was talking about, nor did she care. All she knew was that she needed to get away from this guy, fast. Deacon gave her the creeps.

She inched her chair away from him. "You need to go. He's going to be here any minute."

Deacon leaned his elbow on the table and pointed at her. "When Jason suggests running away, you bring him back to the hotel where he belongs. You hear me?"

"He'll get hurt. The loan shark—"

"Doesn't rough people up for no good reason."

"Do you need help, ma'am?" Jason's driver materialized at her side. "You look distressed."

"I'm fine." Ari was furious, too furious to think.

Deacon grinned and tipped his baseball cap. "I will see you at the hotel, Ms. Perconti."

"I wouldn't hold my breath." Ari scowled and watched Deacon retreat. As soon as he was out of sight, her underwear vibrated. She gasped and sat back down. Then, just as soon as it started, it stopped.

"Ma'am?" Ari looked up to find one of the baristas standing over her.

"Yes?"

"I was told to give this to the woman with the wide-brimmed hat." She held out an envelope.

Ari took the piece of paper from her fingers. "Thank you."

The barista's features turned pensive. "Do I know you?"

"I don't think so." Ari stood and pulled out the handle on her rolling suitcase. "Excuse me, but I really have to get going." She waited for the barista to go and opened the note.

Meet me at the Main Street parking garage. ~ J

Shoving thoughts of Deacon aside, she jammed the note into her pocket, grabbed the handle of her suitcase, and started moving toward the parking garage. Her driver-turned-bodyguard followed, quickly catching up to her.

"Allow me." He moved to take the suitcase from her hand.

"No, thank you, I've got it." Despite Jason's sending him, she still didn't trust the driver. He fell into step beside her as they made their way to the garage.

When they got to the entrance of the garage, Ari glanced around her and noticed a tall, sandy-haired man leaning up against a vintage-looking compact car.

"Jason." She hurried over and wrapped her arms around his neck.

The driver put her suitcase into the trunk of the car. "If you don't need anything else, sir, then I'll return the limo to the hotel."

"Thank you, Simon," Jason said as he pulled out a long, slender remote.

"What's that?" Ari asked.

He grinned and pushed a button.

Ari gasped as her underwear vibrated in response. Heat rose up through her center, and she grabbed the car door to steady herself.

"Oh my God." She reached for the remote. "Give me that."

He grinned as he pulled his arm away and pushed the button again, causing desire to ripple over her skin. "You love it."

Damn the man. He was too astute. "It's too bad I don't have a control, too."

He chuckled. "Now that's something to think about." He opened the passenger's side door. "Let's get out of here."

She briefly thought about telling him about his brother, but decided against it. Jason seemed so happy and relaxed. She didn't want to ruin the mood.

"Where's the McLaren?"

He opened the car door and ushered her inside. "Back

at the hotel. Sorry this isn't anything fancy, but I didn't want anyone to recognize us."

"I totally understand." Actually, it was a little fun. All of her life she had been riding in luxury cars and limos. Sitting in an old compact car felt . . . nice. Refreshing. She understood why her younger sister, Gianna, had renounced the family fortune. In this car, she felt as if she could do anything, be anybody. There were no restrictions, no expectations. It was just her and Jason against the world.

Ari nibbled her lower lip as he rounded the car and got inside. Her gaze slid past him, to a spot across the street. There, on the corner, she saw Deacon once more. Immediately, her sense of freedom vanished. He was watching them, she realized. He had probably seen them approach, probably watched them kiss. As she stared, Deacon nodded and tipped the rim of his baseball cap toward her. Whether it was a gesture of approval or a reminder of her promise, she wasn't sure. She guessed it was probably a little of both. He never wavered from his position, holding her gaze as she sat in the car. Jason seemed oblivious to his brother's presence as he pulled away from the curb and out into traffic.

Jason glanced over at Ari. "If you keep looking so distracted I'm going to get jealous." When she snorted, Jason waved the remote in the air between them. "Don't make me use this."

"You wouldn't dare. Not while we're driving."

"Just sit back and enjoy the ride." He pressed a button on the remote, and Ari's underwear vibrated. She raised her eyes as the sex toy rubbed against her sensitive flesh, sparking desire deep inside her core.

"That's better." He grinned at her reaction and hit the button again. Another blast of desire rolled through her body, making her squirm.

"You're evil," she said as she reached for the remote.

"I am." He shifted the remote out of reach and hit the button again.

"God, Jason, you're killing me."

"Good." He smiled. "You're far too serious. I needed something to distract you." He pushed the button again. Ari whimpered as desire rushed through her veins. "Trust me, princess. I've got everything under control."

They drove for the next hour in relative silence, with the exception of the buzzing noise from the sex toy. Jason was relentless with the button, stimulating her body until Ari felt weak with need and then backing off before things got too intense.

The foul man enjoyed torturing her, and by the time they were over the Sagamore Bridge, Ari was shaking with need.

"Where are we?"

"A place on the Cape. It's a small motel my last foster parents used to take Deacon and me when we were kids." He cleared his throat. "It's the one happy memory I have of my childhood." He dropped his hands from the steering wheel and slipped the remote into his pocket. "It's off season and secluded, so no one will bother us."

"You spent your time here?" She looked out over the small rise overlooking the ocean. She was desperate to get out of the car and rub her body up and down his like a cat. Nibbling her lower lip, she looked at the scenery, trying to distract herself with the small, family-style hotel and expansive beach. A small family had put out their blankets there, and the kids were playing in the sand while the parents watched. It was peaceful here, serene. If Ari hadn't been tortured for the past hour, she might have enjoyed it.

Jason rounded the car and opened her door. As soon as Ari was on her feet, Jason pulled her into his arms and kissed her hard.

"The family," she said, pulling back with a gasp.

They both looked toward the beach, where the family was picking up their things and heading back to the hotel. "They'll be gone in a minute."

He kissed her again, and it was several long seconds before she had the presence of mind to pull away.

"What if someone else comes?"

"I told you—it's the off season. Don't worry about it."

"But—"

"I must be losing my touch if you're worrying about what is going on around us." He backed her up into the hood of the car and kissed her again.

Ari moaned as his body enveloped her. As his tongue entered her mouth, the world around them faded away and she concentrated on how good he felt pressed up next to her. She leaned back, taking him with her, until her back was flat against the top of the car. Lifting her legs, she hooked them around his hips as he ran his hands up and down her sides.

"Did you enjoy my little gift?" he asked as he shifted from her lips to her jaw.

"Like it? I love it."

He stopped caressing her sides and fumbled for something in his pocket. Before she could ask what it was, her underwear vibrated, sending waves of pleasure through her core.

Ari gasped and arched her back, pressing her breasts into his chest. He set the underwear on continuous vibrate as he tore open her shirt and freed her breasts from her bra.

"This is torture. Jason—"

"I want to make sure you're ready for me." He placed his hand in between her legs, over her underwear. As he kissed her again, the vibration intensified, and Ari groaned as she spread her legs wider.

"Do you want more?" he asked.

"Of course."

"Good, then you'll love this." He left it on the higher setting as he ran his tongue around her nipple. He flicked and sucked, stimulating her sensitive tip. Ari squirmed beneath him, causing him to hold her second breast to keep her steady.

"Tease." She bucked and wiggled with pleasure as he used his teeth, tongue, and hands to torture first one breast, then the other.

"Jason . . ."

"Soon." He reached once more between her legs and slipped his fingers underneath the elastic of the underwear. "While I loved our little game, I'm afraid it's time to end it."

"End it?"

"There's another game I'd much rather play." He hooked his fingers under the waistband and pulled them off. Within seconds he was back again, zipping down his pants and preparing himself.

"Let me help." She sat up and slid off the hood as she reached for his cock. Jason braced his weight against the car as she crouched down until she was at eye level with his shaft. Freeing his erection, she ran her tongue around the tip and then pushed him deep inside her mouth.

"Yes." He bowed his head and curled his fingers into the metal frame. "God, that feels good."

Ari glanced at the beach and saw that it was deserted. For now. At any moment, another couple could enter, or a group of staff members could come and clean the beach. They were high up, people would have to really look to find them behind the bushes and dunes, but they could be seen. The thought of being caught made her even more brazen.

"Ah," Jason said as she slid her tongue down his length and took one of his balls into her mouth. She gently sucked, focusing on first one, then the other. She heard him gasp.

"Are you okay?" she asked after she retreated.

"Okay? I'm more than okay, honey." He grabbed her hand and pulled her into a standing position. "But if you do too much more than that, I won't last very long."

"There's nothing wrong with that."

"No," he said. "I need to last for what I have planned." He kissed her again, then turned her until she faced the car. When her naked breasts hit the cool metal, he stepped back and pulled his pants down to around his ankles. She heard the distinct tear of a condom wrapper and shivered with anticipation.

"You are so lovely." He palmed her backside and squeezed it between his fingers. Ari whimpered and arched her back, pushing her hips up to his eager hands.

He slid his fingers around front and easily found her clit. He rubbed it in a circular motion, just the way she liked it, as he positioned himself against her slit.

"Open wider," he whispered against her skin.

Ari hurried to follow his command. With a swift thrust, he was inside of her, filling her. He continued to push, spreading her folds open with his fingers as they came close to the car. Her clit pressed against the smooth metal hood, giving her a ripple of pleasure.

"That's it, princess," he soothed. "Just like that." He removed his hand and grabbed her hips as he retreated and thrust deep inside her core.

He pushed hard, moving her body forward into the car. Her breasts rubbed up against the metal hood and her clit pressed against the side of the car as his hips came flush with hers. The extra jolts of stimulation pumped through her system, driving her desire higher.

"Yes," she said as she adjusted her elbows so she sank more toward the car.

He retreated and thrust again, quickly finding a rhythm. Ari glanced ahead of her at the empty road, knowing that at any time someone could come around the bend and park in this secluded rest area and see them together. She widened her stance, loving how their bodies sounded as they came together.

"Work with me, princess," he said.

Ari pushed back as he thrust forward, and their bodies crashed together as one. Again and again they pushed, and each time her need soared. Ari turned her head and glanced at the ocean as her nipples slid against the smooth metal of the car. Jason felt so good, so right. If he was going to make her live in the moment, then she didn't ever want this moment to end.

Once, twice . . . their bodies came together like the crashing waves, breaking against the shore. The pressure on her clit was amazing, and Ari groaned as she felt her body strain toward release.

Higher and higher she raced, until she was hovering on the edge of something vast and amazing. Then Jason adjusted his stance and slid his hands up around her shoulders. The adjustment made him penetrate deeper, push harder. Ari gasped as he hit a sweet spot in her core.

Her orgasm hit her hard, bursting through her system like a summer storm. Ari cried out his name as bliss rained through her body, blanking her mind to everything but pleasure. Behind her she felt Jason stiffen and his movements become more intense. Within seconds he followed her over into oblivion, pouring every last ounce of his passion deep inside her body.

They silently hung onto the moment together, and as Jason curled his body around hers, Ari sighed her contentment. If only every moment could be this good.

Jason buried his face in Ari's shoulder and inhaled her sweet scent. He didn't want to think about his hotel, his brother, or anything else at the moment. Part of him wished that he could just run away with Ari, but he knew that could never be the case. On some level, Deacon was right. Jason would never be able to outrun his past. No matter where he went, he'd always be that kid that nobody wanted.

He carefully withdrew and helped Ari to dress.

"My shirt's ruined," she said.

"You didn't seem to mind earlier."

"No, I suppose I didn't." She chuckled and inched closer. "I'm surprised you keep coming back here. This hotel doesn't seem very . . . you."

He supposed she was right. "The hotel is part of my past. One of the families I had stayed with used to bring Deacon and me down here in the summer. The times I had spent here were the only happy memories from my childhood. Too bad it didn't last."

"What happened?"

"My foster parents were busted for dealing drugs. When they went to jail, Deacon and I went back into foster care." He slid his arms around her and tugged her close. "Later, when I was just starting out in the hotel business and found it difficult to mingle with the Boston elite, I came here because it reminded me of where I came from and where I wanted to go," he said. "This hotel centered me and helped me to regain focus."

Ari rested her head on his shoulder. "And where do you want to go?"

Good question. At one time, Jason would have had a ready answer—he wanted to be the richest, most influential person in the world. Someone no one would ever want to cast aside again. Unfortunately, the unwanted and unloved little boy in him wouldn't go away quietly. The more power he got, the more he felt like an imposter. No longer was he sure that success would slay the memories of his childhood.

"I want to feel like I fit in somewhere." His words

surprised them both, but the more he thought about it, the more it felt right.

She lifted her head off his shoulder and squinted up at him. "Like you're making a difference?"

"Yes."

"Me, too. That's why I have the charity. I just wish that the accounting wasn't such a mess."

"Deacon has always been good with numbers. When we ran the business together he kept track of all the finances."

She frowned and eased away from him. "I don't think that's such a good idea."

"What do you mean?" Jason thought it was perfect. It would give Deacon a job and Ari someone she could trust. It would solve so many problems.

She crossed her arms over her middle, pulling her shirt together. "Promise you won't get mad?"

Red flags went up in Jason's mind. "What happened?"

"First you have to promise."

"You know I can't promise that when I don't know what you're talking about."

She swallowed and averted her gaze. "Deacon . . . your brother . . ."

"Yes?" he asked when she didn't continue.

"We've had a couple of conversations now and each time I get the feeling he doesn't like me very much."

"It's in your head, I'm sure. Let me talk to him—"

"He thinks that I'm changing you." She took a step closer. "He said that you are ignoring family because of your concern for me."

Jason thought back to the handful of conversations they'd had and shook his head. "He's just upset that I've changed. I'm no longer the conning gigolo who would blindly hand him money to manage." Jason shrugged. "He'll get over it once he realizes that I no longer want to revive the old business." He tightened his hold on Ari. "I've moved on."

"Maybe." She widened her eyes and put her finger to her mouth. "Oh my God. Jason, I forgot."

"Forgot what?"

"Deacon saw me while I was waiting for you. He told me to tell you that plans had changed and the loan shark wanted to talk with you personally."

"Are you sure?"

She nodded. "I'm so sorry."

"I was an idiot to let my brother do this on his own. This isn't his problem. It's mine." He glanced at his watch and realized that if he left now, he'd make it just in time. "Come on. Let's go check you in."

She glanced down at his outstretched fingers. "Check me in?"

"Yes."

"Oh, no, you don't. I'm going with you."

He shook his head. "You can't. I won't risk your safety again."

She glared at him.

He let out a long breath and took her fingers. "I can't concentrate if there is a chance you could get hurt. Humor me on this. Stay here, where it's safe, and I'll come back for you when this is all over."

"I've been sitting on the sidelines all my life, Jason. I refuse to do it anymore."

He ground his teeth as he tried to think of a solution that would appease them both. "Okay, here's the deal," he said as he hooked his finger under her chin. "I'll send my driver—"

"No."

"Don't be so stubborn."

"No, you don't be so stubborn. Let me do this, Jason. I want to help you. We're a team."

"Your safety comes first." He lifted his finger, shutting her mouth as she was about to protest. "Humor me on this. I need to have my head clear to deal with this situation, and I can't do that when I know that there is a possibility that you might get into trouble."

She considered him for a moment before responding. "Okay, how's this. I stay with my family until this blows over." She inched forward. "I just can't stand the thought of being down here, so far away from you, when you're dealing with so much back in Boston."

He relaxed his shoulders as he considered the compromise. With Leo, Marco, and Dante watching out for her, she'd be much safer there than in some run-down motel with no one to look out for her. It would mean confessing his problems to his rival, but he felt his relationship with Leo was beginning to turn a corner. A little honesty might not be so bad after all.

"Okay, we'll go to the Palazzo first." He opened the passenger's side door and motioned her inside. As she got into the car, he realized that she'd given in a little too easily. He wouldn't put it past her to have some plan up her sleeve, but he didn't have time to think about it. He had to get her back to her family before the exchange was to take place.

The ride back to Boston was mostly quiet, for which Jason was thankful. An accident on the road caused traffic to back up, which in turn made them late getting back to the city.

"You need to go straight to Stone Suites," Ari said as they pulled off the highway.

"Not until you're safe."

"Be reasonable, Jason. If you were to drive up to the North End now you'd miss the exchange." She waved her hand in the air in front of them. "Just go to Stone Suites. I'll stay in the car and out of sight while you and Deacon do your thing." She slid out her cell phone and waved it in the air. "I'll even call my brother if things get too intense."

Jason glanced at the clock on the dashboard and realized that she was right. There was no time to get back to the Palazzo before the exchange. Steeling his jaw, he considered her offer.

"Okay, but promise me you'll stay out of sight."

"I will."

A sense of foreboding rose up inside of him as he pulled into the Stone Suites parking garage. Nothing seemed out of place, and no strangers were milling around. Despite this, he couldn't seem to shake the uneasy feeling in his stomach.

He glanced at the clock on his dashboard. It was ten minutes past eight, ten minutes past the time the exchange was supposed to take place in the parking garage. Deacon was nowhere to be found. Neither was the loan shark or his goons.

Jason pulled into his parking spot, grabbed Ari's hand, and tugged her closer. Ari gasped and he took advantage, sliding his tongue across her lips and into her eager mouth. He groaned and placed his hand on the back of her head as desire surged up through his bloodstream once more.

"Get down," he said as he pulled away.

She wrinkled her brow. "There's no one here. Are you sure it was supposed to happen at eight o'clock?"

"Plans may have changed," he said. "I'm going to find out." Jason opened the driver's side door.

"There you are."

Someone grabbed his arm and dragged him away from the car.

"Wait." Jason grimaced as something hit him on the back of the head. He fell to his knees as stars blinked in front of his eyes.

"That's for trying to get out of your appointment."

He tried to stand, but everything was spinning. "I don't understand. My brother was supposed to be here—"

Something long and hard hit him across the shoulder blades. Jason fell forward and barely got his hands up in front of him before his face hit the concrete.

"And that's for leaving your brother to do your dirty work," someone said as a foot hit him in the ribs. "You're lucky that our boss is forgiving. If it was me you double-crossed, I would have killed you."

Ari screamed from somewhere behind him. Jason turned his head and saw a man pull her from the car. To her credit, she fought hard, but she was no match for the large man. The thug easily pinned her arms behind her back and started pulling her away.

"Wait." Jason pushed himself up, only to get kicked in the ribs one more time.

"One more chance, you hear me? That's all you get."

"She has nothing to do with this," he gasped.

"She has everything to do with this," the man, their leader, said. "She's our collateral."

Jason started to protest, but someone else kicked him again, robbing him of breath.

Jason opened his eyes and tried to see through the pain, but the men had closed in around him. Ari was nowhere in sight.

"Let go of me, asshole." Ari's voice rose up through his haze of pain. "Do you have any idea who I am? Jason!"

"Ari!" Jason winced as blow after blow hit him in the ribs. He had no idea how many people were kicking him, and he didn't care. The only thing that mattered was Ari.

Then suddenly, blissfully, the kicking stopped. Jason squeezed his eyes shut and curled into a fetal position as pain blasted through every muscle and organ.

"Tomorrow night. A courier will stop by tomorrow

morning and give you the location. You better have the money, or the girl will experience an unfortunate accident."

From somewhere in the distance, Jason heard a car engine start. It sounded like a large car, or perhaps a van. He tried to open his eyes so he could see the make and model, perhaps get a license plate number, but everything hurt too much. As the car peeled out of the garage, blackness hovered on the edge of his vision. He fought through it as a wave of nausea washed over him. It took forever to pass, but once it did, the reality of his situation hit him like a brick wall.

Ari was going to die, and it was all his fault.

Chapter 19

Jason struggled up into a sitting position and rested his back against the stone pillar. "Fuck!"

The outburst caused pain to blast out through his skull and vibrate along every bone in his body. *Get your shit together, man. She's counting on you.*

Jason squeezed his eyes shut as helplessness washed over him. He glanced over at his vintage car collection as his chest squeezed with agony. Most of the cars had been damaged. Some were totally destroyed. Windows were bashed in, tires slashed, and hood and doors were dented in. Only his McLaren had remained unscathed, mostly because it was parked away from the rest of the cars.

Not that it mattered. Jason was in no shape to drive. Even if he was, he had no idea where those bastards had gone with Ari, or what they intended to do with her.

Pay us, or you'll never see your little woman again. Blackness hovered on the edge of his vision, and Jason ground his teeth as he struggled to remain conscious. Ari's life depended on what he did next. He moved to pull out his cell, grinding his teeth in pain as his bruised fingers slid into the fabric of his torn suit jacket.

"Ah!" He winced as he pulled out his cell and swiped the screen.

Who could he call? His mind raced with possibilities. This situation, although desperate, needed to remain discreet. If word got out that the Perconti heiress was missing again, things were going to get ugly fast.

He had to get to her, and to do that, he had to figure out where they were taking her. Grinding his teeth to get through the pain, he dialed the only person who could give him any answers.

"You have reached the mailbox of Deacon Stone . . ." Jason leaned his head back against the pillar and closed his eyes as his brother's voice mail droned on.

"Where are ya, bro?" Jason said after the beep. "Did you give 'em the money?" Another round of pain blasted through him, causing him to wince. "Get ova to Stone Suites. I need ya help." He ended the call and did a mental inventory. He hurt like hell, but nothing was broken. At least, he didn't think anything was broken.

Ari. If those bastards hurt one hair on her head . . . Jason blinked back the surge of emotion at the thought of never seeing her again. If something happened to her, he'd have no one to blame but himself. What would he tell the media, or her family? Fuck, Leo would blame him, of course, not that he didn't deserve it. If only he had taken her someplace else and not to the hotel. He had been so obsessed with getting his dick back into her that he didn't consider the fact that those goons would be waiting for him. Now Ari was in trouble, and it was all his fault.

He had been a fool not to acknowledge what was growing between them, what had been growing ever since that first date. He could see that now. She needed more from him than a casual fuck. She deserved more. The woman knew all about his sordid past, had even accepted his dysfunctional brother, and yet she still wanted him. Ari deserved so much more in life, and he had held her back. Now, thanks to his selfishness, she could be facing her death.

"Fuck," he said again. He was so stupid. If he ever got them both out of this mess, he was going to tell her just how much she meant to him. Jason couldn't imagine his life without Ari in it in some way. He'd do anything to protect her, even if that meant running his own business, a hotel empire that had taken over a decade to build, into the ground.

He swiped the screen of his phone and punched in his assistant's number. "Micki," he said, not waiting for her greeting. "Come out to the staff parking garage as soon as you're able."

"Sure thing, Mr. Stone."

The phone clicked, signaling the end of the call. Jason's muscles protested as he slowly slid his feet underneath him and used the pillar to ease himself into a standing position. "Damn."

He closed his eyes and leaned on the pillar, waiting for his muscles to stop screaming. His side hurt like hell. One of those guys must have had a boot with a steel toe.

"Oh my God, what happened?" Micki said from the door to the hotel. She dropped her duffle bag and hurried to his side. "Are you okay?"

"No." He wasn't okay, and he wouldn't be all right until Ari was safe and back in his arms once more.

"You need to see a doctor."

"Not now." He swiped his phone. Micki grabbed it from his fingers.

"What are you doing?" he demanded.

"I'm not letting you do anything until you tell me what happened."

Jason sighed. "It's complicated. Basically, some guys jumped me as I was parking my car."

"Oh my God." Micki put her hand over her mouth. "Did you get a good look at them?"

"Where's my security?"

"What?"

"I asked for extra security in the garage tonight."

She furrowed her brow. "I didn't know that. It's been business as usual. I don't think they ever got the orders." She nibbled on her lip in thought. "I might be able to pull the security tapes. If we call the police—"

"No, no police."

"Are you crazy?"

Jason winced and held out his hand. "Not crazy, just cautious. Give me my phone."

She flashed him a skeptical look, then placed his cell in his palm. "I don't like this. You need to go to the hospital."

"Later." Jason swiped his phone once more and tried a different number.

"I'm taking you inside."

"No."

"Humor me." She situated herself under his arm as he dialed.

"Stone." Leo's voice crackled on the other end of the line. "What do you want?"

"Arianna is in trouble."

"What?" Leo's voice rose and tension crackled over the line. "If you've hurt her—"

"Not me." He grimaced as Micki started walking toward the door to the hotel. "But yes, someone hurt her. She doesn't have much time, Leo, and I need your help."

"I'm on my way."

Deacon's cell buzzed, disturbing the perfect moment he had spent all day creating. Frowning, he glanced at the screen, noted the number, then turned the damn thing off. It had been a long time since he had been in a position like this, and he wasn't going to let anything disturb him. Especially not his high-and-mighty brother. Let the bastard panic for a little while. It would probably do him good.

The waitress he had been eyeing all evening with a nose ring and purple hair glided over to his table and took his order. As she stood there, seductively chewing on the end of her pen, he appreciated how the tight, round globes of her breasts pushed over the edge of her low-cut tank. God, he'd love to taste those breasts. He had been sleeping with men for so long he had forgotten how wonderful the softness of a woman felt against his skin. It would be the perfect ending to a perfect day.

Everything was going according to plan and he was in the mood to celebrate. As the waitress winked at him and sauntered back to the bar to get his drink, Deacon considered taking her to one of the side rooms in Dark Desires and fucking her senseless, but then dismissed the idea. That woman's ass was made for anal, but he had always preferred watching sex to participating in it.

Fucking always took stamina and strength. To do it right, you had to pace yourself and be in tune to another person's needs. Deacon had to pretend that he gave a shit about his partner, at least until he got his rocks off. It didn't matter if it was a man or a woman, people wanted to be complimented and cuddled before offering up their sexual wares. Everyone wanted to feel like a princess, even if it was only for a short while. No one wanted to just have sex anymore, and Deacon didn't have the patience or the inclination to open himself up in that way to anyone.

No, he had learned the hard way what becoming vulnerable did to a person. He had trusted his brother once with his livelihood a long time ago, and Jason had betrayed him. Something had snapped inside of Deacon the day Jason had left their business to strike out on his own. In that moment of darkness, Deacon had learned a valuable life lesson and vowed to never be hurt like that again.

And so it began. The long journey of revenge that had brought him to this point in his life. It was a moment he was going to savor for months and years to come.

"Your drink, sir." Miss Purple Hair bent over low as she placed the microbrew on the table, giving Deacon a healthy view of her ample bosom. The woman's breasts were perfectly round and pert, like two round, ripe fruit, waiting to be plucked. Fuck, they were lovely.

"How much do I owe you?" he asked, dragging his gaze up to meet hers.

"Oh, you don't owe me anything."

"I don't?" He raised his brows.

"No, this drink is already paid for." She moistened her lips and glanced over her shoulder at the scene being played out on a small stage not far away. "The woman over there paid for it. Said it was a 'thank you' for her new toy."

Deacon looked up and met the gaze of a tall, thin domme with inky hair and crimson lips. He started to smile, but then caught himself. They were in public. His mistress had strict rules about public displays of affection.

"She said that I'm supposed to give you anything that you ask for tonight." The waitress slid her long fingernails across his thigh. "So if you have any particular needs you want fulfilled . . ."

Deacon dragged his gaze away from the domme and focused on the waitress. "Not right now, sweetheart, but thank you. I'll keep your offer in mind." With a wave of his hand, he dismissed her. Miss Purple Hair sashayed back to the bar and he promptly dismissed her and her large tits from his mind. There were much more important things requiring his attention.

Deacon settled back in the chair of his private booth

and raised his drink at the beautiful domme. She really shouldn't thank him for finding the hottest BDSM spot in town. It wasn't Deacon who had discovered Dark Desires, but the handsome Southern boy he had brought to her last night. As soon as Deacon saw the tall, thin blond in his brother's hotel's foyer, he knew that he'd be perfect for her. For them. Having a club to act out their scene just made everything that much easier.

But the Southern boy didn't show up tonight, so they'd had to adjust. This new toy wasn't quite as good as the last. He was far too accommodating for his tastes. Deacon liked some fight in a submissive. It showed some character. This one seemed as if he had already been broken by someone and was just going through the motions.

But they would make do with what they had. They always did.

His mistress nodded to him, then turned her attention back to the man on his knees before her. She cracked her whip in the air, and aviation tycoon Landon Blake's eyes widened in surprise.

Deacon groaned as he set down his drink and unzipped his pants. He fucking loved it when she used that thing. This was going to be quite the show.

Chapter 20

When Arianna had urged Jason to let her come back to Boston with him, she'd had no idea it would involve being kidnapped by a bunch of thugs.

"Jason already paid you," she said as they dragged her to a large gray sedan that could be found anywhere in America. Every muscle in her body was sore, and her head throbbed to the beat of some unknown tune.

"No, he didn't, but he will now."

"What do you mean? His brother was supposed to make the exchange tonight."

"Our boss told those two that she wanted to speak to Jason directly. He didn't play by the rules, so now he must pay the price." Someone placed a mask over her eyes and shoved her into the backseat. "That's why we took you—to make sure she gets what she wants."

"It wasn't his fault. He—" Someone pushed her from behind, cutting off her words. As Ari tumbled onto the leather, two rough hands grabbed her wrists and tied them together with a zip tie. Another zip tie was used around her ankles. She complained, of course. Then her complaining quickly turned into pleading. Her cries of mercy went unanswered as the men efficiently went about their work. It was obvious they had done this with others before.

She concentrated on the sounds around her. Mostly she was trying to determine whether Jason was still alive, or if there was anyone around who might come to their aid if she screamed for help.

"Don't even think about it, lady," the man said from the seat beside her.

"Think about what?"

"Screaming." Something cool and metal pressed against her throat. "I'd hate to silence you."

She swallowed and leaned her head back on the seat, desperate to get away from the blade. From somewhere outside the car, she heard a man speak.

"Tomorrow night. A courier will stop by in the morning and give you the location. You better have the money, or the girl will experience an unfortunate accident."

Then the other two men got into the front of the sedan and dove off.

Ari didn't know how long she sat in the backseat, but it felt like hours. The men were quiet, too quiet, and she wondered just what they had in store for her.

"I'm rich," she said into the silence. "I can just give the money to you now and we can forget the whole thing."

It was a long time before anyone responded. "This is bigger than the money." The man's voice rumbled through her.

"Bigger than ten million?"

"Stone had his chance to pay, and he refused."

"He's not the one who racked up the debts, you know," she said, trying to keep her hopes up. "Someone stole his identity."

"We just do as we're told, lady. The boss wants her money, and she wants Jason to hand it to her personally."

"But it isn't fair!"

A different voice rose up from somewhere in the front seat. "Put a muzzle on her, will ya? I don't want to hear her yapping for the next thirty minutes."

The large man next to her grunted his agreement and reached for something.

"No—wait. I'll be quiet, I promise."

"Sorry, lady," The man's voice sounded apologetic, almost compassionate, as he shoved some ball-like plastic object into her mouth. "I have to do what I'm told." He secured the straps behind her head. The strong smell of leather and plastic hit her hard, and she wondered what the hell he'd put into her mouth. She hoped it wasn't laced with drugs or poison or anything.

Ari slumped back onto the seat in defeat. Working her jaw, she tried to make it so the object in her mouth moved to a more comfortable position and failed miserably. She couldn't move, couldn't speak. As the car drove on, her mind raced with what she could do to escape.

It was odd that the men wouldn't consider taking money from her. Why would they care where the money came from? And this loan shark's need to speak directly with Jason seemed odd. Things weren't adding up.

Not that she could do anything about the situation while she was bound and gagged in a moving car. The first thing she needed to do was escape. Then she needed to talk to Jason about her suspicions. She had no idea what these people were after, but it seemed as if money was only a small part of it.

Perhaps there was something she could do once they stopped. Wherever they wanted to take her, Ari was sure she didn't want to go there. Her only chance of escape was to get away while they took her out of the vehicle.

She strained her hearing, listening for movement. At some point during the drive, someone turned on the radio, and the local sports station was talking about the upcoming Red Sox series starting tomorrow. Ari blocked it out and concentrated on other movements, listening for something that would suggest that the men weren't paying attention to her.

Hearing nothing, she gently tested her bindings around her ankles and wrists, learning their tightness without making it look like she was trying to get out of her restraints.

The men knew what they were doing. Instead of rope or cuffs, the thugs had used zip ties, which provided very little in the way of movement. In fact, they had been tied so tight that she was starting to lose feeling in her hands. She had no idea how she was going to get away while her limbs were tied, but she knew she had to try. Who knew what was going to happen once they got her to their destination?

The car eventually stopped, and she heard movement around her. The men were eerily silent, as if they had done this so many times that they needed no further instruction. The door opened beside her and a big, meaty hand reached out and grabbed her elbow. He hauled her to her aching feet and, once able, she swung into action. She jerked her arms up behind her hard and hit something soft and yielding.

"Fuck." The grip around her arms loosened, and she flung her body forward, away from her captor. She hit something else hard—a chest—and was rewarded with a loud "oomph." Triumphant, she jerked her head up and hit someone in the chin. Laughter ensued around her, but she paid it no mind. Ari flailed and wiggled as best she could, hitting everything that came within inches of her body.

"Let her struggle." A man's voice, the same one that had been in the front of the car, rose up over the yelps and howls. Immediately, the soft barriers of flesh that were holding her upright melted away. Without the use of her limbs, Ari had nothing holding her up and she tumbled to the pavement. She landed on her side, and pain shot out from her head and numbed her body. She wanted to scream with frustration, but the gag prevented her from doing more than mumbling. Tears streamed down her cheeks as she jerked back and forth on the ground like a fish, trying to stand.

Male laughter rose up around her, and Ari became even angrier. She rolled onto her stomach and tried to get her knees under her.

"Enough," a man said. Someone grabbed the back of her shirt and hauled her to her feet.

"Look at those breasts," someone else said. Ari did a mental check of her body and realized that her tits were poking out of her torn shirt. They were still covered by her bra, but such things probably didn't matter to these men.

"They're so firm." Someone grabbed her boob. Ari screamed through the gag and tried to push him away. Her efforts were only met with laughter.

"Enough," said the man who had sat in the front of the car. "The boss said not to harm her. Yet."

"Later maybe?" someone asked.

"Maybe." Someone grabbed her, and Ari pulled away. Something hard hit her in the ass, causing pain to vibrate up her body.

"Behave." The man crouched low and lifted her up off the ground. The world tipped upside down as he flung her over his shoulder.

Ari blinked back the tears as best she could and tried to think past her rising panic. They were taking her to their boss. Hopefully this loan shark would be more willing to negotiate than these guys. If she could just figure out what they really wanted, then she could use it to gain some leverage. It was a long shot, but right now it was her only hope.

They took her into a building, and then down a long corridor. Through the edges of the blindfold, Ari saw that the place they were taking her was dark. They seemed to walk for hours. She thought about kicking the guy carrying her and making a run for it, but decided to preserve her energy. Perhaps when talking to this loan shark, there would be a chance for escape.

There were voices, speaking in low murmurs. Ari wasn't sure what they were talking about, nor did she care. She just wanted this all to end.

A door opened from somewhere up ahead, and the men took her through it. They were immediately met with the voice of an angry female.

"Oh, for the love of all things holy, put the woman down. And be careful." Ari heard some mumbling about incompetent males as she was lowered to the floor.

"Take off that thing around her head, too," she ordered. Immediately, the blindfold came off, and Ari found herself standing in a dimly lit, musty room surrounded by about six men, all in suits and bigger than trucks. The room was some sort of office, impeccably decorated in a contemporary style, with soft pinks and cream accents and solid oak furniture. There were gold-trimmed mirrors and ornately framed abstract art decorating the walls.

It wasn't quite what one would think of when they thought of a loan shark's office.

"I see that these knuckleheads at least brought you in one piece."

Ari stared at the woman, who was strikingly beautiful, if not a little frightening. She wanted to ask who she was, but couldn't with the gag.

"I'm sorry, let us remove those for you. We want you to be comfortable, after all." She jerked her head in the direction of two men, who moved forward to remove her bindings. As they worked, Ari caught her reflection in one of the mirrors. She looked a mess. Some type of pink ball had been shoved in her mouth, held there by leather straps. The zip ties were neon pink, and were cutting into her flesh. One man slipped a knife between the tie and her skin, then jerked his hand outward, cutting her bindings, while the other removed the gag.

"Be careful not to cut her," the woman said.

The men finished their work, and Ari rubbed her wrists as circulation started to flow once more.

"Now, that's better, isn't it?"

Ari nodded. "Who are you?"

"I'm sorry," the woman said as she stood and rounded the desk. "How terribly rude of me." She held out her hand as a warm and somewhat sinister smile spread out across her face. "My name is Burke. Felicia Burke. I'm so sorry to capture you, but it seems as if your boyfriend owes me quite a bit of money, and this is the only way I can get his attention."

"You're the loan shark?" Ari asked as she took the woman's hand.

Her smile appeared forced. "You don't think that a woman can be a loan shark?" She shook her head in disappointment. "It appears as if you have a lot to learn, little one. I now see why Jason made you a target."

"What do you mean?" This was all so confusing.

She turned and slowly walked back to her desk. "I've been watching you. You let your brothers lead you around by the nose. Such behavior only supports the stereotype that females are weak and simpering, and makes you a target for con men like Jason Stone."

"Weak and simpering? I run my own charity."

Felicia settled in her seat. "Funded by your brother, who was willing to marry you off to the highest bidder." Felicia rolled her eyes. "It's as if we were all shot back to the Dark Ages."

"I'll have you know that I'm my own woman."

"Not yet, but you could be. You just need to know how to handle men correctly. When treated properly, they'll fall over themselves to do whatever you desire. *You* will control *them,* and not the other way around."

"I don't understand."

Felicia flicked her wrist, holding her hand out, palm up. Two large men materialized out of the shadows. One picked up her fingers and kissed her palm, while the other slowly trailed kisses up the inside of her arm.

"See what I mean?" the woman asked. "All of these men are eating out of my hands."

Ari stared at her, dumbstruck. This woman was crazy. Certifiably crazy.

"Only once did a man defy me," she continued. "He managed to get away before I could have him fully trained." She pulled her hand away and the men went back into the shadows, like palace guards protecting their queen. The woman turned her gaze back to Ari.

"Jason Stone will pay for embarrassing me," the woman continued. "Soon I'll have him eating out of my hand too, just like his brother."

Deacon hated getting up before the sun, especially after a night of erotic fun, but sometimes it was necessary. He had to speak to Jason, and if he didn't catch his brother early, he'd be impossible to reach for the rest of the day. After a quick cup of high-test coffee and a shower, Deacon passed the restaurant with the complimentary breakfast and ignored the temptation to grab a few slices of bacon. Instead he focused on making his way to his brother's office. As he neared the closed door, he found both his brother and the famous hotelier Leo Perconti arguing.

"We need to go to the authorities," the Perconti patriarch said. "This is my sister we're talking about."

Deacon opened the door and stepped inside. "No," he said before his brother could object. "No authorities."

"Who is this?" Leo asked, waving his hand in Deacon's direction.

Jason frowned and straightened. "This is my brother, Deacon. Where the hell have you been? Where's the money?"

Deacon took a step into the room, closing the door behind him. He hated how Jason always seemed to talk down to him. Even back in their conning days, Jason had always wanted to work alone, leaving him in the shadows to watch and learn. Things were too dangerous, he'd say. You need more finesse.

He glanced from Jason to Leo and back again as the tension rose in the room. "I got a note that the drop-off had changed to a different location. I waited hours there for them to show up." He held up the suitcase of money. "But no one ever came."

"Where was this new location?" Leo asked.

"Why didn't you answer your cell?" Jason said at the same time.

Deacon took a step back as the anger the other men felt radiated through the air at him. "Look, I didn't have my phone on me—they said no electronics. And it was at that club downtown." He scratched his head, as if trying to remember the name. "Dark Desires, I think it's called."

Leo fisted his hands. "This is ridiculous. We're being led around the city like dogs on a leash."

"I agree," Jason said. "I'm done playing games."

"What's going on?"

"I've been texting you for hours. Haven't you gotten my messages?"

Deacon glanced from one billionaire to the other. "Sorry, I've been busy. When they didn't show up at the club, I started to leave, but then this woman came up to me . . ." He placed the suitcase on the floor. "I'm only human."

"Jesus, Deacon. Did it ever cross your mind to fucking call me?"

"They took my sister," Leo said. "Those bastards took my sister." He turned to Jason. "And I say it's time to get the authorities involved."

Deacon shook his head. "No, no authorities."

"Why?"

"Because we're guaranteed to lose," Deacon said. When both men looked at him in confusion, he took a deep breath and tried to explain. "Don't you see? These aren't normal people we're dealing with. Loan sharks are used to working outside the law. You call the cops, they could disappear with the girl and you'll never find her again."

Jason swore and pushed his hair from his face. "What a mess."

"And it's all your fault, Stone." Leo pointed his finger and scowled. "She never should have come to you in the first place, not when she has family."

"Yeah, family who forced her into a marriage she didn't want."

"Ari wanted this marriage. She said so herself. I made it clear that if at any time she wanted to back out, all she had to do was ask."

"She was too intimidated."

"That's ridiculous."

Jason crossed his arms. "Admit it. You can come off as rather intimidating at times."

Leo glowered. "And you don't?"

"Of course not."

Leo snorted. "No, you just use people to further your business and dump them on the sidewalk."

"At least I didn't use my own sibling—"

"Listen, guys." Deacon inserted himself between the men. "Arguing about the past isn't going to help her. We need to work together if we're going to get this girl back."

The men stared at each other with hatred in their eyes.

"None of this is helping Ari," Deacon said.

After a few tense moments, Leo seemed to back down. "I just want my sister back."

"I want that, too. Believe me." Jason pushed his hair back from his face and leaned up against the wall. "If I'd had any idea what they were going to do, I never would have brought her back to Boston."

Deacon was fascinated at how ruffled the normally cool and collected hoteliers were. Never before had Deacon seen his brother so out of sorts, not since he said he wanted out of the family business.

He cleared his throat. "I came in here because I ran into a courier outside. He asked me to give this to you." He pulled out a small, square envelope from his jacket and handed it to Jason.

"What does it say?" Leo asked, rounding the desk to peer over Jason's shoulder.

"It's the pickup point," Jason said after a few moments. "They want me to meet them at Sabrina's restaurant tonight with the money. No cops, no personal security. Just me. I provide the funds, and in exchange, I'll get Ari back unharmed."

"But if we try to pull something," Leo said, reading over his shoulder. "Then Ari will get hurt." He fisted his hands. "I'm calling the police."

"No," Jason said. "My brother's right. We need to do things exactly as they say. If this Burke guy senses that we've double-crossed him, then we put Ari in more danger than she is in now."

Leo made a frustrated noise and began pacing. "So

what do we do? Just hand this guy the money?" He stopped pacing and stared at Jason. "Really, Stone, it's not like you to lose so much to the tables."

"It wasn't him," Deacon said. "His identity got stolen."

"You should be more careful—"

"You aren't being helpful, Perconti." Jason dropped the note on the desk. "From now on, we do things by the book. They just want me, so I'll show up at Sabrina's at the assigned time with the money. I'll get Ari and then we can put this nightmare behind us."

"No," Leo said. "I'm going with you."

"But—"

"She's my sister, Stone. There's no way I'm going to sit back and leave her fate in the hands of the likes of you."

"Hey now." Deacon took a menacing step forward. "That's uncalled for."

"No, he's right." Jason put his hand on Deacon's chest, stopping his advance. "This could be a trap. If it is, then I'll need help." He lowered his hand and frowned in thought. "Calling the cops will just make everything more complicated, and having all of the Perconti brothers hanging around outside will only bring unwanted attention." He turned to Leo. "But if it was just you outside, and you were well hidden, perhaps it could work." He extended his hand. "What do you say?"

Leo hesitated, then shook it. "You realize that my sister's safety is my first concern."

"If things go bad, get her out. Forget about me."

"Jason." Deacon turned to his brother, aghast. "You'd really put your life on the line for a girl?"

"She's not just a girl to me," he said as he lowered his hand. "She's everything." He turned away from Leo to face his brother. "If anything happened to Ari, I wouldn't be able to live with myself."

"What time does this loan shark want to meet you?" Leo asked.

"Eleven o'clock tonight."

"Good. We'll meet back here at ten and iron out the details." He stared at Jason a moment, considering. "We're going to get her back, Stone."

It wasn't a question, but Jason seemed to answer anyway. "Yes, that's all that matters. Keeping Ari safe."

Leo flexed his fingers as if he was turning things over in his mind. "Okay. I've got work to do. I'll see you in a few hours with the money."

"No, this is my mess. I'll pay for it. Besides, you don't have the funds."

"This is my sister, Stone. I wasn't there for her. I'm paying for this, end of discussion."

Jason stared at him for a long moment before responding. "We split it down the middle." He held up his hand before Leo could protest. "I am as much to blame as you for this. Perhaps more. We messed up together, so we'll get her back together."

Leo grunted his approval and headed for the door. "Don't forget, ten o'clock, sharp."

"I won't forget." Jason let out a long breath as Leo turned his back to the room.

Deacon waited for the Perconti patriarch to go before he spoke. "What about me?"

"You're to stay out of this," Jason said. "I have enough to worry about with Ari, I don't think I could keep it together if something happened to you, too."

"But—"

"No, and that's final."

Deacon steeled his jaw. He was being dismissed—again. Just like Jason had hurt him the day he left the business. There was no warning, no "Hey, bro, come join me." He'd just picked up his stuff and cut his older brother out of his life.

Well, this time, Deacon wasn't going to let him go quietly. "There's another way, brother," he said as he watched Jason pull out the chair behind his desk.

"Is there?" Jason said, collapsing into his seat. "Because I'm all out of ideas."

"We could double-cross them." Deacon moved into the seat opposite him and scooted to the edge.

Jason frowned. "You just argued that if they suspect a double-crossing, they'll take Ari away and we'll never see her again—"

"I'm not talking about getting the cops involved. Hear me out." Excitement rippled through Deacon as an idea formed in his mind. "You're putting the cash in a briefcase, right?"

"Yes . . ." His voice sounded hesitant.

"What if, instead of taking it to the loan shark, you head out back to my bike and we drive away with the money?" Deacon became more animated, waving his hands in the air as he spoke. "We'll have five million from Perconti Enterprises and five million from your company. The gig would be clean. Just like old times. We'd be able to start over and—"

"You're kidding me, right?"

Deacon stopped and stared at his brother. "No, I thought—"

Jason held up his hand in the air. "I'm not walking out on Ari. She needs me."

"But don't you see how beautiful this is? You can take five million of your rival's money, and five million from your investors. We both know how to go under the radar. We'll assume new identities and—"

"No."

"But—"

"I said no." Jason's firm tone had a note of finality to it. "I'm not leaving her, Deacon, and there is more to life than money."

Deacon stared at his brother as a sense of hopelessness welled up inside of him. "You just don't get it, do you?"

"Get what?"

"Whatever happened to blood is thicker than water?"

"What do you mean?"

"All I ever wanted was to be important to you." And it was the truth. He'd dump all of this revenge nonsense in a heartbeat if Jason would just treat him like a brother again.

"You *are* important to me. I gave you a home—"

"You walked away from our business without warning. Even employees give a company two weeks before they leave. You didn't give me two hours."

"Because I had to get away from Felicia. You know that. Her narcissism had taken a dark turn and I couldn't deal with it anymore."

"I could have helped you escape Felicia. You didn't have to leave me, too."

"It wasn't just Felicia." Jason let out a long breath. "The business hadn't felt right for a long time. I felt lost, Deacon. I needed to find myself again."

"We could have done something to make it work." Deacon inched forward. "I miss you, Jason. Remember the fun we used to have together?"

"We could have that again, you know," Jason said. "But you need to stop using people, Deacon. You need to stop trying to devise ways to con people out of their livelihoods."

"Isn't that what you do? Buy up people's ideas and profit from them?"

"These people need money to continue their work. Sometimes I just let them borrow money. Sometimes, they recognize that I can take their product further than they could on their own. In those cases we enter a partnership. I never cheat people, and I never buy ideas outright unless it's something the person wants." Jason straightened and patted him on the shoulder. "At the end of the day, manipulating people will leave you empty. Helping them achieve their dreams is much more fulfilling."

"As long as you profit from it." Deacon took a step back, out of his brother's reach. "I'm sorry Jason, I just don't see the difference."

"There's a huge difference."

Deacon snorted. "This is all temporary. It could be gone in a moment's notice." He waved his hands between them. "This is real, brother. I'm real, and you've been ignoring me for years."

"Deacon, I haven't been ignoring you. You've been going underground with your fighting and gambling. I can't be a part of that."

"No, not when you have such a good racket going on all by yourself." Deacon took a deep breath and tried to steady his rising temper. "Good luck saving your pretty girlfriend. I hope she's worth it." He stormed out of the office before Jason could reply and marched down to the garage. Grabbing his helmet, he shoved it on his head and sped away from the hotel, the city, and anything that reminded him of his brother.

Things weren't going the way he'd planned, and he needed some time to think.

Chapter 21

"Are you okay?" Leo asked. "Perhaps I should—"

"No, I'm fine." Jason took a deep breath in and let it out. Leo had wanted to have Jason come with him in his limo, but Jason argued that the loan shark would be expecting him to come alone. Besides, they didn't want to appear intimidating. The most important thing was Ari's safety. Once she was out of harm's way, then all bets were off.

"You can do this," Leo said as he put his hand on Jason's shoulder. "Sabrina placed the suitcase and cell phone in the men's room about an hour before they arrived. All you need to do is to go in there and pick it up. One phone call, and I'll have my men storm the place."

Jason nodded. "I know." He shook his hands out, as if he was getting ready for a prizefight, not a negotiation. "I'm hoping I won't need it. Hopefully this Burke person is reasonable."

"I can't understand why your brother would do that to you," Karin said from her place at Leo's side. Leo had forbid her to come along, citing that it was too dangerous, which only made her want to come more. He had eventually agreed to bring her, but only if she promised to stay out of harm's way.

"I thought I told you to stay in the limo," Leo growled at her.

"I wanted to show my support," she said, turning to Jason.

"You aren't mad at me?"

"For screwing around behind my back?" She slid her arm around Leo's. "No. If I never left Stone Suites, I never would have come to work at Perconti Enterprises. I never would have met Leo or his wonderful family."

Pain sliced through Jason as Karin cast a loving gaze at Leo. He had seen Ari look at him like that, dozens of times. He just wished that he'd known what a good thing he had when he had the chance.

"Besides," she said as she refocused on Jason. "I don't like to live in the past."

"Neither do I," Leo said. "You get my sister back, Stone, and we'll have a clean slate."

"That's very generous of you."

"It just shows how much I care about my sister."

Jason's thoughts drifted to Deacon. He couldn't help it. How he wished that he and Deacon had shared a close bond like Ari and her siblings. Deacon was probably long gone by now, traveling down the East Coast to somewhere warm and filled with lonely widows. Once again, the last words they had spoken to each other had been in anger.

Life was odd sometimes. For years, he had been sparring with Leo and his family, figuring out ways to squeeze them of money so that he could come out ahead in business. Now, here Leo was, supporting him in his time of need. Sure, he was concerned about Ari, but he was willing to work with him, not against him, and he seemed concerned about his welfare, too. The difference between Leo and Deacon was striking, and made Jason realize just how self-centered his brother really was.

"I don't know what to say," he said. "I truly don't deserve all of this support after the terrible things I have done to your family."

Leo twisted his lips into a half-smile. "Just get my sister back, and we'll call it even."

Jason nodded. The Percontis were counting on him, and he could make a real difference in their lives. This was what life was all about—bonding with and improving the lives of others. Not living from one adrenaline rush to the next. For years he had been chasing the next high, hoping to outrun any true emotions. Now, in this moment, he suddenly realized how empty his life had become.

His life didn't have to stay empty, however. He had the power to change things for the better. Starting by saving the woman he loved.

They went over the final plans. Jason was to go in alone, and Leo would stay outside the restaurant, just in case they were keeping Ari somewhere close by. If it became apparent that Burke wouldn't negotiate, Jason would go into the bathroom to retrieve the money and check in. If Leo didn't find her, then Jason would give the loan shark the money. If she was safe, then all bets were off.

Since it was her restaurant, Sabrina was already inside, behind the bar. The goons had paid her well to close the restaurant down a little early and for her to keep quiet. They weren't aware of her connection to the Percontis. If they were, Jason was sure they would have met at another venue.

Jason glanced at his watch. "Okay, it's showtime." After one last "good luck" they each headed back to their cars, and Jason climbed into his McLaren. His hands shook as he put his favorite vehicle into gear and drove it the two blocks down to the restaurant.

He parallel parked and stepped out onto the sidewalk.

Immediately, two of the loan shark's men emerged from the shadows of the restaurant and told him to put his hands on the car.

"You both look familiar," Jason observed as the larger man patted him down. "Any chance you could just give me the girl?"

"Afraid not. Where's the money?"

"Somewhere safe. I need to talk to your boss first." He hesitated, then added, "You could come work for me, you know. I'd pay double whatever you're getting."

Satisfied that Jason was unarmed, the larger man stepped back. "There are some things in this world more precious than money."

Jason turned around to face them. "Whatever this loan shark has over you, I can make it right."

The older man chuckled. "You and your brother are a lot alike, you know that? He had no idea who he was dealing with, either. He learned soon enough, though. So will you." He led Jason up to the front door of the restaurant.

As he walked, Jason turned over the men's words in his head. The men hinted at a connection between Deacon and the loan shark that he wasn't aware of. Had his brother held something back from him?

Jason was missing something, some giant piece of the puzzle, but then his thoughts scattered as the larger man opened the door and ushered him inside. A quick glance around told him that Sabrina stood behind the bar, wiping the same spot on the counter again and again with a dishrag. She nodded to him, then motioned over to the far corner of the room. The loan shark was sitting down at one of the booths. She sat away from the light, so it was difficult to make out her features. Her bodyguards sat on either side of her.

Wait a minute . . . "A woman?" Jason asked the man beside him. "This loan shark is a woman?"

"Not only a woman, but one of the most powerful women in the northeast."

"A businesswoman? Why haven't I heard of her then?"

"She works under a fake masculine-sounding name so she gets more respect." The men led Jason toward the table where she sat. Uneasiness rippled down his spine with each step. As Jason came closer, the shadows dispersed, and a very familiar face looked up to greet him.

"Jason." Felicia smiled and motioned to the seat across from her. "So nice for you to join us."

"Felicia Killington," Jason said on an exhale.

"Oh, I haven't gone by that name in a long, long time. I go by my maiden name now. Burke sounds much stronger, don't you think?"

Jason felt dizzy as he was led to the seat across from her. "How . . ."

"I've been a busy girl since you ran away from me." She patted his hand. "We have a lot of catching up to do."

Jason pulled his hand away and straightened in his chair. "Our relationship ended years ago."

"I'm sorry to hear that." She glanced at something behind him and the two guards who had brought him over inched in closer.

"Why are you doing this? You know who I am. You *must* be aware that I'd never rack up such a large gambling debt."

"Of course you wouldn't do such a thing, but your brother did." She waved her hand in the air in dismissal. "And he proved to me that he had access to your money many times over."

"But he doesn't have access."

Felicia smiled. "So you say."

He'd had about enough of her games. "What do you really want from me, Felicia?" Jason asked.

"Ms. Burke. You lost the right to call me Felicia when you stopped playing my favorite bedroom games."

Jason locked his jaw as he remembered how she liked to use the flogger and the St. Andrew's cross in her basement. "Is that what this is all about? You want me to sleep with you again?"

Felicia laughed. "Don't flatter yourself. I've moved on, and my new lover is much better equipped to handle me than you were." She considered him for a moment. "You were the only one who got close enough to hurt me, Jason." She tapped her long, manicured fingernails on the table. "Not even my poor, deceased husband was able to cause me such grief."

"Your husband was a good man. He'd roll over in his grave if he had any idea what you have done with his investments."

"They are my investments now, not his, and my husband was afraid to take risks. Now, the company is under new—and better—ownership."

"I never meant to hurt you. You have to believe that. The relationship had run its course."

"But you *did* hurt me, Jason. And now it's my turn to hurt you."

Jason pushed back his panic and tried to clear his head. "Arianna is innocent and you know it."

"She's the object of your affections, sweetheart, and therefore a pawn. Now." She leaned over the table and took his hands in hers. "Let's talk about your debt to me."

"I don't have any debt."

"Ah, but your name is on the papers now, isn't it?"

Jason ground his teeth. "Someone forged my name. I'll be able to prove in court that—"

"Details, and this will never make it to court, not if you value your woman." She squeezed his fingers. "If you come back to me, I'll forgive your little slight, and you can keep your money."

"I thought you didn't want me back."

"Not in a relationship, of course, but on my team." She waved her hand around them. "Swear your allegiance to me, give me half of your earnings in your business, and in exchange, I will offer you your girl and protection."

"Protection from what?"

When she smiled, her features turned sickly sweet. "From me, sweetheart."

"You can't do anything to me." Jason pulled his hands from hers and sat back. "And I can't possibly have anything you want."

"That's where you're wrong, darling. I want what you took from me—my money, my pride, and my influence."

"I didn't take anything from you. You lost it when news surfaced about your stay in a mental institution."

"And whose fault was that?" She leaned back in her seat and crossed her arms. "You can't tell me that the information just happened to come out all by itself, and no one knew about my little stay except my poor deceased husband, your brother, and you."

"Deacon must have—"

"Stop blaming your brother for your faults. It's unbecoming." She leaned her elbows on the table and toyed with the stack of gold bracelets on her arm. "All I wanted from you was a little respect, Jason. Not once did you think about my needs. All you wanted to do was to manipulate me into giving you what you wanted. And I gave it all to you—my knowledge, my connections . . ."

"I'm a different person now. I've changed."

"Have you?" She raised her brows. "I wonder if we asked that woman I have in back if she feels you take her seriously. I wonder, if we learned of her aspirations and dreams, if they would be a surprise to you." She hesitated for a moment and nodded. "You haven't changed, Jason

Stone. Your eyes give everything away. You are hurting that poor girl, manipulating her to stay with you so you can get what you want from her."

A chill rippled through Jason's body as the loan shark's words hit a little too close to home. "What could she possibly give me that I couldn't get myself?" Jason adjusted his cuff links. "I assure you, I'm no longer the poor boy who worshipped at your feet. I have my own money and influence—"

She narrowed her gaze. "Money and influence you stole from me."

"That I created myself."

Felicia waved her hand in the air in dismissal. "It doesn't matter. The woman gives you something else."

"What?"

She considered him for a moment. "Sex."

"I could have sex with anyone."

She tightened her jaw. "Yes, I suppose you could." She signaled Sabrina to come fill her glass of water. Tension filled the air as the redheaded waitress moved next to Jason and poured from a pitcher into a glass. She caught his gaze, held it, but for the life of him, Jason couldn't figure out what Sabrina was trying to tell him. Within moments, she glanced at the men's room and moved away.

She's telling me to get help. Jason realized that he was getting nowhere on his own. If they'd ever have hope of getting Ari back, then he needed to be smarter, less confrontational. He fisted his hands under the table as he thought about what the loan shark had said. He had never considered the fact that Ari might be putting aside her own aspirations to give him what he wanted. While she had said that she had never wanted anything more than sex, she might not have meant it, or fully understood what she was getting into. He had spent his entire life manipulating people, and didn't know any other way to behave in a relationship. He might have inadvertently manipulated Ari into something she didn't really want.

The realization filled him with self-loathing. His relationship with Ari had been one-sided. She was always meeting him on his terms, doing things his way. Even when she asked to stay in his home, he'd manipulated her into staying at the hotel, then used her as an escape from his problems.

Jason swore that if he ever got himself and Ari out of this mess, he'd listen to her more, perhaps do something grand to make it up to her.

"What do you want from me, Felicia?" he asked.

The woman shook her head. "I already told you—your money. With that, I can restore my husband's company to its former glory."

Jason knew it would take a lot more than some quick cash to salvage that sinking ship. She had been mentally unstable for far too long. Things were in disarray. It would take a strong hand to put all of the pieces back together.

"Deacon tried to give your goons the money. They never showed up."

"You're lying to me, just like you did when we were together. Now give me back what's mine."

Jason started to tell her where she could shove her money, but then stopped. This was getting him nowhere.

"Fine, I have the money, but I need some assurances that Ari is okay first."

She raised her brows. "You want assurances, but what assurances do I have that you have brought the money?" She glanced at his feet. "I specifically asked for cash, and unless you are hiding one-hundred-dollar bills in your pants—"

"I have the money, not on me, but close by."

"Close by." Her voice revealed her skepticism.

"It's in the restaurant."

"My men have searched this restaurant."

"Not all of it." He leaned on the table and placed his finger on the hard surface to emphasize his point. "You can have your money, but I want to know that Ari is safe first."

She tilted her head to the side for a moment and considered him. "Very well." She waved her hand in the air and one of her goons produced a cell at her side. She punched in some numbers and then waited for the other person to pick up.

"It's me. We want to talk to the girl." She hesitated for a few moments, then added, "Well, make sure it doesn't happen." She handed Jason the phone. "You have sixty seconds."

Jason noticed that his hand shook as he took the phone from her. "Ari?"

There was a brief moment of silence, and then a weak voice rose up from the other end of the line. "Jason?"

"Ari, is that you?"

"Oh, Jason! Where are you? Get me out of here."

"Are you all right?"

"I—I think so, but these men, they keep looking at me, like they want to . . ."

"Calm down. It will all be over in a moment. Where are you?"

"Oh, Jason, please hurry, I—"

Felicia pulled the phone away. "Time's up."

Jason stared, dumbstruck, as she put the phone away. "Now, where's my money?"

"I'll get it in a moment. I just need to use the men's room first." Tension built as Felicia's gaze narrowed on him. "If you don't mind," he added.

"Alex, go with him," she commanded.

Jason was about to protest, but realized that he had no choice. Slowly he stood and walked to the bathroom with the younger guard in tow.

With each step, his mind worked over what to do. He had to get rid of the guard, but how? They walked past the bar, where Sabrina was still cleaning the counter. She nodded to Jason as he passed in reassurance.

"Hey, big boy," she called out. "Could you help me lift something for a moment?"

The guard hesitated, and Jason kept walking, not wanting to draw attention to himself.

"Come on," Sabrina said. "It will just take a few seconds."

"Okay, but better make it quick."

Jason glanced over his shoulder and saw the guard move toward Sabrina. It would only buy him a minute or two, but it would have to be enough. Jason rushed to the bathroom, eager to get this whole mess over with so he could hold Ari in his arms once more.

Chapter 22

Jason opened the men's room door and quickly slipped inside. Remembering Leo's instructions, he moved to the end of the long line of sinks and opened the lid on the trash container. Inside, as promised, was the briefcase and a small cell phone. Jason quickly grabbed the suitcase and checked the money. Satisfied that it was all there, he placed the suitcase on the counter and slid his finger across the phone's screen.

"What the hell?" The phone's screen remained blank. He tried it a second time, and then a third. Still, there was nothing.

"It's busted."

Jason looked up and saw his brother leaning against the wall close to the stalls. He had crossed his arms and was studying Jason intently.

"How?" Jason asked.

"I don't know." He straightened away from the wall. "I tried calling your friends, but it wouldn't work."

Shit. "How the hell did you get in here?" Jason asked, crossing over to him.

Deacon nodded toward the window. "I slipped in up there. No one saw me. When I peeked out and saw you having trouble, I tried to call for backup." He glanced at the phone in Jason's hand. "You'd think that they'd check the phone before they dropped it off."

Jason tossed the phone in the garbage. "What are you doing? I told you to stay away."

"I'm here in case things go wrong." He fisted his hands and bumped Jason's shoulder. "If things turn south, you're going to need all of the help you can get."

"That's what Leo's for."

"Yeah, and he's done a stellar job so far, don't you think?" He frowned at the trash bin. "My guess is that he's double-crossed you."

"Leo would never abandon me, not when his sister's in danger."

"Is she really in danger?"

"I told you, I talked to her on the phone." Jason grabbed the briefcase off the counter. "I don't have time for this." He started to push by his brother, but Deacon put up his hand, stopping him.

"Think about what you're doing—and who you're dealing with."

"I know very well who I'm dealing with. Felicia is a monster who is set on getting revenge on me for something I didn't do. And she has Ari."

"No." Deacon shook his head and tightened his grip. "Felicia is a businessperson."

"She's insane. She spent months in a mental institution after having a nervous breakdown."

"Because her husband never paid attention to her. Think about it, Jason. She's just looking for attention."

"She has a funny way of going about it."

"Stop and think for a minute. If these thugs were really out to hurt you, do you think you'd still be walking around? Do you honestly think Felicia cares about your girl?"

He had a point. "What are you getting at?"

Deacon lowered his hands. "It's a bluff." He glanced at the suitcase. "I bet if we were to take that suitcase and climb out that window right there, they'd let the girl go."

"I'm not following." Jason tightened his grip on the suitcase.

"Wow—it's been a long time since you've been in the game, hasn't it?" Deacon shook his head. "She doesn't want Ari. She wants you. Your money, your attention. Felicia has always been all bark, no bite."

"So?"

"So . . . How do you con a con artist?" He pressed his finger on the top of the suitcase, emphasizing his point. "With a better con."

"I don't get it."

"We take the money and run." Deacon nodded his head. "There's plenty in there, far more than we need to set up new identities and a new life."

"We've already been through this. I told you, I don't do that anymore."

"Jason."

"No." Jason dragged the suitcase off the counter. "I'm not bargaining with Ari's life."

"They won't kill her. The only reason why Felicia is interested in her is because you're showing an interest in her. As soon as you demonstrate that this girl means nothing to you, Felicia will let her go. She's not a monster."

"Could have fooled me." Jason started toward the door. "I'm not taking that chance."

"Think about what you're doing. We could get away and start over. It will be like old times, just you and me against the world."

"No, I can't. It's too risky." Jason placed his hand on the door.

"Where's the ambitious, adrenaline junkie I used to know? He's in there somewhere—I just know it."

Jason hesitated, then dropped his hand.

"Think, Jason. If you go out that door, then sure, you'll get the girl, and all of the boring, dull things that come with a steady relationship. She'll want a commitment, types like her always do. She'll want reassurances and fancy things. She'll make you into her slave."

"No."

"Yes. Perhaps she won't flog you in the bedroom, but she'll scar you just the same. Women like to manipulate people, Jason." He started to close the distance between them. "No one knows that better than us. Hell, you ran away from Felicia because she was starting to get too intense. This is no different."

"It's completely different, Deacon."

"How?"

Jason couldn't put it into words. There was something special about Ari. She had something Felicia didn't, something no other woman could give him. All she had to do was be herself.

"It's just different," he murmured.

"The only way to survive is to beat them at their own game." He placed his hand on Jason's shoulder. "Come with me, brother. Leave all of this behind. We'll become like leaves in the wind and no one will be able to find us. We'll go wherever we want, do whatever we want. There will be no responsibility, no routine. We'll do whatever strikes our fancy."

Jason looked at his brother's smiling face for a long time, remembering all of the adventures that they had gone through together.

"We had some good times, didn't we?" Deacon asked as he inched closer. "We could have that all again." He placed his hand on Jason's shoulder. "I miss you, bro. Come back to me. Come back to us."

They'd had good times, yes, but at what cost? They

had lied and manipulated people. Jason had assumed personalities like a chameleon, burying his own emotions so deep that he didn't know who he was anymore.

Ari had changed that for him. Now, not only did he know who he was, but what direction he was going. There was comfort in that, as there was comfort in forming real friendships with the Percontis. He wasn't sure what was going on with the phone, but Leo wouldn't leave him high and dry. It wasn't his style. All of his life, Jason had trusted his gut and it had never steered him wrong. His gut was telling him to make the exchange and ensure Ari's safety, so that was what he was going to do.

"I'm sorry, Deacon, but I can't. I'm not the person you think I am." He reached out and pulled open the door. "Not anymore."

Before Deacon could protest, Jason left the bathroom with the suitcase. No matter what happened next, he was going to stay true to himself. He owed that not only to Ari, but to his new friends. Deacon was right about one thing. Jason was going to start a new life, just not the life that his brother had envisioned for them.

Ari sat in the back of the large van, trying to get comfortable in her tight bindings. At least they hadn't blindfolded or gagged her this time.

"There he is," one of the guys in the front of the van said as he pointed to something moving on the screen.

"It's amazing how well she predicted all of this."

"I thought you told Jason to come alone," Ari said.

One of the men, the one with the bald head and a round face, turned and flashed her a frown. For a moment, Ari thought that he would try and gag, her, but the planets must have aligned in her favor, because he decided instead to answer her question.

"It looks as if your boyfriend didn't listen. Your brother is poking around in an alley next to the restaurant."

"What? Leo's here?"

"It looks as if he's waiting for something." The other man chuckled.

"A phone call perhaps?" The two men grinned at each other.

Ari leaned forward and stared at the small screen the men held between them. "What's that?"

"Surveillance. We set it up before they arrived," the bald man said.

"I'm surprised that Sabrina let you do that to her restaurant."

"She doesn't know."

"What do you mean? How could she not know that you were setting up cameras in her restaurant?"

"She already had the cameras. We just altered them so that we get the feed as well." The bald man exchanged glances with his younger friend. "And it's amazing what people will believe."

"You lied to her?"

The bald man grinned. "Not us, pretty lady, but your friend."

"What? What do you mean, my friend?"

"There he is now," the younger guy said, pointing to the screen.

"Deacon. He's in on this?" She should have known.

"He's the one who's behind the whole thing." The younger man chuckled, which got him a jab in the ribs from the older man in front.

"What?" the younger guy said, rubbing his ribs. "It's not like it matters. By the time he gets in there, it will all be over."

The older man rolled his eyes. "Just keep your mouth shut."

They sat in silence for a time as they all watched Jason stroll in and sit down in front of the loan shark.

This was a trap, she realized. A carefully calculated plan set up by Deacon to rob Jason blind. His brother had orchestrated this whole thing from the beginning. Ari sat back in her seat and tried to wrap her head around what could make someone so thoroughly betray his own flesh and blood.

She had to warn Jason. That meant that she had to get out of the van and into the restaurant.

"How do Deacon and your boss know each other?" she asked. She didn't really care, but she wanted to keep the men talking. If she could distract them, perhaps she could find something sharp to help her out of these bindings.

"Deacon and his brother tried to steal money from Felicia years ago."

"Back when they were nothing more than a couple of con men," the other agreed.

"Our boss was too smart, however. She caught them and decided that instead of confronting them, she'd make them pay."

Ari found a set of keys on the seat across from her. It wasn't much, but perhaps the jagged end could help her get through the bindings. She picked up the keys and rubbed them against the zip tie holding her hands behind her back.

"Make them pay, how?" she asked.

"By destroying them, of course," the older one said. "She thinks the Stone brothers robbed her of her wealth. She won't stop until they're both destitute."

"And she won't stop with money. Family, friends . . . she wants to take everything away from them."

"Just like they took everything from her."

"When Deacon discovered what she was up to, he gave her an offer she couldn't refuse," the younger one said. "He would help her get Jason, if she'd leave him alone."

"That explains why Deacon is helping her, but why are you two helping her?" she asked, wondering if there was something she could leverage against her freedom. "If it's money—"

"She's giving the signal," the older one said. Silently both men left the front of the cab.

"Wait, come back. I swear I can help you if you help me."

The back doors of the van opened. "There's nothing you can give us, child," the older one said. "Nothing anyone can give us." Both men moved as one as they grabbed her elbows, hauled her out of the van, and dragged her into the restaurant.

The young guard put the rest of the money back into the suitcase and looked up at his boss. "It's all there, Ms. Burke."

Felicia nodded and pointed to the back door. "Then go get her." The room fell silent as the man set the suitcase by her side and moved to go get Ari. Footsteps echoed along the hardwood floors, grating on Jason's nerves. He wished that they would just get on with it already. The sooner Ari was back in his arms, the better.

Muffled cries rose up from outside, causing panic to shoot up through Jason's chest. He straightened in his chair, but one of the loan shark's bodyguards put a hand on his shoulder, keeping him still. Jason shot a glance out the window, but couldn't see anything. He knew that Leo was out there, somewhere. Hopefully he had a handle on the situation and could get Ari to safety.

"If you harm one hair on that poor woman's head . . ."

The loan shark laughed. "Don't worry, my dear. I wouldn't harm your little plaything. Although she does have a certain charm." She tapped her lips with a well-manicured finger. "I can see why you like her. She has a lot of spunk." She tilted her head and considered him for a moment. "My offer still stands. I'll forgive your debt if you come and work for me. I'll even let your little woman come, too."

"I have my own business, Felicia."

"For now."

What the hell was that supposed to mean? Jason went to ask, but then the door opened and a furious and gagged woman stumbled into the room ahead of the thug who had left moments ago.

"Ari." Jason started to stand, but was shoved back into his seat. "Hey."

"Be patient, my dear." Felicia waved her hand and motioned for the thug to bring Ari to the table. Her eyes went wide when she saw Jason. She tried to say something, but couldn't through the gag.

"Did you really have to do that?"

Felicia smiled. "Like I said, your girl has a lot of spunk. I had to tie her mouth and hands for my people's safety."

"That's ridiculous."

Felicia shook her head. "You haven't changed a bit, have you, darling? Very well. I will remove the gag, but I'll tell you now that you won't like what she has to say."

The loan shark waved her hand, signaling her follower to remove the gag. As soon as he did, Ari started coughing and sputtering.

"Ari, are you all right?" Jason asked.

"It's a trap." Ari's voice sounded hoarse and strained. She had to say the sentence twice before Jason understood her.

"A trap?"

"You didn't pay her, did you?" Ari asked.

"It was a condition of your release. I should have paid it long ago. I'm so sorry." He reached out for Ari, but she shrunk back.

"Get it back."

"What are you talking about?"

"The money, get it back."

"I can't do that." He shook off the goon behind him and went to Ari's side. The men around the room started closing in, but Felicia waved them away, just like she always did. It sickened him how she made human beings into her playthings. Hopefully, within the hour they would be done with her and would never have to deal with her ever again.

"Forget about the money. It's not important." He rubbed Ari's arms and searched her face for signs of abuse. "Are you okay? Did she hurt you?"

"Jason, listen to me." She grabbed his shirt and yanked him close. "She's after revenge, not settling some gambling debt. She wants to ruin you."

"What do you mean, ruin me?"

"She means that Felicia wants to humiliate you, and cause you to lose credibility with your investors and the press," Deacon said as he came out of the shadows and stood at Felicia's side. "It's one of the many things we have in common."

Chapter 23

"Deacon." Jason shoved Ari behind him and shifted his gaze between Felicia and his brother. "What are you doing?"

"I offered you an escape."

"I couldn't leave Ari and Leo—"

Deacon held up the phone from the bathroom between them. "This Leo?" He shook his head and studied the phone. "Too bad he got sent on a wild-goose chase."

"How?"

Deacon returned his focus to Jason. "Turns out the phone wasn't broken after all. It was just low on batteries." He swiped the screen, and the phone lit up in his hand. "Someone drained them, I'm afraid. Good thing I had a charger on me." He dropped the phone to the floor and stepped on it with the heel of his boot, crushing the screen. "Now it's broken."

"This is a new low, Deacon, even for you."

Deacon shook his head. "You should have taken my advice and left when you had the chance, bro."

"You wanted me to abandon my company, my friends, and the woman I love."

"Love?" Ari asked. Jason ignored her.

"And in exchange I was offering you something better.

Life, excitement, unpredictability." He shook his head in disgust. "Remember when old lady Crosby came home and found us eating her brownies in her kitchen? How we jumped out the window and through her garden while she chased us with a stick?"

"We were ten and seven."

"We were wild. And then, when we got older, we took that priceless piece of art out from under Mrs. Holmes's nose. And she thanked us for it." He shook his head. "That was amazing."

"It was stealing."

"You convinced her that the abstract would be better suited in your hands than hers. What did you say?" He paused and pretended to think. "Oh yes, it would be more appreciated in your museum, rather than in some private living room. As an art appraiser, you know just the people to make sure that the painting will be seen and appreciated by thousands."

"I was a different person back then." Jason glanced at Ari, who was staring at him with wide eyes. "And I gave her money for the painting."

"Despite her refusal. The woman gave you the painting willingly. It was money in the bank."

"It was handed down through her family. It wasn't right." He fisted his hands at his sides.

"You've changed, brother, and not for the better. It used to be that you'd get so excited about the prospect of running a con. Now . . . now you may drive fast cars and hang out with fast women, but your life has gotten stale and boring."

"My life is what I want it to be. No one can change that, Deacon. Not even you."

"Oh, I think I already did," he said as he put his hand on the back of the loan shark's chair. "After you left me to pick up the pieces with Felicia, we came to an understanding.

We've been working together for quite a number of years, my friend, the fruition of which we didn't see until today." He picked up the suitcase beside her and ran his hand over the side. "Ten million. One million for each year we have been apart." He turned his angry gaze to Jason. "One million for each year I was forced to fend for myself."

"Not so fast." Felicia plucked the suitcase from Deacon's fingers and motioned to her thugs. "Don't worry, my friend." She patted his cheek. "We shall reap the fruits of our labor soon. First, we have a few more appointments to keep."

"You won't get away with this," Jason said as she picked up the briefcase.

The loan shark raised her brows. "It's always the same with you men. You're all about who wins." She let out a long breath. "Rest assured, I have thought of every angle. Even as we speak, my people are leaking to the papers how you have been hiding Ari from her family, lavishing her with gifts while your business suffers."

"I've done no such thing." Jason glanced out the window, wondering what had happened to Leo.

Felicia scoffed. "Like I said, we have a lot of appointments to keep. Shall we?"

"It's not too late to change your mind," Jason said to Deacon as Felicia led her thugs to the door. "You don't have to follow her."

"And if I don't follow her? What then?"

Jason shrugged. "You can come and stay with me."

Deacon shook his head. "And continue to be talked down to and brushed aside? Sorry, but I think I'll pass." He turned to go.

"Why Felicia, Deacon?"

He glanced over his shoulder. "Why?"

"I mean, I get why you hate me, but why follow her after everything she's done to us?"

"Because she treats me like family, Jason. She cares for me, which is more than I can say for my own flesh and blood."

Jason swallowed the lump in his throat and watched him leave the building. Within seconds, the sound of engines revving filled the air as the group made their getaway.

Seconds later, Leo burst inside the restaurant. "Did they leave?"

"I'm afraid so," Jason said, pulling Ari close. "What's on your head?"

Leo winced as he touched the cut on his temple. "Deacon called and told me he found something in the alley out back. I went to check it out and someone struck me in the head. When I came to, I saw the cars pulling away." He scanned the restaurant until his gaze settled on his sister. "Ari." He rushed forward and enveloped her in a bear hug. "I thought I'd never see you again."

"It's okay, Leo. Jason saved me."

Leo flashed Jason a skeptical look. "I wanted to be there for you."

"Where is she?" Dante said as he stormed inside. Marco quickly followed.

"God, you guys run faster than the wind," Sabrina said as she and Karin brought up the rear. At Jason's questioning glance, she explained. "I called them for backup, but it took them a while to get here. I stumbled into Karin as she was looking for Leo."

"He had been gone longer than expected and—oh my God!" She hurried to Leo. "What happened to you?"

"I'm fine, *cara*." He jerked his head away from her touch. "It's just a scratch."

"It looks like more than a scratch."

Jealousy rippled over Jason as he stepped back and let the siblings hug each other and fuss over Leo's wound. They had this easy manner with each other, as if nothing stood between them. All of his life, he had strived for that with Deacon, but somehow, it was never meant to be. Lately, he had been so concerned with preventing people from finding out about his past that he never allowed himself to get close to anyone. As a result, he had been missing out on some of the best parts of life.

"What happened in here while I was out?" Leo asked Jason in an effort to draw the attention away from his wound.

Jason relayed the events of the past hour. "So she got away with the money. I'm sorry, Leo."

Leo smiled and slapped him on the back. "You got my sister back, that's all that matters." He put his arm around Jason's shoulder and led him into the group.

"Thanks, man," Dante said as he extended his hand.

"Yeah, thanks. I don't know what we would have done without our girl here," Marco said.

"I'd be outnumbered, for one," Karin said as she threaded her arm around Ari. "Thank goodness you're back, Ari. It was tough managing all of these men on my own."

As they laughed and fell into an easy banter, Jason realized that the Perconti siblings accepted him as one of their own. After all of the snide remarks, after all of the fighting for control of businesses, the Percontis were treating him as an equal. Even Karin, whom he had tossed to the curb, seemed to accept him into the inner circle.

Then again, watching her interact with Leo, it was obvious why she'd forgiven Jason. She had moved on, and judging by Leo's possessive arm around her side, she had made the right choice. As his gaze settled on Ari, he realized that he wanted the same for himself. Unfortunately,

Ari was now back with her family, and he wasn't sure if she needed him as much as he needed her.

Ari watched Jason with her brothers and her heart warmed. Despite being on opposite sides of the fence in business, they had managed to come together for a common cause—her. She hoped that this comradery would extend beyond clearing their names and getting back their money. Jason had offered to reimburse Leo and her family for the money, but her brothers wouldn't hear of it. They knew to what lengths Jason had gone, putting his own life at risk in order to save their sister. They agreed that they would work together to get the money and reputations back. If they all made a united front, they should be able to squash rumors pretty quickly and boost the confidence of their investors. They all agreed that Ms. Burke probably wouldn't be back, now that she had what she wanted, but they'd keep feelers out if either she or Deacon showed their faces in Boston again.

None of them touched on why Ari had been staying at Stone Suites in the first place, or why Jason was the first person she ran to when she felt she could no longer go through with her wedding. She knew that this would have to be dealt with at some point, and Leo probably wouldn't approve of her answers, but that was a battle for another day. For now, Ari decided that she'd take Jason's advice and stop worrying about the future and enjoy this moment, or what was left of it.

Sabrina had declared the rescue mission a victory, despite the loan shark getting away with a good chunk of change. Within the hour, she had large pasta dishes, salad, and sauce served as an impromptu celebration. Others were invited, and soon the restaurant was filled with family and friends. Dean Martin and Frank Sinatra—her favorite singers—streamed in over the speakers and Ari was surprised to find that Wes and Karin knew all the words. Soon they were singing and laughing, just like a regular old family reunion. Even Sabrina and Dante seemed to hold a fragile truce in order to enjoy the moment. It was amazing to have everyone in one place. Ari felt truly blessed.

"You have an amazing family," Jason said as the party began to wrap up and disperse.

"Thanks," she said.

"I always wondered what it would be like to have siblings who cared about you more than making money."

"Well . . ." She nudged him in the arm. "They seem to like you." She grinned. "They're not your real brothers, but sometimes friends can be closer than siblings."

"Friends, I like that." He brushed his finger under her chin.

"I feel bad about Felicia taking your money and trying to ruin your business. I can't believe that anyone would be so cruel."

He shook his head. "I realized something tonight."

"What?"

"The business, the money, all of it, means nothing."

"You can't possibly mean that."

"Oh, but I do." He inched closer. "Everything I have, everything I've worked for, means nothing if I don't have you." He brushed his fingers over her cheek, sending heat rippling down her spine. "I really thought I was never going to see you again."

She touched his wrist and felt the electricity spark through her veins. "Me, too."

"If anything happened to you . . ." He pressed his lips together as some strong emotion crossed over his features.

"Hey," she said as she inched closer. "I'm still here."

"I know." He glanced over her shoulder. "And I plan to take full advantage of it."

She furrowed her brow. "What do you mean?"

He returned his gaze to hers. "Remember our game?"

She widened her eyes in surprise. "Here? With my family? Jason, I don't—" Before she could finish her sentence, Jason took her hand and tugged her in the direction of the coatroom.

"Jason, stop." She tried to dig in her heels, but he wouldn't be swayed.

"Stop fighting it," he murmured over his shoulder. "You'll make a scene."

"But my family." She glanced around the room at everyone milling around the tables. How much time did they have before someone went to get their coat? Five minutes, ten?

Jason pulled open the door to the coatroom. "Then that will just give you more incentive to win, won't it?" He winked and pulled her into the darkened room, shutting the door behind him.

Chapter 24

Ari started to protest, but Jason kissed her hard, making her insides melt. She molded herself to his body as the fire inside her rose.

"The counter . . ." She gasped as he pulled away for breath.

"Good idea." He grabbed her hand.

"No." She waved to the long, polished counter that connected the coatroom to the rest of the restaurant. "Anyone can see inside."

"Not if we do it right." He pulled her close again and covered her lips with his. His touch was amazing—like fire. It was all too easy to let him take the lead, especially since hours before she hadn't known if she was ever going to see him again.

He wrapped his arms round her waist and edged her back deeper into the coatroom as he invaded her mouth, filling her with his taste. She had no idea what he was planning, nor did she care. As long as they were together, nothing else mattered.

He pulled away from her lips and kissed a long, hot trail along her jaw. Ari leaned back into the coatrack and curled her fingers into his hair as he feasted on her skin.

"Yes," she whispered as he inched lower. "God, Jason."

"I'm never letting you out of my sight again," he whispered against her skin.

Ari shivered as he undid the buttons on her shirt with his teeth. One by one, they popped open with agonizing slowness.

"Jason . . ."

"Shh." He ran his tongue along the canal between her breasts. "Let me enjoy this."

She could hardly argue. She held onto his head and closed her eyes as he created a trail of heat and desire along the curve of her breast.

Suddenly he straightened. "Not good enough."

"What?"

He glanced above her, then pulled a scarf off one of the hangers. Without a word, he took her hand and began securing the scarf to her wrist.

"What are you doing?"

"Cheating."

"Wait a minute . . ." But she was too late. He had already secured both hands behind her back with the scarf.

"This hardly makes the game fair."

He flashed her a wry grin. "I never play fair, you know that." He tugged her shirt out of her skirt and reached around to unclasp her bra.

"Jason—"

He knelt before her and pushed the lacy pink material aside. "Ah, much better." He ran his tongue over one taut nipple, creating lazy circles of heat.

"Oh, God." Ari swallowed and glanced down at his dark head as he flicked and teased her sensitive tip with his tongue.

"Feel good?" he asked.

"Yes." Too good. At this rate she was sure to lose the

game and they both knew it. She had to up the stakes, but how?

Jason shifted his head and worked on the other nipple, making it difficult to think. Spirals of heat danced up through her veins, robbing her limbs of strength. Ari swayed on her feet, and Jason put his hands on her hips to steady her. His quick movement gave her an idea.

"I think I need to sit down," she said.

He eased her onto the bench a short distance away. "Better?" he asked as he straightened.

Ari opened her eyes to find herself at eye level with the fly of his pants. "Much." She reached out and pulled the zipper down with her teeth.

"Now who's cheating?" he asked, but made no move to stop her. Emboldened, Ari grabbed the top of his pants with her teeth and tugged open the button. Jason helped her ease down his clothes until they gathered around his knees. His cock sprang up between them, thick and eager. Ari moistened her lips and then ran her tongue around the tip.

"Wow," he whispered. "I never thought I'd feel those lips again."

She smiled then repeated her movements, running her tongue around the tip and teasing him just like he had moments before.

Jason uttered a low groan, and it was hard for Ari not to smile. This game was going to be like taking candy from a baby. She took him into her mouth, easing down his shaft as far as she could go. Jason shuddered and placed his hands on her temples, holding her steady. Slowly, Ari eased back, running her tongue along the underside of his erection as she did so. Jason shivered as she moved, making her feel beautiful and wanton. As she took him into her mouth once more, she made a low, throaty groan, just loud enough for him to hear.

"You like that, eh?"

She retreated and repeated the movements, moving slightly more quickly. Not having the use of her hands made everything more intense. She concentrated on his salty taste and how he felt in her mouth. With each stroke, his cock swelled. Soon he was undulating against her lips.

"God, Ari." She pushed once more, relaxing her throat so she could take more of him into her mouth. Back and forth, in and out. Ari increased the pace, until Jason curled his fingers into her hair.

"Stop." When she didn't relent, his voice took on a pleading tone. "Ari, please."

She eased away from his body and met his gaze.

"I want to be inside of you when I come." He slipped on a condom and straddled the bench beside her. He kissed her lips and eased her back on the hard surface. Slipping his hands up her skirt, he lingered at her thighs, tickling her slightly as he rubbed them lightly with his fingers. Then he hooked his fingers under the seam of her panties and pulled them off her body.

"I need to taste you."

"No. Jason, that's not fair." He knew how his mouth made her scream.

He flashed her a wicked smile. "I told you, sweetheart, I don't play fair." Ari leaned back helplessly as he lifted her legs in the air and set them on his shoulders. She was trapped, at the wicked billionaire's mercy. Ari closed her eyes as Jason slid his warm tongue over her sensitive folds.

"Oh, God." She lifted her legs off his shoulders and spread them wider, granting him better access.

Jason chuckled and ran his fingers up and down her thighs, imitating the motions he made with his mouth. Up and down, back and forth. The man was relentless. She squirmed and moaned, desperate for more.

"Soon, princess. Soon." He slipped his hands underneath her backside and lifted her up to his eager mouth.

Ari gasped as he assaulted her senses, using both his tongue and teeth to send her desire soaring to new levels. He'd tease her opening, slipping inside just far enough to give her a taste of what was to come, then sweep up and focus on her clit. He knew just where to touch, just how hard to press to drive her wild. Ari's breath came out in short hard gasps as Jason plunged deeper, pushed harder.

"Oh, God. Jason, I'm going to come." She felt her muscles tighten and steeled her jaw against crying out. She wasn't going to lose the game. She wasn't.

Jason adjusted his hands. On the next rotation, he slid his finger inside her opening. Ari saw stars as her orgasm blasted through her body, leaving her light-headed. Again and again he assaulted her senses, causing pleasure to burst through her system again and again.

Ari closed her eyes and soaked it all in, determined not to make a peep. Sweat beaded at her temples as she clamped down on his finger. He felt good, too good. As wave after wave of joy washed through her, she realized he was watching her as he was touching her, waiting for his moment of victory.

"You lose," she whispered when the last ripple of pleasure faded away.

"Not yet." He put down her legs, slipped on a condom, and placed his hands on the edges of the bench, along either side of her head. "Guide me."

"I can't." She smirked. "My hands are tied, remember?"

He swore under his breath, making her laugh, as he positioned himself against her opening. "There." With a swift thrust, he entered her, filling her to the point of breaking.

"God, Ari." He pulled back until only the tip of his cock remained inside of her, then pushed again. Within a few thrusts, Ari felt her desire begin to rise once more.

"Wait," she said as another idea floated through her mind.

"Did I hurt you?"

"No." She lifted her head and kissed him. "Sit up."

He started to move back, but she shook her head. "Take me with you."

Confusion etched his brow, but he wrapped his arms around her and brought them both up into a sitting position. Ari swung her legs over the bench and was thrilled to learn that they rested perfectly on the small stepladder.

"My turn." She used the stepladder to support her weight as she lifted herself off the chair and up his shaft.

"Ari." He clung tighter as she relaxed her legs and sunk back down on his erection until their hips were flush once more.

"Wow."

She repeated the movements, moving herself up and down his cock as if she was enjoying her favorite ride. The sweet friction caused heat to build deep inside her core, and it wasn't long before that heat rose up through her entire body.

"Yes." Jason slid his hands down until one was on her ass and the other on her lower back. "That's it." He helped her move, clinging to her as their bodies came together as one. He tilted his head back and leaned against the wall in between the coats as he locked his gaze with hers.

"You feel so good."

"You do, too."

He moistened his lips and groaned as she moved faster. Tension filled the air, and Ari felt her muscles begin to stretch once more. "Untie me," she pleaded. "I want to touch you."

Untie me . . . Delirious with desire, Jason moved quickly to obey her request. Fuck, she felt so good. This was more than just having sex, more than two bodies coming together. Ari was his everything. He didn't want to be anywhere else, with anyone else.

She braced herself against the wall and moved faster. The conversations in the restaurant fell to a background whisper as he focused on the sweet sound of their bodies coming together. Never before had he felt so connected to anyone. He curled his fingers into her flesh and used his head on the wall as leverage as he began to move with her, desperate to be as deep inside of her as possible.

It wasn't enough. Nothing with Ari was ever enough. As he felt his body begin to race toward oblivion, Jason closed his eyes and let the emotions take control. This was his woman, his moment. He needed more, wanted more. As Ari's soft, feminine whimpers rose up between them, Jason let out a low, throaty moan.

"Ari . . ." He felt the familiar tingling along the base of his spine. "I'm close."

He pushed harder, moved faster as the emotions threatened to rise up and swallow him whole. Suddenly the game was no longer important. Neither was the fact that her family was on the other side of that wall. All that mattered was Ari and this moment, and the fact that he would never be so stupid as to let her get away from him again.

"Arianna," he cried out as his emotions overwhelmed him. His orgasm erupted through his center, causing him to tremble. Passion consumed him as he drove deep into her center. Ari bit her lip hard and shuddered as she spasmed around his cock. The sensation was too much, everything was too much. Jason moaned as his orgasm blasted through his body, rocking him to his core. He filled her again and again, and with each thrust, only one word pounded through his mind. *Mine.*

When the last of his orgasm faded, Jason lifted his head off the wall and buried his head in her shoulder. She held him close and as he struggled to get his breathing under control, he noticed how good she smelled, like flowers and sex. She was soft too, like a welcoming garden where he could rest and feel safe. His sanctuary.

"Is someone in there?"

Jason stiffened at the familiar voice. *Karin.*

"Jason, is that you?"

Ari's body shook against him. He realized she was chuckling.

"Yeah, it's me," he said.

"Leo and I need to go. I was trying to get my coat, but the door's locked. You wouldn't mind handing it to me?"

He cleared his throat. "Sure. What does it look like?" Despite his best efforts, his voice shook with emotion.

"The pink peacoat—with a scarf."

Jason bit back a groan as he realized he had used Karin's scarf to tie up his girlfriend.

Girlfriend. He liked the sound of that.

Ari shifted off his lap and grinned at him like a Cheshire cat. Jason flashed her his best scowl, straightened his clothes, and brought Karin her coat.

"I really hope that's Ari back there with you." Karin smirked as she took the coat from him.

He leaned on the counter, more for support than anything else. Who knew that having sex in a coatroom could be so exhausting? He tried to recover the best he could and gave her a lazy smile. "You know I'm never one to kiss and tell."

"No, you weren't, were you?" She shrugged on her coat. "Leo's is the black one there."

He grabbed it off the rack and handed it to her, then shifted so he stood in her line of vision when he realized that she was using it as an excuse to see around the corner.

Karin tossed Leo's coat over her arm. "Some things never change, I guess."

"What do you mean?"

She flashed him a knowing smile. "You always had an affinity for supply closets and coatrooms."

It took him a moment to realize she was talking about their failed relationship and how he never wanted to be seen with her in public. "Yeah, about that."

She waved her hand in the air between them. "Water under the bridge." She smiled and patted his hand. "Ari means a lot to us, so don't screw it up, okay?"

"She means a lot to me, too."

"I know." She peered over his shoulder. "Good-bye, Arianna."

"Bye." Ari's delicate voice rose up from the back of the coatroom. Karin chuckled as she moved away.

With Karin safely gone, Jason returned to Ari's side to find her completely dressed. "Well, that was unexpected."

"I won." Ari turned from the door to face him. "I won!" She grabbed his sleeves and grinned from ear to ear.

"Now, I don't think—"

"I finally won the game!" She wrapped her arms around his neck and hugged him hard. "It was *you* she heard, not me."

Jason ran his fingers down her spine and cupped her backside. "What can I say? You're irresistible."

"I can't believe I won," she said as she stepped out of his embrace. "How long have we been playing this game?"

"Almost a year."

"And I've never won—until tonight." She giggled, feeling giddy. "What do I get?"

"Excuse me?"

She nibbled her lower lip and took his hand. "Come on, this is a memorable moment. I think I deserve some sort of prize or something, don't you?"

His expression turned hungry as he raked his gaze over

her disheveled frame. "You're right." He squeezed her fingers and pulled her toward the door.

"Where are you taking me?"

"Home."

"To the Palazzo?"

"No, to my apartment, where you belong." He pulled her out of the coatroom, eager to get her back home so he could ravage her properly.

She tugged on his hand, stopping him. "Are you sure? There's no need to protect me anymore, and I know how much you like your privacy."

He stopped and closed the distance between them. "Our privacy," he corrected. "I don't want us to keep anything from each other, not anymore."

She couldn't help but smile. "And if the two of us moving in together becomes routine and boring?"

"Oh, princess . . ." He brushed his lips against hers. "Life with you is never boring." He pulled her toward the door as Ari quickly said good-bye to her family. As soon as he got her outside to his car, he eased her back up against the McLaren and kissed her, hard. Ari's body immediately molded to his as she parted her lips in invitation. He seized the opportunity to touch her chest, her sides, her backside.

"Jason—"

He broke the kiss and opened up the door to his favorite car—his sanctuary. "Come on, beautiful," he said as he ushered her inside. "The sooner we get home, the sooner I can get a rematch."

Ari smirked and ran her finger along his jaw. "Expect to be disappointed."

"We'll see, princess. We'll see."

"Ari!" Jason bellowed as he walked into his sky-rise apartment. "Ari, come quick." He moved into the large, spacious living area and started to put the garment bag down, then thought better of it. Instead he paced the open space, smiling as he passed Ari's collection of princess figurines in the curio cabinet by the window. It was hard to believe that she had moved in ten months ago. Time moved so fast.

"What is it?" she asked as she came out in a bathrobe and with a towel around her head. "I was taking a shower."

"Never mind that. Come over here. I got you a gift."

She flashed him a skeptical look. "A gift?"

"Here, sit." He motioned to the large, cream-colored couch. She moved aside the crimson throw pillows and scooched to the end to make room for him. Instead of sitting, Jason draped the garment bag over the end of the couch and told her to open it.

"What did you do?"

"I got you a present."

"But I thought that we were both watching our spending. My brother lost a lot of money in the wedding and ransom."

"And I lost a lot due to the media dragging my name through the mud. I know. But that's changing."

"Changing, how?"

He shifted from one foot to the next. He felt like a kid on Christmas morning. "Come on, just open it."

"Okay." She shifted her position on the couch. Her robe fell away, exposing her smooth, creamy thigh. Jason bit back a groan as his cock immediately responded to the change in scenery.

"Oh my God, Jason." She stood, taking the dress out of the bag and holding it up. "It's beautiful."

"It's a Cinderella dress," he said as he sat on the arm of the chair.

"It's just like the movie when the fairy godmother changed her rags into a beautiful gown."

"And she went off to the ball to dance with the prince."

She lowered the dress and flashed him a skeptical look. "Yes."

"Well," he said, suddenly nervous. "You're going to a party."

"A party?"

"A celebration of sorts. I wanted you to have something beautiful to wear."

"It certainly is beautiful," she said, admiring the shimmering fabric once more. "But I don't understand." She placed the dress gently on the domino-styled coffee table as Jason moved closer to her on the couch.

"You know how I lost investors and could no longer buy those hotels from your brother in Asia?"

"And you even had to stop renovations and put some of your hotels up for sale to consolidate and focus your business. Yes, we've been through this." She shook her head. "The two of you have been going crazy trying to outdo each other with how much you're saving and how fast you can recover."

He grinned. "What can I say? We're both competitive." But the truth of the matter was that the competition had changed. While they still loved to go at each other in the boardroom, the jibes were more in jest, and the language had softened. After seeing how crazy his sister and Jason were about each other, Leo had forged a fragile friendship with Jason, and while there were still a lot of things to work out, that friendship had been growing stronger every day.

Strong enough for Jason to put the next phase of his plan into action.

Ari smirked. "At least you two aren't going after each other's throats anymore. You were even buying drinks at the bar of my charity event last week."

"All in an effort to get him to spill his secrets, my dear," he joked.

"You can't be serious."

He wasn't serious, but he liked how he could get her riled up. "Oh, it's true—didn't you read the tabloids? We're in competition about everything, even when it comes down to winning a certain woman's affections."

She shook her head and chuckled. "I can't believe that the tabloids think I could choose between the two of you."

"You don't have to yet, but Leo's feelings may change once he's learned that I just inked a deal that will gain the upper hand in the hotel business."

"Upper hand? How?" She shifted in her seat as she widened her eyes. "You have a buyer?"

He nodded, unable to keep the grin off of his face. "After two long months, I finally have someone willing to purchase those damn hotels."

"You're kidding."

He took her hand and stroked her fingers as he talked. "This person is offering enough money for me to get back on my feet and start up the renovations again."

"Oh, Jason. I'm so happy for you!" She hugged him, and Jason felt a tightening in his chest as he inhaled her sweet scent. She pulled away slightly and met his gaze. "And I'm sure Leo will be happy for you, too."

Jason wasn't so sure, but he wasn't going to argue when there were more pressing matters to discuss. "I'm going to finish the renovations to the German suites first."

"The hotels shaped like old castles? Get out—I love those buildings."

Jason nodded. "You see, I want to do those first, because I know how much you like castles, and I want you to have someplace nice to stay for your honeymoon."

"For my . . ." She gasped as Jason pulled out a ring and got down on his knee.

"Oh, Jason."

"Arianna Perconti, will you do me the honor of becoming my wife?"

She reached for the ring, then hesitated. "I thought you said that marriage was boring?"

"It is. Wonderfully, beautifully boring."

"But you hate boring."

"Correction—I used to hate it. I find that, as of late, predictability is growing on me."

She grabbed the ring from his hand and put it on.

Jason chuckled. "Is that a yes?"

"Only if we get married in one of the renovated hotels."

"My thoughts exactly." He glanced at the dress. "Which is why I bought the dress."

"It's perfect," Arianna said. "Just perfect."

As Jason's lips closed over hers, he decided that he couldn't agree with her more.

Epilogue

Jason steered Ari into the conference room at the Prudential Center as a sliver of unease rippled down his spine.

"What are you doing here?" Leo asked from his position by the window.

"The same could be asked of you." Jason lowered his hand from the small of Ari's back as she went to kiss her brother.

"Please, Leo, not today," she said as she gave him a welcoming hug.

Leo embraced his younger sister then turned his dark gaze on Jason. "If you think to come here and sabotage this deal—"

"Me? Why on earth would I do that?"

"So you didn't come here to stop the sale from going through?" Marco asked as he started to close the distance between them.

Ari moved into his embrace. "We came here to finalize a deal of our own," she said.

"Deal, what deal?" This was getting worse by the minute. Jason glanced around the large space and found nothing out of sorts. The cream-colored walls held various prints from contemporary artists, including a painting of a girl on a swing he had remembered seeing at the Palazzo. A long buffet table with coffee supplies lined the wall to his right, while a projector screen pulled over a Dry-Erase Board filled the left. Straight ahead were large, floor-to-ceiling windows and in the middle sat a large conference table with ergonomic office chairs. In the center of the table sat a laptop, connected to some power source through a hole in the table.

"We have a buyer for those hotels in Asia you refused to take off my hands," Leo explained.

Jason shrugged. "Money's tight. Besides, I know how much you like to remind me of your stronghold in China."

"Not anymore. This buyer is willing to pay double their worth. It will mean losing most of our Asian market, but the extra money will allow for some much-needed renovations to our existing buildings." He nodded to Marco. "If everything goes according to plan, we will start with Karin's renovation plan for the Palazzo next month. She also picked out a publicist to help improve our image."

"I told her I could do it myself," Marco muttered.

Leo smiled. "I'm sure you could, but Karin believes that a second opinion by someone trained to work with the media could really help us revive our reputation." He held up his hand as Marco started to protest. "And I agree."

"Something similar happened to me," Jason said in an effort to dispel the rising tension in the room. "A few days ago, an offer came in from a buyer for my properties in South America. I'll lose most of my holdings there, but the added capital will allow me to finish the renovations."

"He's renovating the hotels in Germany," Ari said, grinning. "You know, the ones that look like castles."

Jason slid his arm around her waist. "If everything works out, we hope to be married there next spring."

"Married?" Leo asked, raising his brows.

Ari grinned and held up her hand, showing off the large, princess-cut diamond.

The brothers immediately moved to hug both Ari and Jason, offering them their congratulations.

"You better take care of her," Leo said as he patted Jason's back. "She means a lot to me."

"She means a lot to me, too."

Leo twisted his lips into a half-smile. "I know, although I think Italy would have been a better choice."

"We're getting married in Germany," Ari said as she slid her arm through Jason's. "That's what I want—my choice."

"I give you a little control over the company, and it's gone completely to your head," Leo joked.

"I've had a good teacher," Ari shot back, smirking.

"I can hardly wait," Marco said. "Germany." He hugged his sister again. "You're going to make a beautiful bride."

"Something about this doesn't feel right," Jason said as he broke free from Ari and began to pace.

"How do you mean?" Marco asked, disentangling himself from Ari.

"It seems very coincidental that we both received offers from a mysterious buyer within days of each other."

"And that we were both asked to be here on the same day to close the deal," Leo added.

"You have a point," Marco said as he rubbed his chin.

"Who did you say made the offer to buy your South American holdings?" Marco asked.

"I didn't say, but—"

"Good morning." The familiar voice cut off Jason's train of thought. He glanced around the room, but no one new had joined them.

"The computer," Ari said, her voice full of strain.

"Deacon," Jason said as he moved in front of the laptop screen. "What are you doing?"

Deacon smiled at his brother. "I'm doing what I do best—running a con."

"You're what?" Leo asked as he pulled up a chair and squinted at the screen.

"Oh no." Jason fell into the chair next to Leo. "No."

"Oh, yes. I do a good job, don't I, brother? Felicia wanted to get revenge on both of us for stealing her connections and credibility by sending her to a mental hospital. I convinced her that it wasn't me who took her power and influence, but you. One only has to look at your massive hotel chain to prove it."

"What is he talking about?" Leo asked.

Jason suddenly felt sick. "I didn't steal anything, and she ended up in the hospital because of her own actions, not mine. It wasn't my fault that her creditors pulled out because of her mental collapse."

"But you were there to soothe their wallets and pick up the pieces, weren't you, little brother?" Deacon corrected. "Go on, ask him who his first investors were."

"Jason?" Ari asked.

"It was their choice," Jason said. "I had nothing to do with it."

"You manipulated them and then left both me and Felicia in the dust while you took all of the glory."

"Well," Leo said. "That was a long time ago. Stone has proven time and again that he can not only manage a hotel chain, but make it thrive."

"For now, yes." Deacon smirked. "But what will the future bring?" He glanced at each of them in turn. "The best part of this whole thing was that we used your own money to buy you out."

Marco leaned on the back of Leo's chair and frowned at the computer screen. "But ten million isn't nearly enough—"

"It was only the last in a long line of cons." Deacon

glanced at his brother. "Jason has been paying into our fund for months by investing in the 'starving artists' we threw in his path." He glanced at Leo. "And all of those reporters you bribed to stay away from your family?" Deacon shrugged. "The only one I couldn't secure was that Amanda Vaughn." He shook his head. "Some people have far too much integrity for their own good."

"If you forged our signatures, then the paperwork is illegal. It can't possibly stand up in court," Leo said.

"Yes, it can. You all dealt with a company called Harris Incorporated, which is a subsidiary of my employer's holdings, Killington Corp. Ms. Burke is thrilled by her new acquisitions. These hotels are the perfect addition to her company."

"Ms. Burke owns Killington?" Leo asked.

Jason rubbed his temples as a dull ache formed behind his eyes. "Felicia was married to Robert Killington. When he died, he left her everything, including his company. I thought she sold it off."

"I convinced her that it was so much more fun to play the game than to cash in and sit on the sidelines."

"But she knows nothing about the hotel business," Jason said. "It's complicated and—"

"That's why she has me." Deacon smiled. "I have been studying you, brotha, and I've got a few tricks up my sleeve."

"You can't possibly think to run us into the ground," Leo said. "You have no experience."

"It takes years of hard work to build an empire," Jason added.

"And now, thanks to the two of you, the hard work is done. All we need is a little branding and marketing spin, and we'll become the largest hotel chain in the world."

"Why, Deacon?" Jason asked. "At any time you could have come to me—"

"I tried, little brother, but I'm too much of an embarrassment for you to deal with, aren't I? Well, things are going to change around here. You've had your chance in the spotlight. Now it's my turn."

"What has she done to you?" Jason asked. "You know Felicia as well as I do. She's unstable—"

Leo fisted his hands. "This is a family fight. It has nothing to do with the Percontis."

"You are one of the most successful hoteliers in the world. I'm afraid that makes you collateral damage." Deacon glanced at each of them in turn. "You will find copies of the paperwork over on the side table in the corner." He smirked. "As you can see, we have countersigned and witnessed the documents. Everything is legal and in order. May the best hotelier win."

"Jesus," Jason said as the computer screen went black.

"What do we do now?" Marco asked.

Jason stood and walked over to the side table. Sure enough, two large stacks of legal papers were there, waiting for them. "Now, we fight."

"Fight?" Leo asked.

Jason turned and faced the room. "My brother is counting on us fighting separate battles against him. What he doesn't realize is that united, we are stronger than anything he can do to us." He walked up and put his arm around Ari. "I say we fight for our hotels, and our positions around the globe. If we fight together, I'm confident we can overpower him and set things right."

"Together," Ari said as she put her arm out in the middle of the circle. Each of the men covered her hand in turn.

"I like how you think, Stone," Leo said. "We shall fight this new threat together."

Don't miss Suzanne Rock's first novel in this blazing new series

AT HIS SERVICE

Available from